WHAT DISTANT DEEPS

DEEPS

THE REPUBLIC OF CINNABAR NAVY

DAVID DRAKE

TITAN BOOKS

What Distant Deeps
Print edition ISBN: 9781785652332
E-book edition ISBN: 9781785652349

Published by Titan Books
A division of Titan Publishing Group Ltd
144 Southwark Street, London SE1 0UP

First Titan edition: July 2018
2 4 6 8 10 9 7 5 3 1

A CIP catalogue record for this title is available from the British Library.

Printed and bound in Great Britain by CPI Group UK Ltd.

What did you think of this book? We love to hear from our readers. Please email us at: readerfeedback@titanemail.com, or write to us at the above address.

To receive advance information, news, competitions, and exclusive offers online, please sign up for the Titan newsletter on our website:

www.titanbooks.com

To Jason Williams and Jeremy Lassen
of Night Shade Books

AUTHOR'S NOTE

I'll start out with what in my days as a lawyer we would call boilerplate: I use both English and metric weights and measures in the RCN series to suggest the range of diversity which I believe would exist in a galaxy-spanning civilization. I do not, however, expect either actual system to be in use in three thousand years. Kilogram and inch (*et cetera*) should be taken as translations of future measurement systems, just as I've translated the spoken language.

I really wish I didn't have to say that. I've learned that I do.

The situation on which I based the plot of *What Distant Deeps* is the crisis that overtook but did not—quite—overwhelm the Roman Empire in the third century A.D. The extremities of the empire went through striking (and strikingly different) convulsions. For the action of this novel I'm particularly indebted to what happened in the East, but there is by no means a direct correspondence between this fiction and historical reality (even to the extent that we know the reality).

I write fiction to entertain, not to educate; but Aristophanes proved it was possible to do both, and on a good day a reader might learn something from me as well. Empires have generally used proxies to fight wars on their borders. The problem—as Rome learned with the Oasis of Palmyra—is that the proxies have policies of their own. Not infrequently, things go wrong for the principal when the proxy decides to implement its separate policies.

For a recent example, in the 1970s the US hired a battalion of troops from Argentina, called them "the Contras" and employed them to fight the socialist government of Nicaragua. The military dictatorship running Argentina at the time was more than happy to support the US effort.

Unfortunately for everybody (except ultimately the Argentine people), General Galtieri and his cronies (some of whom, amazingly, were even stupider and more brutal than he was) decided that their secret help to the US meant that the US would protect them from Britain when they invaded the Falklands and subjected the islands' English-speaking residents to what passed for government in Argentina. Galtieri was wrong—the tail didn't wag the dog during the Falklands War—and Argentina ousted the military junta as a result of its humiliation by Britain; but there might not have *been* a Falklands War if the US had not used Argentina as a military proxy in Nicaragua.

I could mention cases where US proxy involvements have led to even worse results. If the shoe fits, wear it.

Finally, a word about the dedication. I could simply let it stand

(I've many times dedicated a book to an editor or publisher), but there's an aspect to this one that won't be obvious to anyone outside my head (including Jason and Jeremy).

I came back to the World in 1971 and began writing the Hammer stories as a way of dealing with my experiences in Vietnam and Cambodia. The stories were successful, but they made me a pariah to a number of very vocal people.

Jason took me aback when he approached me about putting the series in limited-edition hardcovers. Nobody had ever suggested the stories were worthy of that before. Indeed, the people who said anything were likely to be protesting them being in print at all, even in mass market editions.

When I opened the box that contained the beautifully produced *Complete Hammer's Slammers, Volume 1,* I had an unexpected emotional reaction: I'd finally come home to the America which sent me to Nam in 1970. It was something that I didn't know I'd been missing until Night Shade Books gave it to me.

—Dave Drake

david-drake.com

In what distant deeps or skies
Burned the fire of thine eyes?
On what wings dare he aspire?
What the hand dare seize the fire?
—*The Tyger*
William Blake

CHAPTER 1

THE BANTRY ESTATE, CINNABAR

"Come and join, Squire Daniel!" called a dancer as she whirled past. "I'm not partnered!"

Daniel vaguely recalled the face, but he knew he must be thinking about an older sister. Ten years ago, he'd left Bantry to enter the Republic of Cinnabar Naval Academy. This girl was no more than sixteen, though she was undoubtedly well developed.

Mind, he didn't recall the sister's name either.

Steen—Old Steen since the death of his father, who'd been tenant-in-chief before him—elbowed Daniel in the ribs and said, "Haw! Not just a dance she's offering you, Squire! Going to take her up on it? You always did in the old days!"

Steen's wife was hovering nearby, though she hadn't presumed to enter the group of men centered on Daniel and the cask of beer on the sea wall. Foiles, the commodore of the fishing fleet, and Higgenson, the manager of the estate's processing plant, were from Bantry, like Steen, but also present were the owners of three nearby estates who had come to the festivities. Waldmiller of Ponds was over seventy and Broma of Flattler's Creek wasn't much younger; but at twenty-five, Peterleigh of Boltway Manor was a year Daniel's junior.

Before Daniel could pass off the comment with a grin and a shake of his head, Mistress Steen clipped her husband over the ear with a hand well used to hoeing. Fortunately Steen hadn't gotten his earthenware mug to his lips, so he merely jerked the last of his ale over his bright purple shirt instead of losing his front teeth.

"Where's your manners, you drunken old fool?" Mistress Steen demanded in a voice that started loud and gained volume. "Can't you see Lady Miranda close enough to spit on? You embarrass yourself and you embarrass the Squire!"

Daniel caught Mistress Steen's hands in his own, partly to forestall the full-armed follow-up stroke she was on the verge of delivering. "Now, Roby!" he said. "My Miranda's a sensible woman who wouldn't take note of a joke at a celebration, or even—"

He bussed Mistress Steen on the cheek. It was like kissing a boot.

"—this!" he concluded, stepping away.

"Oh, Squire!" Mistress Steen gasped in a mixture of delight and embarrassment. She put her hand to her cheek as though to caress the memory.

"Oh, you do go on!" she said as she stumped off, seemingly half-dazed. Daniel thought he heard her titter when the piping paused.

The original piper, gay in a green vest with blue and gold

tassels, was snoring in a drunken stupor behind the bench. His son—who couldn't have been more than twelve—was making a manful effort to replace him. All the will in the world couldn't increase the boy's lung capacity.

Daniel's eyes touched Miranda, who was with her mother Madeline a good twenty yards away—Roby Steen had been exaggerating. She waved with a merry smile, then went back to describing the stitching of her bodice to more women than Daniel could easily count.

The wives of the neighboring landowners were there, but Bantry tenants made up most of the not-quite-crush. The tenants observed protocol in who got to drink with Daniel, but their wives and daughters weren't going to give way to outsiders from other estates at their first chance to meet the Squire's lady.

"A pretty one, Leary," Peterleigh said. "Your fiancée, is she?"

Daniel cleared his throat. "Ah, Miranda and I have an understanding," he said, hoping that his embarrassment didn't show. "There's nothing formal at this moment, you'll understand, until, ah, some matters have been worked out."

Miranda herself never raised the question. She was an extremely smart woman, smart enough to know that others would prod Daniel regularly.

"For the gods' sakes, boy," Waldmiller said with a scowl at Peterleigh. "If you weren't raised to have manners, then at least you could show enough sense to avoid poking your nose in Speaker Leary's affairs, couldn't you?"

Peterleigh could probably buy and sell Waldmiller several times over, but seniority and the words themselves jerked the younger man into a brace. "Sorry, Leary, sorry!" he said.

"Don't know what I was thinking, asking about a fellow's private affairs. Must've drunk too much! My apologies!"

Bringing up Daniel's strained relationship with his father was calling in heavier artillery than Peterleigh deserved, but the young man could have avoided the rebuke by being more polite. Corder Leary was one of the most powerful members of the Senate—and certainly the most feared member. He hadn't visited Bantry since Daniel's mother died, and Peterleigh—who was both young and parochial—had obviously forgotten who the estate's real owner was.

"Not at all, Peterleigh," Daniel said, smiling mildly. "But as for drinking, I think it's time for me to have another mug of our good Bantry ale. It's what I miss most about Cinnabar when the RCN sends me off to heaven knows where."

So speaking, he stepped to the stand beside them where a ceramic cask of ale and a double rank of earthenware mugs waited. He knew his neighbors—Bantry's neighbors—would be surprised at having to pump their own beer, but Daniel was providing a holiday for *all* the Leary retainers.

He'd thought of bringing in outside servants, but city folk would mean trouble. One of them would sneer at a barefoot tenant—and be thrown off the sea wall, into the Western Ocean thirty feet below.

Daniel was dressed more like a countryman than a country gentleman, but he *was* wearing shoes today. He generally wouldn't have been at this time of the year when he was a boy on Bantry.

A pair of aircars landed in quick succession, drawing the men's attention. "That's Hofmann in the blue one," Broma said. "I don't recognize the gray car though."

"I think that's...," Daniel said. "Yes, that's Tom Sand, the contractor who built the Hall. I, ah, invited him to the dedication."

Broma squinted at the limousine which was landing a hundred yards away, on the field of rammed gravel laid for the purpose beside the Jerred Hogg Community Hall. "That's quite a nice car for...," he began.

He stopped and turned to Daniel in obvious surmise. "You don't mean the Honorable Thomas Sand of Archstone Construction?" he said. "By the gods, Leary, you do! Why, they're one of the biggest contracting firms in the whole Capital Region!"

"They did a fine job on the Hall," Daniel said with a faint smile, turning to look at the new building itself. All four sides had been swung onto the roof as they were designed to be, turning the building into a marquee. The drinks—no wines or liquor, but ale without limit—and the food were inside, where Hogg was holding court.

Hogg had been the young master's minder when Daniel was a child, and his servant in later years. He'd taught Daniel everything there was to know about the wildlife of Bantry which he and his ancestors back to the settlement had poached. He'd taught Daniel many other things as well, much of it information which would have horrified Daniel's mother, who was delicate and a perfect lady.

Hogg had a tankard of ale and a girl half his age ready with a pitcher to refill it. His arm was around a similar girl, and as many tenants as could squeeze close were listening to his stories of the wonders he and the young master had seen among the stars. Daniel was probably the only man present who knew that the wildest stories were absolutely true.

Hogg was royalty in Bantry today. Daniel smiled faintly. That was a small enough payment for the man who'd taught the young master how to be a man.

Tom Sand walked toward Daniel in the company of half a dozen children including at least one girl. They could claim to be guiding Sand, but they were more concerned with getting a good look at a stranger who was an obvious gentleman. Sand had weather-beaten features and more chest than paunch, but his suit—though gray—shimmered in a way that neither wool nor silk could match. Daniel suspected it had been woven from the tail plumes of Maurician ground doves.

"You'll be spending more time in Bantry now that we're at peace again, Leary?" Waldmiller asked, letting his eyes glance across their surroundings. His tone was neutral and his face impassive, signs that he was controlling an urge to sneer. This was a working estate, not a showplace.

They stood in the middle of the Bantry Commons, a broad semicircle with the sea front forming the west side. The shops bounded its south end and the sprawling manor was to the north; tenant housing closed the arc. The dwellings facing directly on the common were older, smaller, and much more desirable than the relatively modern units in the second and third rows. Younger sons and their sons were relegated to the newer housing.

Instead of turning the manor into a modern palace to reflect the family's increased wealth and power, Daniel's grandfather had put his efforts into a luxurious townhouse in Xenos. Corder Leary had visited Bantry only as a duty—and not even that after the death of his children's mother. The house looked much as it had three centuries ago.

Birds screamed overhead. The fish processing plant was shut down for the celebration, and they were upset at missing their usual banquet of offal.

Daniel grinned. At that, the flock wasn't much less musical than the piper...and there'd been enough ale drunk already that the dancers could probably manage to continue even if the boy on the bagpipe gave up the struggle he was clearly unequal to.

"It's true that many ships have been laid up since the Truce of Rheims," Daniel said, "and that means a number of officers have gone on half pay."

In fact almost two thirds of the Navy List had been put on Reserve status. That meant real hardship for junior officers who had been living on hopes already. Those hopes had been dashed, but they were still expected to have a presentable dress uniform to attend the daily levees in Navy House which were their only chance of getting a ship.

"But I've been lucky so far," Daniel continued. "I'm still on the Active list, though I don't have an assignment as yet. And anyway, I wasn't really cut out to be a—"

He'd started to say "farmer," but caught himself. Thank the gods he'd drunk a great deal less today than he would have even a few years earlier. Daniel hadn't become an abstainer, but he'd always known when he shouldn't be drinking; and the higher he rose—in the RCN and in society generally—the more frequent those occasions were.

"—a country squire."

Sand joined them; the entourage of children dropped

behind the way the first touch of an atmosphere strips loose articles from the hull of a descending starship. Miranda was leading Mistress Sand to the house, having shooed away a similar bevy of children.

Waldmiller opened his mouth to greet Sand. Peterleigh, his face toward the sea, hadn't noticed the newcomer's approach. He said, "Well, I think the truce is a bloody shame, Leary. You fellows in the navy had the Alliance on the ropes. Why the Senate should want to let Guarantor Porra off the hook is beyond me!"

"Well, Peterleigh...," said Daniel. "You know what they say: never a good war or a bad peace."

"And maybe it was a good war for folks who live out here in the Western Region and don't leave their estates," boomed Thomas Sand, "but it bloody well wasn't for anybody trying to make a living in Xenos. Off-planet trade is down by nine parts in ten, so half the factories in the Capital Region have shut and the rest are on short hours."

Peterleigh jumped and would have spilled ale if he hadn't emptied his mug. Waldmiller and Broma masked their amusement—Broma more effectively than his elder colleague. The tenants, Foiles and Higgenson, maintained their frozen silence. They'd been quiet even before Maud Steen had torn a strip off her husband, and that had chilled them further.

"Didn't mean to break in unannounced," Sand said. "I'm Tom Sand and I built the hall there."

He nodded in the direction of it.

"And not a half-bad job, if I do say so myself."

"These are my neighbors," said Daniel. "Waldmiller,

Broma, and you've already met Peterleigh, so to speak. Have some ale, Sand. We're setting a good example for the tenants so that none of them bring out the kelp liquor they brew in their sheds."

Sand laughed, drawing a mug of ale. "I understand, Leary," he said. "I have a capping party for the crew on each job, but it's beer there too. It doesn't hurt a man to get drunk every once in a while, but I'd as lief give them guns as hard liquor for the chances that they'd all survive the night."

He shook his head, then added, "No offense meant about trade being strangled. The RCN did a fine job. But any shipowner who lifted at all got a letter of marque and converted his hull into a privateer. In the neutral worlds, chances are he's got warrants from *both* us and the Alliance. That was better business than hauling a load of wheat from Ewer to Cinnabar— and likely being captured by some privateer besides."

"No offense taken, Sand," Daniel said. "Every word you say is true."

He swept his neighbors with his eyes. "You see, Peterleigh," he said, "our tenants work hard and they live bloody hard by city standards. But they never doubt there'll be food on the table in the evening, even if it's dried fish and potatoes. The folk in the housing blocks around Xenos don't know that, and I'm told there were riots already last year."

He flashed a broad grin and added, "I wasn't around to see them, of course."

"Right!" said Sand, turning from the keg with a full mug of ale. To the others in the circle he said, "Captain Leary was chasing the Alliance out of the Montserrat Stars with their tails between their legs. Splendid work, Leary! Makes me proud to be a citizen of Cinnabar."

"That's the Squire for you!" blurted Higgenson, pride freeing his tongue. "Burned them wogs a new one, *he* did!"

There was commotion and a loud rattle from the Hall. Hogg and a tenant of roughly his age were dancing with rams' horns strapped to their feet. The curved horns made an almighty clatter on the concrete floor, but the men with their arms akimbo were impressive as they banged through a measure to the sound of the bagpipe.

"That's Hogg himself, isn't it, Leary?" asked Broma. The hammering dance had drawn all eyes, though the tenants around the Hall limited what Daniel and his fellows could see from the sea front.

"Aye, and that's Des Cranbrook who's got a grain allotment in the northeast district and a prime orchard tract," said Foiles. Since Higgenson had spoken without being struck by lightning, the fisherman had decided it was safe for him to say something also.

"Plus the common pasturage, of course," Daniel said, speaking to Sand; his fellow landowners took that for granted. The dancers—both stout; neither of them young nor likely to have been handsome even in youth—hopped with the majesty of clock movements, slowly pirouetting as they circled one another.

"Haven't seen a real horn dance in—law!—twenty years if it's been one," said Higgenson. His social betters were intent on the dancing, which gave him a chance to speak from personal knowledge. "The young folk don't pick it up, seems like."

"That'll change now," said Foiles. "The young ones, the ones that didn't know Hogg before he went away with you, Squire—"

He dipped his head toward Daniel.

"—they all think the sun shines out of his asshole. And some of the women as did know him and so ought to know better, they're near as bad."

The dancers collapsed into one another's arms, then wobbled laughing back to their seats. Girls pushed each other to be the ones unstrapping the rams' horns. Cranbrook was getting his share of the attention. The lass hugging him and offering a mug of ale might have been his granddaughter, but Daniel was pretty sure that she wasn't. He grinned.

"Ah...?" said Higgenson in sudden concern—though he hadn't been the one who'd actually commented on Hogg's former reputation. "Not that we meant anything, Squire. You know how folks used to say things, and no truth in them, like as not."

"I suspect there was a lot of truth in what was said about Hogg," Daniel said, thinking back on the past and feeling his smile slip. "And about me, I shouldn't wonder. It's probably to Bantry's benefit as well as the Republic's that the RCN has found the two of us occupation at a distance from the estate."

Georg Hofmann approached the group. He looked older and more stooped than Daniel had remembered him, but that was years since, of course. His estate, Brightness Landing, was well up the coast.

"I didn't recognize the woman who got out of the car with Hofmann," Daniel said in a low voice. She was in her early forties and had been poured into a dress considerably too small and too youthful for her.

"He remarried, a widow from Xenos," said Waldmiller with a snort. "Damned if I can see the attraction."

"And she brought a son besides," said Peterleigh. "Chuckie, I believe his name is; Platt, from the first husband. That one might better stay in Xenos, *I* think."

The youth was tall and well set up. He looked twenty from Daniel's distance, but his size may have given him a year or two more than time had. Accompanied by two servants in pink-and-buff livery—those weren't Hofmann's colors, so they may have been Platt's—he was sauntering toward a group of the younger tenants on the sea wall not far from the manor house.

Daniel's eyes narrowed. Platt took a pull from a gallon jug as he walked, then handed it to a servant. His other servant held what looked very much like a case of dueling pistols.

Hofmann joined the group around Daniel. Up close, he looked even more tired than he had at a distance. He exchanged nods with his neighbors, then said, "It's been years, Leary. Good years for you, from what I hear."

"It's good to see the old place, Hofmann," Daniel said, "though I don't really fit here any more, I'm afraid. Hofmann, this is Tom Sand, who built the new Hall."

"I heard you were doing that work, Sand," said Hofmann, extending his hand to shake. Hofmann was the other member of the local gentry who'd been active in national affairs; though not to the extent of Corder Leary, of course. "How did that come to happen, if I may ask. It's not—"

He gestured toward the new building.

"—on your usual scale, I should have said."

Daniel heard the low-frequency thrum of the big surface effect transport he'd been expecting and gave a sigh of relief. He'd set the arrival for mid-afternoon. He hadn't wanted his Sissies to party for the full day and night with the Bantry tenants, but he'd been so long in the company of spacers that the rural society in which he'd been raised had become strange to him.

"I asked for the job," said Sand, squaring his broad shoulders. "I wanted a chance to do something for a real hero of the Republic."

He gave Daniel a challenging grin and a nod that was almost a bow. "Hear hear!" said Peterleigh, and the others in the group echoed him.

"Much obliged," said Daniel in embarrassment. He drew a mug of ale for an excuse to turn away.

The bid for the Community Hall had seemed fair. Deirdre, Daniel's older sister, had handled the matter for him; she'd been handling all his business since prize money had made that more complex than finding a few florins to pay a bar tab. Deirdre had followed their father into finance with a ruthless intelligence that would doubtless serve her well in politics also when she chose to enter the Senate.

The building that appeared wasn't the simple barn that Daniel had envisaged, though. The wall mechanisms were extremely sophisticated—and solid: Daniel had gone over them with the attention he'd have given the lock mechanisms of a ship he commanded. Only then had he realized that this was more than a commercial proposition for the builder; as, of course, it was for Daniel Leary himself.

The transport rumbled in from the sea, a great aerofoil with a catamaran hull. It slid up the processing plant's ramp—which had been extended north to support the starboard outrigger—and settled to a halt.

The reel dance had broken up for the time being. All eyes were on the big vehicle.

"This something you were expecting, Leary?" said Waldmiller, frowning. To him such craft were strictly for trade, hauling his estate's produce to market in the cities of the east.

The hatches opened. Even before the ramps had fully deployed, spacers were hopping to the ground wearing their liberty suits. Their embroidered patches were bright, and ribbons fluttered from all the seams.

"Up the *Sissie*!" someone shouted. The group headed for the Hall and the promised ale with the same quick enthusiasm that they'd have shown in storming Hell if Captain Leary had ordered it.

"It is indeed, Waldmiller," Daniel said. "These are the spacers who've served with me since before I took command of the *Princess Cecile*. I invited them and some of my other shipmates to share the fun today."

Officers waited for the ramp, not that they couldn't have jumped if they'd thought the situation required speed rather than decorum. For the most part they wore their second-class uniforms, their Grays, but Mon—a Reserve lieutenant, though he'd for several years managed Bergen and Associates Shipyard in Daniel's name—had made a point of wearing his full-dress Whites.

The shipyard had been doing very well under Mon's leadership. That had allowed him to have the uniform let out professionally, since his girth had also expanded notably.

Two slightly built women were the last people out of the transport. Adele wore an unobtrusively good suit, since she was appearing as Lady Adele Mundy rather than as Signals Officer Mundy of the *Princess Cecile*. Tovera, her servant, was neat and nondescript, as easy to overlook as a viper in dried leaves.

"I say, Leary?" said Broma. "Who're the civilian women there? Your Miranda's meeting them, I see."

Miranda, accompanied by another flock of children—generally girls this time—waited at the bottom of the ramp. Mothers and older sisters were running to grab them when they noticed what was happening.

"That's my friend Adele and her aide," Daniel said with satisfaction. "And I'm *very* glad to seem them again!"

The transport had four files of seats running the length of the fuselage, arranged in facing pairs. Only when the exit ramps began to open did Adele shut off her personal data unit and slide it into the pocket which she had added to the right thigh of all her dress clothes. The cargo pocket of RCN utilities worked very well without modification.

Adele had found over the years that bespoke tailors gave her more trouble when she demanded the PDU pocket on civilian suits than RCN officers did when they saw her out of uniform. On the other hand, even the snootiest tailor gave in eventually for the honor of dressing Mundy of Chatsworth, a member of one of the oldest families of the Republic and a decorated hero besides.

Adele was in fact the *only* member of the Mundys of

Chatsworth to have survived the Proscriptions which had decapitated the Three Circles Conspiracy nearly twenty years earlier. At the time she was a sixteen-year-old student in the Academic Collections on Blythe, the second world and intellectual capital of the Alliance of Free Stars. Though her family had been extremely wealthy, her personal tastes were simple. That fitted her to survive if not flourish in a poverty too deep to be described as genteel.

Recently, the prize money that had accrued to her as an RCN warrant officer in the crew of the most successful captain in a generation had allowed Adele to live and dress in a fashion that befit her rank in society. She was amused to reflect that she owed the recovery of her fortunes to the son of Speaker Leary, the man who had directed the execution of every other member of her family.

She stood; Tovera, with her usual neutral expression, waited in the aisle to precede Adele as soon as she decided to leave the transport. Tovera's expression sometimes implied that the pale, slender woman was pleased about something. Those "somethings" weren't the sort of matters that amused most other people, however.

Adele shared much of her servant's sense of humor. That, and the fact that Adele was a crack shot whose pistol had killed indeterminate scores of people during her service in the RCN, made her a suitable role model for Tovera. In order to survive in society, a murderous sociopath needs someone to translate the rules of acceptable behavior for her.

Adele started down the aisle. Lieutenant Cory and Midshipman Cazelet were waiting by the hatch. Tovera gave them a minuscule nod which sent them down the ramp. This wasn't a social event for Adele; at least not yet.

The two young officers were her protégés, though she wasn't sure how that had happened. Rene Cazelet was the grandson of her mentor at the Academic Collections, Mistress Boileau. When the boy's parents were executed for plotting against Guarantor Porra, Boileau had sent him to Adele.

That was perfectly reasonable. Adele didn't understand why, however, after she'd helped Rene get his feet under him on Cinnabar, he'd continued to follow her in the RCN instead of finding a civilian occupation. Adele's contacts could have opened almost any door for him.

Cory was even more puzzling. He'd been a barely marginal midshipman when he was assigned to the *Princess Cecile*. Some of his classmates had blossomed under Daniel's training, but Cory had remained a thumb-fingered embarrassment...until Adele had more or less by accident found that the boy had a talent for communications—and used him. To the amazement of herself and Daniel both, Cory had managed to become a more-than-passable astrogator as well.

Well and good; Adele was of course pleased. But Cory apparently credited her with his turnaround, whereas Adele would be the first to say that she would be better able to fly by flapping her arms than she would be to astrogate. She didn't even know how to direct the astrogation computer to find a solution the way many of the senior enlisted personnel could.

Tovera led the way out of the transport, her hand within the half-open attaché case she carried in all circumstances which didn't allow her to show weapons openly. There was almost no chance of someone trying to attack Adele here at Bantry, but Tovera would say that no one had ever been murdered because their bodyguard was too careful. Tovera wasn't going to change her behavior, so it was a matter on which mistress and servant would simply disagree.

The assorted spacers were already mixing with the crowd of Bantry tenants. Both groups were in their party clothes, but they were as distinct as birds from lizards. The Sissies wore ribbons and patches, while the Bantries were in solid bright colors— generally in combinations that clashed. Muted good taste wasn't seen as a virtue either by spacers or farmers, it appeared.

Adele smiled. "Mistress?" said Tovera, who flicked quick glances behind her as well. Presumably she was concerned that the transport's driver might enter to creep from the cockpit to shoot Lady Mundy in the back.

"I was wondering...," Adele said, "how my tailor would react if I asked him to run me up a liberty suit."

"Any of the Sissies would be proud to do the work, Mistress," Tovera said with a straight face and no inflection. "They'd fight each other for the honor."

She paused, then added, "Woetjans would win."

"Yes," Adele agreed dryly. "Woetjans would win."

A sociopath shouldn't be able to joke, but Tovera had certainly learned to counterfeit the act. At least the comment was *probably* meant as a joke.

The *Princess Cecile*'s bosun was six-foot-six and rangy rather than heavy. She—Woetjans was biologically female— had always struck Adele as abnormally strong even for her size, and the length of high-pressure tubing she swung in a melee was more effective than a sawed-off shotgun.

Miranda Dorst had just reached the bottom of the ramp. She waited in the middle of a group of children, smiling up at Adele.

Daniel had kept company with many women in the years Adele had known him. Most of them had been prettier than Miranda—a healthy girl, but not a raging beauty; and none of them had displayed half Miranda's intelligence.

Adele respected Miranda, which permitted her to like the younger woman as well. She hoped that matters went well for her and Daniel, which didn't—Adele smiled briefly, coldly—necessarily mean that they would marry. But Miranda was adult, *quite* smart, and certainly knew her own mind.

Women with floral aprons and contrasting bonnets were descending on Miranda's gaggle of children like jays on a swarm of termites, whisking them off one at a time by a sleeve or an ear. A boy remained, but a girl of sixteen or so was coming at a run with her eye on him.

"Adele, I'm so glad to see you," Miranda said, sounding as though she meant it. "Is this your first visit to Bantry? I'm sure it's a wonderful place when one learns to appreciate it, but I'll admit that I've always been a city girl."

"Lady Mundy, Lady Mundy!" squealed the boy. He couldn't have been more than six.

"Robbie!" cried the girl running toward him.

"Are you the Squire's girlfriend, Lady Mundy?" Robbie demanded. "*We* all think you are!"

The girl clouted Robbie over the ear. He yelped; she smothered his outrage in folds of her scarlet apron which overlay the blue/green/yellow checks of her skirt.

"Your Ladyship, I'm *so* sorry!" the girl said. Her cheeks were almost as bright as the fabric. "He's my brother and it's my fault, I was supposed to watch him, I'm so sorry! I'm Susie Maynor and I shouldn't have let it happen!"

"Thank you, Mistress Maynor," Adele said. Her voice and expression were emotionless, but she had made the intellectual decision to find the business amusing. That was the proper response, especially with a child; though it wasn't the direction her thoughts had first turned. "You may assure Master Robbie when he reappears that I am not the Squire's girlfriend."

"Oh, Your Ladyship!" the girl gasped. She strode toward the main gathering with determination, ignoring the muted wails from her apron.

Adele, grimacing internally, met Miranda's eyes. As she—and probably both of them—wondered what to say or whether better to ignore the business, Tovera said, "I've been in Captain Leary's company for a number of years now, but no one has made similar assertions about me. If I had human feelings, they would be hurt."

Miranda blinked at Tovera, then smothered a giggle with her hand. Adele only grinned slightly, but the expression meant more in her case than it would for most people. Aloud she said, "Would you like a raise, Tovera?"

Her servant gave her a wintry smile. "What do I need money for, mistress?" she said. She had closed her attaché case. "You provide my food and lodging, and you point me to plenty of people to kill."

Which may be a joke, Adele thought. "Yes," she said, "but not here."

"Daniel asked me to take you to the house," Miranda said as she turned. She started back along the arc of the commons instead of the chord of the sea front. She cleared her throat, perhaps still embarrassed. She said, "He isn't really the Squire, you know. His father is, and Deirdre will inherit if, well … when …"

Her voice trailed off.

"I don't believe Speaker Leary is immortal, either," Adele said, letting the words rather than her dry tone supply the humor. "But 'Squire' is a term of custom rather than law. If the Bantries choose to grant the title to Daniel who grew up with them rather than to his father to whom the estate is merely a muddy asset, then I applaud their judgment."

They walked close to the tenant houses. Adele could see that the fronts were decked with swags of foliage and flowers, not bunting as she'd thought from the transport's hatch. Dogs barked from some of the fenced dooryards.

Miranda followed Adele's eyes. With quiet pride she said, "They really love him, don't they?"

"Yes," said Adele. "Just as the Sissies do. The tenants don't find their lives at considerably greater risk from associating with Daniel, but even so I don't think a computer could have predicted the depth of feeling."

Miranda laughed. She was a cheerful person, a good fit with Daniel in that way. She hadn't had an easy life, but the troubles didn't appear to have marked her.

Whereas Adele—she smiled wanly at herself—hadn't been particularly happy even when she'd been the heir to one of the wealthiest and most powerful houses of the Republic. She'd often been content, though; as she was generally content now, except the nights that she lay in the darkness, surrounded by dead faces that she'd last seen over the sights of the pistol which even now nestled in her left tunic pocket.

The piper was taking a break, and at least a dozen men had begun singing "The Ring That Has No End" without accompaniment. They stumbled up to " ... when you find one who'll be true," but by the time they reached, "Change *not* the old friend for a new," their voices had blended into a natural richness which Adele found beautiful. Her hand reached for her data unit as it always did when she was really engaged by her surroundings, but she had nothing to look up.

Her lips twitched, though her expression couldn't have been called a smile: she reached for her data unit, or she reached for her pistol. Either way, she preferred to keep a mechanical interface between herself and the world.

"I'm so glad they're getting along," Miranda said, also watching the festival. She and Adele walked side by side. Tovera followed at a respectful distance of two paces. "I was afraid there'd be, well, fights between spacers and tenants."

"There probably will be," Adele said. "And fights among spacers *and* fights among tenants. Most of both groups will be drunk before the night's out, and those who aren't falling-down drunk will include some who want to knock other people down. But they all respect Six—or the Squire, depending—too much for it to go beyond fists. And remember, at least a score of the present Sissies were tenants before they enlisted."

And anyone who wasn't sufficiently respectful to begin

with would have a proper understanding beaten into him by Woetjans or Hogg, each policing the group they came from. They would certainly be drunk also, but Adele couldn't imagine them too drunk to do their duty.

She took that sort of implicit violence for granted now. Her father, knowing that a leading politician was open to many pressures, had seen to it that not only he but his wife and daughters were known to be crack shots who would certainly kill anyone who challenged them to a duel. That hadn't helped him the night troops arrived with the notice of the Proscriptions, but it had kept Adele alive during her years of slums and squalor.

This was different, though: this was force applied in the service of order, not chaos. Her mother, who had believed in the innate decency of the Common Man, would have been horrified; her father would have been disgusted.

Adele, who had lived in very close quarters with the Common Man ever since the Proscriptions, took the same sort of detached view that she had of lice: there were discomforts which you alleviated if you could and bore if you couldn't. There were no moral questions involved, just practical responses.

And a crack on the head with plenty of muscle behind it was often a *very* practical response.

The double leaves of the manor's front door were standing open onto the veranda; guns and fishing tackle hung from hooks in the hallway behind. The gear looked well cared for, though there wouldn't have been anyone living in the building since Daniel had left Bantry to join the RCN.

Tovera skipped ahead; her right hand was within the

attaché case again. The hall and the rooms to either side along the central passageway were empty.

If Miranda was surprised by Tovera's behavior, she didn't comment on the fact. Instead she said, "I'll take you through to the library, Adele, and then go back to the party."

She smiled fondly. "I need to give my mother a bit of a break, I'm afraid," she said. "When the Bantry women learned we'd both made our own dresses—"

She touched her skirt. The fabric was sturdy, but the pattern of magenta flames on the white background made it stand out even in these festivities. The lines, though loose enough to be comfortable, flattered what was already quite a good figure.

"—nothing would help but we had to show them every seam."

Miranda knocked on the last door to the right, where the passage jogged into the new wing. "Enter," called a voice that had become familiar to Adele over the years.

Tovera reached for the latch; Adele stepped past and said, "No."

She opened the door and entered what passed for a library here.

"Did you have a good trip, Mundy?" asked Bernis Sand, seated at the reading table with a bottle of whiskey, a carafe of water, and two glasses before her.

"No worse than I expected," Adele said to the Republic's spymaster. When the door closed behind her, she went on, "What did you wish to speak to me about, mistress?"

CHAPTER 2

THE BANTRY ESTATE, CINNABAR

"You're not one for small talk, are you, Mundy?" said Bernis Sand. She tapped the bottle. "Help yourself to the whiskey."

"No," said Adele, "I'm not. And I expect the sun to rise in the east tomorrow, if you choose to discuss the obvious."

Adele had known she was in a bad humor, but she hadn't been aware of exactly how bad it was until she heard herself. Despite that, she took the bottle and poured a half-thimbleful into the glass. After swirling the liquor around, she filled the glass from the carafe.

It was what she'd done in the years when the water where she lived wasn't safe to drink. The liquor wasn't safe either, of course, but in small doses it would kill bacteria without being immediately dangerous to a human being.

It wasn't precisely an insult to treat Mistress Sand's whiskey that way. But it wasn't precisely *not* an insult, either.

Adele took a sip. Very calmly, Sand said, "What's wrong, Mundy? The last mission?"

Adele set the glass down. She swallowed, trying to rid herself of the sourness which—she smiled—was in her mind, not her mouth.

"I'm sorry, mistress," she said. "I—"

She paused, wondering how to phrase it without being further insulting. The things other people said or did would always give room to take offense, if you were of a mind to take offense. Therefore the fault wasn't in the other people.

"Yes, I suppose it was the most recent mission, the battle above Cacique at least," Adele said. "It affected me more than I would have expected."

"Your ship was badly hit," said Sand as Adele paused to drink. "I understand that it will probably be scrapped instead of being rebuilt. You could easily have been killed."

Adele smiled faintly and refilled the glass with water. Her mouth was terribly dry. When she laughed, the ribs on her lower right side still ached from where a bullet had hit her years ago on Dunbar's World. Fortunately, she didn't laugh very often.

"I'm not afraid of being killed, mistress," Adele said, meeting the spymaster's eyes over the rim of her glass. "I haven't changed that much."

"Go on, then," Sand said quietly. She was a stocky woman on the wrong side of middle age. In the brown tweed suit she wore at present, she could easily have passed for one of the country squires Adele had seen with Daniel on the sea front.

Mistress Sand had been more important to the survival of Cinnabar in its struggle with the much larger Alliance than any cabinet minister or admiral in the RCN. What Adele saw in the older woman's eyes now were intelligence and

36

strength...and fatigue as boundless as the Matrix through which starships sailed.

"Debris flew around inside the ship after the missile hit us," Adele said. "A piece of it struck Daniel—that is, Captain Leary—"

Sand flicked her hands in dismissal of the thought. "Daniel," she said. "This isn't a formal report. It's two old acquaintances talking. Two friends, I'd like to think."

"Yes," said Adele. "Debris struck Daniel in the head."

She raised the carafe, but her hand was trembling so she quickly put it back. Sand reached past and filled the glass.

"It cracked his helmet and gave him a concussion, but the injuries weren't life threatening," Adele said. "If it had struck an inch lower, however, it would have broken his neck. Severed it, like enough. That would have been beyond the Medicomp or any human efforts to repair. And I don't believe in gods."

"An RCN officer's duties are often dangerous," Sand said, carefully neutral. Adele realized that the spymaster still didn't understand the problem. Sand was afraid of saying the wrong thing—and equally afraid of seeming uninterested if she didn't say anything. "That might have happened to any of you."

"Yes," said Adele, "exactly. Whereas I'd been thinking—feeling, I suppose—that it might happen to *all* of us. That is, if a missile hit our ship, we would all be killed. That event, that incident, proved that there might well be a future in which Daniel was dead and I was alive."

She took her glass in both hands and drained it again. This wasn't coming out well, but she wasn't sure there was a better way to put it.

"Mistress," Adele said, "I've built a comfortable life. Rebuilt one, perhaps. The RCN is a family which accepts and even appreciates me. The Sissies, the spacers whom I've served with, they're closer than I would ever have been with my sister Agatha in another life."

In a life in which two soldiers hadn't cut off Agatha's ten-year-old head with their belt knives and turned it in for the reward.

"And Daniel himself...," Adele said. She didn't know how to go on. She hadn't expected this conversation. She hadn't expected *ever* to have this conversation. It was obvious that she was in worse shape than she had imagined only a few moments ago.

It was less obvious to see how she was going to get out of her present straits.

Adele felt her lips rise in an unexpected smile. The RCN prided itself that its personnel could learn through on-the-job training. No doubt life would prove amenable to the same techniques by which Adele had learned to be an efficient signals officer.

"There's no one like Daniel," Adele said simply. "I don't mean 'no one better than Daniel,' though in some ways that's probably true. But my entire present life is built around the existence of Daniel Leary. I would rather die than start over from where I was when I was sixteen and lost my first family."

Mistress Sand sighed. "I have my work, Mundy," she said. "And my—"

Her face went coldly blank, then broke into an embarrassed grin. "I may as well be honest," Sand said. "I have my children. That's how I think of them."

With a hint of challenge she said, "That's how I think of *you*."

"I wasn't a notably filial child when I was sixteen," Adele said. "Perhaps I'll do better with the advantage of age."

Sand laughed and pushed the bottle another finger's breadth across the table. From her waistcoat she took a mother-of-pearl snuffbox. She sifted some of the contents from it into the seam of her left thumb closed against her fingers.

Adele poured two ounces of whiskey and sipped it neat. It was a short drink but a real one, and an apology for her previous behavior.

"You were wondering why I wanted to see you," Sand said. Her eyes were on her snuffbox as she snapped it closed. "Are you ready to go off-planet again, do you think?"

"Yes," said Adele. She'd considered the question from the moment she'd been summoned to this meeting, so she spoke without the embroidery others might have put around the answer.

Sand pinched her right nostril shut and snorted, then switched nostrils and repeated the process. She dusted the last crumbs of snuff from her hands, then sneezed violently into her handkerchief. She looked up with a smile.

"There's a Senatorial election due in four months, perhaps even sooner if the Speaker fancies his chances," she said. "All the parties will attempt to use Captain Leary. He's a genuine war hero and, shall we say, impetuous enough that he might be maneuvered into blurting something useful."

"Yes," Adele repeated, waiting.

"That would be a matter of academic import to me," Sand continued, "were it not for the fact that Leary's close friend is one of my most valued assets, and that asset would become involved also."

Sand cleared her throat. "Do you suppose Captain Leary would be willing to undertake a charter in his private yacht to deliver the new Cinnabar Commissioner to Zenobia?"

Adele set her data unit on the table and brought it live. Sand knew her too well to take the action as an insult, but that wouldn't have mattered: Adele had done it with no more volition than she breathed. If asked whether she would prefer to be without breath or without information, she would have said there was little to choose from.

"I had understood...," she said as her fingers made the control wands dance. She found the wands quicker than other input devices—and so they were, for her. Adele used them as she did her pistol, at the capacity of the machine. "...that Daniel was to be kept on full pay despite the fact that the *Milton* is scheduled to be broken up."

"That's correct," Sand said, pouring herself another tumbler of whiskey. She controlled her reactions very well, but Adele could tell that the older woman was more relaxed than she had been since Adele entered the room. "The officers and crew will serve as members of the RCN—"

Sand used the insider's term instead of referring to "the Navy."

"—but as a matter of courtesy to the Alliance, they will be in civilian dress while in Zenobian territory, and their ship will be a civilian charter rather than a warship."

Adele smiled slightly as she flicked through the holographic images which her data unit displayed. Common spacers generally wore loose-fitting garments, whether their ship was a merchant vessel or a warship—of the RCN, the Alliance Fleet, or one of the galaxy's smaller navies. The colors were all drab, but the particular hue depended on where the fabric had been dyed rather than who was wearing it. If they were worn by Power Room crew, lubricant and finely divided metal had turned them a dirty black.

Officers wore RCN utilities on shipboard duty. For most of the crew, utilities were dress uniform—and formed the base for liberty suits.

"A voyage to Zenobia will certainly keep the brave Captain Leary out of the political arena for a suitable period of time," Adele said dryly as she skimmed information on Zenobia. There were specialist databases—virtually every database on Cinnabar was open to a combination of Adele's skill and the software which Mistress Sand had supplied—but it scarcely seemed necessary here. Unless the readily available material—which included the *Sailing Directions for the Qaboosh Region*, published by Navy House—was wildly wrong, Zenobia had no depth to go into.

"Yes," said Sand. "It fits that criterion amply, since it's a sixty-day run for merchant vessels."

She smiled wryly and added, "I have no doubt that you'll tell me that Captain Leary can better that estimate, Mundy. Nonetheless, the distance justifies our hero being absent for as long as the campaign season requires."

"*Any* RCN vessel could better the estimate, I suspect, mistress," Adele said, hearing a touch of asperity in her tone. She smiled, amused to realize that she had become just as protective of the honor of the RCN as she was that of the Mundys of Chatsworth. "It's as much a factor of the larger crews of a naval vessel as it is of the much higher level of astrogation training to be expected of the officers."

"I bow to your greater experience in the matter, Mundy," said Sand. Adele wondered if the older woman would have been less amenable to the pedantry if she weren't so relieved to be past the awkward scene with which the interview had opened.

Clearing her throat, Sand continued, "Zenobia is typical of the Qaboosh Region, meaning it's of no particular account. Both we and the Alliance have tributaries and a naval base there, but the region is such a backwater that both parties chose to ignore it during the recent hostilities. Sending a real fighting squadron to the Qaboosh would have wasted strength which was needed closer to home."

"Is Zenobia an Alliance possession?" Adele said, scrolling rapidly through data without finding the answer she wanted. "It appears to be one, but there shouldn't be a Cinnabar Commissioner if it were."

"Zenobia is technically independent, with a Council and an executive—the Founder—elected for life by that Council," Sand said. "Foreign policy and realistically everything more important than the level of the food subsidy for Calvary, the only real city, is in the hands of an Alliance Resident. I suspect that if the Resident cared about the food subsidy, he could change that also."

Adele nodded, her eyes on her own data streams. Now that she knew what she was looking for, she found considerable detail.

"You're probably wondering why we even have a Commissioner

on Zenobia," Sand said. She tapped the bottle forward again, but Adele was absorbed in her information gathering.

"Not at all," Adele said, more curtly than she would have done if her intellect hadn't been focused in other directions. "A good quarter of the region's spacers appear to be from Rougmont, one of our client worlds. I suspect very few of them are actually Cinnabar citizens, but based on what I've noticed on the fringes of civilization, most will *claim* to be Cinnabar citizens when they're jailed for being drunk and disorderly. Their normal state when they've been paid upon landfall."

A Resident was a senior official in the Cinnabar's Ministry of External Affairs. He or she directed the local leaders of worlds which were Friends of Cinnabar: that is, tribute-paying members of the Cinnabar Empire.

Not that anybody put it that way. Those who did were promptly imprisoned for Insulting the Republic.

"Ah," Adele said with more satisfaction than most people would have packed into that simple syllable. "I was wondering why I wasn't finding more evidence of piracy. Our ally, the Principality of Palmyra, patrols the region and appears to do a very good job of it."

Her lip quirked in a wry smile. She said, "It would seem that they do a better job than dedicated anti-pirate squadrons in other regions, whether mounted by us or by the Alliance."

"Just for my curiosity, Mundy...," Mistress Sand said. Despite her attempt to seem casual, her eyes had narrowed slightly. "How do you determine the effectiveness of the patrols? Do you have Admiralty Court records in your computer?"

Adele laughed. "I could get them from the database in Navy

House," she said. "Or for that matter from the duplicate set that the Ministry of Justice is supposed to keep. I doubt if they'd tell me much, though. Our own patrols are rumored to take shortcuts when dealing with pirates, and the Palmyrenes *certainly* do."

She met Sand's eyes for the first time since she'd brought up her data unit. "It's much simpler," she said with a cold grin, "to check insurance rates for the region. They're as low as those for the Cinnabar-Blanchefleur route."

Sand laughed ruefully. "Rather than say, 'Oh, that's simple,' I'll note that the mind which went directly to that source wasn't simple at all," she said. "And yes, Palmyra has nominally been a Cinnabar ally for several generations, though that's basically been a matter of the Autocrators choosing a policy which is in keeping with the aims of the Republic. Palmyra has become a major trading power—*the* trading power in its region, certainly—and has put down piracy for its own ends."

Adele collapsed her holographic display to meet the spymaster's eyes directly. "Is Palmyra my objective, mistress?" she said.

Sand placed her hands palm-down on the scarred leather tabletop and laughed. "You've just demonstrated the limits of logic, Mundy," she said. "You know there's a reason I'd be asking you to go to the Qaboosh Region, and the only thing of even moderate significance in the region is the Principality of Palmyra, on whose intentions you've noticed that my information is strikingly scanty. Not so?"

"You're correct," Adele said with clipped tones. The humor of it struck her. She didn't laugh, but her lips formed a self-mocking grin.

"Arrogance is the claim of greater power, here in the form of knowledge, than one actually has," she said. "You're quite right to bring me up short when I display arrogance."

Sand looked at her in appraisal. "Sorry, Mundy," she said. "You give me too much credit: I was priding myself on having finally beaten someone who regularly runs circles around me. And it was a trick, because there was no way you would have known that Guarantor Porra's favorite of the past three years was Lady Posthuma Belisande."

Adele's smile reformed itself into tight, triumphant lines. Her display sprang to life.

"A relative of the present Founder of Zenobia," she said. Her wands flickered further. "The younger sister of Founder Hergo Belisande, twenty-four standard years old. Called Posy, although I don't know when that datum was gathered. It might be embarrassing to greet the lady by a nickname she'd last heard when she was eight."

Adele shrank her display again. She said, "You said Belisande was, rather than that she has been, Porra's mistress for the past three years. The relationship has ended?"

"So we understand," said Mistress Sand. "Officially the lady is visiting relatives on Zenobia, but it's generally understood that she isn't expected to return. That she's expected *not* to return, in fact—though some of that may be put around by rivals."

Adele's eyes narrowed. "Do you expect her to confide in me?" she said, trying to restrain the irritation that threatened to sharpen her tone. "Because I have no skill whatever at Human Intelligence, mistress. I have no skill at human *relationships*, one might say."

"My thought was that electronic security on Zenobia would be a great deal less sophisticated than it was on Pleasaunce," Sand said calmly. "While there's no evidence that the lady will be writing her memoirs, I'm confident that you will be able to penetrate all her files in short order."

Adele grimaced. "Sorry," she said. "I've been on edge. As you know."

The room held three waist-high bookcases, one against each wall; the door took the place of the fourth. Two of the six hinged glass fronts had been replaced by wooden panels. Those must have been lovely when waxed and buffed, but they hadn't received any care in decades.

The shelved books were standard sets of the classics, published in the second and third centuries after society on Cinnabar had begun to rebound from the thousand-year Hiatus in interstellar travel. Old learning had been assembled and reprinted in lovely editions. Every prominent landholder and every tradesman with pretensions to culture had sets just like these.

Adele had seen scores of similar collections when she haunted the libraries of her parents' friends before going off to Blythe to finish her education. Most of them, like these at Bantry, appeared to have remained unopened throughout their long existence.

Any unique items—journals from the settlement, handwritten memoirs; perhaps a list of flora and fauna by one of the first Learys to settle at Bantry—had been removed from this collection. They were probably in Xenos if they existed at all. How would Corder Leary react to a request from Lady Adele Mundy to view his library?

Adele's smile was terrible in its cold precision. Her honor didn't require her to seek out Speaker Leary. If by some mutually bad luck she met him, she would shoot him dead unless his guards shot her first. She would bet on herself there: she had a great deal of experience in shooting people.

"I...," said Mistress Sand and stopped. Adele would have thought that Sand had forgotten what she intended to say had she not kept her eyes focused on Adele's. Sand finished the whiskey in her glass, poured another four ounces, and drank half of it. Adele waited.

"You're wrong about lacking skill in manipulating people, Mundy," Sand said as she lowered the glass. "You're remarkably good at it, simply by being yourself. I don't think you appreciate how powerful an effect absolutely fearless honesty has on ordinary people."

She smiled, but the expression was unreadable.

"It's something many of them will never have encountered before, you see," Sand added.

Adele grimaced; the conversation was making her uncomfortable. "I'm afraid of many things, mistress," she said. "And it's easier to tell the truth than to lie."

"Of course it is," said Sand. "*If* you're not afraid of what other people will think. That's where the rest of us run into problems, even—"

She paused to drain her tumbler in two quick gulps. She wasn't doing justice to what Adele supposed was very good liquor.

"—when we've been drinking more than perhaps we should be."

Sand shrugged. She looked at the bottle but placed her

hands flat on the table instead. "Regardless, I won't ask you to use a talent that makes you uncomfortable. Not unless the safety of the Republic requires it."

Sand didn't move except to tremble from the effort with which she pressed down on the leather. She seemed—not right. Adele was used to people showing emotion, but it was a new experience to see Mistress Sand showing emotion. Adele disliked it in the spymaster even more than she did in others.

"You know I'll use up my assets if the Republic requires it," Sand said. "You *do* know that, don't you?"

"Yes, of course," Adele said. She paused, then went on, "There are twenty rounds in the magazine of my pistol."

She tapped her left tunic pocket.

"They wouldn't be of any use to me if I weren't willing to expend them."

"That doesn't bother you?" Sand demanded. Her face sagged into a lopsided smile. "I suppose it doesn't at that. You understood it from the beginning, when I first approached you; so of course you're not going to complain about a choice you made willingly. *You* wouldn't."

Adele said nothing. She realized, not for the first time, that anger was a common human response because it was a comfortable one. The mood in which she'd started this interview was much easier to bear than quietly listening to Mistress Sand say things that Adele would rather not hear. She could solve the problem by hurling the water pitcher to the floor and storming out of the room....

She smiled. "Easy" had never been the major criterion for her decisions.

Sand shook her head slowly. She took out the snuffbox again, but instead of opening it she raised her eyes.

"Sorry, Mundy," she said. Her voice was normal again. "I realize there's no need for me to say anything, not to you; but I started this, so I'll finish it. I expect you to extract whatever useful information Posy Belisande has. I expect you to considerably expand my information on Palmyra and on anything else in the Qaboosh Region which is material to the Republic of Cinnabar. This is a real mission."

Though she was obviously trying to seem cheerful, the impression Adele got from Sand's sudden smile was sadness. She said, "Mundy, we—the Republic—are as much at peace as it's possible for an entity of our size to be. If I thought it would do any good, I'd suggest you take a research fellowship in Novy Sverdlovsk. Captain Leary would make a splendid Naval Attaché at our embassy there, I'm sure. I didn't think that would work out, however."

Adele felt the corner of her mouth twitch in the direction of a grin. "No," she said. "I don't think it would. For either Daniel or for me."

Sand nodded agreement; she was relaxing again. "It appeared to me, however," she said, "that this business in Zenobia might be a useful stage for you both—for servants of the Republic like yourselves—to transition from the business in the Montserrat Stars back to normal life."

"Thank you, mistress," Adele said as she rose. "I appreciate your ..."

She paused, searching for the way to phrase what she wanted to say.

"I appreciate your intelligent concern."

Sand remained seated. Adele made a slight bow, then turned to the door. As she reached for the latch, she heard a shot in the near distance.

Adele was striding down the hallway in the next heartbeat, her left hand dropping to her pocket. Tovera led with a miniature sub-machine gun openly displayed in her right hand. There was another shot from outside, toward the sea front.

The trouble with normal life, Adele thought, *is that it doesn't stay normal for very long*.

Daniel felt his eyes narrow slightly as he looked past Peterleigh's ear to watch the group centered on Chuckie Platt some twenty yards north up the sea front. Peterleigh was giving a full discussion of the formal garden he was building at Boltway Manor, complete with a grotto populated with—fake—crystalline formations which were meant to suggest petrified trolls.

"Just like they'd been touched by sunlight and turned to stone, don't you know?" Peterleigh burbled. It was the sort of fashionable nonsense that would have bored Daniel to tears if he hadn't had Platt and Lieutenant Cory to worry about. Both young men held dueling pistols.

Peterleigh said, "Of course, that's where the paradox is that you need for real art. They're underground in the grotto, don't you know, so the light *couldn't* have touched them! That's a paradox!"

Platt was aiming out to sea. His body was edge-on, making a single line with his outstretched right arm; his lift arm was rigidly akimbo as though he were executing a ballet posture.

"I don't see what you mean by a paradox," Broma said, scowling. He sounded as bored with the description as Daniel felt. "Isn't a troll a bloody paradox enough? They're not real, so they're a paradox."

Platt fired; his right forearm lifted straight up with the recoil. The *whack!* of the hypersonic osmium pellet accelerating down the barrel made the others around Daniel jump. The birds overhead screamed, chattered, or croaked, depending on their species.

Waldmiller snarled, "Hofmann, what's your boy playing at, hey?"

"Don't call him my boy," Hofmann muttered. He hunched over his mug of ale and didn't meet the older landowner's eyes. "He's Bertie's boy and she insisted on bringing him. I swear by all the gods, Leary—"

He looked up in abject misery.

"—I didn't think he'd want to come. And when he said he did, I said maybe we ought *all* to stay home, but Bertie insisted because she'd heard Lady Mundy was going to be here. And now it looks like she was wrong about that, but here we are with Chuckie anyway!"

Daniel didn't bother to inform Hofmann that Adele had arrived—but with the rest of the Sissies instead of in the private aircar that he and his wife were apparently expecting. The Bantry tenants knew of Adele as the Squire's friend. It hadn't occurred to Daniel that Bertie Hofmann was from Xenos and would hope to scrape acquaintance with Mundy of Chatsworth.

"I think it'd be just as well if your son put those pistols

away for the time being, Hofmann," he said. "There's a lot of people here. And some of them have been drinking, of course."

Cory fired. They were shooting out to sea, presumably at bobbing flotsam. Spray fountained only twenty feet from the base of the sea wall; Cory had let his muzzle dip as he pulled the trigger.

Platt hooted and called in a loud voice, "Why, you weren't within a mile! Not a mile! What wets you navy men turn out to be!"

The coils wrapping the barrel generated an electromagnetic flux which ionized the pellet's aluminum driving band. The plasma hung in the air, a quivering paleness which faded as it stripped electrons from the atmosphere and returned to steady state.

One of the effete servants was loading the pistols; the other held the case for him as a table. Platt had taken the gallon jug.

"Oh, he won't listen to me," Hofmann mumbled. "I may as well save my breath."

Platt laid the jug on the crook of his elbow to lift it, then drank. He passed the liquor to the man on his right. There were about a dozen people in the group, none of them as old as twenty-five.

Cazelet was one of them. Daniel supposed he and Cory had joined a youth whom they knew only as someone of their own age and class. The sons and daughters of a few Bantry tenants had drifted over also.

"I think then that I'll have a word," said Daniel, starting forward. He thought sourly about how much more easily he could handle matters aboard the *Princess Cecile*, but he knew this sort of business could occur in a military environment as well.

His Academy classmate Oudenarde had served as midshipman on a light cruiser whose captain allowed his pet Tertullian swamp monkey to wander freely on A Level. The animal's career of rending, fouling and eating the possessions of the junior officers ended when it gobbled a package of aphrodisiacs which the Second Lieutenant had concealed among his socks.

Apparently the pills worked better on swamp monkeys than Daniel had ever known them to do with humans. The beast had been shot on the captain's screamed orders while it made a very respectable job of buggering him through the trousers of his Dress Whites.

"I figure a wet like you hasn't any business with a pretty bint," said Platt, seizing the arm of the girl in a scarlet apron who'd been standing with Cory. She tried to pull away. "You don't resent this, do you, navy boy?"

Platt grabbed a handful of the squealing girl's hair and bent to kiss her.

"Cazelet, grab him!" Daniel shouted as he broke into a run.

Rene Cazelet wrapped his arms around Cory and dragged him back. Thank the *gods* he'd been smart enough to understand what Daniel understood but hadn't adequately put in words. Cazelet touching Platt would have been just as bad as what Cory was lunging to do.

It was possible though unlikely that Cazelet was a better shot than Cory, but in either case RCN officers had to resign their commission in order to fight a duel. A hundred puffed-up bullies like Chuckie Platt weren't worth the career, let alone the life, of an RCN engine wiper.

The girl scratched at Platt's arm; his fist balled. Daniel knew he wouldn't get there in time.

Adele slapped Platt's left cheek. The boy straightened and cried, "What?"

"Sir," said Adele, "you have insulted my friend, Mistress Maynor. You will apologize to her at once."

The girl pulled herself free; Platt had forgotten her. Two of the male tenants helped her get clear but stayed to watch; the girl ran sobbing toward the huts.

"Who the bloody hell do you think you are?" said Platt, touching his cheek in amazement.

Daniel paused. This wasn't what he'd wanted to happen, but it had happened—and the situation was certainly under control now.

Hofmann's wife, gasping with emotion and the strain of running in a ridiculously tight dress, thrust herself between her son and Adele. "Chuckie, this is Lady Mundy!" she said. Her voice had a shrill edge that didn't seem to belong with so fleshy a body. "What are you thinking of?"

Platt flung his mother aside with a sweep of his arm. She gave a despairing cry as she fell. *He's more drunk than I realized*, Daniel thought. *He's wobbling on his feet.*

Eyes locked on Adele's, Platt repeated, "Who the *hell*—"

Hogg and Woetjans had the boy from behind. The complaints of people they'd knocked down added to the general bedlam.

"Think a swim'd sober him up, Six?" the bosun said, nodding toward the sea. She held Platt's right arm straight up and was stepping on his foot to anchor it.

54

"*Or* there's the old cesspool from before we cut the sewer through from the third row houses," Hogg suggested in a gruffly hopeful voice.

"Dear gods, Leary," Hofmann said. "Dear *gods*."

Daniel had forgotten the fellow. He said, "You can—"

Hofmann bowed to Adele. "Lady Mundy," he said, "I sincerely apologize for any offense my son may have given in his delirium. I was remiss, *grossly* remiss, in not keeping him at home when I knew how ill he was."

Adele's face changed, though Daniel didn't know how he would have described the difference. Adele looked human again; he supposed that would do.

"Yes," she said. "Home would be the best place for him. My colleagues—"

Her eyes flicked toward Hogg and Woetjans.

"—will help you put him in the car, if you don't mind."

"Yes, of course!" Hofmann said. "And I will apologize personally to Mistress Maynor in the place and manner you wish, Your Ladyship."

"A moment if you please, Hofmann," Daniel said. Woetjans thumped to attention; even Hogg's expression showed that he understood that there weren't going to be any arguments now. "May I borrow these for a moment?"

Without waiting for Hofmann's response—it was a blurted, "Yes, of course, anything!" when it came—Daniel lifted the pistol from the tray with his right hand and the one the servant had just finished reloading with his left. Holding each by the balance, butt forward, he turned toward Adele. She waited impassively.

55

"Adele?" he said. "There are two Dravidian maws above us, the large pink birds. They're an introduced species which I consider to be a nuisance. Would you please take care of it for me?"

He held out a pistol. Adele glanced at the raucously circling birds. Smiling faintly, she took the weapon in her left hand.

The maws wobbled between a hundred and a hundred and fifty feet in the air, higher than most of the other birds. The bare skin of their wings was, as Daniel said, pinkish below, though the upper surface was opalescent and rather attractive in sunlight.

That was the birds' only attractive aspect. Their heads were roughly the size of clenched fists and resembled beaked gargoyles, their call was as shrilly unpleasant of that of a tortured rabbit, and they spread their liquid green feces widely as they flew. One could scarcely ask for a better—

Adele presented her pistol and fired as part of the same motion. Spectators jumped at the shot; a few reflexively clapped their hands over their ears.

One of the birds had been over the sea. Its head vanished in a pink mist; the heavy body tumbled, motion making the wings flutter like unstayed sails. The bird splashed but did not immediately sink.

Adele tipped the butt of her pistol up; Daniel took it in his free hand as he offered her the loaded weapon. She held that one for a moment, judging the balance. The pistols should have been identical, but Daniel wasn't going to try to tell his friend her business.

Some of the birds had scattered at the previous shot, but

the remaining maw continued its circle. It shrieked as it sailed over the sea wall, apparently in general peevishness. Adele presented and fired, her motion more like someone netting butterflies than anything lethal.

The bird's skull splashed, though this time the lower half of the beak remained attached to the neck by a strip of skin. The throat sack filled like a parachute, halting the maw in mid flight.

The bird dropped, spilling air and swelling again twice more before it hit the water; it floated within an arm's length of its mate. The new splash drew some of the fish which had begun to nibble the previous carcass.

"Thank you, Adele," Daniel said as he took the emptied pistol. He beamed at Platt.

The youth had stopped struggling. He stared at Adele, then turned gray and threw up. Hogg grinned to Woetjans. When they both let go, Platt toppled face-first into his own vomit.

Hogg elbowed one of the liveried servants. "I guess you two can get him to the car, right?" he said. "Do it *now*."

The servants took their master by the arms, but they fumbled badly. Platt dropped to the ground again before they got him to his feet. They finally stumbled off in the direction of the aircar.

Daniel turned. He threw the pistol in his right hand as far into the sea as he could get it, then followed it with the other. He managed to get an additional three or four feet on the second throw. Fish, made hopeful by the maw corpses, shivered toward the fresh disturbances.

"Very sorry about dropping the guns, Hofmann," Daniel said. "I'll pay you for them, of course."

Hofmann was helping his wife to her feet. He looked over his shoulder toward Daniel. "I wouldn't think of it, Leary," he said. "It's just another of the several favors you've done me this day."

Then, to his wife, "Come along, Bertie. We have things to discuss when we get home."

The landowners and Sand remained where they had been. Daniel gave them a quick, hard smile to show that all was well.

Bantries sidled away from Daniel and Adele, whispering to one another with a variety of expressions. Cazelet had headed for the hall, his arm around Cory's shoulders.

Hogg and Woetjans were moving back also. That surprised Daniel until he realized that the gallon liquor jug had somehow vanished from sight.

They've earned a drink this day, he thought. He ostentatiously turned his back instead of peering more closely at his servant's baggy tunic.

Adele was standing at his side. "I don't know about you, Daniel," she said quietly, "but *I'm* ready to leave Cinnabar for a place where the rules are simpler."

"Yes," said Daniel. "Though with the Peace of Rheims in effect, we can't hope to find a war zone."

CHAPTER 3

XENOS ON CINNABAR

Daniel, holding the ivroid chit inset with 444 in black which he'd just gotten from the receiving clerk, turned and looked for an empty place on the benches. The General Waiting Room was as full as he'd ever seen it.

Navy House had grown into a complex of buildings as the Republic of Cinnabar Navy expanded into the sword of an empire. What people ordinarily meant by Navy House was the Navy Office, built around the hall in which RCN officers waited to be summoned for new assignments.

Generally they waited in vain. They would return tomorrow and following tomorrows until they either lost hope or received an assignment. A third of the RCN's ships had already been paid off in response to the Treaty of Rheims, and perhaps as many more would follow over the next few months. Today's crush of unemployed officers could only get worse.

Daniel wondered if officials in the Procurement Bureau had ordered additional ivroid chits. The highest number he recalled having seen was in the seven hundreds. He smiled faintly: the apparatus of the waiting room might have to expand because of the demands of peace, just as Navy House itself had grown due to the needs of war.

Someone ten benches back waved in the air, then pointed to Daniel. His grin spread as he recognized Pennyroyal, a friend—or at least friendly acquaintance—from his Academy days; he strode down the aisle toward her.

He wouldn't have said there was a real space beside Pennyroyal, but she was widening what there was with animated whispers to the officers in both directions as she mimed shoving them aside. The result was still tight, but that was in part a result of Captain Daniel Leary having put on a few pounds. A few *more* pounds, unfortunately. He sat with a grin of apologetic embarrassment to the older lieutenant to his left.

"I'm surprised to see you slumming with us poor sad jetsam, Leary," Pennyroyal whispered. From another's mouth that could have been a bitter gibe; from hers, it was ruefully appreciative. "I heard you got a Cinnabar Star for that business off Cacique, didn't you?"

"Ah, yes," Daniel said. He was wearing his best set of Grays. Medal ribbons were proper but were not required with Grays, the second-class uniform; Daniel had chosen not to wear his.

In fact he'd gotten a Wreath for the Cinnabar Star which he'd been awarded after the Battle of Strymon while he was still a lieutenant. "We had a great deal of luck there, I must say."

The Annunciator stood with the receiving clerk, beside the gate in the bar separating the assignment clerks from the ranks of benches. The printer beside him whirred out a length of flimsy. He pulled it off, glared at it, and said, "Number One-Seven-Two, come forward!"

A thin, almost cadaverous lieutenant scraped up from one of the back benches and strode toward the front. She was trying to look nonchalant, but she stepped a little too quickly. She was wearing her Whites; when she passed, Daniel saw that fabric of the elbows and trouser seat had been polished by long use.

Daniel felt uncomfortable discussing his career with former classmates. He *had* been lucky, very lucky; and particularly, he'd been lucky in gaining Adele's friendship and support, which were matters he couldn't discuss. Indeed, Adele's intelligence duties—her spying—made Daniel even more uncomfortable than discussing his victories did.

"Well, I'm hoping for some luck myself," Pennyroyal said. "Vondrian—you remember Vondrian, don't you?"

"Of course," Daniel said truthfully. Vondrian, who'd been a class ahead of him at the Academy, had private money. Instead of lording it over his less fortunate fellows, he'd been liked and respected by all who knew him. "He has a ship of his own, I understood?"

"That's right, the *Montrose* in the Tattersall Flotilla—which Vondrian says is three destroyers on a good day but generally less," Pennyroyal said. "Tattersall is an Associated World of the Republic but not a Friend, you see. It gives the RCN an observation base in the Forty Stars where every other world worth mentioning is part of the Alliance."

"I dare say Vondrian's breathing easier for the Peace of Rheims," said Daniel, shaking his head. The trouble with a detached command like what Pennyroyal described was that if the enemy decided to get rid of you, you probably wouldn't have enough warning even to run away.

"I wouldn't be surprised," said Pennyroyal. "And I hope to be able to ask him personally soon, because he swears he's requested me as his First Lieutenant. I don't mind telling you, Leary, it's going to be bloody short rations for me if I have to live on half pay for very long."

"Vondrian's as straight as a die," Daniel said. It was the truth, but he added verve to the words to buck up Pennyroyal. "If he told you he was going to request you, you can take it to the bank that you'll have your berth shortly."

That wasn't quite so true. Captains had a great deal of influence in the choice of officers serving under them, and Vondrian's wealth gave him more influence than most. At a time like this, however, when any posting was worth fighting for, there was always the risk that an admiral's nephew was going to be appointed into the place a lieutenant commander had requested for a friend.

Partly because Daniel was afraid his smile would slip if he looked directly at Pennyroyal, he focused on the bench ahead of him. Faintly visible in the wood was a pentacle about three inches across from flat to the point opposite. The illumination from the skylights thirty feet above was so diffuse that he first noticed the texture rather than the slight difference in color.

"Why, I'll be!" Daniel said. He was glad to change the subject, but his enthusiasm was real. "Here, Pennyroyal—do you see the fungus growing through the wood? The gray pentacle?"

"I suppose I see the pentacle," Pennyroyal said—*agreed*

would be too strong a word. "If you say it's a fungus, I'll believe you."

"You remember that some of these benches were supposed to have been made of paneling from the Alliance flagship captured in the Battle of Cloudscape?" Daniel said. Burbled, he supposed—but he'd always found the *wonder* of the universe more interesting than tensile strength or power-to-weight calculations. "Well, that must not be just a legend. This is a Pleasaunce species!"

He grinned in satisfaction at having dredged up another datum. "A male. They're bisexual, and the females grow in circular patterns."

"That's your number, isn't it, Leary?" said Pennyroyal.

For a moment Daniel tried to fit her words into a context of history or natural history, which between them were absorbing his attention. *The bench in front of me is over three hundred years old!*

"Four-forty-four?" Pennyroyal said.

Oh, dear gods!

"Yes, and I thank you sincerely," Daniel said as he rose. The two officers between him and the aisle turned sideways to let him slip past. Their faces were stoical, but Daniel didn't think he was imagining a touch of envy on the face of the overweight commander.

The receiving clerk looked up at Daniel. The sour disdain with which he greeted an expected new suppliant turned to fury when he saw the person approaching was an officer who'd been to see him only minutes before.

"If you're looking for a luckier number, Captain—" the clerk sneered. When he realized that the chit Daniel was displaying face-out was the number that had been called a moment earlier, he swallowed the rest of whatever the comment would have been.

"This one seemed lucky enough to me," Daniel said with a pleasant smile; he handed the chit to the Annunciator to drop back into the wire hopper. "Four-four-four, if you please."

He was in too good a mood for a minor functionary to spoil it. Besides, he was pretty sure that just being cheerful would irritate the clerk as much as anything else he could do.

The twelve or fifteen personnel at desks on the clerical side of the Waiting Room bar were civilians. The only RCN officer in their chain of command was the Chief of the Navy Board. No one else in uniform, not even a full admiral, could give a valid order to an assignment clerk. That was a necessary feature of a job which would often lead to outbursts of fury from frustrated officers.

But facing anger and resentment day after day would have taken a toll on a saint, in the unlikely event that a saint applied for the job. The receiving clerk in particular had to be ruthless, but his duties had curdled necessity into cruelty.

"Yes, of course, Captain," the clerk muttered. The Annunciator gave Daniel the flimsy printed with 444—DESK 7 and nodded to the usher, who lifted the gate.

Desk 7 was in the second row, identified by a rectangular sign on a short post; the letters were tarnished silver. The clerk was a woman in the process of passing middle age; her throat was wrinkled and her jowls were slipping, but her figure was still good.

She beamed at Daniel, an expression he had never expected to see on the face of an assignment clerk. "Do be seated, Captain," she said, gesturing toward the straight chair across the desk from her. "May I say that I regard it an honor to meet you professionally?"

"I...," said Daniel. He didn't know where to go with his response. Here on this side of the bar, the noise of the hall was more noticeable than it had been among the hundreds of waiting officers whose whispers and shuffling were responsible for it. "I, ah, thank you."

"There are a few formalities to take care of first," she said, sorting through a file of hardcopy. "As the final commander of RCS *Milton*, you're to initial this Finding of Loss and Disposal."

Sliding a sheet of paper and a stylus across the desk, she added peevishly, "They haven't attached the court-martial decision, though. There's normally a copy of the court record."

She raised her eyes to Daniel's. "Not that there was anything to be concerned about in your conduct, of course," she added hastily.

The document was a form whose blanks had been filled in by someone with casually beautiful handwriting. Daniel began to initial each paragraph that had holograph additions. He said, "A court martial is required for any captain who loses his ship, mistress. We—because it wouldn't have been possible without an exceptional crew—were able to sail the *Milton* home. The surveyors declared her a constructive loss, but that was decided after I'd handed her over to the dockyard."

Daniel returned the finding and stylus. Smiling to make a joke of what he was about to say, he added, "There wasn't much doubt about their decision, I'm afraid; even without the end of hostilities, the *Milton* couldn't have been economically repaired . . . and there was a prejudice against her design, as well. But I, ah, regret her loss nonetheless."

Sixty-three spacers had died when an Alliance missile vaporized the *Milton*'s stern. Daniel felt for every one of them; but he felt for the cruiser herself as well. A theologian might claim that ships don't have souls, but Daniel was a spacer and knew things that no landsman would ever fathom.

The clerk replaced the form in her file folder, then handed Daniel another document. "Here is your new assignment, Captain," she said. "Oh! I should have told you to keep the stylus, I'm afraid. You're to sign the upper copy."

"Thank you," said Daniel dryly, retrieving the instrument which was only six inches from his hand. He scanned the document, smiling with satisfaction—and, truth to tell, with relief.

The past generation had been one of constant war or looming war between Cinnabar and the Alliance. The Peace of Rheims appeared to be a different animal from the brief truces of the last twenty years, if only because both empires were on the verge of social and economic collapse.

Peace had put the RCN in a state of flux like nothing before in Daniel's lifetime. It had been possible that someone very senior in the RCN or even the Senate was going to trump the cards that Captain Daniel Leary and his friends could play.

"Captain," the clerk said earnestly, "I realize that being assigned to a chartered vessel may appear to be a slight after your command of a heavy cruiser. I assure you that it is not: the Cinnabar Commissioner died suddenly on Zenobia. It's necessary to rush a replacement there, but the world is in the Alliance sphere. We can't send a warship without giving offense, which might have the most serious implications for the recent treaty."

"Mistress...," Daniel said, looking up from his orders. He was faintly puzzled. "I understood that the needs of the service were paramount from the moment I enlisted. I've never objected to a lawful order."

There had been times when Daniel Leary's superiors might have complained regarding the speed and manner in which he *executed* his orders—but he wasn't going to say that to a civilian.

"Oh!" said the clerk, touching her fingertips to her lower lip. "Oh, of course not, Captain! But surely the needs of the service include the proper treatment of officers who have done so much for the Republic. Why, the peace treaty might not have been signed without your victory at Cacique!"

Daniel blinked. He supposed he ought to be pleased that the clerical staff was treating him as an individual rather than a cog to be put in whatever bin a computer decided.

In fact he found he preferred to be a cog. If the clerks treated Captain Leary as a person, then he had to think of them as people. It took much less energy to view clerks as minor irritations to the life of an RCN officer, much like the gnats that rose from the marshes at Bantry to clog the eyes, noses, and food of everyone who had to be outdoors in early spring.

But after all, it might be just this clerk at Desk 7. Perhaps he could go on being callously dismissive of all the faceless others here in Navy House and beyond.

Daniel smiled broadly; the clerk seemed to glow in reaction.

That was fair even though she probably misunderstood his expression: she'd led him to the train of thought, after all. Anyway, it made the world a better place than it would have been after another sneering exchange like his with the receiving clerk.

The woman was forty years past the age that Daniel's smile would've meant what she apparently understood from it, though.

Aloud he said, "Well, since I'm to have my pick of spacers to crew her, I'll see if we can't get Commissioner—"

He glanced at the document he'd just signed.

"—Pavel Brown and his family to Zenobia before the vacancy causes problems for distressed Cinnabar spacers in the Qaboosh Region."

Simply being in the Qaboosh Region would be distressing enough for an RCN officer; the place could be used as the illustration of the term "backwater." Though peace meant that there weren't *any* postings which were likely to be a springboard to higher rank.

The clerk took the signed copy of the orders. As Daniel stood she said, "Using a chartered yacht means money in the pocket of some well-placed civilian, but we mustn't complain about reality. I only hope that this *Princess Cecile* is well found."

Daniel grinned again. "The ship is as tight and nimble as any vessel in the RCN, mistress," he said. "And the charter fee won't be going to a civilian—because I own her myself."

He had to remind himself not to begin whistling as he strode toward the door to the street.

* * *

HARBOR THREE, NEAR XENOS ON CINNABAR

"Ma'am?" said Benthelow. He was a Power Room tech who'd been on guard duty when Adele boarded the *Princess Cecile* an hour before. He probably still was, but he'd left his submachine gun back in the boarding hold with his fellow guard before he came up to the bridge. "There's a guy here that, well, I thought you might talk to him."

Adele was alone on the bridge. Tovera had gone off on her own business; Adele made a point of not knowing what her servant did in her free time. She sat at the Communications console, going over the software she had just installed.

Every time Adele landed on Cinnabar, Mistress Sand's organization provided her with updates for the codes she might encounter. The top Alliance military codes were still effectively closed to her if they were applied properly, but the computing power necessary to guide a starship through the Matrix could by brute force gut almost any commercial code like a hooked fish.

And even unbreakable codes were often misused. Adele found that people were frequently careless.

Other people, that is.

She got to her feet. Adele was wearing civilian clothes because she had come from her townhouse and hadn't bothered to change into utilities before she went to work. Her garments were similar in cut to RCN utilities but were light brown instead of mottled gray on gray, so she could wear them in public without violating regulations.

"Yes, sir?" she said to the man in the hatchway behind

Benthelow—who really shouldn't have brought the fellow up with him, but Signals Officer Adele Mundy wasn't the proper person to give lectures on following protocol. Nor was Captain Daniel Leary, if it came to that.

"I apologize, mistress," the man said. He was over six feet tall; well over, in fact, though the way he hunched forward tended to conceal his height. He had limp, sandy hair and a high forehead, making him look older than his forty or so standard years. "I asked to see the captain for permission to view our quarters, but this man brought me to you. I'm Pavel Brown. Ah, my family and I are to be his passengers."

"I'll take care of this, Benthelow," Adele said. "And yes, Commissioner Brown, I'll be happy to show you your quarters. I'm Adele Mundy."

She patted her trousers with a smile that was mostly for show. People liked other people to smile.

"When I'm in uniform, I'm Signals Officer Mundy. A moment, please."

She sat again, this time crossways on the bench. The data unit which she used as a control interface was on her lap. Nobody was likely to meddle with Adele's console in her absence, and nobody except Cory or possibly Cazelet would be able to get into it anyway. Nonetheless she made sure everything was switched off before she rose, slipping the PDU into her cargo pocket.

"Surely not *Lady* Mundy?" Brown said as he followed her into the corridor and down the forward companionway. "I was told that she might be a passenger on this voyage as well, though I assumed that was one of those silly departmental rumors."

"Watch your footing," Adele said as their footsteps echoed within the armored tube. Her clumsiness on shipboard was something of a joke among the spacers she'd served with, but the slick steel treads of the stairs between levels of the ship had never given her trouble: she'd spent years trudging up and down similar steps in the stacks of research libraries. A warship's companionways were a memory of home to her.

"I'm Mundy of Chatsworth," Adele said as she exited onto D Level, the deck below the bridge. In harbor on Xenos the companionway doors were left open, but in combat they would be closed and could be locked both for structural strength—maneuver and battle damage both twisted a ship's hull, which the transverse tubes resisted—and to limit air loss in event of penetration. "But not aboard the *Sissie*, where I'm a warrant officer, not a passenger."

She led the way briskly down the corridor. Several spacers were about their business in the compartments to either side; they murmured "Ma'am," or bobbed their heads when they saw Adele.

She paused at the hatch of what would ordinarily be the Captain's Suite. On previous voyages, she had lived in the Captain's Office, which had a fully capable computer though with a flat-plate rather than holographic display. She would be with the midshipmen until the Browns were delivered, and Daniel would live in his space cabin adjacent to the bridge.

"I don't know what you may have heard, Commissioner," she said. "But as you're already aware, most rumors are silly. And in any case, they have no bearing on my duties or our relationship while the *Sissie*—"

She smiled coldly. "While the *Princess Cecile*, I should say, is under way. Forgive me for dropping into jargon."

"Your pardon, Officer Mundy," Brown said. He looked miserable, at a loss in all possible fashions; but she'd *had* to say it. "I didn't intend to give offense."

"Your quarters," Adele said instead of replying directly. She found it best to let matters drop when they were embarrassing. "The stateroom here. The door to the right is the sleeping cabin, and on the left is the office, which now has a bunk as well. I gather there are three of you?"

"Yes, Clothilde and Hester, our four-year-old, will accompany me," Brown said sadly. "Clothilde wanted me to bring Hester's governess along, but the wages Mistress Beeton demanded to come such a distance from Xenos were beyond my resources, quite beyond them. I told Clothilde that perhaps we could hire a governess when we reached Calvary, but she seems to believe that the inhabitants of Zenobia are all barbarians who might be expected to eat babies. The governess was of a similar opinion."

The Commissioner's glumness seemed to be the mindset he— like others whom she had met—found most congenial. That puzzled Adele. She was bleak—how could any intelligent person view the universe and mankind without being bleak?—but there seemed neither pleasure nor profit in a negative attitude.

And then there was Daniel's example: an intelligent man who was also cheerful. Knowing Daniel had made Adele question the primacy of data and reason, the elements on which she built her life.

She couldn't do anything to change her attitude, of course,

even if she were wrong about the pointlessness of life. And presumably Brown couldn't help but be negative even if he had enough common sense to realize that his attitude was silly.

"I think you'll find the culture of Calvary on a level with that of most provincial cities on Cinnabar," Adele said dryly. "And even in the countryside, I believe that the staple meat is goat rather than babies. Though my information is no doubt incomplete."

Brown looked at her in amazement, then realized that the comment had been ironic. He forced a smile.

"Yes," he said. "And I believe Clothilde knows better as well. I'm not sure Mistress Beeton did."

He crossed the stateroom and peered into the sleeping cabin. Rather than try to replace the single fold-down bunk into something suitable for a couple, Pasternak and the shipyard crew had left the bedroom as it was—for the child, presumably—and put a double bed in the office where the desk and terminal had been. That also required expanding the office some distance into the stateroom, but internal partitions were expected to be moved.

"It's very small, isn't it?" Brown said sadly. "Clothilde won't be happy. And such a long voyage, a month and a half."

"I doubt the *Princess Cecile* will take anywhere near that long on the passage," Adele said. It was natural for her to keep her tone unemotional, but she felt a spike of irritation at Brown's comment. *What does the fellow expect?* "But unquestionably, interstellar travel is uncomfortable."

She cleared her throat. She hadn't researched the Browns' backgrounds as thoroughly as she should have. "This is your first voyage, then?"

He turned and nodded as he walked to the refitted office. "Yes," he said. "I've been on Xenos my entire career with the ministry. I'm an accountant, you see."

Brown smiled in embarrassment, though Adele couldn't imagine why he should think an accountant had to apologize to a librarian. Both vocations were necessary to civilization, and both involved organizing data, making them—

She grinned minusculely, but in her heart she believed it.

—the highest forms of human endeavor.

Adele nodded noncommittally. "If you've seen your fill of the suite," she said, "we'll go back down the corridor to the wardroom where you'll be eating."

She wondered whether Brown had received any briefing from his superiors. She was beginning to suspect that he had not.

"You can either bring along your own food, which will go in a storage locker on A Level...," she said, stepping back into the corridor, "or you can pay a subscription and mess with the officers. I suppose you'll at least want to bring, well, whatever your child eats."

Or do four-year-olds eat adult food? That wasn't a question Adele had previously considered; nor, she realized, did she need to do so now.

The hatch to the wardroom was open. The hanging table was fast against the ceiling, so she gestured to call attention to it and said, "It will be lowered for meals, of course."

"I see," Brown said sadly. "Thank you, ah, Officer."

"The purser can help you with questions of what stores you should bring," Adele said. "He'll be in Warehouse 73, I believe...."

She took out her data unit and sat on the nearest of the

chairs bolted to the deck plates. A few flicks of her control wands gave her the answer.

"Yes, he's there now," she said with satisfaction. "Master Reddick. I can send a spacer with you as a guide, if you like?"

"No thank you, Officer Mundy," Brown said as though he were announcing the death of his mother. "The Bureau's handbook gives extensive information on supplies for off-planet assignments and I've read it thoroughly."

"Well, then...," said Adele. "If you don't have any more questions...?"

"I'd intended to stay in the accounting department until I retired," Brown said. He was looking toward the holographic seascape on the compartment's outer wall, but his eyes were on something far more distant. "Clothilde thought that I should be promoted more quickly, and of course promotion in Accounting isn't very fast. We don't have the casualties that you naval personnel do, you see."

Adele smiled; Brown smiled back shyly.

"I transferred to the Representational Service," he said. "It was a two-step promotion, which made Clothilde very happy. The trouble is, accounts have to balance in life as well as finances. Now that Clothilde is beginning to realize what the higher pay grade cost, she isn't so happy."

He smiled wider. The expression showed both misery and genuine amusement.

"I think you'll find the voyage more congenial than you now think, Commissioner," Adele said truthfully. With that sense of humor, Brown might get along well after all.

CHAPTER 4

HARBOR THREE, CINNABAR

Daniel was familiar with the *Sissie*'s Power Room. He was the captain: he must have at least a working acquaintance with every aspect of the ship he commanded.

Having said that, he always felt like an unwelcome visitor when he passed through the armored hatch which, unlike the ship's other internal hatches, was always closed and dogged when not in use. Larger vessels even had airlocks between the Power Room and the rest of the ship, but a corvette like the *Princess Cecile* couldn't spare the space.

If the *Sissie*'s fusion bottle vented while someone was entering or leaving the Power Room, it was just too bad for the rest of the ship. Realistically, that was true even if the containment bulkheads retained their integrity. For the technicians themselves it made no difference whatever.

"Anything I should know about, Chief?" Daniel said, looking about the steam-hazed chamber with appreciation if not affection. To him, star travel meant standing on the masthead, feeling his soul merge with the cosmos, while infinite bubble universes glowed in pastel splendor all around him.

That magnificence wouldn't be possible without the energy developed by the fusion bottle cradled here in muggy discomfort in the Power Room. Thank the gods there were people like Chief Engineer Pasternak who not only accepted this environment but who thrived in it.

Pasternak turned and glared at Daniel in grim satisfaction. *"Like enough there is, yes,"* he said. *"I've never lifted yet but there was a seal that cracked or a fleck of corrosion to scale off the inside of a line and clog a converter inlet or the like. But—"*

The glare didn't become a smile, but it suggested that the engineer's face was capable of smiling. Years of association with Pasternak hadn't given Daniel any evidence that the suggestion was true, however.

"—I'll say that the Sissie *could—could, mind you—become the first one."*

Though they stood side by side, Daniel and the Chief Engineer were using a two-way link through their commo helmets. The noise in the Power Room was as omnipresent as the steam. Though no single machine was particularly loud, in combination they were overwhelming. Pumps ran constantly, to maintain the fusion bottle's equilibrium as well as to circulate the water that when vaporized drove the generators which in turn powered everything else on shipboard.

There were many possible working fluids with higher thermal efficiency than water. The reason they weren't used was that starships were closed environments which were subjected to all manners of strain. Everything within a ship's hull was certain to become part of the atmosphere eventually. Crews readily accepted lower efficiency in the power train so that they could avoid poisoning by minute concentrations of whatever heat, pressure, and bad luck could turn metals and long-chain molecules into.

Daniel beamed. That was perhaps the most positive statement he'd heard from Pasternak in all their years together. "Very good, Chief," he said. "You and your team have dealt with every problem you've been thrown, but I'd say that you've earned a chance at an uneventful voyage. Mind, I *will* be pushing this time."

"And when have you not pushed, Captain?" Pasternak said. *"In your cradle, you were trying to rock faster than the other lads, were you not?"*

Both Power Room watches were present, crowding the space which wasn't given over to machinery. Liftoff was in six hours. Though there wasn't much to do by this time, everybody down to the engine wipers wanted to make sure of that.

Gauges were being calibrated, synchronized, switched off, and checked again to make sure they had held their zero. Flow rates were calculated, compared against the lines' logged history, and compared again with that of the other feed lines.

A pair of very serious assistant engineers were even running density checks of the contents of the reaction mass tanks. That determined the quantity of impurities in the water being sucked up from the harbor to be later spewed out as plasma through the thrusters or converted to antimatter and recombined in the High Drive motors. Since the reaction mass was cleared by centrifugal filters before it even left the tanks, Daniel couldn't imagine how the answer could matter—but maybe it did; and in any case, Pasternak's assistants were bent on learning it.

Daniel looked directly at the Chief Engineer. Despite the crush and bustle around them, the very noise gave them complete privacy. Further, though Daniel found the atmosphere—in all senses—of the Power Room to be oppressive, Pasternak was in his element and as relaxed as he ever seemed to get.

"Chief?" Daniel said. "Why did you sign on for this voyage? Don't mistake—I couldn't be happier to have you. But, well, not to pry, but—"

Bloody hell. He *was* prying, that was all he was doing.

"If you don't mind telling me, I mean. Because it can't be the pay, after what you've salted away in prize money over the years."

For a moment, Pasternak's face had no more expression than the Tokomak squatting in the center of the compartment; then it creased into a smile that suggested ice breaking up on the Bantry shoreline as the tide came in. Daniel swallowed a sigh of relief.

"You've made me a rich man, Captain," Pasternak said. *"And no, I haven't pissed it away in the alleys behind dram shops and knocking houses like half the crew has. Half the crew and nigh all the riggers."*

The Chief of Ship—Pasternak—and the Chief of Rig—the bosun, Woetjans—had to work together to make the *Sissie* the first-rate fighting ship she was. The rivalry between the two sides from top to bottom was also a factor in that success, however.

"When I first signed on with the RCN," Pasternak said, *"I started saving for a piece of land in Wassail County where I*

come from. I'm not a farmer, no, but my dad, he was chief mechanic on the Tomlinson Estate there. And now, because I shipped with Captain Leary, I own the Tomlinson Estate, sir, I own it. Lev Pasternak is the richest man in Wassail County and everybody calls his children squire or lady, they do."

Daniel clapped his hands in delight. Heaven knew what the other people in the Power Room made of that, but they'd all shipped with Captain Leary before so it wouldn't greatly surprise them.

Senior warrant officers took a significant share of prize money. Land prices in Wassail County, far south of Xenos, were moderate, and Daniel's commands had captured a fortune in prizes while Pasternak served with him.

"Chief," he said, "that's marvelous! By all that's holy, I'd never have dreamed it! I mean—not that you could become a country squire, but that you'd *want* to be a country squire."

Which the *gods* knew, Daniel Leary—though raised as he was and full of fond memories of his childhood—did not. But if vaccinating swine and talking to stodgy neighbors about corn prices really were Pasternak's ideal, all the more reason to wonder what he was doing aboard the *Princess Cecile*.

"Testing only!" snarled a male voice over the ceiling loudspeakers, adding to the cacophony. Power Room personnel would be getting the warning through their commo helmets as well. *"Testing only!"*

A blat of sound and pulsing red light followed immediately and lasted much longer than Daniel thought it should have. He wondered, as he often had, whether alert signals weren't distractions that interfered with an intelligent response.

Though when the alerts were real, he'd always been too busy to notice.

"*Well, between you, me, and the bedpost, sir,*" Pasternak said, "*a month or two every year or two, when we're on Cinnabar between voyages—that's pretty much my limit. But the wife likes it, and the little ones like it, not that they're so little any more, and those're good things.*"

"I understand exactly how you feel, Chief," Daniel said. "But I hadn't thought of you as needing adventure; and, well, there's houses to be had in Xenos or another place if you fancied."

Pasternak touched the side of his commo helmet as though he'd forgotten he was wearing it when he tried to knuckle his head. He was frowning; perhaps the question puzzled him as much as it did Daniel.

"*I been shot at enough times now to know I don't like it, that's a fact,*" he said. "*But you know, sir? I find I'm happy being around people who're good at their jobs and who understand that I'm good at mine. You don't see that on many ships, and you bloody never get it with civilians. Does that make sense?*"

Daniel thought of his sister Deirdre. He was pretty sure that the personnel of the Shippers' and Merchants' Treasury were just as sharp and hard-working as his Sissies. But trying to imagine Pasternak working in a bank—

Daniel clapped the engineer on the shoulder. "It makes perfect sense, Chief," he said. "Perfect. Now I'll leave you to it and get up to the bridge and my own job."

Daniel pressed the touchplate in the center of the hatch and waited for the hydraulic systems to open it for him. He was grinning.

Pasternak working in a bank would be almost as silly as me working in a bank!

Adele sat upright at the signals console—she rarely reclined—as she skimmed the data from the battleship *Euclid* which was pouring into her data banks. Tovera moved into the corner of Adele's vision and swayed back and forth very slowly.

Adele froze her holographic display—though the data dump continued—and met Tovera's eyes directly. She could no more have ignored her servant than she could have ignored an onrushing fire—though if needs must, she could have worked through the distraction in either case.

"Yes?" she said crisply. She was irritated, but she tried to keep her feelings out of her voice. She knew Tovera wouldn't interrupt without what she considered a good reason; and in all truth, there was no reason for Adele to enter the *Euclid*'s data banks except to prove that she could.

Mind, the data might come in handy for some unexpected purpose. But the exercise was reason enough.

It should have been impossible to breach a battleship's electronic security, but when the *Euclid* was docked to replace half her thruster nozzles, the Communications Officer—a lieutenant commander, not a mere junior warrant officer as on a corvette—had failed to complete his shut-down procedures. By reversing the instructions which Adele found echoed onto the command console, she was able to copy all the *Euclid*'s data except the codes which were housed in a separate computer and not linked to the main system.

Adele had become too familiar with that sort of carelessness to even become angry about it. Well, very angry. Which was an even better reason not to vent her transferred displeasure onto her servant.

"The Commissioner's wife would like a word with you in private, mistress," Tovera said. She didn't point, but her eyes flicked in the direction of the bridge hatch, open but guarded by technicians Munsing and Rawls.

Adele let her gaze follow the minuscule gesture. Clothilde Brown looked furious, but the *Sissie* was within an hour of liftoff, so personnel were restricted to their stations.

Rawls wouldn't have let the woman pass anyway. He'd been a labor organizer as well as a machinist at Harbor Three. When a squad of Militia had suddenly arrived at the dockyard, he'd decided to ship out on the RCS *Aglaia* under a false name to avoid discussing his recent activities.

Rawls had learned very quickly that everybody aboard a starship pulled together or none of them saw home again. He'd stayed with the RCN and with the newly promoted Lieutenant Daniel Leary after the survivors of the *Aglaia*'s crew transferred to the corvette *Princess Cecile*. But Rawls wasn't going to forget his orders because a civilian with a snooty accent told him to.

Adele looked around the bridge without expression. Pasternak hadn't lighted the thrusters yet, so there was time for a short conversation...and no reason not to have one, except that Officer Mundy was in a bad mood.

Smiling faintly, Adele stood up. "I'm going to my quarters for a moment, Cazelet," she said to the midshipman on the jumpseat opposite her on the console. "Take over until I return, if you will."

"Ma'am," Cazelet said, his face and tone neutral. There was a flat-plate terminal in the midshipmen's quarters; he would watch the interview through it unless Adele told him not to, which she had no intention of doing. If Clothilde Brown wanted to believe that her privacy was being respected, she was free to do so; but civilians didn't give orders on an RCN vessel.

Before Clothilde could speak, Adele said, "Since you want privacy, mistress, we'll go down to my quarters."

"If you'll follow me, mistress," Tovera said. "Please be careful of the treads."

The midshipmen's compartment was the point of the bow on B Level, directly below the command console. The hatch was locked open; Tovera bowed Clothilde through, then stood in the hatchway when Adele had followed.

Clothilde frowned. "Does your servant have to be present, Lady Mundy?" she said.

Adele grimaced, though for the most part the reaction didn't reach the muscles of her face. "Yes," she said. "She has to be present."

She didn't offer an explanation. She didn't *have* an explanation, except that she now understood the purpose of this conversation and that added to her existing ill temper.

Clothilde Brown blinked. "Ah," she said. "Well, this is embarrassing. Lady Mundy, I most sincerely apologize for waiting this long to pay my respects. If you can believe it, it was only a few minutes ago that my husband finally told me who you are! I was furious, of course. I told him that he must watch Hester while I saw you—since he refused to allow me to bring Hester's governess on this horrible trip."

Adele considered a number of responses. She would not, of course, shoot Clothilde. If she had been Commissioner Brown, however, that option would have been closer to the top of the list.

"On this voyage," Adele said aloud, "I am Officer Mundy—as I believe I told your husband. It would be regrettable, mistress, if you were to object to the Commissioner having obeyed my instructions."

"Oh!" said Clothilde, touching her mouth with the fingertips of her left hand. "Oh, no, Your Ladyship, I didn't mean that at all."

"Very well, Mistress Brown," Adele said. "I'll return to my duties, then."

Clothilde's face scrunched up; she began to cry. "Oh, please," she blubbered, "I'm sorry but I'm so miserable and I'm afraid! This is so awful, all of it."

Adele recoiled in horror, though she hoped she managed to keep her face blank. *Daniel would know what to do.* Of course one of the reasons Daniel had more experience with crying women was that his own behavior was often the cause of the tears. Adele had done nothing to provoke this unpleasant outbreak.

"I assure you that there's less danger now than you'd face crossing the Pentacrest at rush hour, mistress," she said. "Captain Leary and his crew are very skilled, uniquely skilled I might say. There'll be no trouble."

Clothilde produced a handkerchief from her sleeve and

blew her nose thoroughly. "Ah," said Adele. "Would you care to sit down? There's just the bunks, I'm afraid." She released her own, the bottom portside unit. Midshipman Cazelet was on the starboard side.

"No, no, I'm all right," Clothilde said, then snuffled again. As she folded the handkerchief, she looked around the compartment for the first time. "My goodness, L— *Officer* Mundy. I would have expected you to have, well, larger quarters."

I did, until you and your husband came aboard.

Aloud Adele said, "This isn't so bad, mistress. Though it would be tight if the *Sissie* had five midshipmen instead of the present one."

Clothilde's carefully neutral expression—she clearly hadn't wanted to be too damning of Lady Mundy's present lodgings—turned to open amazement. "You mean you *share* this—"

Her tongue froze before it framed the word "closet" or the like. She had a stricken look.

Adele began to find the business amusing. Smiling faintly, she said, "Space is at a premium on a starship, mistress. Even on a large ship, which the *Princess Cecile* certainly is not. But I've slept in worse conditions in civilian life."

"*You* have?" Clothilde said. "That is, I don't of course doubt you, La— La— *Officer*. But I'm surprised to hear that."

"I lived in straitened circumstances for years following the Proscriptions," Adele said calmly. "For a time I slept in a flophouse where the beds were fenced off from one another by barbed wire. Most of the other residents were drunks who were likely to urinate through the wire in the night."

Clothilde stared without speaking, her eyes wide. She was

quite a pretty woman, the sort men called doll-like. She wasn't as young as she dressed to appear, but Adele guessed she was still several years short of thirty . . . and therefore fifteen years younger than her husband.

"Did you . . . ?" she said, glancing toward Adele's left tunic pocket. The stories about Lady Mundy and her pistol were common property in the RCN and probably a long way beyond it by now. "Threaten them?"

"No," said Adele, her smile a little wider but as cold as an asteroid's core. "It wouldn't have done any good—they were drunk, as I say, and drunks simply can't process information in a useful fashion. And there would have been repercussions had I shot them, you see."

"Nowadays they'd hush it up, of course," Tovera said primly. The fact she spoke—and what she said—implied that Clothilde's behavior had irritated her as well.

"Perhaps," said Adele. "At the time I expect it would have been a brief criminal court proceeding. Fortunately I didn't have to learn."

She smiled again. The matter wasn't humorous, even in memory, but the fact that she had solved a difficult problem was worth a smile of satisfaction.

"The manager was sober," Adele said, "or at any rate not so drunk that he couldn't rationally respond to a threat. His office wasn't much bigger or cleaner than an individual sleeping cell, but it did have walls. I slept there."

Clothilde swallowed with difficulty, but she didn't look away as Adele had thought she might do. Instead she managed a smile and said, "You must think I'm very foolish to be concerned about such little things when you've gone through so much. Well, I apologize again."

"Problems are only large or small when one is able to look back on them," Adele said. She looked into her own past and smiled, faintly and very crookedly. "When they're happening, they're all huge. Or so it has seemed to me."

Right now my problem is how to get free of you without giving offense. Although—as a puzzle, Clothilde Brown was at least as interesting as entering the *Euclid*'s data banks, and the information to be gleaned was likely to be of more immediate importance.

Instead of taking her leave immediately as she probably could now have done, Adele said, "The discomfort of the voyage will be over in a few weeks, mistress. And you may find cramped conditions less burdensome than you thought. I did."

"It isn't that, Officer Mundy," Clothilde said, "as I'm sure you know."

Unexpectedly she sat on the bunk, then slid over and patted the portion nearer Adele. Adele shrugged mentally—this was what she had decided she wanted, after all—and accepted the invitation. She preferred to have personal discussions while standing, but here as generally the other party's ease was of more importance.

"It's Pavel's career," Clothilde said. She'd apparently decided to treat Tovera as a door panel rather than a pair of ears. "On non-career. I understand that one can't expect a plum appointment immediately unless one is a member of one of the Great Houses—"

Her face changed as her intellect caught up with her

emotions. "Oh!" she said. "I didn't mean you, La—"

"The Mundy name took my family to a very high place, mistress," Adele said dryly. "To the top of Speaker's Rock, in fact."

Clothilde Brown wasn't stupid, but the words came from so unexpected an angle that it took her a visible moment to process them. When she *did* understand, she lurched halfway to her feet, then sat down heavily. Her face was white.

"I'm sorry, mistress," Adele said in real embarrassment. "I've lived so closely with my family's execution that I forget that treating it as simply a fact of existence will disturb other people. I didn't mean to offend you."

"Oh, not you, Your Ladyship," Clothilde said. "How could I have been so, so ... ?"

Throwing the other party off-stride was sometimes a useful interrogation technique, but here the effect had been closer to having Woetjans club the poor woman over the head with a length of high-pressure tubing. At least Tovera hadn't snickered, as she sometimes did when she saw a civilian discomfited by Adele's sense of humor.

"I misspoke, Mistress Brown," Adele said. "You were discussing your husband's career, I believe."

"So to speak, I was, yes," Clothilde said, giving Adele a wry smile. "I'm—"

She paused.

"*You* are a very remarkable woman, Officer Mundy," she said, fully composed again. "As I was saying, I know that one must expect to start at the bottom, but after Pavel accepted the posting, I learned that the previous Commissioner had been left on Zenobia fifteen years. *Fifteen* years. And he died there!

I couldn't bear that, and Hester shouldn't have to bear that!"

"Georg Brassey, the previous Commissioner," Adele said, "was the third son of the Brasseys of Chorn. He wasn't a professional diplomat, just an unambitious man whose family had enough influence to arrange for him to have the quiet life he wanted. Your husband won't remain on Zenobia for longer than the normal two-year posting unless something goes badly wrong either there or in Xenos."

"I see," said Clothilde, shaking her head with the same wry smile as a moment before. "My, it's certainly my day for embarrassing myself, isn't it?"

With a slightly sharper expression, she said, "Do you know the Brasseys, Officer?"

"I did, slightly," Adele said in a neutral tone. "There were marriage connections. And I knew the de Sales family, to the same slight degree."

"Yes, of course you would have known my family," Clothilde said. "The de Sales homestead wasn't far from Chatsworth Major, though it was all gone by the time I was born; and my father was of the cadet line anyway. Well, I *am* a fool. You knew everything about me before I even came aboard."

"I'm a librarian by training and vocation, mistress," Adele said, rising. "Information fills the part of my existence that others choose to give over to life. I think they're wrong, of course, but I realize I'm in a minority."

The *Princess Cecile* began to shudder, and a low roar permeated the ship. Stains on the bulkheads blurred from the vibration.

Clothilde jumped up again. "Is something wrong?" she

asked in a tone that meant, *"Are we all going to die?"*

"Chief Pasternak is testing the thrusters," Adele said. "Which he wouldn't do unless he and Captain Leary believed that everything is in order. It does mean that I need to return to my station, however."

Clothilde sucked her lower lip in and nodded. "Thank you, Officer Mundy," she said.

"If I may volunteer some advice," Adele said, "your husband will need all the help he can get to be sure of obtaining a better posting for his next assignment."

"He'll have it," Clothilde said as she followed Adele out of the compartment. "And thank you again."

Adele Mundy understood better than most how much everyone needed help. *Some of us need the help of others just to find a reason for going on with life.*

Daniel Leary, captain of the Cinnabar-registered private yacht *Princess Cecile*, stretched by working his muscles against the couch of his command console. He grinned and on a whim shrank his holographic display to look sternward across the bridge.

All eight thrusters were running at half volume with the petals of their Stellite nozzles fully open. Their plasma exhaust sprayed into the water of Harbor Three, dissipating its energy as steam, while two great pumps in the vessel's stern refilled the reaction mass tanks from the harbor. The noise would have been deafening if the commo helmets hadn't had active sound cancellation; vibration made loose objects walk across flat surfaces.

Everything was as it should be. Daniel was in his element.

He'd lifted the *Princess Cecile* hundreds of times by now, and he'd commanded much bigger ships. There was still a unique thrill to this moment, a visceral memory of the first time they'd lifted from Kostroma—a newly made lieutenant at the controls of a corvette which had never been close to anything more dangerous than the fireworks of a national celebration.

They'd showed the Alliance fireworks on that day, and on many later days.

Daniel grinned. The Republic was at peace now, and that was a good thing; a necessary thing if the civil government was to survive. But by the *gods*, the *Sissie* and her crew had proved themselves against anything the Alliance could throw at them!

Sun, the Gunner and one of the original Sissies, sat at the console to Daniel's immediate left. With the record he'd compiled in the years since, he could choose his own assignment, up to and probably including a battleship.

Sun had chosen to stay with the *Princess Cecile* and her meager two pairs of 4-inch cannon: a turret on the dorsal bow and another in the ventral stern. He liked *using* his guns, not just having the rank of gunner. If Captain Leary was commanding a corvette, then Sun was happy to be gunner on a corvette.

On most warships, the Chief Missileer would be at the Attack Console on the port side of the bridge. Because Daniel liked to control at least the initial launches himself, that warrant officer—Chazanoff, on a corvette rated as a missileer's mate— was in the Battle Direction Center in the stern. The *Sissie* would be fought from the BDC if the bridge were destroyed.

At the console here sat an engineering tech named Fiducia who was striking for a missileer's rating. He was compulsively checking the status of the *Sissie*'s missiles, the two ready to launch in her tubes and the eighteen additional rounds in her magazines. A corvette's punch was minuscule compared with the eighty and more missiles which a battleship could launch in a single salvo, but used shrewdly she could be effective.

Daniel grinned. Many of the Republic's enemies could testify to how effective the *Sissie* had been in the past.

Lieutenant Cory was at the Astrogation Console to Daniel's immediate right; there was unlikely to be anything for him to do in that line. Lieutenant Vesey, in the BDC as normal for the first lieutenant, had started as an exceptionally skilled astrogator and had become better: long service with Daniel Leary had taught her to read the Matrix the way his uncle, Stacey Bergen, had taught him.

But Cory's position wasn't as much of a joke as it would have seemed a few years ago. He had become a pretty fair astrogator, which initially Daniel would have said was as unlikely as a pig learning to dance ballet.

The final console on the bridge was Signals. Midshipman Cazelet, in the backup postition in the BDC, could do everything an ordinary signals officer did. Nobody—nobody in the human universe, in Daniel's considered opinion—could equal Adele. The chance that brought her and Daniel together had been fortunate for both of them, and more fortunate still for the Republic of Cinnabar.

Daniel stretched again. Everything that could be checked in harbor was in the green. The thrusters' steady output was rocking the *Sissie* as plasma boiled away the water in which she floated. The input hoses had withdrawn into the hull.

"Ship," said Daniel on the general push, "this is Six. We will lift under my control in thirty, that is three-zero, seconds. Prepare to lift."

"*Ready/ready/ready,*" replied Pasternak, Vesey, and Woetjans.

The bosun stood in the forward rotunda with a crew of riggers wearing hard suits. They were prepared to go onto the hull as soon as the *Sissie* reached orbit. The antennas and sails were hydraulically controlled, but the hard knocks the rigs took on liftoff through an atmosphere meant that there were always kinked cables and frozen joints to clear.

"Ship," said Daniel, his left hand on the throttle control of his virtual keyboard, "we are lifting—"

He ran the thrusters up to full output; then, with his right hand, he sphinctered the thruster nozzles to narrow aperture. "Now!"

The *Princess Cecile* trembled thunderously, then started to rise. Daniel laughed with joy. It was pure magic and wonder, this time and every time.

"Up Cinnabar!" he shouted, and the crew's triumphant cries echoed him.

CHAPTER 5

EN ROUTE TO STAHL'S WORLD

"Why, this is interesting," said Cazelet from what was meant for a training position across from Adele at the back of the signals console. *"The Councillors of Zenobia, that's the oligarchy, claim to be autochthones."*

"That's odd," Adele said. "The record of the settlement vessel *Lombard* arriving from Earth are quite detailed, including passenger lists. Hmm. It must have been one of the last settlement ships, too; it landed less than a generation before the wars that led to the Hiatus. Zenobians wouldn't have had as much contact with Earth as most colonies, but there doesn't seem to be any doubt that they know they *were* an Earth colony."

The compartment was quiet enough that they could have talked directly. Besides the two of them and Sun at the gunnery console, nobody was on the bridge. Vesey was conning the *Sissie* from the BDC, though while they were in the Matrix there wasn't really anything for her to do either.

Nonetheless, by mutual choice Adele and Cazelet used a two-way link. It wasn't that she was worried about Sun overhearing them while he set up gunnery simulations—besides being totally disinterested, the gunner was as trustworthy as Daniel himself—or that the discussion involved anything that could be considered a security matter.

Adele had gotten into the habit of not talking about the things that interested her in front of spacers, however. Cazelet had automatically followed her lead in this as in all other matters. A starship was a tightly closed environment, and spacers tended to think the worst of any situation.

People who reacted fifty times as if to a threat when they were faced with unfamiliar occurrences would live to be embarrassed when the events turned out to be benign. Ignoring what was a real danger was likely to be fatal the first time. Spacers might not be logicians, but the survivors didn't have to be.

Because of who Adele was, whatever she said aboard the *Princess Cecile* would be the subject of general attention, and she had learned that there was nothing, absolutely nothing, that there wouldn't be somebody who could give it a negative spin. That interpretation would become the common property—and common dread—of the company.

Spacers were used to operating in a state of dread, so it wouldn't affect their efficiency. Nonetheless, it offended Adele to be—no matter how innocently—the instrument of negative misinformation. If she kept her thoughts secret, that wouldn't happen . . . though she supposed the secrecy itself caused rumors.

"*My goodness,*" Cazelet said in wonder. "*Zenobia retains*

blood sacrifice, can you imagine that. The Councillors slaughter a bird on the altar after they elect the new Founder following the death of his predecessor. Or her predecessor. I can't recall a planet with star travel where they were still sacrificing living creatures."

"Perhaps the Browns' former governess was right," said Adele as her wands raked data through her holographic display. "She claimed the Zenobians were barbarians who might eat strangers. Do you find any reference to cannibalism?"

"No, but they'd probably hide that from outsiders," Cazelet said. *"I could do a search for records of off-planet visitors disappearing on nights of the full moon if you'd like."*

"Perhaps later," Adele said. "Though if I remember correctly—"

Her wands flicked.

"—yes, there it is. Zenobia has three moons, but none of them are large enough to be distinguished from stars without a telescope."

The most interesting thing Adele had learned thus far from the great mass of data was that Zenobian singing marmosets were not only popular pets in the Qaboosh Region but also were widely distributed throughout the Alliance. She didn't imagine that would affect her own mission one way or another, but she copied the material in case Daniel would be interested in it.

Reminded by that thought, Adele began sorting out information on Zenobian natural history from the material which she had acquired as soon as she learned where they were going. The *Sailing Directions for the Qaboosh Region* would be adequate for most purposes, but they were unlikely to differentiate among, say, the amphibian species to be found on the margins of Calvary Harbor. And Daniel might want to know.

"Adele?" Cazelet said. He was properly formal in public, but though he was now wearing an RCN uniform he remained, like her, a civilian of the better classes in his self-conception. *"This may be significant. We'll be arriving just after the closing of the Qaboosh Assembly. On Stahl's World, that is, not Zenobia."*

Adele switched her search parameters. She'd put Cazelet to combing the data for regional data; she, using the same material, had been sorting for items specific to Zenobia.

In the days before liftoff from Cinnabar, she had busied herself in gathering as much information as she could which might be useful for the current mission. Anything with possible bearing was grist for her mill: memoirs, logbooks, histories; even fiction which touched on the Qaboosh Region. The Mundy name, her personal connections, and her very considerable experience in knowing where something of significance *might* be stored, had allowed her to cast a very wide net.

All the material had been converted to electronic form. Adele had an affection for hardcopy documents that went well beyond their utility, but what she needed now was the ability to search quickly.

She'd retained electronic facsimiles of the documents, however, to edit and inform what the text-only versions provided. If she wanted to, she could pore to her heart's content over the manuscript records of Captain Christopher French, the semi-literate drunk who had made the initial landing on the world now called Zenobia.

"Yes," she said, scrolling quickly through the data. She had two streams running on her display simultaneously, a regional handbook from External Affairs and news reports from Stahl's World as archived in the Library of Celsus in Xenos. "Yes, good work, Daniel will want to know about this."

The Qaboosh Assembly had been instituted some three hundred years in the past, but the leaders who set it up claimed to be reinstituting a pre-Hiatus gathering. Such statements were common—every other planetary strongman claimed to be of pure Earth blood descended in direct succession from the captain of a colony ship—but in this case there was some substance to them.

One of the documents Adele had just perused, *The Rambles of a Misspent Life*, described the author, the younger son of an unnamed family, posing as an official observer from Cinnabar at a meeting of the Qaboosh Assembly and profiting from the bribes he took from all sides. The work had been published in Xenos in the year 878 Old Style, thus antedating the Hiatus by almost a century.

"The Assembly is supposed to occur every other year," Cazelet said, *"but this will be the first in eight years because of the war. Since they're held on Stahl's World from before it was a Friend of Cinnabar."*

"And before Palmyra became so important in the region," Adele noted aloud. But the Autocrator of Palmyra had been present eight years ago, and so were heads of state or at least delegations from a score of other worlds in the region—including the Founder of Zenobia.

"A pity we're not going to arrive a little sooner," Cazelet said. *"The Assembly will be over by two days by the time we reach Stahl's World. Though perhaps at least some of the dignitaries will still be present."*

"And perhaps…," said Adele, "when Daniel learns about the timing, he'll find a way to shave a little more time off our run. Break. Lieutenant Vesey, where is Six now, if you please, over?"

"Mistress," Vesey said, replying instantly. *"The Captain has taken Commissioner Brown out to show him the Matrix. Would you like me to summon him, over?"*

"No, thank you, Vesey," Adele said. She grinned ruefully. "I'll get him when he returns. Mundy out."

Daniel had probably gone onto the hull through the forward airlock, which Adele could see when the bridge hatch was open—as it was now. She'd been so focused on her work that she hadn't noticed the considerable noise and commotion which must have occurred when Daniel had fitted a layman into a vacuum suit. Well, they had been none of her present business, and her business could be expected to absorb her completely.

Quirking a grin, Adele set a signal to flash across her display when the inner airlock next cycled open. Otherwise she was likely to miss Daniel's return as completely as she had his exit.

Then she went back to work on her data. Of course.

Daniel leaned back at the waist to look upward, a complicated task while wearing a rigging suit. The rigid panels, including protective sleeves over each joint, made the hard suits much safer for the personnel who actually worked on the hull. The edge of a slipping tool or the frayed end of a whipping cable would bounce off instead of tearing a long, probably fatal, gash.

The suits weren't even clumsy once people got used to them. The riggers who wore them throughout their daily watches executed acrobatics, regularly swinging through the rigging and even leaping from antenna to antenna.

RCN regulations required riggers to wear safety lines and always to grip a fixed element of the ship with one hand. On no vessel Daniel knew of did riggers wear safety lines, and most bosuns—including Woetjans—felt that the ship's needs took precedence to what the regs said about crew safety. Despite that, there were very few accidents involving veteran riggers.

Daniel wasn't quite as nimble as a rigger, but he wore his hard suit with ease and a lack of concern. At the moment, his concern was wholly directed at the civilian he'd brought out with him.

Commissioner Brown wasn't the clumsiest person Daniel had ever seen on the hull—that would probably be Adele, despite her having what was by now a great deal of experience—but walking in magnetic shoes took some practice. The Commissioner hadn't learned the trick yet.

Daniel pointed upward with his left arm. "The lights you see," he said, checking through his side lens to make sure that the communication rod was firmly against Brown's helmet, "aren't stars, Commissioner. They're universes, every one as real as our own."

Brown wore an air suit: light compared to a rigging suit, flexible, and not nearly so bulky. It was safer for a layman because it was less awkward to move around in, and it was much more comfortable: the interior of a hard suit bruised and scraped an unfamiliar wearer. Air suits were regulation for ship-side crewmen when they went out on the hull, though veterans like those aboard the *Sissie* had often found rigging suits for their own use.

"I—" Brown said, but he turned his head as he spoke and took his helmet away from the rod. Daniel waited, expecting Brown to realize his mistake and lean back into contact.

He did. "I'm sorry, Captain," he said. "I'm not used to having to hold my head in the same position in order to speak. Well, to be heard, that is."

The suits aboard starships were not fitted with any means of communication in the electrooptical band. In sidereal space, radios or modulated lasers would have been harmless; but such a device if used by accident in the Matrix would throw the ship unguessed—and possibly unrecoverable—distances off course.

Spacers didn't add to the risks they faced. They knew—the survivors knew—better than anyone else just how good their chances of being killed already were.

Riggers talked with hand signals when they needed to talk at all; the personnel of an experienced rigging watch knew their own duties and expected their fellows to do the same. Daniel and Adele, for their own individual reasons, needed privacy to discuss ideas more complex than "Help Jones clear the frozen block on the A3 topsail lift."

Until recently they had touched helmets to hold conversations. Daniel had improved the technique by having mechanics at Bantry fabricate eighteen-inch-long brass tubes which allowed people to speak in vacuum with fewer contortions.

"As I was saying," Brown resumed. "I can't see what you see, but I think I understand what you see, Captain. I—"

He turned carefully, gripping the rod to keep it in contact with his helmet. "Numbers mean more to me than they are, you see," he said with a wistful grin. "More than they are to other people, that is. Here I see a—"

He gestured with the fingers of his gloved left hand spread.

"—pattern of light, rather like the streets in a business district on a rainy night. Only less intense. Whereas from the way you've described the Matrix to me, I think you see religious significance. Do you not?"

Daniel blinked. That wasn't what he'd expected from the Commissioner. And it was very close to being correct, which he also hadn't expected.

He guffawed. If they'd been inside and he weren't wearing a rigging suit, he'd have clapped Brown on the shoulder in startled camaraderie.

"I don't know that I'd call it religious, Commissioner," he said, "but I won't object if you do. Do you see the string of green, well, blurs there, off the port bow?"

He pointed with his full arm, shifting his feet slightly so that Brown could watch without adjusting the communication rod again. "That's the direction we're going," he said. "Though 'direction' isn't really correct. Our brains are used to seeing in three dimensions, so that's how they translate the images they receive through our eyes."

They stood in the far bow at the base of the Dorsal antenna in the A ring. The mainsail wasn't set but the topsail and topgallant were cocked a few degrees to port.

The sails of metalized fabric, tough but only microns thick, gleamed with their own light. They blocked the Casimir radiation which was the only constant in the Matrix where otherwise time, distance, and all other factors varied among the bubble universes.

Radiation pressure served to shift starships among universes, using the variations between adjacent bubbles. Ships circumvented the limitations of the sidereal universe simply by travelling outside it. A computer with the right software could calculate a course. A trained astrogator using the same software could calculate a shorter course than a machine alone could do.

Someone who had developed an instinct for the Matrix could tell at a glance what the energy states of other universes were in respect to that of the bubble of the ship herself. Such an astrogator could do subtle wonders in company with a crew which translated those calculations into the set of the sails. Cinnabar had never raised a more gifted astrogator than Commander Stacey Bergen and he—Daniel's Uncle Stacey—had worked hard to bring his nephew up to his own high standard.

Daniel tried to pass his uncle's knowledge on to the officers under his command. Now on the masthead high above him and Commissioner Brown, Lieutenant Cory stood with an ambitious technician named Loomis and took the line of descent a generation further. *Uncle Stacey would be proud of me.*

"I cannot see the order, Captain," Brown said. "But I can see that there *is* order, and it's obvious to me that you see it. I'm fortunate to be making this voyage under your care."

"I realize that star travel isn't ever comfortable," Daniel said, meaning comfortable for a civilian. "But the crew and I will continue to do whatever we can to minimize the discomfort. We should be on Stahl's World in ten days—"

Which is a bloody good run, if I do say so myself.

"—and after a layover for you and your family to catch your breaths, it'll be only three days more to Zenobia."

"It's not the discomfort of the voyage that concerns me, Captain," Brown said, turning toward Daniel. He held his end of the communications rod against his lower face shield, hiding his mouth, but his eyes looked sad. "It's what awaits me when I get there. I know numbers, perhaps as well as you know..."

He made a circular gesture with his right hand. Daniel winced mentally, but it was perfectly safe. Two safety lines were clipped to the hasp on the Commissioner's waist belt, attaching him to the stanchion just outside the forward airlock and to Daniel's belt as well.

"Know the path through those universes. But I don't know much about people, I'm afraid."

"I don't believe...," Daniel said, trying to word this so it wouldn't be taken as an insult. "That the duties of a Commissioner in a quiet area like the Qaboosh Region will prove too arduous, sir."

"It's not the distressed spacers that I'm primarily worried about, I'm afraid," Brown said. Then he said, "Are you married, Captain?"

"Ah...," said Daniel. "Ah, no I'm not, though I've, ah, reached an understanding with a fine woman. A very fine woman."

"Ah," said Brown with a nod that might have meant anything. "No doubt it will work out well for you, Captain. You're obviously a forceful young man. Whereas I am an accountant."

He barked a laugh that nobody could have mistaken for humor.

"Better," he said, "I should be an accountant. Instead I have become the Cinnabar Commissioner to Zenobia, in order to please my wife. As I said, I don't know very much about people."

Daniel saw the semaphore station ahead of the airlock clack its six arms upward, then begin to chop out a message. It was hydromechanical rather than electrical, the only way to communicate between the bridge and the outside of the hull while the ship was in the Matrix.

"We'd best go aboard, Commissioner," Daniel said. "The *Sissie* will be shaking out her mainsails in a moment, and I don't want you to have to dodge a cable."

He took Brown by the arm and began shuffling with him toward the airlock. What he'd just said was true.

But what he *really* meant was that he didn't want to go any further with the present conversation. Daniel Leary was not a person who had any business giving relationship advice.

CHAPTER 6

ABOVE STAHL'S WORLD

Adele had researched Stahl's World extensively during the voyage from Cinnabar. Nothing she had read had mentioned that the planet looked pink from orbit because—she had just checked—of microorganisms in the extensive oceans. Near the poles the water tended toward magenta; around the equator, its frothy lightness reminded her of cotton candy.

In a manner of speaking, the apparent color of the planet from space didn't matter in the least. Nonetheless Adele was irritated that the first thing that she noticed on arrival above Stahl's World was unexpected. *I need to do better!*

Cazelet's interactions with Raphael Control ran as a text sidebar along the right side of her display. The midshipman was handling the ordinary chores of a Signals Officer while Adele—and Cory, at the astrogation console—were gathering data to be sorted at greater leisure.

The harvest was largely automatic—devouring the logs of all the ships in harbor along with the open files of public bodies and private institutions concerned with trade and shipping—but human oversight refined the work. When files were sealed or encrypted, Cory opened them if he could and otherwise flagged them to Adele's attention. Thanks to software from Mistress Sand's organization and the processing power of an astrogation computer, there was very little in a backwater like the Qaboosh Region which was really unavailable.

"Adele?" said Daniel over a two-way link. *"I recognize the destroyer in the civilian basin below as a 40-series Alliance vessel, but I'm not familiar with the heavy cruiser except that it seems to be a Pantellarian design. Brief me, please, over."*

"Yes," said Adele. Instead of sorting through data on her console, she simply highlighted the link she'd already placed on the command display. She didn't object to the question, because she felt it was her fault that Daniel had to ask it.

Information gathering wasn't difficult: machines did most of it more efficiently and in greater volume than human beings could. The trick—and craft helped, but it really was an art form at the higher levels—was information retrieval. In sufficient mass, unsorted data was as difficult to penetrate as encrypted data.

Adele had put over thirty items onto Daniel's sidebar, ranging from the names and biographies of the dignitaries still present—this was the final day of the Qaboosh Assembly; it was midafternoon in Raphael, the Assembly site and the Cinnabar regional headquarters—to the local weather and the indicia of every ship in the harbor below. That had obviously been too much, so Daniel had called in an expert to sort it for him.

Adele grinned minusculely. That was a typically good decision on his part.

The cruiser was the *Piri Reis*, flagship of Palmyra's naval forces, the Horde. It had been built only five years earlier on Pantellaria which, though an Alliance ally, did considerable business with neutral worlds which lacked the capacity to build larger warships themselves.

Adele had heard Daniel and his fellow officers sneer at Pantellarian design and workmanship, but they sneered at any vessel that wasn't RCN—and often enough at RCN ships other than whichever one they served on. All Adele could say was that *Piri Reis* had clean lines and longer antennas and spars than was usual for a heavy cruiser. Her defensive battery of 15-cm plasma cannon was arranged in three triple turrets—two dorsal, one ventral—instead of the four twin turrets of most heavy cruisers.

Adele was sure that Daniel would say that the design was a bad one and that the *Piri Reis* was more susceptible to damage either from accident or enemy action. That said, the cruiser presumably had a higher rate of fire than an RCN—or Fleet—vessel of the same displacement.

Speaking but directing the console to convert her words to a text crawl at the bottom of Daniel's display so as not to disturb him until he was ready for the information, Adele added, "The ship is carrying the Autocrator Irene to and from the Assembly. There are six Palmyrene cutters escorting the cruiser; I'm—"

Adele's wands sorted, then clicked pale green halos about the Horde vessels. They appeared to be a standard type for the region, as—she counted—seventeen other ships in the civil basin were similar enough to be confused with them.

The highlight color was a good contrast with the water, but

the result made a startlingly ugly combination; she switched to blue, wondering if she would have bothered to do so five years ago. The universe in all its aspects had seemed very ugly then.

"—marking them now."

The Alliance destroyer Z 46—which Daniel had correctly identified, of course—was at the other end of the civil basin from the Palmyrene cruiser. Though Cinnabar and the Alliance were in a state of peace, it was unexpected to find a warship of one party making a courtesy call at a regional headquarters of the other.

Adele couldn't reach the core databases of a Fleet warship without time and a great deal of luck, but the log was a relatively simple proposition and gave her the reason: the Z 46 was serving as transportation for Founder Hergo Belisande of Zenobia. The Founder was accompanied by his sister, Lady Posy Belisande.

Adele smiled wryly. It would be all right to say that this gave her an opportunity to meet her target on neutral ground if she wished to do so but imposed no requirement if she did not. Sand had been clear that the primary purpose of the mission was to give a trusted agent, Lady Adele Mundy, an opportunity to relax in a quiet region while the needs of the Republic didn't require her special skills elsewhere.

Adele's expertise was in databases and information flow. Posy Belisande wouldn't have brought electronic information bearing on Porra's inner circles here to Stahl's World, so Sand wouldn't think her agent was shirking if she spent the entire time out of Posy's sight.

Adele *would* have been shirking. And though she and Sand

both considered this mission to be make-work for a burned-out agent, it was a mission and Adele would carry it out to the best of her ability.

Adele's smile faded. It would no doubt do her good to interact socially with strangers. It was the sort of thing that human beings did regularly. She needed the practice, because she generally thought of herself as a species not dissimilar to humanity but certainly not the same.

The exchange between Raphael Control and Midshipman, Acting Signals Officer, Cazelet had been on hold for several minutes. When the ground controller came back, Adele's sidebar read "Princess Cecile, I have instructions for your captain from Admiral Mainwaring, over."

Without having to think about it, Adele locked out Cazelet and took over the duties. She said, "Go ahead, Control, over."

Cazelet could certainly have handled this, but he shouldn't have to. Admirals could be whimsical; indeed, admirals could be peevish swine. If somebody had to deal with such a person, it wouldn't be a midshipman to whom Adele had delegated what she had thought was a simple task.

"Princess Cecile, *this is Commander Milch, ADC to Admiral Mainwaring,*" said the voice from the other end of the microwave transmission. "*The Admiral requests that Captain Leary join him at the reception being given this afternoon by the Autocrator Irene. I'm leaving the reception now and will pick him up in an aircar at Slip 4 of the Naval Basin. You are to land ASAP, I repeat, as soon as possible. Captain Leary is to wear Dress Whites with all his medals.*"

Milch paused to chuckle. Adele had his face and file—a record of pedestrian competence, with neither exceptional luck nor the interest of powerful figures to push him upward—before her. He might well end his career in a post like this one, aide to the admiral commanding a squadron of ageing ships in a backwater.

"That'll give the locals something to see, won't it?" Milch said. *"Raphael Control out."*

"One moment, Control!" Adele snapped. "If you please. The *Princess Cecile* is a yacht under private registry and not authorized to use the Naval Basin, over."

"The Princess Cecile *is authorized to land wherever on Stahl's World that Admiral Mainwaring says it will,"* Milch snapped. *"And the Admiral said he'd be buggered if Captain Leary was going to set down in the middle of a bunch of wogs. Out, and I mean it."*

Raphael Control broke the connection. Adele was already passing the information on to Daniel and Vesey in the BDC. So much for being polite to the Founder of Zenobia and his Alliance masters.

Adele smiled grimly. She didn't really disagree with the decision, after all. Her highly cultured mother would have been horrified to hear Adele shouting "Up Cinnabar!" after a bloody victory, but her mother hadn't been RCN.

Up Cinnabar! And up the RCN!

RAPHAEL HARBOR ON STAHL'S WORLD

Daniel didn't ordinarily think about how the *Princess Cecile* looked to civilians, let alone civilian children. As he stood beside the Browns, however, watching the little girl—Hester?—cling to the Commissioner's leg, he realized that there was very little to choose between the *Sissie*'s boarding hold and a detention cell.

The steel surfaces were flecked with rust—landings were more often than not made in salt water—and streaked with hydraulic fluid: a working ship *couldn't* be clean, not after the first liftoff and landing. Other than that, the compartment's only features were the hatches which were steel like the bulkheads. They were dogged and sealed more securely than a bank vault, let alone a prison.

The main present feature of the hold was noise: the sighs and wheezes and clanks of the ship's internal workings, and the trip-hammer clangs of the hull and rig cooling, each part at a differing rate. Steam no longer roared—Pasternak had shut down the thrusters—but it continued to sizzle angrily as harbor water boiled from hot metal.

"It'll be over soon now, mistress," Daniel said, bending toward the child with the care his closely tailored Whites demanded. Though they weren't as tight as they might have been: in the Matrix, he ate less than he did in port, and he spent a good deal of time on the hull. Walking in a rigging suit was exercise, and climbing repeatedly to a masthead and back was that in spades.

As Daniel spoke, the multiple bolts—the dogs—which locked the entry hatch into the hull withdrew deafeningly. To someone who'd been aboard while automatic impellers were raking the corvette, the clangor—even when expected—was similar enough to induce a start.

To civilians like the Browns, it probably sounded like a load of anvils had been dropped on them. Clothilde screamed, her husband threw his arms around her, and the child began to bawl as though she'd accidentally smashed her pet hamster. She was trying to climb her father's leg.

Daniel put his hand on the girl's shoulder. "Ah, mistress?" he said. "It's all right, really it is. The noise will stop soon—"

The hatch began to lower into a boarding ramp. Metal squealed against metal, and the pumps driving the hydraulic jacks had a vibration so high-pitched that one experienced it instead of hearing it. Stepping outside his experienced viewpoint, Daniel had to admit that it would have been pretty unpleasant even without the steam and biting plasma which curled in through the widening gap.

The child didn't stop crying, but she transferred her grip to Daniel. That allowed him to lift her and mutter into her ear, "There, there, dear. It's all going to be all right."

He wasn't good on names, particularly women's names. He'd learned over the years that "dear" or "love" were safe, whereas a "Hester" which should have been "Heather" could lead to a very unpleasant discussion.

Hogg hovered close at hand, wearing what for him were dress clothes. His cap, shirt, sash, trousers and shoes were brand new and bright orange. Unfortunately they were five separate shades of orange, and his socks were chartreuse. He looked like a clown, a countryman dressed in what he imagined was sophisticated finery.

That was all true. Hogg was also an expert poacher and as ruthless as a countryman has to be. He would throttle a man with a length of monocrystal fishing line with as little hesitation as he would snap the neck of a snared rabbit. The pockets of his baggy clothing sagged with various weapons, and he was expert with them all.

"She's going to slobber on your Whites, young master," Hogg grumbled. He half-extended his arms, but he wasn't quite willing to take the girl away. Just as well, Daniel supposed. Hogg wasn't really a bogeyman, but it wouldn't be hard for a child to imagine otherwise.

"And if she does, Hogg?" Daniel said. "You've sponged worse than drool off my uniforms, have you not?"

"Aye, but not before you went to a reception with an admiral," Hogg said. "Although not much of an admiral or they wouldn't have stuck him in a bloody dump like this."

He patted the girl on the back and said, "Sure, go ahead and puke, sweetie. It don't matter on this pisspot out in the sticks."

The end of the hatch banged against the corvette's starboard outrigger, extended to provide stability as well as buoyancy. It floated twenty feet from the concrete quay, but members of the harbor's permanent staff were already swinging an extension bridge to meet the ramp.

"I'm not going to whoopsie!" the child said, turning her head toward Hogg with injured dignity. "You shouldn't say that."

"No, dear, I'm sure you're not," Daniel said. "Now can I give you back to your—"

He started to say "Mommy" but switched instead to "—Daddy?"

He bent. The girl obediently got back onto her own feet, but she continued to hold Daniel's right hand.

An eight-place aircar with a closed cabin made a fishhook turn over the harbor and settled crosswise on the quay. "Is that the Governor's car for us, Pavel?" Mistress Brown said. She started forward, tugging at her daughter's free hand. "It must be, thank goodness. Come along, Hester."

Adele had been watching them, which Daniel found about as predictable as there being a sky overhead. The overhead speakers—so that the Browns would hear the information—announced, "Captain Leary, this is Signals. The Squadron Commander's vehicle has arrived for you."

"Oh!" said Clothilde Brown, rocking back on her heels. Hester still gripped Daniel's hand.

"Roger, Signals," Daniel said. "Break. Lieutenant Cory, what uniform are you wearing, over?"

"Sir?" said Cory, using the earbud only. *"Sir, I'm in my Grays, over."*

The second-class uniform was proper public garb—an important consideration, because a regional RCN headquarters wasn't a place to openly flout regulations. Daniel said, "Report immediately to the entry hold and escort the Commissioner and his family to the quay where the—"

Daniel's tongue fluttered an instant. The Governor himself would not be sending anybody to meet the Browns; he would almost certainly be attending the affair on the Palmyrene cruiser.

"—Governor's office will be having them picked up and escorted to Government House, over."

"Sir!" said Cory. "On the way, out."

Daniel smiled faintly, visualizing Cory banging down the companionway three steps at a time. The boy had always been willing, but it was a pleasant change that he'd become competent as well.

"I have to go off now, Commissioner," Daniel said, bowing slightly. He didn't owe that to a civilian official below him in equivalent rank, but courtesy was cheap. Courtesy and kindness were cheap. Brown looked as though he had been staked over an anthill; the glare he was getting from his embarrassed wife explained why. "Lieutenant Cory will be down in a moment to take charge of you while I go play the—"

He fingered the sash that marked him as a Knight of Novy Sverdlovsk. It was one of a number of foreign decorations whose empty magnificence impressed civilians who didn't understand the significance of the Cinnabar Star with Wreath.

"—dashing naval hero for people who don't know any better."

He squeezed the child's hand and firmly released it. "Hester," he said. "Ask Lieutenant Cory to tell you how he helped me steal a destroyer on Bennaria when he was only a midshipman. Can you remember that?"

The girl bobbed her head enthusiastically. Daniel turned and strode briskly down the ramp. He hadn't really felt sorry for Commissioner Brown, who was an accountant. Daniel couldn't get inside the head of an accountant.

But he had been a child; many would say that he still was. It seemed rather hard lines for Hester to be stuck out here in the back of beyond.

CHAPTER 7

RAPHAEL HARBOR ON STAHL'S WORLD

Daniel lengthened his stride. A commander wearing Whites had gotten out of the aircar. Instead of waiting, he marched down the quay to the base of the cantilevered bridge which had been swung out to meet the *Sissie*'s boarding ramp. There he chatted with the riggers under Woetjans who were lashing the free end to bitts on the ramp.

"Do you want an escort today, Six?" the bosun asked as Daniel approached.

"In case I have to shoot my way out of the party, Woetjans?" he answered with a grin. "Thank you, but I hope that won't be necessary."

"Aw, not that, Six," Woetjans said. She obviously wasn't sure whether Daniel really believed that was what she'd had in mind. "Just to show you're important."

"Carry on, bosun," Daniel said, hoping that Woetjans didn't understand his smile. To base personnel, let alone civilians, twenty Sissies with their weapons of choice would be seen as ragged tramps—an embarrassment rather than an honor. Only people who had been in hard places themselves could understand what it meant to have a crew like that at your back.

The commander started down the bridge. It was wide enough for even three to walk abreast, but his steps and Daniel's made the tubular frame flex awkwardly.

If I'd had my choice, I'd just as soon we'd met on the concrete, Daniel thought. But then, if he'd had his choice, he wouldn't be rigged out like this to meet what passed for the Great and Good of the Qaboosh Region.

He grinned. The son of a Cinnabar senator knew who counted in this universe. It wasn't anybody he'd be meeting today.

"Captain Leary?" the commander called. "I'm Milch, and I'm honored to meet you. Or—should I have saluted? Bloody hell, Leary, I apologize! We don't stand much on ceremony out here, you know."

Milch was a little taller than Daniel and a little plumper, but he looked both alert and friendly. Sometimes the officers you found in posts like this were people who for one reason or another—booze was a frequent one—couldn't be trusted anywhere they might actually have to do the job of an RCN officer.

"I don't stand much on ceremony either, Commander," Daniel said, "because I'm so bloody poor at it. Even when I'm not wearing this clown suit—"

He flicked the sash again with a grimace.

"—for which I apologize, but I understood it was the admiral's orders that I wear foreign decorations."

"Oh, don't apologize, Leary," said Milch as they walked back alongside one another toward the car. "You're quite a coup for us. The Palmyrenes have been making all the running at this Assembly, but you've just given Admiral Mainwaring a way to top the Autocrator. The only thing better would be if you'd come in a bloody great battleship instead of a corvette."

"I think a battleship would rather defeat the intention of delivering the new Commissioner to Zenobia in a quiet and courteous fashion, Commander," Daniel said dryly. "Though I'm surprised that Palmyra is, well, so important. I had the impression that it was merely a regional power, and the Qaboosh Region isn't—you'll forgive me?"

Milch chuckled and said, "Isn't worth mentioning in the same sentence as, oh—"

He gestured to the aigrette on Daniel's left shoulder, the Order of Strymon.

"—Strymon, you mean? Or Kostroma? Well, you'd be right—but the people here, *in* the region, don't know that. The Qaboosh is so far from Cinnabar—or Pleasaunce—that the Autocrator gets taken at her own valuation because nobody knows any better. Including her."

Daniel found the quay a subconscious relief because it didn't spring up and down in response to the commander's forceful strides. A starship under way vibrates on many simultaneous frequencies, but one whose hull actually bounces is in very serious trouble indeed.

"But surely one heavy cruiser, even out here...," he said. "And a local crew, I assume?"

Milch didn't bridle, exactly, but there was a slight sharpness in his tone as he said, "Local crew except for specialists, yes, by and large. And you won't find better spacers than the

Palmyrenes, Captain. As for the *Piri Reis*, that's the cruiser, she's enough to handle everything else in the region, ours or the Alliance's. But it's the cutters that make Palmyra important. I'll show you when we get aloft. Simmons?"

"Sir?" replied the driver, opening the car's middle door for the officers. Milch gestured Daniel to a front-facing seat of the middle pairs, then took the one opposite him as the driver got in.

"Take us up to a hundred feet and circle the civil basin clockwise instead of going straight to the Palmyrene do," Milch said. To Daniel he went on, "Palmyra was independent for five hundred years following the Hiatus, but Pleasaunce took over in the First Expansion and held the planet till the Consolidation Wars. It was their regional HQ."

The driver had left his fans idling at zero incidence while waiting instead of shutting down. That allowed him to lift off as soon as he got in, simply by running up the throttle with one hand and coarsening the blade pitch with the other. The lightly loaded car rose in a steep curve.

"The Pleasaunce governor," Milch said, "revolted and declared independence. The regional forces went along with him. By the time the Alliance of Free Stars had formed around Pleasaunce and Blythe thirty years later, it would have taken a major expedition to recover the place. Nothing in the Qaboosh Region was worth the effort."

Daniel grinned wryly. A certain amount of grit had blown over the tops of his ankle boots—the footgear of first-class uniforms was standard space boots in design, though they were glossy black instead of gray suede—but it wouldn't have time to work down to where it would raise blisters. What was presumably good enough for the squadron commander was perforce good enough for the captain of a private yacht.

"I'll grant you the Autocrator has been putting on airs—Odin was bad enough, but to listen to his widow Irene, you'd think you were hearing the Speaker of the Senate," Milch said. "But it's a bloody good thing the Horde is out there or the region'd be overrun with pirates. There's not much we could do with four patrol sloops—when none of them are in the yard—and an old gunboat. The Alliance has two modern destroyers on Zenobia, but besides that it's a handful of gunboats scattered through the region."

"I noticed the *Z 46*," Daniel said. The aircar's wide circle had brought them around to the destroyer's berth. "Frankly, I was a little surprised. The Peace of Rheims is fresh enough—"

He meant "fragile enough."

"—that there aren't likely to be courtesy calls to most squadron bases for a while yet."

"Oh, we've always been more relaxed here," the commander said. "Neither side was strong enough to push matters, and until the past year Irene was busy with two of her husband's sons by mistresses who had their own ideas about who should be the new Autocrator. But the reason the *Z 46* is here is Hergo Belisande, the Founder of Zenobia. He's a very small fish, as you might expect, but he's as noisy as if he counted for something. He's been raising holy hell at the Assembly, claiming that Palmyra plans to attack him and that he wouldn't be safe travelling by anything but an Alliance warship."

Milch shrugged. "The Fleet commander on Zenobia, Lieutenant Commander von Gleuck, asked Admiral Mainwaring through a back channel if it would be all right—it's not a decision for the Governor, you see. And we didn't see any reason why not."

"Are those the Palmyrene cutters?" Daniel said suddenly as the car continued its circle. "There, the slip alongside the cruiser, the six of them?"

"Ah, you noticed, did you?" Milch said in a pleased tone. "I wondered if you would. Yes, they are—and it's just what it looks like. There's a full set of hydraulic linkages for the sails and yards in the dorsal bow, not just a semaphore keypad. The ships can be conned from the hull while they're in the Matrix."

"I'll be buggered," Daniel said. "I've never seen that, though my Uncle Stacey said that it could be done. Some of the little clusters he'd found had people who did it."

He looked from the cutters below to Milch. "Pirates," he said. "It's not good for much except piracy, is it?"

"And anti-pirate operations," Milch said, nodding. "Which is what the Palmyrenes do now. But that's a reason we don't get shirty about the unique glory of Cinnabar here in the Qaboosh Region. An RCN battlegroup could take care of the *Piri Reis* without blinking, but a couple hundred cutters like that—the Horde and private ventures—would pretty much shut down trade in the region for as long as they wanted to."

His face suddenly blank, Daniel glanced at the commander. He'd been mildly contemptuous of the Qaboosh Region and the Cinnabar officials here. Oh, it was natural enough—inevitable, he supposed, for an officer who'd been in the thick of things and had done very well for himself and for the Republic.

But Commander Milch's strategic appraisal was completely valid—and would have been beyond the imagination of most

RCN officers whose service had been limited to big ships and important regions. And those Palmyrene cutters were remarkable by any standards, even Daniel's own.

They were small, displacing five hundred tons or even less. They were armed with clusters of unguided rockets whose only purpose was to damage the rigging of other ships in sidereal space. The more sophisticated rockets had proximity fuses, though pirates often made do with contact fuses and simply got close enough that one or more rockets hit the hull or rigging.

When that happened, a 20-pound bursting charge blew a cloud of shrapnel in all directions, cutting cables and clawing sails to rags whether they were spread or furled against the yards. The hull—even of a lightly built merchantman—was unlikely to sustain any damage worse than scars and perhaps a sprung seam. Pirates didn't want to damage cargos, and the ships might also be of value if only for spare parts.

For the rockets to hit, they had to be launched at knife range. Pirates achieved that by tracking their prey in the Matrix and dropping into sidereal space on top of them. Spacers who'd soaked themselves in the feel of the Matrix could pick up the linear anomalies of other ships passing close to their own. Daniel could do that, and he'd taught the art—it wasn't a skill—to some of his midshipmen.

But to actually conn a ship from the hull instead of depending on computed solutions—that would have been beyond even Uncle Stacey's abilities. All six of the Horde cutters were fitted to do that, and a quick survey of similar cutters in the harbor showed that at least half of them had similar installations. Ordinary warships would be as useless against such enemies as cannon would be to deal with flies.

Daniel pursed his lips and nodded in understanding. "I take your point, Commander," he said. "I surely do. Now I suppose I'm ready to go be a performing monkey for Admiral Mainwaring."

"Take us down, Simmons," Milch said in obvious satisfaction. As the aircar curved toward a parking area near where the *Piri Reis* floated at the west end of the harbor, he added, "The Qaboosh isn't like Cinnabar, not by a long run, I'll admit. But it has its interesting points."

Daniel nodded. Milch was right about that.

Adele was busy and therefore content. Thirty-two separate worlds had sent delegations to the Qaboosh Assembly. Dakota had sent two, from the East Continent and the West Continent respectively, both of which had spent the event in their hotel rooms with liquor and prostitutes. Adele was gathering information on everyone attending, using payment records, imagery, and security logs as well as the Assembly minutes.

Her console whirred softly. She dipped into what blurred past, but for the most part this was a job for machinery. The data couldn't really be digested until there was a use for it. Was it significant that Mortonsonia's President of the Conference was having an affair with the Hereditary Queen of Isis? Perhaps, but not until at least one of those worlds became important—which certainly wasn't the present case.

Adele smiled. In a perfect universe, her data banks would contain all the information there was on every subject. As soon as someone had a use for the information, she would provide it to them.

Information wasn't of any intrinsic use to her, of course. She just wanted to have it available.

Tovera was at the console's training station, viewing feeds from the security cameras recording the Autocrator's gala. Adele had unlocked the station for her, of course, but Tovera could have used another console if she had wished to—the two of them were alone on the bridge. Apparently she found the jumpseat adequately comfortable. Besides, like her mistress, Tovera considered comfort to be a matter of small importance.

Adele would view the imagery later, after the rout had broken up. She wanted to watch Lady Posthuma Belisande conducting herself in public: with whom she interacted, how much she drank, what her expressions were in the moments she wasn't talking to another guest. All of those things had bearing on how Adele might best get close to her target.

Her display registered an incoming call via microwave, from RCN Qaboosh Regional Headquarters to CS—not RCS, because the *Sissie* was a private charter—*Princess Cecile*, Attention Signals Officer. Adele would have fielded the call anyway, though she supposed she was technically off-duty. The routing had piqued her interest.

"Qaboosh, this is *Princess Cecile*," she said. Tovera had shut down her display and was listening intently to the conversation. "Go ahead, over."

"Princess Cecile, *I'm Technician Runkle*," said the female voice on the other end of the signal. *"The communications section here has a problem, and we've heard that your Signals Officer is a wizard. Adele Mundy is your Signals Officer, is she not, over?"*

"Qaboosh, that is correct," Adele said. Her wands flickered

as she spoke; the data stream now in the center of her display told her what she had expected. "What sort of assistance are you requesting, over?"

"We would appreciate it if Officer Mundy would come to the Headquarters Annex 6, that's the white temporary building to the left of the main building, as soon as she can be spared from her regular duties," Runkle said. *"She'll be met at the door. Ah—I'm sorry, but we don't have a car to send, over."*

"One moment, Qaboosh," Adele said. "Break. Mundy for officer-in-charge, over."

"Vesey here," the acting captain responded almost instantly. She had remained in the BDC rather than coming forward to take the command console. Either decision would have been proper, but Vesey was extremely punctilious about not seeming to covet the captain's prerogatives. *"Go ahead, over."*

"Sir," said Adele, "Tech 8 Runkle has requested that I join her in the Headquarters Annex six. She stated that the communications section is having a problem which they would like my help with. Do you have any objection to my going to the Annex as requested, over?"

"Permission granted," Vesey said crisply. *"Do you want any support, Mundy? Or a vehicle? We're supposed to have the use of a pair of motor pool trucks while we're here, over?"*

"Thank you, sir, but that won't be necessary," Adele said, rising from her console. "It's only half a mile. Mundy out."

"I wondered if you were going to tell her," Tovera said. Her smile was a smirk most of the time so that it didn't look as though she were a carnivore preparing to leap.

"I told her everything that was important to her," Adele said.

127

"I have to change out of utilities before I leave the ship, though."

They started for the companionway. Tovera said, "Cory would have known, wouldn't he?"

"Yes, I suppose he would," Adele said. "But he's still standing on the quay with the Browns, and anyway, it doesn't matter."

Cory would have traced the signal back to its source as a matter of course. He *liked* signals. And with that cue, he probably would have found a building manifest. That in turn would have told him that the only occupant of Annex 6 was the Regional Intelligence Section.

The band was playing a song Daniel remembered as being current in Xenos just before he graduated from the Academy, but it had been rescored for what he supposed were Palmyrene instruments: recorders with a swollen air box immediately beneath the mouthpiece; stringed instruments, plucked as well as bowed, with very long necks and rounded bodies; sets of hand-stroked drums; and a sistrum—fourteen pieces in all.

The *Piri Reis* floated in the largest slip in the civil basin, suitable for a bulk freighter or even a battleship, so there was a good deal of water between the cruiser's bow and the peripheral quay. That had been decked for a dance floor with steel beams and thick wooden planks instead of the usual thin plating supported by gridwork attached to pontoons.

Daniel grinned. It didn't flex, although among the dancers was a circle of twelve men in pantaloons and loose tunics whose whirling was definitely on the acrobatic side. Several of them held in either hand green scarves which fluttered wildly as they spun.

"They're from Behistun," Milch said, leaning close to be heard. "The only reason I know is there was a lieutenant commander in Administration when I was first posted here who was doing a study of them. You couldn't shut him up in the mess."

The crowd numbered several hundred. Some wore uniforms, but not nearly so many as Daniel had learned to expect on the fringes of—not to put too fine a point on it—civilization, as a citizen of Cinnabar or Pleasaunce would define the state.

The other surprise was that planetary costumes of various types predominated. Indeed, Daniel would have seen far more women dressed in the latest Pleasaunce fashion at a party in Xenos than he did here. The residents of the Qaboosh Region were so distant from the centers of power that they didn't realize their customs were quaint and laughable.

Daniel smiled wryly. Given their ability to navigate in the Matrix, they had reason to be satisfied with who they were.

"Leary?" someone called. "Daniel Leary, and it's not half a wonder to find you on Stahl's World!"

Coming through the press wearing Grays was Lieutenant Ames, an Academy classmate with whom Daniel had spent a good deal of time when they were both impecunious Cadets. Ames had the same smile and the same unruly black hair. His uniform looked as though it was meant for a larger man and had been cut down inexpertly, so he was probably still impecunious as well.

"By heavens, it's good to see you, Ames!" Daniel said, clasping hands with his old friend. "I'm glad to see you've—"

His tongue twitched an instant, then concluded, "—kept yourself so fit."

"The great thing about being out in the boondocks,

Leary...," said Ames with a quirked smile. "Is that the chances are you won't be thrown on half pay when peace breaks out and your ship is put into ordinary. Our Lords of Navy House can't run down the Qaboosh Establishment very much and still have an establishment here. So yes, I'm still Second Lieutenant of the *Fantome*."

Daniel nodded in embarrassment. He'd always thought Ames was among the sharpest of his classmates, but his combination of being brash, poor, and unlucky was a bad one.

"If you don't mind, Ames," said Milch, who obviously minded the delay quite a lot himself, "I need to introduce our guest to Admiral Mainwaring. Do you know where he is? Perhaps you can catch up with the captain at some later point; but not, I think, today."

"The Admiral is on the quay near the forward boarding ramp, sir," Ames said. "About as far from the band as he could get, I shouldn't wonder. Ah—I wonder, Commander Milch?"

"Well, what is it, boy?" Milch snapped as he started down the quay separating the cruiser's slip from the adjacent one where the six Palmyrene cutters were berthed. They were small enough in all truth, but against the bulk of a heavy cruiser they looked tiny.

"I'd appreciate a chance to introduce Captain Leary to the Admiral myself," Ames said. "We *are* old friends."

He cocked an eyebrow toward Daniel.

"Hear hear!" Daniel said with honest enthusiasm. "We are indeed, Commander."

"And it's a, well, different context from some of those the Admiral may recall me in," Ames concluded hopefully.

Milch guffawed. "You mean, like the time you and Midshipman Jarndyce appeared at the Governor's Ball in silks, claiming to be the Sultan of Patagonia and his Chief Concubine?" he said. "All right, Ames, you can introduce your friend. But make yourself scarce as soon as you have, got that?"

"Aye aye, sir!" said Ames. "And here, most honorable Captain, is the man we're fortunate to have as our squadron commander."

The admiral stood in the midst of Whites and civilian clothing ranging from tweeds to a barefoot woman wearing a poncho of cerise feathers with a mantilla. Mainwaring was a big man; he certainly carried more weight than he needed to, but Daniel's first impression was of power rather than flabby indolence. He was holding a drink in his right hand and gesturing forcefully to the befeathered lady with his left.

"Admiral Mainwaring?" said Ames. "May I have the honor to present my classmate, Captain Daniel Leary?"

"What?" said Mainwaring. He held out his drink to the side; a boy of sixteen or so, wearing Whites without insignia, snatched it away to free the admiral's hand. "Ames, are you telling me that the captain was a *classmate* of yours?"

"He was indeed, sir," said Daniel. By regulation, salutes weren't to be exchanged in civilian venues, but he'd held himself ready to try if Mainwaring's scowl had showed that the admiral was expecting one. "And you can take most of his stories for true, because Cadet Ames was generally in the lead when the more interesting incidents were happening."

Mainwaring laughed, but he gave the lieutenant an appraising look. Ames nodded politely, then said, "I'll be off then, sir. Leary, it's a pleasure to see you, as always."

"You and he really did run around together, Leary?" Mainwaring said.

"Yes, sir," Daniel said. "And based on my experience of Ames at the Academy, I'd venture that Midshipman Jarndyce is a comely young lady."

A lieutenant commander laughed. "You got that in one, sir," he said. "I'm Paxston—" which Daniel had already determined from the tag on his left breast "—of the *Fantome*, young Ames' CO."

Not for the first time it struck Daniel that people were referring to him with deference and his classmates—Ames was thirty-seven days his senior—as "young this-or-that." Apparently success added not only laurels but years.

"Now," said Mainwaring, "we need to find the Autocrator. Milch, do you see anybody in a yellow cap?"

To Daniel he added, "Those would be Palmyrene officers. One of them ought to know."

Milch disappeared on his implied errand. Daniel spread a smile across the group around the admiral, feeling uncomfortable.

One learned in the RCN that a superior officer's whim was the word of god, but he'd much rather that Mainwaring had taken a moment to introduce him at least to the Cinnabar officers present. Nobody likes to be ignored, and—quite apart from being a generally courteous person himself—Daniel had learned that nobody was so insignificant that their resentment couldn't matter.

It also struck him that the quickest way of learning where Autocrator Irene was would be to ask Adele over the microphone concealed under his left epaulette and get the answer through the bud in his right ear. He didn't want to call attention to himself—or to Adele—in that fashion, but the idea was tempting.

"I believe I can help you there, Admiral Mainwaring," said a cultured baritone behind Daniel's left shoulder. "Autocrator Irene is in conference with your Regional Governor, Master Wenzel, in the Admiral's Suite on A Level of the *Piri Reis*."

Daniel turned and backed slightly, though he kept his smile. The speaker, a man of about thirty Standard years, was, by leaning slightly backward, being punctiliously careful not to crowd. That didn't make much change in the distance, but the body language was clear.

His costume was remarkable: loose pantaloons gathered above the ankles and an equally billowy shirt with full sleeves but a deeply cut V neck that displayed quite a lot of muscular chest. Over it he wore a gold chain whose links looked so buttery pure that Daniel suspected he could bend them with his fingers.

"This is Zenobian national costume," the man said, facing Daniel with an engaging smile. They were of a height, but the stranger was undeniably trimmer. Daniel controlled his urge to suck his gut in; he was better off not to try to compete on those terms.

"The colors aren't," said the woman touching the fellow's arm. "If you can even call those colors."

"I'd suspected as much," Daniel said, smiling in growing amusement. The pantaloons were light gray and the tunic was gray-green—field gray, if you were describing a Fleet dress uniform, whose hues the outfit perfectly mimicked. The golden bangle hanging from the chain was three crossed tridents: the rank insignia of a Fleet lieutenant commander.

"Thank you, sir!" said Admiral Mainwaring. "And now if I may ask, who the bloody hell are you?"

The stranger turned and made a half bow to Mainwaring. "Your pardon, Admiral," he said. "I am Fregattenkapitan Otto von Gleuck, commanding the Z 46. We have no friends in common, I fear, so I chose to approach you without a proper introduction. I of course knew of you and likewise knew of Captain Leary."

He glanced again to Daniel and nodded, not as formal an acknowledgment but an apparently friendly one.

"I'm very pleased to meet you both."

"Pleased as well," said Daniel with a comparable nod and an equally friendly smile. "I hope that now that our peoples are at peace, there'll be more chance for the professionals on both sides to socialize."

He offered his hand as though they were civilians meeting; von Gleuck gripped it firmly, but without attempting the silly game of trying to crush a stranger's fingers. They stepped back from one another.

Admiral Mainwaring was turning red. Von Gleuck bowed again to him and said, "Admiral, may I have the honor of presenting Lady Posthuma Belisande of Zenobia. Her brother Hergo, you may know, is the Founder of her planet; so to speak, the President for Life. She has recently returned home from a stay on Pleasaunce."

That explains her fashion sense, thought Daniel. He'd seen his share of attractive women, but no more than a handful whom he would put in Lady Posthuma's class. Her poise gave her a presence beyond what her exceptional face and body could have done by themselves.

She curtseyed to Mainwaring and rose with a smile that could have lighted an arena. "Admiral," she said, "it truly *is* an honor to meet you. And do please call me Posy. All my friends do."

Daniel smiled ruefully. Mainwaring would have had to be a better man than Captain Daniel Leary to resist charm on that level. But from the proprietorial way the lady's hand had rested on von Gleuck's arm as they approached, the Alliance had already won this battle.

"Enchanted, Your Ladyship," Mainwaring said, bending over Posy's hand with the enthusiasm of a starving cannibal. "Is your brother here, then? Not that anyone would care when your lovely self is present."

Commander Milch reappeared with a sharp-featured man of fifty who wore a round, brimless yellow cap. His uniform was tan with silver buttons but no other markings. There was a five-pointed star on the cap, also silver.

"Sir?" said Milch. "This is Commander Bailey, the Chief Gunnery Officer of the *Piri Reis*. The Autocrator gave him a message for you."

"Right you are, Admiral," Bailey said in an accent straight from the spacers' tenements around Harbor Three. "She was just going into conference with your Governor Wenzel when she heard that the ship what just landed had brought Captain Leary. She asked could I show him around the cruiser till she was through, because she really wanted to meet him."

Mainwaring looked thunderous again; then his face cleared. "Well, I wanted to show you off to the Autocrator myself, but it seems she's stolen a march on me," he said. "Run along, Leary, and I'll catch up with you later. I trust you to uphold the honor of the RCN without me nursemaiding you."

"Aye aye, sir!" Daniel said brightly. He had been in an awkward situation for a moment. It was Mainwaring who'd created the problem, by ordering him to be present at the gala and thereby giving his hostess a right to request his attendance. One didn't need much experience of the RCN or of life more generally to know that admirals and their civilian equivalents tended not to blame themselves when their wishes were thwarted, however.

"I wonder, Commander Bailey?" said von Gleuck. "Would you mind if Lady Belisande and I joined you? If it's all right with Captain Leary, that is."

"Perfectly all right, ah, Master von Gleuck," Daniel said, gesturing toward the lieutenant commander's civilian tunic. "The more the merrier, wouldn't you say, Bailey?"

Bailey looked stricken, but he swallowed his confusion and mumbled, "Well, I suppose it'd be all right. Come along, then."

As they followed Bailey up the forward boarding ramp, Posy giggled and whispered, "You men! You're being cruel to the poor little fellow! He'll get in trouble."

"Now, now," von Gleuck said. "I just wanted to chat with Leary here."

Daniel gave the woman a shamefaced grin, knowing that she was right: the Autocrator might be *very* unhappy when she learned that Bailey had given an enemy officer a tour of her flagship. But whatever Bailey's Palmyrene rank might be, he was clearly an oik from the Xenos slums; there was no way he was going to resist the double-teaming of two aristocrats.

And apart from anything else, Daniel wanted to get to know von Gleuck.

CHAPTER 8

RAPHAEL HARBOR ON STAHL'S WORLD

Headquarters Annex 6 was the last in a row of prefabricated single-story buildings behind the stuccoed masonry of the headquarters building proper. It was built from sheets of structural plastic. The walls were beige, while the corrugated roof was reddish brown where it had been in the shade. Where the surface took direct sunlight, it had faded to pink.

"Not a very secure site," Tovera said as they approached. By training she stepped slightly ahead, putting herself between Adele and the door in the center of the building, but neither of them imagined that there would be any real trouble here.

Adele smiled faintly. "My suspicion is," she said, "that if they tried to attack us, they would injure themselves."

"If you follow your training, you have less to think about and so make fewer mistakes," said Tovera in a primly chiding tone. She accepted Adele's ethical decisions without question: Tovera had no conscience, but her sharp intelligence let her act within the bounds of society so long as she had a guide she trusted to tell her what those bounds were.

Tovera did not, however, defer to Adele's judgments regarding doctrine and technique, except under orders. She was apt to honor even direct orders in the breach if she decided they would endanger her mistress unduly.

That wasn't simply a matter of loyalty, though perhaps it was that as well. Tovera knew that she wouldn't survive in society without direction. She had been the tool of a Fifth Bureau officer. After he was killed, she had attached herself to Adele as someone who would appreciate the usefulness of a murderous sociopath the way she appreciated the pistol in her tunic pocket. Either would kill at Adele's direction, and Adele's duties and ruthlessness guaranteed that she was likely to need them.

A hefty middle-aged woman in utilities watched through the glass-paneled door. She pushed it open a moment before Tovera would have had to reach for the latch.

"Officer Mundy?" the woman said. Her voice was the one Adele recognized from the call. "I'm Technician Runkle. Lieutenant Leonard is waiting—"

A thin, very serious looking young man, also in utilities, came out of the office at the end of the hall. "Officer Mundy?" he called.

"Yes, I'm still Officer Mundy," Adele said as she followed Tovera into the building; Runkle locked the door behind them. "Now, shall we go to your office where you can explain what this rigmarole is about?"

"Officer Mundy," Leonard said, looking nervously over his shoulder as he trotted back the way he had come, "I have to apologize for deceiving you. You see—"

Tovera snickered.

"You didn't deceive us," Adele said in a more formal version of the same statement. "You're the Regional Intelligence Section. What do you want of me?"

"Oh!" said Leonard. "Oh, yes, of course. I suppose we should have expected that, Runkle."

"Sir," the technician muttered in agreement. "Sorry, ah, Officer."

Adele said nothing—and Tovera didn't sniff, as she might have done—but that was certainly true: if this pair knew who Adele was, they should have expected her to investigate them.

In fact they probably *thought* they knew who Adele was, but only by reputation. They could no more understand what she really did than they could imagine the processes going in at the heart of a star.

Half the building was an open clerical pool with storage cabinets along one wall. On the other side of the hallway was Runkle's office with ASSISTANT TO THE DIRECTOR on the door, a closed file room, and the door Leonard had come out of. The four of them seemed to be the only people in the building—Tovera would know for certain—but going into the lieutenant's office seemed the choice that would put the locals most at ease.

Which in turn would get them to the point most quickly, though Adele didn't have high hopes for that. People simply *wouldn't* be as direct as efficiency required.

There were only two extra chairs in the office. Runkle, realizing that, said, "Just a second. I'll bring another chair."

"Don't bother," said Tovera. "I'll stand."

She placed herself in the corner to the left of the outward-opening door. Her expression was probably one of amused contempt, but it could be read as friendly openness.

Adele seated herself. She knew Tovera as well as anyone did, she supposed, but she certainly wouldn't claim to know what was going on in her servant's mind.

"Well, if you're sure...?" said Runkle; Tovera didn't deign to answer. Runkle sat gingerly on the open chair.

A Technician Grade 8 was a senior warrant officer, on a level with a bosun or a chief engineer—far superior to a signals officer. The deference Runkle and her commissioned superior were displaying proved, which was scarcely necessary, that they weren't thinking of Adele in the RCN chain of command. It also indicated that they believed that she and they were all in a continuum of the intelligence community. That was a degree of arrogance which would have made Adele angry if it weren't so foolish.

Leonard coughed and crossed his hands precisely on the deck before him. He said, "I suppose it's too much to hope that you've been sent here because of our reports to Xenos, Lady Mundy?"

"With respect, Lieutenant...," Adele said. There was no respect whatever in her tone. "While I'm wearing this uniform—"

She flicked her left sleeve with her right little finger. Her personal data unit was in her lap—she had brought it live without really thinking about it when she sat down—and she was holding the control wands in her thumbs and first two fingers of both hands.

"—I am Officer Mundy."

"I'm very sorry, Officer Mundy!" Leonard said hastily, clasping his hands by reflex. "It won't happen again!"

"And as for the question," Adele continued, "I know nothing about your reports, but I'm inclined to doubt that they had anything to do with me passing through Stahl's World. As I was given to understand the matter, a minor figure of the Representation Service died and the *Princess Cecile* was chartered to deliver his replacement as quickly as practical. I am the Signals Officer aboard the *Princess Cecile*."

The locals looked at one another. Runkle grimaced and said, "I don't wish to speak about matters which shouldn't be discussed generally, Officer, but if I may say—it's public knowledge that you have a reputation beyond the RCN."

"I shouldn't wonder," Adele said dryly. "I won't speculate on what you or anyone else may have heard—about me, or about the inner workings of the Senate, or the true story of this or that video entertainer's love life. I will say, however, that my duties to the RCN brought me to Stahl's World, and my courtesy has brought me to this room."

She paused, then said, "That courtesy is rapidly becoming exhausted, Technician."

The lieutenant opened his mouth but then froze. Runkle looked at him, then blurted, "Palmyra is dangerous, *really* dangerous. We thought, everybody out here thought Autocrator Odin was less an ally than a tin-pot king with delusions of grandeur. After he died, though, we saw—we in the Intelligence Section, I mean—that the real pressure had been coming from Irene all the time. Odin had been holding her back."

She looked again at Leonard. This time he said, "No one

will listen to us, Officer Mundy. You know how the RCN is. Nobody counts except watch-standing officers. They completely ignore us technical specialists."

Adele kept a straight face. The lieutenant had obviously forgotten who he was talking to.

She would agree that spacers, not just RCN officers, tended to treat anyone who wasn't a spacer with good-natured contempt. Space officers of Adele's acquaintance had invariably accepted her as soon as she had given evidence of her abilities, however. Leonard and Runkle hadn't yet convinced even her that they had a point.

"The Squadron staff treats us like a joke," Runkle said. "We've compiled evidence that Palmyra intends to expand by force in the near future, but nobody will pay any attention to our dossier."

"Commander Milch told me that the Palmyrenes were 'good fellows and bloody fine spacers,'" Leonard said bitterly. "As if commanding a light cruiser in the Battle of Dorking made him an authority on political intelligence!"

"You believe that Palmyra intends to attack us, Technician?" Adele said. Her tone was dry, by habit rather than policy. She kept her eyes on the display her wands were manipulating, though she was listening to the locals as she worked.

"We don't know," said Leonard. He spread his hands on the table and scowled at them. "But they have four regiments of infantry confined to base in preparation for embarkation. Plus the Horde on high alert, though that isn't so unusual. The Palmyrenes feel the same way about the importance of the Horde as RCN officers do about the RCN."

"The soldiers are under General Osman," said Runkle. She had her own personal data unit out. It was larger though far less capable than Adele's, but the technician handled the virtual keyboard with skill. "He's a good officer. Probably the only Palmyrene ground officer who you could say that about."

The section's electronic databases were well protected, much better protected than Adele had expected them to be. Their weakness was the provision to allow transfer of files from open storage to locked storage. Adele set her PDU to emulate the Section's administrative computer, then used it to insert a Trojan Horse to take control of the remainder of the system.

"The Palmyrenes have been talking for a generation about their traditional hegemony over the Qaboosh," Leonard said, relaxing slightly now that he and his assistant had begun talking without being slapped down. Since they'd finally come to the point, Adele had no reason to slap them. "If you go back far enough there's evidence for that."

If you go back far enough, Earth rules the human universe, Adele thought. *The reality is that since a dozen asteroids crashed into the home planet to begin the Hiatus, what remains of Earth is either pastoral or barbaric depending on your viewpoint.*

But the present reality in the Qaboosh Region appeared to be the Horde; which did indeed put a different complexion on Palmyrene claims.

"Founder Hergo may well be right," said Runkle. "Though he doesn't do himself any good with his yelping and posturing. And if Irene attacks Zenobia or another Alliance possession, who's to say that the Alliance isn't going to retaliate against our shipping because Palmyra is a Cinnabar ally?"

"You said that two thousand Palmyrene ground troops appear to be poised for invasion," Adele said as her wands moved. She was switching tasks. The data harvest was complete, but it could have continued without her oversight if that were necessary. "My information is that Zenobia has a population of about three million, almost entirely on Setif, the main continent?"

When Runkle referred to Zenobia, she brought up a subject with which Adele had been familiarizing herself. Adele let her tone suggest a question, but she was confident in her statement. Quite apart from anything else, the data she'd brought from Xenos turned out to mirror that which she'd just gleaned from Section files.

"Well, yes, but there's no Zenobian regular army," Runkle said. "A sudden landing at Calvary might capture the government."

"Except for the three hundred personnel of the Founder's Regiment," Adele said, her lip curling in contempt at Runkle's imprecision.

"Besides that," she went on, viewing her display as she spoke, "Calvary Harbor has anti-starship missiles. It would be necessary to capture or disable those, or else to land at a distance—at least a hundred and eighty miles from the batteries. Even then there would be a risk if a battery commander were alert. A landing starship can't maneuver; it's already operating at maximum stress."

"Have you technical specialists ever been on an assault landing?" Tovera said, her voice a buzz as quiet as a wasp's wings. "Mistress Mundy and I have, several times. Even when Captain Leary was in charge, they weren't nearly as neat and simple as they may seem on a computer display."

"Yes," said Adele, "there's that."

She shut down her data unit and rose. The visit hadn't been a waste of time, since she would have found it very difficult to enter the Section's locked files from outside the building. This way she could check whatever information the Section gave her without them knowing she was doing so.

"I will relay your concerns to such persons as might have an interest in them, Lieutenant Leonard," Adele said; she turned her head slightly to include Runkle in her statement. She thrust the data unit away in the thigh pocket she'd had added to her Grays. "For the moment, however, I must repeat that to the best of my knowledge, the fears you express are not shared on Xenos."

"But there *has* to be a reason you were sent to the Qaboosh!" Runkle said, frustration getting the better of her tone. "It doesn't take an agent of your stature to nursemaid some commissioner!"

"I am here, Technician...," Adele said, suddenly coldly angry, "as signals officer to the best fighting captain in the RCN. And now that you've reminded me, I'll get back to my duties. Good day to you both!"

She stalked into the hall, past Runkle who was trying to burble an apology. Tovera followed, walking backward with her hand inside her attaché case. A needless precaution, but she would ignore Adele's objection; and anyway, Adele didn't feel like objecting.

The trouble was that Adele suspected there really was fire somewhere in the smokescreen of sloppy thinking which the Intelligence Section had raised. The best hope was that

Autocrator Irene planned to attack a Cinnabar ally or even Stahl's World itself; such a business could be put down at modest cost in lives and property.

If the attack was on an Alliance world, however, the danger wasn't just commerce raiding in reprisal. It would light a fuse which, when it burned back to Pleasaunce, would engulf the Peace of Rheims and with it, very possibly, *both* exhausted empires.

"This bay houses the Power Room watches," Commander Bailey said as he entered the B Level compartment with Daniel at his side; von Gleuck and Lady Belisande followed closely. Most of the bunk towers had been lifted against the ceiling to clear the huge compartment.

Three spacers squatted near the hatch to play cards on the floor. They hopped to their feet and one—presumably the senior man, but they wore only breechclouts—shouted, "Attention!"

A dozen other personnel leaped up in various stages of undress. "Stand easy," Bailey said with a nonchalant wave. The Palmyrene spacers may have relaxed slightly, but they didn't go back to their previous occupations while the visitors strode down the center aisle.

"The room is very clean," Lady Belisande said as the party approached the rear bulkhead. "But perhaps that is because it's so much bigger than your destroyer, Otto?"

Von Gleuck snorted. Daniel said, "Your Ladyship, I've never seen a ship of any size this neat before. I've seen battleships straight from the builders' yard that had more trash and litter about them, not to mention grease."

"What Captain Leary says is my experience also," von Gleuck said. "Commander, has the ship been cleaned specially for the gathering? Even so it is remarkable—and we are not in the public parts of the vessel where strangers are to be expected."

Bailey led them out into the corridor through the sternward hatch. None of the off-duty spacers had spoken while visitors were present, save for the man who had called the compartment to attention.

"No," Bailey said. "That's how it is in the Horde. It's a good thing, you know, but to tell the truth it gives me the creeps sometimes."

"You're from Cinnabar yourself, are you not, Commander?" Daniel said with a friendly smile.

Bailey had been reaching for the control of the hatch marked MISSILE MAGAZINE #2. He started and gave Daniel a look of nervous surmise. "I'm from Kostroma, born right in Kostroma City," he said. "But, ah, I lived a while in Xenos. And had twelve years as Chief Missileer in the RCN if you want to know the truth. But I didn't desert, I mustered out proper, and anyway I'm an officer in the Horde now and the Autocrator won't let you haul me back!"

"Nothing like that, my good man," said Daniel. "Quite a number of RCN personnel will be entering foreign service or trying to live on half pay very shortly if the peace holds."

He'd slipped into the tone of a superior to a servant rather than speaking as peer to peer. Bailey had merely confirmed Daniel's existing assumption: the fellow was a warrant officer with a commission from barbarians rather than an officer by birth and education.

"Are there many foreign officers in the Horde?" von Gleuck said. "I met a number of cutter captains below at the gala, and they were all Palmyrenes."

"Specialist officers is all," admitted Bailey. He'd apparently decided just to answer what he was asked rather than worry about what he *should* say. "Which means some of us aboard the *Piri Reis* and also the *Turgut*. And nobody from Cinnabar or Pleasaunce, either: I'm Kostroman, remember. The destroyer's got a Palmyrene chief engineer, but Antoniani here on the *Piri Reis* is from Pantellaria."

Daniel looked into the missile magazine without entering. All the cradles were filled, and everything was as precisely arranged as the interior of a mechanical timepiece.

The missiles were single-converter units, however. They had the same terminal velocity as the weapons in front-line service with Cinnabar and the Alliance, but they took twice as long to accelerate.

The units that turned reaction mass into the antimatter which was annihilated with ordinary matter in the High Drive were expensive. Otherwise a missile was a water tank which relied on kinetic energy to destroy its target. Navies which expected to use their missiles—and who could afford them—equipped their ships with dual-converter models, thereby gaining an advantage in combat.

"Is the *Piri Reis* having trouble with her own converters, Bailey?" Daniel asked as he turned away from the magazine.

That got through the commander's cloak of resignation. He blurted defensively, "Why do you ask that?"

"Probably because every Pantellarian ship in the RCN has

converter problems," von Gleuck said. "Certainly that's true in the Fleet, as I know to my cost. I was a midshipman on the *Turbine*. We counted ourselves lucky when we had seventy-five percent of our High Drive motors on line."

Daniel laughed. "Yes, but they have such pretty lines, do they not?" he said, exchanging grins with von Gleuck.

He bowed to Lady Belisande and added, "Though not nearly so pretty as those of her ladyship here."

"Captain," she said with an arch lift of her slim nose, "I will slap you if you do not immediately begin referring to me as Posy. Lady Belisande died at my birth, as you might guess from my given name of Posthuma. *I* am alive."

"And quite lively, in a ladylike fashion," said von Gleuck with an affectionate grin.

"Sometimes ladylike," Posy said. She covered her giggle behind her hand. They were obviously an affectionate couple, comfortable in one another's presence.

The commo unit on Bailey's shoulder gave three shrill beeps. That must have been more than merely an attention signal, for he cracked his heels together and stiffened before replying, "Bailey here, Excellency!"

"Bring Captain Leary to my suite, Bailey," a woman's voice directed. The Palmyrenes used external speakers rather than earbuds. While the tiny speaker might account for some of the harsh tone, Daniel suspected that it gave a fairly accurate impression of the Autocrator's manner. *"At once."*

"This way," said Bailey, gesturing with his hands as though he were shooing his guests toward the companionways in the stern rotunda which widened the central corridor just beyond the missile magazine. "And don't dawdle! The Admiral's Suite, that's where Her Excellency is, is just forward of the BDC."

Daniel took the lead, which would allow von Gleuck to shepherd his lady at the speed they chose. He and the Alliance officer exchanged glances, but they both understood the situation without needing to speak. This way there wasn't a risk that a spacer—well, a rated landsman; no spacer would behave that way—would barrel down the up companionway, nor that someone in a hurry would try to push by from below.

Posy couldn't have a great deal of experience on helical metal staircases, but her steps pattered up quickly enough that Daniel didn't feel a need to slow down for her sake. He grinned, remembering how easily Miranda Dorst took to companionways. In Miranda's case, poverty after her father's early death had meant the elevators of the apartment block where she and her mother lived were frequently out of order.

Pantellarians wearing body armor and carrying mob guns—impellers whose short barrel fired clusters of aerofoils which spread widely when they left the muzzle—stood outside the open hatch just up the corridor. Two guards turned to cover Daniel and his companions, while the third kept his weapon aimed toward the bow.

If the Autocrator is really concerned for her safety…, Daniel thought, *she had better consider how aerofoils would ricochet from steel bulkheads.* He gave the guards an engaging smile.

A man in black Cinnabar formalwear with a white ruff stepped out of the compartment, followed by a young woman with a briefcase; she wore a beige suit with maroon piping, the dress uniform of members of External Affairs. She and her superior strode silently past Daniel and disappeared into a down companionway. The man—Governor Wenzel, by deduction—nodded warily to Daniel's uniform.

The woman who followed the Cinnabar officials into the corridor wore a tiara. Golden robes concealed her body, but there was no fat in her cheeks or hands.

"You're Captain Leary?" she said. "Come into my suite. I want to talk to you."

The commo unit hadn't misled Daniel about her voice, though in person the Autocrator had a resonance that commanded respect. He said, "Yes, I'm Daniel Leary, Your Excellency. May I introduce my friends, Lady Posthuma Belisande of Zenobia and Fregattenkapitan Otto von Gleuck of the Alliance Fleet?"

"A Zenobian?" Irene said on a rising note. "And you—"

Her eyes searched for Commander Bailey. He had stepped behind the visitors as soon as Daniel made his announcement.

"—have brought a *Fleet* officer here?"

"Your pardon, Leary," von Gleuck said politely. He fluffed the sleeve of his "Zenobian" blouse and added, "Aboard this vessel, Your Excellency, I am the Honorable Otto von Gleuck, second son of Count Johann. We on Adlersbild continue the custom of hereditary nobility, foolish though it may seem to you sturdy republicans of Cinnabar."

"I recall my father, Speaker Leary, commenting on that very thing," said Daniel, grinning at von Gleuck.

They were baiting the Autocrator. That certainly hadn't been Daniel's intention when he jumped to obey Admiral Mainwaring's summons, but he knew instinctively that it was the correct response—at least when he had a partner like von Gleuck to support him.

If he didn't make clear the position of Cinnabar relative to that of Palmyra, the Autocrator would begin ordering him around like a puppy. That would force him, as an RCN officer in the middle of an RCN base, to react. She might become angry at being treated with gentle amusement, but that was less dangerous in the long run to the relations among the powers of the Qaboosh Region.

The Autocrator's chiseled features went pale. It occurred to Daniel that it would not be beyond possibility that the ruler of a world so far out on the fringes might order her guards to shoot them all dead. After long moments of silence she smiled coldly and said, "Come into my suite, then, all of you. It is well that you should have seen the *Piri Reis* for yourselves."

She swept back through the hatchway. Daniel exchanged glances with von Gleuck, then led the way. The Alliance officer followed Posy.

Bailey seemed to have disappeared. Goodness knew what this would mean for the gunnery officer, but Daniel couldn't find much sympathy for someone who knew what civilization was but preferred to sell himself to barbarians.

The interior of the large compartment surprised Daniel, though he supposed it shouldn't have. Rugs covered the deck. Over them were piled cushions which must be fixed in place or acceleration and weightlessness would fling them about. The curved tables at two corners were low, and the very capable-looking console against the forward bulkhead was intended to be used by someone sitting cross-legged.

There were four male servants in uniforms like the Palmyrene spacers' but with cloth-of-gold bands at wrists and ankles. The fifth man present was a burly fifty-year-old with a full beard. He wore robes similar to those of the Autocrator but in black silk; only the sash at his waist was gold.

"So, Polowitz," she said. "The tall one is an Alliance officer come to spy on us."

Von Gleuck stood very straight. "I assure you, Admiral Polowitz," he said, "that I am not a spy but rather a naval officer like yourself. And—"

He turned and nodded toward Daniel.

"—like Captain Leary here. Your Excellency—"

Looking back toward the Autocrator.

"—if my presence disturbs you, I will of course take my leave."

"Nothing the Alliance does disturbs me," she said, "except its pretensions and its very existence. Isn't that so, Captain Leary?"

"Quite the contrary, Your Excellency," Daniel said, smiling easily. "The Alliance, and particularly its Fleet, have often done things that disturbed me."

He grinned at von Gleuck and added, "For example, an Alliance missile struck the ship I was commanding less than six months ago and left it a constructive loss. I was lucky to escape that with only a headache, but it was a *very* bad headache."

"I heard reports of the Battle of Cacique," von Gleuck said, "though I was not present. *Fortunately* I was not present, I may say. I believe that since our nations are now at peace, it is proper for me to congratulate you on your victory, Captain; even if it cost you your flagship."

"I have heard you fancy yourself as an astrogator, Leary,"

said Polowitz. Von Gleuck had been the first to mention the admiral's rank, but it didn't surprise Daniel that the Fleet officer had done his homework. "Perhaps you will come with me on one of our cutters and I will show you what real astrogation is."

"I've heard remarkable things about Palmyrene abilities, sir," said Daniel. He kept his lips smiling and his voice pleasant, but he felt his back stiffen despite willing himself to relax. *Who cares what a barbarian thinks?* "And having seen the external controls on the cutters in the basin when I arrived, it's clear to me that the stories were not exaggerated."

"What do you think of the *Piri Reis*, Lieutenant Commander?" the Autocrator said to von Gleuck, showing that she had been not only been listening but was able to convert Fleet ranks to their RCN equivalent. "Now that you've had an opportunity to view her."

"She's a trim ship and well found in all respects that I was able to see," said von Gleuck, neatly finessing the subject of the antimatter converters. They appeared to be absorbing the efforts of both Power Room watches, save for spacers who had been on some other fatigue and exempted. Bailey hadn't taken the visitors through the converter bay. "You and your officers—"

He nodded precisely to Polowitz.

"—must be rightly proud of her."

The Autocrator gave von Gleuck a guarded expression, perhaps because she either thought he was mocking her or because she had expected some form of condemnation. *Tsk!* Adele thought. *He's a gentleman, not a barbarian who picks his teeth with a knife.*

Instead of replying, however, she turned to Daniel and said, "And you, Captain? What is your view of our flagship?"

That I'd be happy to take her on with any light cruiser in the RCN, thought Daniel. Missiles and gunnery would decide a battle between heavy ships, and there the Palmyrenes didn't have the experience an RCN crew would. *Though I suspect she could give me points in dodging her way through the Matrix.*

Aloud he said, "I've never seen a crew as tightly disciplined, Your Excellency, or a ship as well maintained."

He coughed. "Some cables that struck me as worn. But we'll be loading rigging from the base stores here to replace some of ours, also. After we've delivered our passengers to Zenobia, that is."

The Autocrator's head snapped around. "Polowitz!" she said. "Is that true?"

"Your Excellency, cables of the length required for a cruiser's rigging are not standard on Palmyra," the Admiral said. He wasn't pleading, but his voice had lost the bluster of moments before. "We have more on order—"

"It will be ready when we return home!" the Autocrator said. "Or there will be executions, you understand? Perhaps starting with the admiral who failed to see to it that the cables were available when they were needed!"

"Yes, Your Excellency," Polowitz whispered.

The Autocrator's eyes swivelled back to Daniel and von Gleuck. "Well then, Captain," she said, her voice still trembling with fury. "You have criticized my cruiser, well and good. But—"

Daniel would have protested, but he knew that would make the situation worse. The *Piri Reis* was perfectly safe to operate, and her rig was in better condition than that of almost any merchant vessel in Cinnabar registry. The RCN—or the Fleet—would by now have replaced some of the cables on vessels in frontline service, that was all he'd meant.

"—perhaps you will be good enough to show me your ship in turn?"

"Yes, of course, Your Excellency," Daniel said. "When would you like to visit the *Princess Cecile*?"

"Now!" said the Autocrator. "And these others—"

She nodded to von Gleuck and Posy.

"—can come too. If her brother will allow her, that is."

"We on Zenobia are civilized, Irene," Posy said with her nose lifted again. "Hergo does not direct my movements, nor I his."

"Master von Gleuck," Daniel said, standing formally straight, "Lady Belisande. Will you do me the honor of touring the *Princess Cecile* with the Autocrator and me?"

He broke into an honest smile. "I'm quite proud of her, you know," he said.

Von Gleuck clasped Daniel's hand. "The honor would be ours, sir," he said. "And I hope in the future you will call me Otto. There need be no formality between two professionals, need there?"

They laughed together while Autocrator Irene watched in stony silence.

CHAPTER 9

RAPHAEL HARBOR ON STAHL'S WORLD

"Irene has three guards with her," Tovera said, watching a feed from the *Sissie*'s external camera. "My goodness, they have mob guns."

She giggled, then added, "It always seemed to me to be simpler to learn to shoot accurately; but then, I'm not from Palmyra."

Both valves of the forward airlock were fixed open while the corvette was in harbor. Lieutenant Cory, wearing utilities, entered the rotunda from the hull and stepped onto the bridge.

Glancing over his shoulder to see that he hadn't been followed, he said, "Captain Leary and four civilians are coming up the ramp. They've got guards with them."

"The Captain is bringing the Autocrator Irene of Palmyra with her admiral, and the captain of the Z 46 with the sister of the Founder of Zenobia," Adele said. She hadn't been formally told who the guests would be—Daniel had just reported that he would be arriving in half an hour with four visitors—but Adele had of course been watching the proceedings aboard the *Piri Reis*. That was her job, after all.

"The Palmyrenes who came on ahead know what they're doing," Cory said uncomfortably. "Woetjans is watching them run up and down the rigging, and I checked with Pasternak too. He says the ones in the Power Room are sticking their noses everywhere. There were even a couple crawling up the throats of the thrusters."

"Is there enough room to do that?" Adele said, looking up from her display.

"Some of them don't look older than twelve," Cory said with a shrug. "Maybe they're just small."

He grimaced. "Mistress, do you know what they're doing?" he said.

"Captain Leary reported that he would be bringing a party to view the *Princess Cecile*," Adele said carefully. "He then added that a number of Palmyrene spacers would be preceding them, and that they were to be given full facilities to see whatever they wished."

She pursed her lips and, because it was Cory, added, "I don't know what their purpose is either. It may simply be that Captain Leary has a reputation as a skilled spacer, and the Palmyrenes are curious because they fancy themselves in that area as well."

"They're coming up the forward companionway," Tovera said. The echo of footsteps was warning enough.

Vesey was in the Battle Direction Center and most of the crew was on liberty—the *Sissie* was moored in an RCN base, after all. Pasternak and Woetjans had rushed back to take charge of their anchor watches. Both senior warrant officers were in their liberty suits and the bosun was staggeringly drunk as well, but she wasn't too drunk to carry out her duties if they didn't involve fancy footwork.

Daniel came up in the lead. Hogg was immediately behind him, wearing a scowl. The servant hadn't been allowed to join Daniel at the gala, which he had accepted; but he had become thoroughly irritated when he learned that the young master had then gone into the midst of a gang of armed wogs without him.

Hogg would have been carrying a sub-machine gun openly if Adele hadn't told him to return it to the armory before he met Daniel at the entrance to the Naval Basin. He hadn't needed the shoulder weapon for any practical reason, but it would have shown how displeased he was to be excluded from possible danger.

"He had no business going off and leaving me like that!" Hogg had muttered. "*Anything* could've happened!"

Adele smiled faintly. Based on past experience, nobody in Daniel's company had to worry about being kept out of danger. There would be plenty to go around—perhaps not on a mission to Zenobia, but soon enough.

Posy Belisande and her escort, von Gleuck of the Z 46, were next up the companionway. Adele had checked the Alliance captain's record as a matter of course. He not only commanded the naval detachment on Zenobia, but the imagery from the gala made it immediately obvious that he was more than a casual factor in the life of Adele's target.

Von Gleuck's record was very good. He would almost certainly have been promoted above command of a destroyer if he hadn't been quite so well born.

Adlersbild was one of the six worlds which had formed the Alliance eighty years ago. While it wasn't nearly as big as Pleasaunce or Blythe, it had some of the finest shipyards in the Alliance and had given the Fleet some of its most famous commanders. The status of the son, even the second son, of the ruling Count was high enough to be a potential threat to Guarantor Porra. Command of a destroyer on a distant station was safer for both of them.

Adele exchanged a glance with Daniel, then turned and watched the rest of the activities on her holographic display with her back turned to the hatch. She had set the screen to focus, as generally, for her eyes only. Anyone else looking at the display would see a shifting pattern of pastels; attractive enough, she supposed, but not informative.

Adele was in utilities again, making herself virtually invisible to a civilian visiting the corvette. If the Autocrator and Admiral Polowitz hadn't been present, she would have arranged an introduction to Posy Belisande. Since they were, Adele wasn't going to call attention to herself.

"Sir!" said Cory, but Daniel's quick smile and finger twitch toward the companionway warned him to wait. Two Palmyrene guards appeared behind the flaring muzzles of their weapons. They looked to be proper cutthroats, scowling through mustaches which merged with their sideburns.

Adele watched their images with a smile that would have been frightening to anyone who understood it. She would fire twice into each right eye; the last round would be off before either of the victims reacted. There was always a chance that a dead man's convulsion would cause his trigger finger to close, but even a barbarian should know better than to leave his safety off as he climbed slick steel stairs.

And if not? Well, death would come one day or another. Today would suit Adele, though she would regret it if Cory were caught in the crossfire.

Autocrator Irene was a handsome woman, though it was unlikely that the pile of blond hair held in place by the tiara was her own. It galled Adele that she couldn't be sure how old the Autocrator was.

Fifteen standard years earlier she had married Odin, then heir apparent. The records in Xenos—and probably on Palmyra—didn't allow Adele to trace Irene back before that point. The Autocrator appeared now to be forty, but she might be younger by ten years.

Adele's lips twisted into another almost-smile. So far as she was concerned, bad record-keeping was a clear sign of barbarity.

"This is my Second Lieutenant, honored guests," Daniel said with a courtly gesture toward Cory. He didn't bother to introduce them to a warrant officer, of course. "Would you care to see the bridge?"

Irene stepped through the hatchway without replying. Two of her guards—another had followed the group up the companionway—pushed in behind her. Tovera had moved to a jumpseat against the starboard bulkhead, her face as smooth as an egg and her hand resting on something within her half-open attaché case.

"It's small," said Irene, "but the whole ship is small, of course. What do you think, Polowitz?"

The admiral had been whispering with two of the Palmyrene

spacers who'd come aboard earlier to inspect. He entered the bridge and came to attention.

"Your Excellency," he said. "It is very suitable. The converters are all running properly, and my men have inspected the logs. There have been no converter failures in the past six months!"

"The *Princess Cecile* is Kostroman built," Daniel said. Only someone who knew him well would have recognized the hint of caution in his voice. "We've replaced three of her original converters with units of Cinnabar manufacture, from Glanz and Son and from Webbern Brothers, during her service with the RCN and in private ownership, but she came from the builders' yard a very solid craft."

"The rig is well too, Your Excellency," Polowitz said. "Very little of it is original, but the replacement spars are of good quality and have been fitted with skill."

He turned to Daniel with a tiny nod of recognition. The Autocrator clearly intended everyone to focus on her when she was present, but Admiral Polowitz was enough of a spacer to offer respect to an equal when he met one.

"Do you think to run up the price on me, Captain?" said the Autocrator. "I am no tradesman to haggle! I am the Autocrator Irene. You own this ship yourself, that is so?"

"That's correct, Your Excellency," Daniel said. He slid his feet slightly apart and stood with his hands crossed behind his back in a formal At Ease posture. "I bought the *Sissie* when she was sold as surplus to the needs of the service. She's under charter to the Bureau of External Affairs, but she is no longer an RCN vessel."

Von Gleuck shifted slightly, putting himself between Posy

and the nearest guard. He continued to smile, but his features could have been painted on a porcelain doll. Posy moved backward, stepping off the bridge.

Acting on a hunch, Adele fed imagery from the pickup over the hatch to a quadrant of her and scrolled back thirty seconds. She saw, as she expected, the Alliance officer's hand behind his back, motioning Posy away.

Somebody else understands the direction this might be going. The corner of Adele's lips moved slightly upward. She and Tovera had matters in hand, but von Gleuck wasn't taking that for granted.

"So," said the Autocrator, "I have a use for a ship like this, though it is small. I will buy it."

She and Polowitz appeared to be unaware of the sudden tension, but the last Palmyrene onto the bridge had picked up on it. He backed away from von Gleuck but collided with the missileer's console; von Gleuck, with his affable porcelain smile, eased closer again so that the guard couldn't lift his clumsy weapon without sticking it into the belly of a high foreign official.

Palmyra might be barbarous, but the guard clearly understood what that would mean on an RCN vessel in the middle of an RCN base. He looked sick. His experience told him that he would be the first to die—*if.*

"That's very flattering, Your Excellency," said Daniel in a falsely jovial tone, "but the *Sissie* isn't for sale. We'll be lifting off very shortly for Zenobia—"

"Polowitz here says she is worth a half milliard of sequins," the Autocrator said as though Daniel had not been speaking. "That's some eight hundred thousand of your Cinnabar florins. Very well, I will pay you a million florins and a half. You wish it in coin? I will have my bankers on Stahl's World deliver it in the hour."

Cory stepped past von Gleuck and slipped out the hatchway. Adele felt an instant's amazement, then realized he had climbed onto the hull to warn Woetjans. A cue on her display indicated that he was also alerting Pasternak on a two-way link, though the Palmyrenes in the Power Room were too far away to be a factor in whatever happened on the bridge.

"I don't wish to sell, Your Excellency," Daniel said, drawing himself up straight. "I—"

"Did you not understand what I said about haggling?" said the Autocrator, her voice rising. The two duller guards heard her tone but looked bewildered. Polowitz had a worried expression, but from the way he eyed his mistress, his concern was for her anger rather than what it might lead to. "Very well, name your price!"

"I have informed you, Your Excellency...," said Daniel. Irene opened her mouth again; he raised the volume of his voice sufficient to overwhelm anything she might have said. "That this vessel is the property of a Cinnabar gentleman who does not wish to sell her. The discussion is closed."

"You—"

"The discussion is closed!"

"Leary," said von Gleuck in the momentary silence, "Lady Belisande has an engagement elsewhere and must leave. Besides, I believe we have reached what a gentleman of Adlersbild would consider the limits of good breeding on a first visit. I hope to see you again in the future."

"Quite right, von Gleuck," said Daniel, suddenly affable again. "It's been a pleasure to meet another professional."

The Alliance officer continued to smile as he backed to the companionway. Only when Posy was within the armored tube did he face around to follow her.

His interjection had broken the mood on the bridge. "Money will always find a way, Leary," said the Autocrator. She sounded distant rather than furious, though Adele didn't doubt the fury was still there. "Some men cannot be bought, perhaps; but a result can always be bought."

She strode to the companionway, surprising all her entourage except the guard who had brought up the rear before. He reached the hatch before his mistress and preceded her down the stairs.

"I think," said Daniel in the sudden quiet, "that we'll lift tonight."

"I'm calling Commissioner Brown now," said Adele as her wands moved. "He should be at the Governor's Residence, but he hasn't had time to transfer his luggage yet."

Woetjans came in from the hull and stopped in the bridge hatchway. "Cory's out looking over things while the wogs scoot down the stays," he said. "I'll go roust our people home. You keep Pasternak here to pick 'em up as they come in, right? Because some'll be drunk enough to wander on off again."

"Roger, bosun," Daniel said. "My goodness, I hope I didn't harm relations in the region unduly by that."

"From the tone of the Autocrator's remarks," said Adele as she checked for Commissioner Brown's location through the Residence security cameras, "I don't imagine you can have done anything worse than advancing the arrival of trouble with Palmyra by a little. A very little."

There was a gust of wind; rain spattered down again. Daniel turned his head away, but he didn't duck into the guardhouse because he saw the lights of a ground car coming down the approach road to the Naval Basin.

"Six, the hire car with the Browns has entered the naval reservation," Cory reported, confirming Daniel's expectation. Presumably Adele had something more important on her plate and had delegated tracking the Commissioner to Cory. *"Bridge out."*

"Roger," said Daniel. He gave a big smile to the pair of guards—ratings from the base establishment—and said, "These are the ones I've been waiting for. Thanks for your hospitality."

"Thank *you*, sir," said the senior man. "Not often we get to listen to somebody like you."

"You're welcome here any time you want to spend a chunk of your life getting rained on for no bloody reason," said his junior. "Say, sure you don't need a ventilation system tech on your corvette, sir?"

"I'm going to be in enough trouble with the regional command," said Daniel, truthfully without explaining why it was true, "without poaching their personnel. But I appreciate the thought."

The vehicle stopped. The four wheels had rubber tires, but the two on the front weren't the same width; the cabin in the back was built of wood and mounted on a chassis designed for something else. The driver, wearing a slicker, got out and started to open the passenger cabin.

"Carry them to Slip Four, my good man," Daniel said, striding over to him. "I'll ride along so it'll be all right."

"What's happening?" said Clothilde Brown. "Surely we don't have to get out here in the rain, Pavel!"

"I'm not supposed to enter the reservation...," the driver said uncertainly.

"It'll be all right," Daniel said, slipping him a coin. "And I'll have one of my spacers ride back with you so that you won't have any trouble on the way back."

While the driver was surreptitiously checking the denomination of the coin—it was a full florin; more than a day's wage here on Stahl's World—Daniel got into the cabin beside the Commissioner. Bench seats front and back faced one another; there were two small suitcases on the central rack.

"We'll be driving up to the ship," he said to the Browns. "I'll get some of my people to carry your bags in, so you just run up the ramp and get out of the rain."

"Here, I'll ride along," said the younger gate guard unexpectedly, shielding his sub-machine gun under his field coat. "No sense one of your folks get drowned walking back when we've got to be out in it anyway."

The guard hopped in beside the driver; the car shuddered off. The cabin was completely separate from the cab, which with the rattling provided privacy for anything Daniel had to say.

"We were treated abominably!" said Clothilde. The little girl flounced up suddenly to a sitting posture; she had been lying half across her mother's lap. "There was nobody to receive us at the Residence! We would have been treated better if we were tradesmen!"

In a matter of speaking, Daniel had no duty to the Browns except to deliver them safely to Zenobia. Out of courtesy, and perhaps because he felt sorry for the poor Commissioner, he had chosen to make their lives a little easier by saving them the walk to the gate. Cory said they had walked out this afternoon when they realized they would have to depend on a hired car because the civil establishment wasn't going to send a vehicle.

"The Regional Assembly has disrupted everything here, I'm afraid," Daniel said. "Ah—I was wondering if you would mind if we were to lift for Zenobia immediately?"

"I want to go home!" the little girl said, but she said it in the tone of a child making a point of her displeasure, not one who thinks there's any chance that she'll get her way. "I don't know why we had to come here anyway!"

"I'm not accredited to Stahl's World," said the Commissioner quietly. "I had hoped that I might get a little local knowledge here before going on to my station, but that probably wouldn't be the case however long I remained here. I would just as soon go on."

"They were insulting," his wife said with venom. "They didn't care anything about us, *anything*. We could just as well have died in space so far as anyone at the Residence was concerned."

Daniel looked at her set, angry face in the lights of the slips as they passed. Brown would have been dealing with junior clerks or less; anyone of greater importance would have been involved with the Regional Assembly. Zenobia, as an Alliance possession, wasn't even part of the Regional chain of command.

Sure, it was a pity that the clerks hadn't been more welcoming to strangers who weren't properly part of their job, but most people found only themselves of importance. Clothilde Brown certainly fell into that category, but this time the locals had trumped her with their disinterest.

Daniel realized he was grinning. To take the sting out of his expression, he said, "We'll get you to Zenobia promptly, Mistress Brown. In three days, I judge. I know that life this far out from Cinnabar takes some getting used to, but once one learns the tricks it can become very pleasant."

The vehicle drew up alongside Slip 4. Even before Daniel could figure out how to open his door—the latch was a half circle of wood which rotated into a cut in the jamb—four spacers double-timed down the *Sissie*'s ramp holding a tarp overhead. A sheet of rain blew in from the side, but the idea of shelter appeared to raise Clothilde's morale.

More spacers appeared, grabbing the bags that Daniel handed out. Daniel sent them and the Browns up the ramp, then covered himself with the poncho Hogg had brought. He waved thanks to the gate guard as the car turned and headed back.

"You could've sent Cory," Hogg said as they reached the boarding hold. The Browns were headed toward the stern companionway; Hester's voice floated back querulously. "You could've sent an engine wiper. If you needed to send anybody."

A truck pulled up, loaded with spacers from the dives along the harbor front. Daniel dropped his visor a moment to check the running count projected on its upper right corner. Thirteen personnel hadn't reported, but only two weren't listed as accounted for. The *Princess Cecile* would be ready to lift inside an hour.

"It was less trouble all round if I met them at the gate," Daniel said, trotting up the companionway behind his servant. "I told the guards a few stories and they let me bend the rules a little. They wouldn't have done that for a wiper. Maybe a warrant officer, but the chiefs were better put to getting the ship to rights for a quick liftoff."

Adele looked up from her console as Daniel entered the bridge. "Captain," she said with polite neutrality.

Daniel smiled with genuine pleasure at seeing her. "Will we step on the toes of any other ships if we lift shortly, Signals?" he asked.

"No one else is scheduled to lift from either basin tonight," Adele said, switching to a two-way link as she checked her display. *"Nor are any other vessels in condition to lift, as best I can tell. The freighter* Costigan *was testing thrusters earlier this afternoon, but the captain isn't aboard at present."*

"Good," said Daniel as he settled onto the command console. "I'll get clearance from Raphael Control, but because we're on the civil registry now, we don't need naval authorization even though we're on the naval side of the harbor."

"Why don't you want to get naval clearance, Daniel?" Adele asked. *"Is there some reason it wouldn't be granted?"*

Daniel was checking the Power Room statistics. The converters and pumps were in the green, as they had been on landing only a few hours earlier. He would normally have taken aboard fresh fruits and vegetables, but the short run to Zenobia made that unnecessary. The additional cable was already aboard.

"I don't want to discuss the matter with Admiral

Mainwaring," Daniel said. "I'm not under his command, but he would have questions...and I think it better not to have my opinion of Autocrator Irene on record in the regional HQ. Half the personnel are locals, and I would be amazed if half of *them* weren't reporting to Palmyra."

"*Six, this is Three,*" Lieutenant Vesey reported on the command push. "*All our personnel are aboard, though there are forty-odd who had best remain in their bunks unless there's an emergency, over.*"

"Roger, Three," said Daniel. "*Prepare the ship for liftoff. Six out.*"

"*The Autocrator is very clear about her place in the universe,*" said Adele with no more expression than usual. "*It remains to be seen whether the universe shares her opinion.*"

Daniel was grinning as Vesey sent the attention signal through the PA system. With luck, they would have returned to Cinnabar before that question became important. But if not, well—civil registry or not, the *Sissie* was a fighting unit and had proved herself so many times in the past.

CHAPTER 10

CALVARY HARBOR ON ZENOBIA

Adele was contentedly engaged with her duties as the *Princess Cecile* roared down toward the surface of Zenobia. Occasionally she wondered if her "contentment" was what other people referred to as happiness. There wasn't any way to test the hypothesis, however, so she generally ignored the question.

Landing a starship from orbit was a matter of lengthy, thunderous buffeting. Though the antennas had been retracted and clamped as firmly as possible to the hull, every section rattled at a different frequency. The atmosphere howled and whistled; the thrusters pulsed deafeningly as they ionized reaction mass, spewing the plasma out at high velocity to brake the corvette's approach.

Adele was more or less aware of what was going on around her, but she ignored it. The cacophony was familiar from long repetition; and besides, nothing that didn't physically interfere with her work was of great importance when she had something to do. She was quite good at finding things, but first landing on a new planet was always an embarrassment of riches.

She had set Cory at the astrogation console and Cazelet in the BDC to various tasks that she had broken out for them. The *Sissie*'s internal operations would have astounded—appalled—any RCN officer who wasn't already familiar with them: during a landing, all officers should be at their posts, prepared to deal with crises—not harvesting electronic data under the direction of a junior warrant officer.

Daniel—who had the conn—or Vesey, either one, could have landed the *Princess Cecile* and dealt with anything untoward that happened. If both of them—if every watch-standing officer—aboard the corvette suddenly dropped dead, there were a dozen ratings who could have brought the ship in safely. And if Captain Daniel Leary chose to give his signals officer a free hand in directing the crew as she saw fit, then surely the results justified his decision.

Adele grinned slightly while she examined data from the Founder's Palace: regular officers would still be appalled. Which was in part why an irregular officer like Daniel had proved so successful.

The thruster output increased in a smooth curve rather than a series of jolts, showing that a human hand rather than a computerized landing program was in charge of the process. Even so, the perceived increase in the weight of Adele's control wands made her pause until the ship sank fingerbreadth by fingerbreadth into the steam which her exhaust boiled from the harbor.

The Palace's electronic security was conspicuous by its absence: Adele had seen local shops which did a better job of safeguarding their data. Security was so bad, in fact, that her first thought was that the Founder's important files had been concealed so skillfully that she couldn't locate, let alone penetrate, them.

That was paranoia on her part. Founder Hergo *had* no important files. The lack of security was actually a reasonable allocation of resources, since the only risk was that someone would divert the monthly household expense allowance.

When on Zenobia—the *Z 46* hadn't yet returned from the Qaboosh Assembly—Posy Belisande lived within the Palace, as indicated by those household expenses. She had no electronic files whatever. As Adele had expected, if she was to learn anything from Posy, it would have to be a result of personal contact.

She managed a wan smile. The risk of embarrassment shouldn't deter her. She could have spent her whole life without being more than vaguely aware of the Qaboosh and the residents thereof, so it could hardly matter to her if in future years somebody here felt that she had behaved in a self-important or otherwise foolish fashion.

Well, it wouldn't deter her. Nothing would. But she feared embarrassment as she had never feared death.

Daniel brought the *Sissie* in so gently that the first sign that they were down was the relative silence as the thrusters shut down rather than the outriggers splashing into the harbor. The ship gave a long, drawn-out sigh; then hatches rang open all over the hull.

It would be some minutes before the entry ramp could be lowered, but the *Sissie*'s veterans weren't concerned about a little steam or ozone from the exhaust. A pump began to chug, hauling harbor water through twin hoses to replace the reaction mass expended in landing.

Adele went back to work. Her first priority had been military installations, since she put her duty to the RCN—or at any rate, to her fellow Sissies—ahead of Mistress Sand in the present circumstances. Very likely she would say the same in *any* circumstances, but she tended to disregard questions in the abstract.

There were no warships in Calvary Harbor or elsewhere on Zenobia as far as she could tell. The Z 46 was either still on Stahl's World or more likely en route to Zenobia, and her sister ship—the other vessel in the Zenobia detachment, the Z 42—was in powered orbit as it had been since von Gleuck lifted off. A Water Buffalo—basically a tanker with enough thrusters to reach orbit—had replenished the destroyer twice, according to her log.

Von Gleuck was clearly taking the Palmyrene threat seriously. Having met the Autocrator, Adele couldn't imagine the woman launching at attack without herself being present to watch, but von Gleuck had no intention of returning to Zenobia and finding that Irene had stolen a march on him and was in control.

There were no Alliance ground troops on Zenobia, and the security presence controlled by the Resident was only about 20 personnel, fewer than Adele had learned to expect. Apparently Zenobia's independence was less nominal than it had seemed from Xenos.

The Founder's Regiment had a present strength of 319

effectives, with an average of about ten percent over the past six months absent for illness or on leave. They were light infantry trained for urban combat—but they *were* trained: they weren't simply thugs and torturers like the troops of many fringe-world leaders.

The commander was Major Aubrey Flecker, a Norstrilian who had left the Grand Army of the Stars to avoid a prison sentence. Though the regiment's equipment was to Alliance standards, none of the personnel were from Pleasaunce or Blythe. Or from Cinnabar, of course; but again, Adele got an impression of Zenobian independence.

A company of forty-four men was on duty at the Palace now. They appeared to be primarily a reaction force to deal with trouble of a serious nature anywhere on Zenobia, but they also guarded the building itself with a surprising amount of enthusiasm. Instead of fixed guard posts, several four-man teams patrolled at intervals set by a randomizing timer. After checking the surveillance imagery for several days running, Adele was impressed by the way the system appeared to keep the troops on edge.

There was also a battery of anti-starship missiles under three soldiers and a lieutenant; the installation squatted in the middle of what had been a Palace courtyard. Adele's quick check of the records showed that the whole regiment had been cross-trained in missile control; personnel rotated through the installation on the regular duty rota. The battery had links variously across the planet, but the missile controls were only accessible from within the command post.

Adele recalled her discussion on Stahl's World about the

problem of capturing Calvary Harbor. *She* wouldn't be willing to bet against the troops on duty being alert enough to spike the first three enemy vessels attempting an assault landing.

"Ma'am?" said Cory; not in any sense proper communications protocol—or RCN procedure more generally—but sufficient on a two-way link with Adele. *"Would you like me to go down and help the Browns, like before?"*

Adele awoke to her immediate surroundings. She brought up a panorama of the harbor, then shrank the imagery to the quay where the *Sissie* had landed. The large aircar waiting there was military in all respects but one: the identification numbers on the front had been painted over, and on the door the seal of the Representational Affairs section had been appliquéd over what was almost certainly the stencilled legend LAND FORCES OF THE REPUBLIC.

A tall, neatly dressed man stood beside the vehicle. The caret Cory had thoughtfully added above him read COMM M GIBBS/ACTING COMMISSIONER.

"There's nobody from the Palace to meet them, I mean," Cory added, probably concerned that Adele hadn't responded immediately.

"Ship, this is Six," Daniel announced over the *Sissie*'s general channel. *"I'm turning over command to Lieutenant Vesey, who will set up the liberty roster as soon as we have a little better notion of the ah, spirit of the community. Remember, Sissies, Zenobia is an Alliance planet, and it would reflect on my personal honor if your actions harmed the recent peace between our nations. Make me proud of you, fellow spacers! Six out."*

"I have the conn," Vesey reported from the BDC. *"Three out."*

When Daniel rose from his console, Adele noticed for the first time that he was wearing blue trousers and an unmarked blue coat over a gray tunic: the garb of an officer of a civilian vessel. He shot his cuffs, grinned at Adele—this was fancy dress for him—and strode purposefully off the bridge with Hogg behind him. Adele heard him in the companionway starting to whistle "The Ring-Rang-Do."

"I think we can leave the Browns' comfort to our betters, Cory," Adele said. "Have you found a roster of the Zenobian militia? It doesn't appear to be in the Palace, at least not in electronic form."

As she spoke, a much newer, fancier aircar landed on the quay, dissipating a few final swirls of steam remaining from the *Princess Cecile*'s arrival. Acting Commissioner Gibbs glanced sidelong at it, then stepped back into his vehicle.

The man who got out from the back was short, dapper and balding, with a pencil moustache. The men who had ridden in the tonneau walked to either side of him. They were big and wore black clothing which, despite the lack of insignia, was meant to be seen as uniforms.

Adele didn't need Cory's caret to know that the newcomer was Louis Tilton, the Alliance Resident on Zenobia. He sauntered toward the *Sissie*'s boarding ramp as the Browns started to descend.

Daniel reached the entry hold a little later than he'd intended: the Browns had started down the ramp without an escort. He grimaced and lengthened his stride.

Daniel had initially planned to simply hand the ship over to Vesey, but at the moment of doing so he'd remembered that Zenobia was part of the Alliance. Ordinary fights between Sissies and civilians or other spacers took on greater significance.

Hogg, following him into the hold from the companionway, said, "The last time we landed on an Alliance planet, we come in with all guns blazing. I kinda prefer it that way. You know where you stand, then."

Daniel laughed, but he knew just what his servant meant. Peace was a much trickier proposition than open war.

"*Daniel*," said Adele through his earbud, "*the Alliance Resident, Tilton, is approaching the Browns. He's got his bodyguards, over.*"

"Follow my lead!" Daniel said over his shoulder as he galloped forward. He reached the bottom of the ramp just as Brown did. The Commissioner gave him a worried look, but Hester pulled her hand from her mother's and trotted over to attach herself to the fabric of Daniel's trousers. Clothilde's expression was unreadable, at least in the brief time Daniel had to spend on the question.

The walkway from the stone quay was of floating wood, typical for a fringe world harbor. The floats were waterlogged, so that the surface dipped into the harbor at several points. Woetjans, standing at the bottom of the ramp with three riggers, turned to Daniel with a disgusted expression and said, "Hey, Six? Want us to lay out our own instead of this piece of crap?"

The *Sissie* had a metal pontoon bridge in her starboard outrigger. It would save the Browns getting their shoes wet, but the locals might take a Cinnabar captain deploying it as an insult. Daniel made a snap decision and said, "Negative, Chief."

Lifting the little girl into his arms, he smiled past her to her parents and said, "Up Cinnabar, eh, Commissioner?" He strode onto the walkway.

It was five feet wide and even had rope handrails, so there was no danger. Nonetheless, Daniel was a bit concerned when he didn't feel the adults start to follow until he'd almost reached the platform floating up and down between two pilings against the quay. He could have ordered a team of Sissies to carry the Browns to land, but that had seemed, well, *insulting*.

The Alliance Resident stood at the top of the stairs from the platform. Daniel's foot quivered an instant short of the first of five steps, wondering how to handle this.

"Out of the way of the little girl, buddy!" called Hogg in a cheerful voice as he bounded past. He turned on the fourth step and held his arms out.

"Here you go, honey!" he said as he thrust his body the last step up to the quay without looking behind him. "I'll take you now!"

Tilton jumped out of the way. Daniel mounted swiftly, murmuring, "Careful now, dear one, because I may have to set you down."

Hogg didn't try to pass the girl off, of course. That had just been an excuse to slam the Resident onto his butt "by accident" if he hadn't moved quickly enough.

As for what would've happened then, Daniel wasn't sure. He wasn't worried about Hogg and himself being able to handle the bodyguards in normal circumstances, but he didn't want the four-year-old to get hurt in the brawl.

The Commissioner was up beside them in an instant. Daniel wasn't sure how much Brown had seen—or at least understood—of the recent byplay; but the fact that his instinct had been to join the men in front instead of holding back raised him in Daniel's estimation.

Not that there was much Brown could do except hold his daughter. Daniel swept Hester into her father's arms while continuing to smile toward the Alliance Resident. The child gave a squeal of protest, but Brown took her firmly and stepped sideways to let his wife join them.

Hogg looked at the nearer of Tilton's bodyguards and deliberately picked his nose with his left index finger; his right hand was in a jacket pocket. "Are you guys local talent?" he said in a rustic drawl. "Or did they have to ship you in from the big city?"

The guard—they were both young, muscular men, but they'd shambled rather than moved with grace—cocked his fist. Tilton waved him back, snarling, "Stop that, you fool!"

Daniel continued to smile quizzically, as though he were a little bemused by everything around him. If he'd known that coming ashore was going to be this interesting, he'd have brought Woetjans and a dozen Sissies along for an escort. That was what the bosun always wanted to do anyway.

He'd rejected the thought as out of place in the circumstances. And so it was, but Resident Tilton's behavior was out of place as well. He grinned more broadly at the humor of it.

"Which of you is the new Commissioner?" Tilton said harshly. He focused on Brown and went on, "You, of course. You are Cinnabar Commissioner Brown?"

"I am," said Brown, stepping between Daniel and Hogg. Hester was clinging to Clothilde's leg with her face buried against it. "To whom have I the pleasure of speaking?"

The man who had flown up in the Commission aircar got out of the vehicle again and approached slowly. He was tall and rather good-looking, wearing civilian clothing. The flounced jacket would have been fashionable in Xenos about five years ago.

"Pleasure?" Tilton said. As well as being a pushy little fellow generally, he appeared to resent Brown's height. "We will see about that. It will be a pleasure if you know your place, Commissioner. *I* am Resident Louis Tilton."

"Pleased to meet you," Brown said, extending his arm to clasp Tilton's. Instead the Resident stepped past him and stopped in front of Clothilde.

"Well, now," said the Resident. "This is more interesting."

Daniel shifted to stand beside the woman. That meant Hogg would have to handle both bodyguards—which he could do beyond question, but it greatly increased the likelihood of death or maiming for the pair.

"May I present my wife—" Brown said.

"Let's see your profile," Tilton said. He pinched Clothilde's chin between two fingers and tried to turn her head.

Clothilde slapped him; her fingers made an impressive *crack* against Tilton's cheek. "You are a bald little worm," she said in a coldly distinct tone.

Daniel stepped between Tilton and the woman. "Mommie!" cried the little girl.

A score of Sissies was double-timing from the ship, carrying travel cases. Woetjans was in the lead with a suit carrier in her left hand and a length of high-pressure tubing held out in her right as if for balance.

Simultaneously the corvette's dorsal turret rotated. The twin four-inch plasma cannon were probably pointed at the Alliance aircar, but Daniel could only hope that Sun had sense enough to disengage the firing circuit while he was playing his silly game. If the weapons accidentally fired in an atmosphere, their side-scatter would fry everybody on this portion of the quay.

Risk aside—and spacers weren't especially concerned about risk—the squeal of the turret got the Resident's attention. His face went white except for the mark of Clothilde's fingers. He backed away until he was standing behind his two guards. Hogg put his folding knife away.

"Well, Commissioner Brown," Tilton said. "We will see if you become more forthcoming when you've had a little time to reflect, no? Alternatively, you may find that import charges for private ventures by Cinnabar officials have risen prohibitively!"

He turned and stalked off, followed by his guards. One of them glanced back several times on his way to the aircar, but it wasn't a very impressive demonstration of their training in personal protection.

Woetjans mounted the steps in two movements, balancing the case and the cudgel. It was like watching a fish mount rapids to spawn. An extremely ugly fish, but Daniel had felt as though he'd lost his left arm when the bosun took a burst of slugs through the chest. She'd made a good recovery, though....

"Got anything you want us to do quick-quick, Six?" Woetjans said, bobbing the tip of her tubing in the direction of the disappearing Alliance personnel.

"Negative, Chief," Daniel said, repeating his words of a few minutes before but in a very different tone. "But for a moment, I thought I might have some work for you if Hogg had any leftovers."

"I wouldn't've," Hogg said firmly. "But I like to see that kind of spirit, my girl, and I'm proud to have your acquaintance."

The Alliance aircar lifted and made an immediate low-altitude turn, heading back into Calvary. Hogg said in a regretful tone, "I kinda thought they might try to buzz us, you know?"

"Yeah," agreed the bosun. She flipped her cudgel a dozen feet in the air and caught it neatly by the end as it came down. She grinned with satisfaction. "I kinda wondered that too."

The Browns were talking with the fellow in Cinnabar clothing. Daniel walked over and joined them, now that he had leisure to. The child and all three adults looked at him.

"Commissioner Brown, my spacers have brought your baggage," Daniel said brightly. "Would your driver here like to show us where to stow it?"

He didn't see any point in discussing what had happened: it had worked out, which is all that mattered. Besides, he was rather afraid that he'd make a comment about the driver's courage which—however true—would be neither necessary nor helpful.

"This is Assistant Commissioner Gibbs, Leary," Brown said. "He's a commander in the Navy, I'm surprised to learn."

Not nearly as surprised as I am, thought Daniel. The RCN rank was higher in the governmental pay scale than an assistant commissioner on the civil side.

"I've been seconded from the RCN," Gibbs said airily. He

didn't offer to clasp hands. "Very glad to meet you, Leary. You can have your people put the baggage anywhere they please. This car was meant to carry a squad in combat gear, so there shouldn't be any difficulty with no more truck than that."

Adele's voice whispered metallically in Daniel's right ear canal, *"Gibbs became involved with an admiral's daughter but turned out to have a wife already. He couldn't divorce her because he couldn't pay back the jointure which he appeared to have mortgaged fraudulently. Reading between the lines, he wasn't cashiered because that would have brought the admiral's name into the public's attention, but he was given what is listed as a lateral transfer into the Representation Service and sent here."*

Daniel continued to smile, though a trifle more tightly. Hard lines on the wife, but he supposed she'd made her own bed when she chose to marry Gibbs.

"The Resident made a comment about Cinnabar private ventures here on Zenobia, Gibbs," said Commissioner Brown. "Do you know what he was talking about? That wouldn't be permitted under the regulations on an Alliance planet, would it?"

"I have no idea, Brown," Gibbs said. "We should be getting you to Cinnabar House, such as it is, I suppose."

"Well, I'll want to go over all the late Commissioner Brassey's accounts immediately," Brown said. "Tonight, if you can get them together."

Daniel smiled faintly. Brown was a decent fellow but completely at sea in his new duties. He was focusing on the thing he knew how to do: audit accounts. In fairness, that was probably as important as any of the other duties he would face as Commissioner on this benighted world.

"Did you serve with Captain Leary, Gibbs?" Clothilde said unexpectedly. She was holding Hester firmly by the hand; the girl wanted to follow what was probably her personal case: it was pink and covered with broadly smiling blue fish.

"No, mistress, I did not," Gibbs said with a hint of hauteur. "I realize the distinction may be lost on laymen, but Master Leary is a civilian and I am an officer of the Republic of Cinnabar *Navy*."

"As a matter of fact, Gibbs," Daniel said, hearing his voice grow a little harder in response to the other man's implied sneer, "I'm RCN also. I'm wearing these—"

He flicked the cuff of his plain blue jacket.

"—out of courtesy to our hosts, which I suppose is why you're in that old—"

Goodness, he was angrier than he'd realized. The nerve of this little cheat, to try to patronize Daniel Leary!

"—outfit yourself."

"Captain Six is a *great* hero!" piped the little girl. "He beat the bad people in M-M-*Montserrat* and all sorts of places! He's killed ever so many bad people!"

Who's been talking to the child? Daniel thought; and at once the answer: *almost anybody aboard the* Princess Cecile.

Only he wished she hadn't put it in just that way, because Daniel suddenly flashed back to his missiles ripping open the guard ship *Heimdall*, spilling out her many hundreds of crew before they even knew they were in danger. And they hadn't been bad people, just spacers like Daniel Leary and his Sissies; and now they were dead.

"Captain Leary?" Gibbs said, his face scrunching in anger. His expression blanked, then became one of horror. In a quiet voice he said, "Great heavens. Captain *Daniel* Leary? That Leary?"

Daniel cleared his throat. "I'm sure the stories you've heard are exaggerated," he said. "Certainly the ones that have gotten back to me have been. But yes, I suppose I'm 'that' Leary."

Gibbs moistened his lips with his tongue. He looked like an animal turning on its pursuit at the base of a high wall. He said, "What are you doing here, then, with a record like yours?"

"Well, with my lack of seniority in peacetime...," Daniel said, choosing to overlook the discourteous form of the question. Gibbs seemed stunned rather than deliberately insulting. "I consider myself lucky not to be on half pay. And of course in the RCN, it's always 'the needs of the service,' not so? For both of us."

Gibbs swallowed, then nodded. He turned to the Browns and said, "Your baggage is loaded, I see. I'll drive you to Cinnabar House. We don't have a staff here except for a pair of local menials."

He turned and walked toward the aircar. Little Hester hopped along sideways with her mother so that she could wave to Daniel with her free hand the whole way.

Daniel smiled, but his mind was on other matters. *What in the name of heavens is wrong with Gibbs?*

CHAPTER 11

CALVARY ON ZENOBIA

A middle-aged servant wearing an outfit of slanted black-and-white stripes opened the door of Cinnabar House to Adele and Tovera. For more than a generation the garb had been standard for servants in Xenos households that couldn't claim livery.

This woman was obviously local, however, and the tailored garment made her look more dowdy than she might have in the looser national costume. Behind her was a tile courtyard with a roof but no furniture.

"Lady Adele Mundy!" the woman bellowed, then turned and waddled toward the arched gateway at the back. "Come this way if you please, Your Ladyship!"

They followed; Tovera looked wary. Adele smiled faintly and said, "She was directed to announce us when we arrived. She appears to be a little fuzzy about the details, however."

Clothilde Brown had risen from her seat in the garden to meet Adele. She gave the servant a despairing glance, but managed to sound cheerful—albeit brittle—as she chirped,

"Lady Mundy, I'm *so* glad you could come. And may I present my friend—"

She turned to gesture to the other young woman rising from a chair in the garden.

"—Lady Posthuma Belisande?"

"Posy, please, Your Ladyship," the Founder's sister said, offering her hand and a bright smile. "Clothilde tells me that you too were aboard Captain Leary's yacht when it landed during the Assembly. I had no idea until I called on Clothilde yesterday. Do please forgive me for my oversight."

"There's nothing to forgive," Adele said, taking Posy's hand briefly and releasing it. "We both had our duties on Stahl's World, I'm sure, and we properly focused on them at the time."

She had been concerned that Posy would remember her from their proximity on the *Sissie*'s bridge. Adele's present outfit, a lavender pantsuit with a thin white stripe, seemed to have driven out all recollection of the RCN signals officer in utilities.

"Please, do sit down, both of you," Clothilde Brown said, extending her hands to her guests and walking toward three chairs set at arm's length apart, facing their common center. "Lady Mundy, what would you like to drink?"

"A white wine, I suppose," Adele said. "A local vintage, if such a thing exists."

"Braga," Clothilde said to the male servant at the refreshments table. He looked even more uncomfortable in his uniform than his presumed spouse did. "Pour Lady Mundy a glass of Knight's Reserve."

Adele smiled, hoping her expression was pleasant. Social interactions were almost entirely a matter of acting for her, and she knew that she wasn't very good at them. Fortunately, most people heard and saw what they expected, so they mentally corrected Adele's missteps.

She probably wouldn't have accepted the invitation had she not known—from an intercepted call—that Posy had asked Mistress Brown to arrange a meeting with Lady Mundy. It seemd the best way for Adele to meet her target; and a meeting was necessary, because in the two days the *Princess Cecile* had ridden in Calvary Harbor, it had become obvious that electronic means were not going to unveil any of Posy's secrets.

The garden was a square fifty feet on a side. A service building, probably a kitchen, and a wall of open brickwork set it off from what may have been intended as a park. Now it was a tangle from which trees with coppery foliage emerged.

The enclosure wasn't in a great deal better shape. The shrubs had been pruned within the past day or less, so that statues of cherubs with gardening tools were again visible among the lopped stems.

The "lawn" had been hacked off also. Short tufts of something grasslike were surrounded by circles of dirt which their foliage had shaded bare until the recent shearing.

The clearance work—calling it yardwork seemed akin to describing a heart attack as indisposition—might explain why Braga glowered so fiercely as he handed Adele a glass of faintly greenish wine. Unless the job market in Calvary was very tight, Mistress Brown would be looking for new servants shortly.

The wine tasted all right, despite the hue. The glass was etched with the monogram dS, marking it as a piece Clothilde de Sales Brown had brought with her to the marriage.

"Quite good," Adele said to her hostess. That was a bit of an exaggeration, but it was close enough. Some of the Mundys and their affines had been experts in vintages and liquors, but Adele's interests ran to colophons and Pre-Hiatus incunabula.

The maid standing behind Posy's chair wore a white cap and pants suit with a broad black sash, a servant's uniform in the Pleasaunce style. Adele wouldn't have paid particular attention—it wasn't surprising that Lady Belisande would have brought a maid when she returned home from civilization—were it not that the servant was looking at Tovera.

Adele's lips squeezed into a tiny, cold smile. Posy's servant was from the same mold as Tovera herself. That wasn't surprising either, given who Posy had been. That left the question of whether the "maid" was a bodyguard or a minder to the Guarantor's former favorite; or most likely both.

"When I left Zenobia five years ago," Posy said, sipping a glass of what was probably the same wine, "I thought I'd love the excitement of Pleasaunce society. After I'd been there a time, well—"

She gave Adele and Clothilde a dazzling smile.

"—it *was* very exciting, but sometimes a little too much so. I wasn't altogether sorry when events made it prudent for me to come back home. And I do like it in Calvary, really, but when I first arrived I found no one to talk to. I'm so glad that the new Commissioner's wife is a lady."

She saluted Clothilde with her glass.

"Commissioner Brassey was an old bachelor, and he neither visited nor entertained." Posy smiled again. "I gather he found our local vintages, ah, compelling."

"And it was wonderful to meet you, dear," Clothilde Brown said with warm sincerity. "Pavel would be happy anywhere that he had accounts to check—that's what he's doing now. But I thought I was going to go mad here until I met you. There's *no* one to talk to!"

"There's an Alliance Resident on Zenobia, is there not?" Adele said, raising an eyebrow as she sipped. She'd watched Daniel deal with Resident Tilton, but she was interested in Posy's description of the man.

"He's a reptile!" spat Clothilde, slashing her hand before her face. She wrinkled her nose.

"Tilton is certainly a reptile," Posy said. "He's a tradesman's son, and from Pinnacle besides. I don't know how familiar you are with the Alliance, Lady Mundy . . . ?"

"I was educated on Blythe," Adele said. "And yes, it's possible that there are good people on Pinnacle, but they certainly seem to have sent their scum to other worlds."

She paused. Posy giggled; Clothilde nodded with grim enthusiasm. Adele added, "And I would prefer to be 'Adele,' Posy."

"Well, you understand then, Adele," Posy said, gesturing with her glass again. It was nearly empty, but even so the remaining thimbleful sloshed perilously close to the rim. "Tilton made a, well, an infamous suggestion when he first called on me. Not only that, but I think he might have tried to use force if Wood hadn't been present. He ordered her out of the room, of all things. Giving orders to *my* maid in my brother's palace!"

Wood smiled faintly at the reference. The expression reminded Adele of Tovera, or of a predatory bird.

"He touched me on the pier," Clothilde said with another grimace. "If it hadn't been for Captain Leary and his man, I don't know what might have happened. Pavel isn't any use in that sort of business."

Your Pavel might not be as used to knocking people down as Hogg and Daniel, Adele thought. *But a woman with pretensions to culture might consider that an attribute rather than a flaw in her husband.*

Aloud she said, "Surely there's a foreign community on Zenobia in addition to the government representatives, is there not? The warehouses facing the harbor include the names of several trading firms which I know have their headquarters on Pleasaunce. At least some of them have off-planet managers, do they not?"

Clothilde looked hopeful, but Posy grimaced and said, "When I was young, I thought the foreigners on Ship Hill— that's where they live, most of them—were arrogant swine. All us Zenobians did, and we despised them. Now—"

The grimace turned to a sneer.

"—I know what they really are: failures from the core worlds, the drunks and fools, the embarrassments whose families shipped them as far away as they could get. Some of them sent their cards when I returned, trying to scrape acquaintance with Guillaume's mistress...."

Posy paused, giving Adele a speculative glance. Adele met it with no hint of emotion or understanding.

"That's what I was, you see," Posy said after a moment. "Guillaume Porra's mistress, Guarantor Porra. Perhaps you knew that?"

"My parents were executed for treason, Lady Belisande," Adele said evenly. "In fact, my ten-year-old sister was executed for treason as well. I'm scarcely in a position to make moral judgments, even if I were the sort of person who approved of doing such things."

Wood was staring at her. Adele glanced up, and the maid looked away.

"I'm sorry," Posy said. She reached out and touched Adele's left hand, then settled back on her chair. "Others *have* made judgments, you see—though generally women who would have liked to know Guillaume as well as I did. And please—Posy."

"Adele?" said Clothilde Brown. "If you don't mind my asking?"

"Asking *what*?" said Adele, more sharply than she had intended. She raised her hand in apology. "Please, I'm sorry; but just ask the question, Clothilde. It's wasting time, which is likely to make me snappish."

"Well, it's about you being on the ship," Clothilde said. "I know you say that you're Officer Mundy when you're there, not Lady Mundy, but you *are* still Lady Mundy. How do you stand it?"

Adele wondered what the other women saw when they looked at her. Something quite different from what she was in the mirror of her own mind, certainly. The thought made her smile, but she suspected some of the sadness she felt showed in her expression also. Sometimes she wished she could be the person that other people saw.

"I'm not a gregarious person," she said, "but I escape into my work, so cramped physical surroundings don't bother me.

Nor do I feel the lack of elite society with whom to—"

She started to say "natter," but she caught her tongue in time to change that to "exchange views."

Posy Belisande's hinted smile showed that she understood the word or at least the type of word that Adele had barely avoided, but she didn't seem offended. Clothilde remained intently quizzical. She had recovered from Adele's verbal slap, but she obviously wasn't looking for another one.

"As for being in close confinement with spacers," Adele said, "I assure you that they're far better companions than the neighbors I was generally thrown together with during the years I was very poor. Besides, on a starship I don't have to deal with people like Louis Tilton. Space is a very dangerous environment, and people of his sort don't last long."

"I wish Resident Tilton could drift off into vacuum," Posy said. Lifting her glass to shoulder height, she added, "More wine, Wood."

Wood carried the glass to the serving table, sidling so that she didn't have to turn her back on Adele and Tovera. *Which of us is she more concerned about?* Adele wondered.

The truth was—if Wood was anything like Tovera, and she certainly appeared to have been trained in the same school— she probably worried even that the Commissioner's wife might smash her stemware into a spike of crystal and lunge for Lady Belisande's throat. Once you start down the path of paranoia, there's simply no line that you can't cross.

Adele smiled—internally, because Posy would have misinterpreted the expression. She fought her own tendency to consider everyone as a potential enemy and every place as a potential ambush site. That was madness.

But Adele had the luxury of knowing that Tovera was being paranoid on her behalf, unasked. That didn't seem fair, but the world *wasn't* fair. And since madness was a word used to describe human beings, perhaps Tovera wasn't at risk.

Posy gulped half her refilled glass, then lowered it and forced a smile. "Tilton fancies himself a ladies' man. He isn't interested so much in the sex, I think, as the degradation of his victims. He particularly fastens on the wives and daughters of the Councillors of Zenobia."

"They don't give in to him, do they?" Clothilde said with a look of revulsion. "Ugh! That bald little pervert!"

"I'm told that Councillor Pumphrey objected forcibly, not long after I left Zenobia," Posy said. Her voice was frighteningly colorless. "I remember his daughter Chris quite well, though we weren't close. She was a very proper girl, and I'm afraid I was too wild for her."

"Did he use the secret police," Adele said, her voice equally detached, "or members of his own security detail?"

Her personal data unit was in its thigh pocket—of course—but she would send the wrong signal if she brought it out now. She wanted the wands in her hands to keep her from reaching for her pistol, which would be even more undesirable.

Adele had to make do with the wine glass and conscious control. Her control had always been sufficient in the past.

"The police," Posy said. "Some of them objected also, till the security detail executed two for treason. The rest were willing to carry off Chris Pumphrey. She hasn't been seen since."

"Oh, dear heavens," Clothilde Brown said, the knuckles of

her left hand in her mouth. "Oh dear heavens, where has Pavel *brought* me?"

"Are Tilton's security personnel from the Fifth Bureau?" Adele asked, still sounding as though she were asking about the color scheme in the kitchen.

"No, Residential Services," Posy said absently. Her gaze sharpened. "How do you happen to know about the Fifth Bureau, Adele?"

Taking a calculated risk, Adele said, "My servant, Tovera—"

She cocked her head slightly to indicate the woman standing behind her.

"—used to be associated with the organization. Before she retired and went into personal service."

Tovera and Wood had obviously recognized one another—at least as types, but probably as individuals as well. There was no point in refusing to acknowledge what the other party already knew; and with luck, the admission would prove disarming.

"I see," said Posy in a puzzled tone that proved she did not. *No* one retired from the Fifth Bureau, the intelligence service which reported directly to Guarantor Porra. "Perhaps one day we will discuss mutual friends, Adele. Without boring Clothilde—"

She gave the Commissioner's wife a dazzling smile.

"—that is."

"With all respect to your maid," Adele said, glancing up at Wood, "I would think a security detail of...eighteen or twenty Residential Services personnel?"

"About that, yes," Posy agreed.

"Eighteen," said Wood, the syllables as short as successive clacks from a pair of wood blocks. "But two of them haven't been sober for months on end. If they were issued live ammunition, they would shoot themselves."

"Sixteen, then," said Adele. "A large enough body to seriously endanger your safety, Posy, if Tilton is the sort of man you describe."

"I could have gotten rid of him when I was on Pleasaunce," Posy said, glancing at her empty wine glass. "I didn't realize, though. Perhaps if someone had told me; my brother could have, I think. But nobody did. And now, well—"

Her mouth twisted in a mixture of anger and disgust.

"—I no longer have that kind of authority."

Her smile became impish. She said, "I do, however, have a friend in Otto von Gleuck. Otto is a dear man and of very good family. There are five hundred spacers on his ships, and they love him like a father. Perhaps you understand that, Officer Mundy?"

"I might," Adele said with her usual lack of expression. "But—and I don't mean to raise an awkward question . . . but how long will Lieutenant Commander von Gleuck be stationed on Zenobia?"

"Yes," said Posy. "Fleet appointments are of limited duration, and a destroyer doesn't have the facilities for passengers that a heavy cruiser does."

She glanced sidelong to see if Adele would react. Lady Belisande had left Zenobia five years ago as the mistress of Captain Karl Volcker, commander of the *Barbarossa*. The heavy cruiser was showing the flag in the Qaboosh Region during an interval of peace between Cinnabar and the Alliance.

The well-connected Volcker had brought Lady Belisande to

a court ball following the cruiser's return to Pleasaunce. There she caught the Guarantor's eye, and very shortly thereafter Volcker had been promoted to command a battleship on distant assignment.

Of course I won't react.

Posy smiled faintly at Adele's bland silence and continued, "And that wouldn't be a practical response anyway, since it was suggested at the time I left Pleasaunce that I might want to remain on Zenobia until I was informed otherwise. I suspect—"

She glanced up toward the servant behind her.

"—that I would be reminded of that suggestion if I seemed to be forgetting it."

Wood didn't react either. Of course.

"Perhaps Tilton will be recalled or, or something?" Clothilde said. Her hands were tight together on the stem of her glass. Adele suspected their hostess was considering the possible results of her having slapped the Resident when they met.

"Perhaps," Posy said, with the unvoiced implication, that perhaps pigs would fly. "I only hope that he doesn't provoke a rebellion first. Because I didn't need Otto to warn me what the response to that would be."

She gave Adele a tired grin and added, "I know Guillaume even better than Otto does, you see. He reacts badly to betrayal, which is how he would view the murder of his representative."

Adele rose to her feet. "I'm afraid I need to return to my duties," she said. "I hope I'll be able to see you both again before we lift, though. The *Princess Cecile* has to remain on Zenobia for some time while her rigging is being replaced, Captain Leary informs me."

Tovera whisked the empty glass out of Adele's hand. She circled with it to the refreshments table, keeping at least one eye on Wood at all times; but she was smiling.

"Oh, surely there's nothing for you to do while you're on the ground?" Clothilde said, rising to squeeze Adele's hands. Braga stood like an unattractive statue; it hadn't occurred to him to take his mistress' empty glass the way Wood and Tovera had done. "Can't you stay?"

"Another time, then," said Posy, coming forward also. "Meeting you has been an even greater pleasure than I expected, Adele. I hope we can talk often while you're here."

"Yes," said Adele truthfully. "It *has* been pleasant."

Clothilde's maid had been watching from the covered courtyard. A light dawned in her dull eyes and she trotted toward the outside door.

Wood's presence had made this a very different conversation than the one Adele had planned. Very likely her task, to elicit secrets which Posy had gained in pillow talk, was now impossible.

Mistress Sand would be interested to learn that Resident Tilton had created disaffection among the Zenobian elite, but that was of no real importance at present. There was no gain for the Republic in destabilizing so distant an Alliance world in peacetime, though Adele knew there were Cinnabar agents who would have worked to raise a rebellion here on general principles.

To Adele, that sort of behavior was simply grit in the gears of civilization. And civilization was in bad enough shape without people actively trying to sabotage it.

* * *

Daniel stood at the head of the Dorsal C antenna, which was extended to its full height of 120 feet. His excuse was that the location gave him the best view of Woetjans and her crew stripping the rigging from one antenna at a time and reeving fresh cables through the blocks. That was true, but the *Sissie*'s veteran riggers could have done the work blindfolded and blind drunk besides; they didn't need their captain's eye on them.

The other thing the location gave Daniel was privacy, or as close to privacy as anybody could have aboard a starship. Certainly everybody could see him perched above them. They could even approach him, but they had to want to do so enough to make a long climb. On the masthead, he had figurative as well as literal distance from the rest of the world.

Primarily Daniel was on top of the antenna because he liked to be on top of antennas: in harbor, as here; in sidereal space; and especially on a ship in the Matrix, where all space and time would have been visible if his eyes had been able to comprehend it.

The ground car driving up the quay stopped at the *Sissie*'s slip. Daniel didn't think anything of it: the four Sissies on guard there would be polite, but they had weapons within easy reach if it turned out to be a visit from Resident Tilton's thugs.

The vehicle was obviously local. It appeared to be a high-sided farm wagon with a canvas roof and pneumatic tires. A fifth wheel supported the wagon tongue, on which an engine putted and rattled. The whole installation showed a great deal of ingenuity, combined with a marked lack of polish.

The passenger got out of the box and walked forward to pay the driver. Daniel had considerable experience in watching people foreshortened by his high vantage point, but Commissioner Brown's tall, stooped figure and jerky walk were easy to identify. He moved like a shore bird mincing through the shallows.

Without having to think about it, Daniel grasped the forward stay and began sliding down it as the quickest route to the hull. Woetjans saw him coming and bellowed, "Stand clear! Here comes Six!"

Daniel wore utilities as he ordinarily would aboard the *Princess Cecile*. Before he started up the antenna, however, he had donned the boots and gauntlets of his rigging suit. They sparked and screeched against the cable as gravity carried him down.

The cables were woven from filaments of beryllium monocrystal, the toughest flexible material available to shipbuilders. Even so, hair-fine fibers snapped as a result of wear and fatigue, leaving the rigging covered with an invisible fuzz of broken ends. Running a bare hand along a shroud would have the same effect as trying to pet a bandsaw.

Hard suits—rigging suits—were made to be used by personnel handling the cables in brutal haste and under the worst conditions. There were lighter gloves and footgear available that were supposed to be equally protective if you weren't working in vacuum, but Daniel had never met a spacer who used them.

Hogg was lounging at the base of the antenna, turning his head to check each line of approach alternately. He had his hands in his pockets and looked as lethargic as a sheep digesting her supper.

He glanced upward, saw Daniel, and immediately slung the

stocked impeller which until that moment had been concealed between the antenna and his baggy garments. So far as Hogg was concerned, the spacers guarding the end of the boarding bridge were simply decoys to absorb an attacker's attention till the real hunter on top of the hull could put slugs through the problem.

The Commissioner looked up at the squeal of Daniel's descent. Daniel hit the hull with a double *bang!* of his soles against the steel plating.

"Toomey," he said, verbally keying his commo helmet to the Tech 3 who was the senior member of the guard detachment, "this is Six. Link Commissioner Brown with me if you will. Give him a helmet, over."

"Roger, Six," Toomey said. She was built like a fuel drum, but her voice was as light and cheery as a schoolgirl's.

There was brief confusion on the quay. Daniel remained where he was so that all those involved could see him. In theory, that didn't matter, but human beings aren't theories. At last Brown settled a helmet borrowed from Hilmer, the junior guard, over his head.

"Commissioner, this is Leary," Daniel said with determined cheeriness. "How can we help you, over?"

Visor magnification made Brown's discomfort obvious, even a hundred yards away. *"Ah, Captain Leary?"* he said. *"I was wondering if I could speak with you privately. I don't want to take you away from your own duties, but..."*

"Certainly," said Daniel. "Meet me in the BDC. Ah—I'll have Hilmer guide you, over. Break. Toomey, send Hilmer up to the BDC with Commissioner Brown, over. Break. Six to

Cory, have the BDC vacated immediately. I'm going to confer with Commissioner Brown there, over."

"Thank you, Captain."

"Roger, out."

"Yes sir, out."

All that was simple courtesy. Daniel really had no duties on Zenobia except to invent make-work until Adele got the information she had been sent for or decided the task was impossible. The rerigging could be spun out for a month if necessary, so even planning the make-work was complete.

"What do you s'pose he's got in mind?" Hogg asked quietly as he helped Daniel take off the pieces of his rigging suit in the rotunda. "Because he looked more upset even than when we were playing games right after we landed."

Midshipman Cazelet and Chief Missileer Chazanoff bustled out of the Battle Direction Center. They were off-duty at present, but Cazelet was trying to learn the fine points of missile attacks and Chazanoff, like most experts whom Daniel had met, was delighted to have an audience to expound to.

They muttered, "Sir," and bobbed their heads as they passed Daniel on the way to the bridge where Cory was on watch. It would have vacant consoles to practice on also.

"I'm not sure the Commissioner fully appreciated what was happening on the quay," Daniel said, smiling. "It isn't the sort of interaction that ordinarily takes place in the offices of auditors."

The comment opened a train of thought. "I would guess he's worried about something to do with the late Commissioner Brassey's accounts," Daniel said as Hogg eased off his right boot, the last bit of gear. "That's what he was going to work on, he said when he left us. But how that would involve me is beyond my imagination."

They reached the BDC well before Hilmer could chivy his charge up the stern companionway, so Daniel waited at the open hatch. Hogg glanced into the armored chamber and scratched himself.

"You'd best be elsewhere," Daniel said. "Since the Commissioner wants privacy."

"I figured," Hogg agreed. "Well, I guess you'll be safe alone with him, young master."

He snorted and said, "You know, it looks like a bank vault, but Cory can watch and listen to any bloody thing that happens in there."

"Yes," said Daniel, "but I don't think he will. And anyway, I'm just making Commissioner Brown comfortable. If I were worried about whether one of my officers could be trusted to keep information secure, he wouldn't be my officer for very long."

Hilmer, a rigger who'd lost two fingers from his left hand, came up from the companionway and waited. Long moments later, Brown stumbled out, winded by the fast climb. He was carrying a small case; now that he no longer needed a hand for the railing, he switched it from his left to his right.

"Let me help you with that, Commissioner," Daniel said, lifting off the commo helmet which he returned to Hilmer. "The BDC will give us both privacy and good displays."

"I'm embarrassed to be doing this, Leary," the Commissioner said. "After all, you have your own duties. But—"

He waited till the hatch had closed—it was hydraulic,

since the armored valve was impractical for even someone of Woetjans' unaided strength—and the dogs had clanged into their mortises, then continued, "—I don't know who else to turn to. Since it involves naval stores, I thought of you."

"Sit down here, Commissioner," Daniel said. Five consoles identical to those on the bridge formed a star in the center of the BDC. Daniel rotated the seat of the nearest one sideways, then sat on an adjacent one which he turned so that he and Brown were facing one another.

He cleared his throat and went on, "Your predecessor was stealing RCN stores?"

How in heaven's name would Brassey have managed that on Zenobia, where there wasn't and couldn't be an RCN presence? But it would explain Commissioner Brown's discomfort.

"Oh, good gracious, no!" Brown said in surprise. "I've gone over Commissioner Brassey's accounts, and so far as I can see they're quite in order. Making allowances for sloppiness, that is, but I assure you that I've seen worse. He certainly wasn't fiddling the secret accounts, which is where in the past I've most often found problems."

Daniel blinked. He'd been leaning slightly forward; he felt himself straighten. "Ah," he said. "Could you be mistaken, Commissioner?"

Brown's smile was wry and surprisingly engaging. "About many things, Captain," he said, "yes, I certainly could be. But not about accounts of this sort, filed by a man whom I may charitably say was not one of the great intellects of his age. You have every right to dismiss my opinions on most subjects, but I've spent nearly twenty years becoming an expert on matters of this sort."

Daniel grinned. "Your pardon, Commissioner," he said. "I spoke without thinking. But if there's no problem with the accounts, then why are you here?"

"If I may give you some background...," Brown said. "When we took possession of Cinnabar House, we found the Commissioner's private apartments were nearly full of empty wine bottles. My wife informs me that they had contained decent local vintages."

He shrugged. "I had access to Commissioner Brassey's private accounts as well as his official ones," he said, "so I went over those also. You may object that this was improper if you wish to."

"It doesn't appear improper to me," Daniel said with what he hoped sounded like sincerity. Actually, it probably *was* improper, but he couldn't bring himself to care. Nothing about accounting seemed to him worth caring about.

"Well, anyway, I did," said Brown. He'd opened his case; it contained a personal data unit and pockets to hold over a hundred data chips. "Brassey had a private remittance from relatives at home as well as his official salary. His outlays for wine almost perfectly balanced those sources of income, leaving very little overage for food and what I might call general maintenance. From the state of his quarters, the figures were accurate."

"Go on," said Daniel, nodding. He'd learned not to anticipate the Commissioner, who appeared to be telling his story in an orderly fashion. If his hearer was still completely at sea as to where that story was going—well, the answer to that was to shut up and listen.

"There's simply no evidence that Brassey had any private venture on Zenobia," Brown said firmly. "Or that he would have been able to manage it if he had. Gibbs did all such business as the Commission required."

He frowned. "Which I must say isn't very much. Now, I admit that Gibbs says that the late Commissioner wasn't as incapable as I believe and that he had secret meetings outside Cinnabar House, though Gibbs knows nothing of the purpose or the other parties involved. But—"

Brown's voice was animated. He had lost the diffidence and confusion with which he had begun the discussion. The accountant was very different from the embryonic Commissioner, let alone the husband.

"—we have learned, that is, I learned, in the Audit Division to ignore verbal testimony when it conflicts with written documentation. I am almost certain that Resident Tilton's suggestion about 'Cinnabar private ventures' was false. As false as one would expect any statement by a man of that sort to be."

He paused with what approached being a smug smile. Daniel had picked up on the key word. Suppressing a smile of his own—he found himself liking the suddenly competent Brown—he said, "'Almost,' Commissioner?"

"Exactly!" said Brown. "Look at this item, if you will."

He typed quickly on the virtual keyboard of his data unit, but the display winked to life on the console at which he sat. With a quick adjustment, Brown moved an omnidirectional hologram to hang between himself and Daniel. It was a series of figures and legends.

This was the sort of thing Adele did all the time. It was surprising to see a stranger—and one who until moments previously had been something of a joke—accomplishing the task with the same reflexive skill.

"I normally work on my own unit," said Brown, who had apparently understood Daniel's expression. "I frankly don't trust linked computers when I'm dealing with financial records. And, ah—I hope you don't mind, but I've disconnected the reporting and export functions of the consoles in this room for the duration of our conference."

"Quite all right, Commissioner," Daniel said. Smiling faintly—had Adele spent time with this fellow during the voyage? He didn't think she had—he added, "There's a separate recording function built into the lighting circuit. It's part of the log. If you like, I can have my signals officer wipe it when she returns to the ship."

"Ah!" said Brown in surprise. "Ah. No, I don't think that will be necessary, Captain. But I appreciate your candor."

He cleared his throat, then touched a point in the air. On the display Daniel was viewing, line items expanded while the background faded. The excerpt read:

ITEM PN425-9901SJ:

REQUISITIONED REGIONAL NAVAL STORES 9-13-45. NO CHARGE.

DELIVERED CALVARY HARBOR 12-07-45.

INSTALLED 12-09/10-45 AT 4PP10418653. BARGE RENTAL 100 FLORINS. CASUAL LABOR (OFF-PLANET SPACERS) 100 FLORINS PLUS 30 FLORINS ALCOHOL BONUS.

"The fund charged is the secret account," Brown explained. "This is the *only* charge on the secret account during Brassey's tenure as Commissioner. Do you have any idea what it could mean?"

"Well...," Daniel said, turning to his own console and bringing it live. "I can find out what the item is easily enough."

Perhaps not as easily as Adele could. Regardless, it didn't take long to find an RCN equipment catalogue. Indexing was almost instantaneous once he'd entered the item number.

Brown stared at the image and description blankly. "It's a portable landing beacon," Daniel explained. "Not something that you ordinarily need, but I suppose it might be more useful in the Qaboosh than in most regions, so it's reasonable they'd have a few in stock on Stahl's World."

Brown still looked blank. Daniel grinned. *Now you know how I've been feeling*, he thought. Aloud he said, "It's for bringing ships in on ground control at a place where there isn't a proper port installation. Colonies usually do it that way: send down a lifeboat with a portable rig, then bring the main ship or ships down on ground control."

"Ah," said Brown. "Now I see. But why a colony?"

"I don't know that it is," Daniel said. "That's what came first to mind. As for where the beacon was placed—"

He switched to a global display, assuming that the grid reference was to Zenobia. If it wasn't, then all bets were off.

"Here," Daniel said, viewing the cursor which seemed to be pulsing in the middle of the Green Ocean, some six hundred miles east of Calvary. He expanded the display, hoping that something that made sense would appear. The detail wasn't very good, but at high magnification the point appeard to be a marshy islet in a scattered archipelago.

"What does it mean?" Brown said, frowning in puzzlement.

"It means...," said Daniel, grinning as he keyed an alert signal to Adele's personal data unit. "That I will make inquiries."

Just as soon as Adele returned.

CHAPTER 12

CALVARY ON ZENOBIA

Adele stepped onto the bridge with Tovera behind her. There was a nearly full house, which was mildly surprising when the *Sissie* was at rest in a friendly harbor. Well, a reasonably friendly harbor.

Cazelet was at the gunnery console, refining missile trajectories under the tutelage of Chazanoff from the missile station. Since Sun was on liberty, there was no reason the midshipman shouldn't use a fully capable console instead of the training station at the back of the missile console. Cory, the watch officer until Vesey returned from liberty, was at astrogation, and Daniel had moved from the BDC, where he'd been when he summoned Adele, to the command console.

Adele sat at the signals console. She was fairly sure that no one else would use her station in anything short of a serious emergency, though she wouldn't have objected. She was *quite* sure that nobody could have accessed the files which she didn't want others to see. Even so, it would have bothered her and seemed discourteous.

The Sissies were a courteous group. Any newcomer who didn't understand the group's internal rules would be informed of them firmly. If the transgressor were one of the midshipmen, who were rated as Common Spacers though their duties were those of commissioned officers, and the person informing them were Woetjans, the process was likely to be very firm indeed.

Adele brought her console live. Daniel's image stared at her from the upper left corner of her display, an eyebrow lifted.

"Ah!" Adele said when she figured out what had surprised Daniel. She looked down at her civilian suit, then back at the display with a slight smile. "I suppose technically I'm out of uniform. Your summons seemed urgent enough that I didn't take the time to change."

Since she was speaking over a two-way link and their consoles had active sound cancellation, their discussion was as private as the thickness of the ship's steel hull would have made it. Daniel grinned and said, *"You're only out of uniform if you're acting officially, and I'm not sure that you are. At least, not officially on behalf of the RCN."*

"Ah," Adele repeated in a different voice. She knew that Daniel preferred not to discuss the work she did for Mistress Sand, though she had only intellectual understanding of his attitude.

To Adele, information was important, but how one obtained that information was of no significance. She preferred written or electronic means over—her lips quirked with amusement at the anachronism—listening at keyholes, but that was simply because listening at keyholes was inefficient.

Her face went hard. And of course, she preferred the

means that most distanced her from human contact. Well, for many years human contact had been the cause of most of her considerable discomfort.

"*I have a map reference ...,*" Daniel said, exporting the image from his display to Adele's console. "*Which Commissioner Brown found in his predecessor's files. I can't find any information or even good imagery about it, though. Can you help me?*"

"Yes," said Adele as her wands flickered. That she spoke at all was simply courtesy to a friend; in the old days—in the days before she had the RCN or friends, either one—she would simply have ignored the silly question.

She'd echoed Daniel's display on her own as soon as she sat down, so his attempt to send it to her was superfluous. There was no reason to point that out, of course.

She first replaced the old, low-resolution image from the astrogation database with a composite of the surface images which the excellent optics of the *Princess Cecile* had captured while they orbited before landing. Over that she laid the global positioning grid, then cross-indexed the point with the data she had accumulated while preparing for the mission to Zenobia.

"Diamond Cay," she said with satisfaction. "Six hundred and twelve miles from the bridge of the *Princess Cecile*."

She smiled, though only someone who knew her well would recognize the expression. "More or less, that is."

"*You know that you're a magician, don't you?*" Daniel said, making her smile a little broader. Though it wasn't true, of course. He expanded the image; it stayed bright and clear instead of fading to a muddy blur as the stock one had.

"The island has the ruins of a Pre-Hiatus building," Adele

said aloud. "Nobody is sure what it was intended for. The structure is rock crystal, not diamond, but that's how the island got its name. Some of the commentators claim that the so-called building is a natural outcrop, in fact."

Daniel continued to increase his magnification; the eight-digit designator indicated a square three feet on a side, directly in the center of the glittering mass.

"That's no natural outcrop!" he said in disgust. *"Did whoever said that ever take a look at the site?"*

"Probably not," said Adele. The image clearly showed a tower at one corner of a hollow square; not, as Daniel had said, anything that nature could have contrived. "There's no reason to go there except the ruins, and they don't repay close study, according to the three personal accounts that I've located."

Daniel chuckled, but his face fell back into crisply intent lines. He wore a smile, of sorts; but it made Adele think of a hunter waiting for just the right moment to squeeze his trigger.

"There's supposed to be a portable landing beacon here, Adele," he said, *"but I can't see anything except the rocks. Can you...?"*

"Would it be manned?" Adele asked as she began combing data according to new criteria. Daniel hadn't finished his question, probably because he didn't know how to go on, but he had provided her with sufficient information to make a start.

"Umm," he said. *"Normally, yes, but I suppose it wouldn't be necessary if the ships to be landed were already equipped with the code set. That isn't safe—there's a chance of a reciprocal, among other things. But you could."*

"Star travel isn't safe," Adele said. "But I take your point.

I asked because none of my imagery shows any visitors whatever to Diamond Cay in the past thirty days."

She fanned the images in two rows across the top of his display. They overlapped slightly: there were twenty-one of them. The quality ranged from fairly good to low-resolution black-and-white, but even the worst would show movement.

"Where did you find these?" Daniel asked in delight. *"Zenobia doesn't have surveillance satellites, does it?"*

"No," said Adele, trying to keep pride out of her voice. Otherwise she would be bragging. "But I've extracted imagery from the logs of all the ships in harbor that have recorders. Some of the smaller country craft do not, of course. The result isn't comprehensive, but twenty-one random checks is a good basis for confidence. If there were a human crew, one of these would show signs of their presence."

"But there's something...," said Daniel, expanding one of the videos. *"And here, on this one too—what are these? They're not people, but they're something!"*

Adele brought up the zoological database she had loaded for this voyage. She had done it because of Daniel's personal interest, not because she expected to need it in their mutual work. That they *did* need it provided further support for her belief that there was no useless information.

"I have an answer to that too," she said, smiling a little more broadly than usual.

Daniel stared in delight at the image which Adele placed in the lower right corner of his display. He immediately expanded it to full size, save for the left sidebar on which the *Sissie*'s diagnostics ran. The latter weren't going to show anything important with the ship on the surface and most of her crew on liberty, but he would have worried if he didn't have them available.

He smiled at himself. Besides, if the fusion bottle suddenly lost its magnetic field or an outrigger strut cracked, he wanted to know about it instantly.

"The local name for them is seadragons," Adele said. *"They're only found on Diamond Cay, so they're not very well known even by Zenobians. They're supposed to get as long as thirty feet."*

"Oh, this is *very* interesting...," Daniel murmured, speaking more to himself than to Adele. "This is remarkable."

The seadragon had a lizardlike body. Its head was long and broad, and the eyes were on the extreme sides of the skull. The creatures had four stumpy legs with paddles instead of feet; imagery showed that they could make quite good speed over soft ground. From the base of the short neck sprang a pair of arms barely long enough to transfer items to the jaws with prehensile fingers.

According to the written description which sprang to life when Daniel highlighted an icon, the seadragons spent most of their lives in water but came out to breed and hatch their eggs. The adults shared the work of guarding the clutch.

"The only thing they eat are pin crabs," said Adele, adding another image—also in the lower right, from which Daniel had expanded the seadragon. *"And those live only in the shallow water around the cay. The dragons might be able to cross deep water, but the crabs can't."*

Daniel expanded the new image to the right half of his display. The "crabs" looked more like toy balls, slightly underinflated and covered with spines which pivoted at the base but didn't bend.

Video showed a crab the size of a pomelo staggering across the sea floor while spiking bits of food—both weed and smaller animals—which it transferred toward its mouth at the front with rhythmic pulses of its spines. When the morsel reached the vicinity of the mouth, the crab's gullet everted around the food, then withdrew to digest within the protection of the hard shell.

"Adele," Daniel said, scrolling through further information on the biota of Diamond Cay, "please connect me with Commissioner Brown. And you'll loan me Tovera to fly the Commission aircar, will you not?"

In past years, he might have said, "*Can* you connect me?" as though there were doubt as to whether Adele could enter the civilian telecommunications system from the *Sissie*'s bridge. What would pass unnoticed as a figure of speech with another signals officer struck Adele as an insult—albeit an unintended one.

"*Tovera can drive the vehicle, yes,*" Adele said tartly as her wands moved. "*But it appears to me that if there's a piece of electronics hidden on Diamond Cay, my skills are better chosen for finding it. As well as the matter being more within the scope of my duties.*"

Switching to a clipped, almost disinterested, tone, she said, "*Commissioner Brown? Hold for Captain Leary, if you will. Go ahead, Captain.*"

"Commissioner?" Daniel said, keeping his tone buoyantly

cheerful. "My officers appear to have the rerigging well in hand. I was hoping you could lend me your aircar to do a little exploring and maybe even some hunting. I'll get stale if I don't take a break away from the ship for a day or two, you see."

"*Why, my goodness, Captain,*" Brown said. "*I didn't realize that this terminal was linked to the communications net. But yes, certainly. Would you like Master Gibbs to drive it? I'm afraid I can't myself. And to tell the truth, I'm more comfortable in an office than I would be in the wilds.*"

"That's no trouble at all," Daniel said heartily. "We've got a number of drivers aboard the *Sissie* who'd like to get some fresh air also. Ah—could we pick the vehicle up as early as six hundred hours tomorrow, do you think?"

"*Why, yes, certainly,*" Brown said. "*I'll tell Gibbs to make sure that the batteries are fully charged.*"

He paused, then added, "*He's really a very able man, you know, Gibbs is. But I can't imagine what he's doing in his present position in Representation.*"

"I can only assume that our lords and masters in the ministries had their reasons, Commissioner," Daniel said. "At any rate, thank you again. I'm really looking forward to getting away."

He felt a tiny twinge as he broke the connection. Should he have told Brown about Gibbs' background? But it wasn't as though Clothilde Brown couldn't spot and deal with a womanizing scoundrel without her husband's help, assuming that she wanted to; nor that the Commissioner would *be* much help. Warning Brown would just make him uncomfortable without changing the result.

Daniel thought for a moment, then looked across the compartment toward Adele's profile. Smiling at his image on her display, she said sardonically, *"We have a number of aircar drivers? I'm trying to remember a landing by Barnes that I didn't consider a controlled crash. And as for Hogg, the modifier 'controlled' might be excessive."*

"Well," he said mildly, "I didn't want to be too forthcoming about our intentions. Brown probably has some notion of what Tovera is. Or thinks he does."

Daniel called up the visuals of Diamond Cay again, this time focusing on the terrain. Musingly, he said, "We'd best land as close as we can to the castle or whatever it is. That seems to be high ground and ought to be firm, but the rest of the island is marsh or at best a mudbank. You know, we might be better off going in the *Sissie* herself. The pontoons wouldn't care how thin the muck was."

"It might be a little hard to explain using a corvette for a leisure trip," Adele said dryly. *"But I suppose a bluff, honest naval officer wouldn't be concerned about that."*

Daniel laughed, though of course he hadn't been—really—serious. Sobering slightly, he said, "So? Would you like to go hunting with me and Hogg in the morning?"

"Certainly," said Adele. *"I continue to believe that this is more a matter for me—and Tovera—than for you."*

"If this were a matter of duty alone," said Daniel, returning to imagery of seadragons paddling with slow menace through the shallow water, "that might be true. But there's something else that you may not have noticed. The seadragons have arms and four legs."

"*Yes,*" said Adele, frowning slightly. "*But six-limbed animals aren't unusual. I recall that some of the birds at Bantry had legs and four wings.*"

"So they did," said Daniel. "*All* the native vertebrates on Cinnabar have six limbs. But the native species here on Zenobia have four. That means that the seadragons came from off planet, and from someplace—because I checked the very complete zoological database which my signals officer thoughtfully equipped the *Princess Cecile* with as soon as you showed me the images—which hasn't been discovered."

Daniel brought up a close-up of the crystal structure. "You mentioned that the castle is Pre-Hiatus," he said. "I'm wondering now if it might not date from before the human settlement of Zenobia."

He grinned like a child holding a toy he's always dreamed of.

CHAPTER 13

OVER THE GREEN OCEAN, ZENOBIA

Daniel leaned out the port side of the open aircar, angling his face slightly backward so that the 200 mph airstream didn't slap his helmet broadside. It wasn't a lot more comfortable that way, but it helped a little.

"The water's changing color from gray-green to bottle green!" he shouted. "And the weed here looks different too. See, bunches branch from one root instead of floating in single long strips the way what we saw off the continental coast did. I wonder if the weed is extra-planetary too?"

Ordinarily a car travelling at this speed would be closed up, but Daniel liked to be able to look straight into the sea a hundred feet below. Hogg and Tovera in the cab hadn't complained, and Adele didn't seem to care.

She was looking at her data unit's display. She'd set it to be omnidirectional, probably to forestall the curiosity that she knew Daniel would feel even if he didn't ask her directly. The hologram was a real-time image of the sea ahead of them. She must have linked to the car's bow camera rather than look at the landscape with her own eyes.

Daniel smiled, as much at himself as at his friend. What Adele was doing actually made more sense than him being buffeted into a headache by the airstream despite his helmet. But their choices were personal ones which had very little to do with logic or reason. He and Adele complemented one another perfectly.

The car had slowly been tilting its starboard side downward. Tovera corrected with a violent lurch that would have thrown Daniel out if he hadn't been used to that and worse every time he brought a starship shudderingly down through an atmosphere.

Hogg grunted and tapped the steering yoke in front of his— co-driver's—seat. Shouting to be heard over the wind rush, he said, "Look, you're probably tired. Want me to take over?"

Daniel looked forward and said, "That won't be necessary, Hogg. Besides, we're almost there."

In truth, Tovera wasn't a particularly good aircar driver: she drove by the book and tended to overcorrect when real conditions varied from what the book expected. Furthermore, the present vehicle had been run hard by the Land Forces and had gotten a minimum of maintenance after it had been transferred to Commission ownership.

Having said that, Hogg was a simply *terrible* driver, a fact he would never admit and which he probably didn't believe. He'd been driving ground vehicles through the woods and pastures of Bantry before he was a teenager, and for that sort of rough-and-ready service he was the right man.

Hogg tried to drive aircars the same way, however. In the

air, his ham-handed, seat-of-the-pants style combined with recklessness to make him not just dangerous but suicidal. If he drove at low altitude, he hit the ground. The one time Daniel had allowed him to go well up above the treetops with an instructor, he set the vehicle oscillating so wildly that he would have crashed tumbling if the instructor hadn't grabbed the controls, landed, and adamantly refused to go up with him again.

When Daniel glanced forward to squelch Hogg, he saw Diamond Cay through the windscreen. The crystal building was unmistakable, but the heavy vegetation of the shoreline was hard to separate from the weed-choked green waters. The island seemed to be a mudbank. If storms of any significance crossed the Green Ocean, they must sweep over the land without even slowing down.

"Throttle back, Tovera," Daniel shouted. "And when you get closer, start to circle with the castle on my side."

An aircar could hover, but he doubted whether Tovera's skills were up to the task. If this had really been merely a sightseeing expedition, Daniel would have borrowed Gibbs to drive for them. He didn't particularly like the commander, but the man had driven with smooth skill when he picked up Brown and his family.

A seadragon had been coiled around a clutch of eggs. It raised its long neck from a bed of reeds and challenged the car's fans with a steam-whistle shriek. Though the creature was ten feet long, its wet-looking, mottled green scales were a close enough match for the vegetation that Daniel hadn't noticed the creature until it moved.

"That's a ramp inside the tower, not steps," Hogg said,

pointing left-handed. He had a stocked impeller upright on the seat beside him, his right hand on the grip just in case he needed—wanted—to throw the weapon to his shoulder. Daniel's similar weapon—they were supposed to be hunting, after all—was on the rear-facing seat ahead of him. "Unless they're really worn, maybe?"

Tovera had reduced speed to about 40 mph. She was holding the car commendably steady as she circled a hundred feet out from the crystal structure. One wall of the square was puddled, and part of the tower's adjacent side had been sheared away. Through the gap, Daniel saw a ramp curling around the axis of the tower to serve rooms against the exterior walls.

The damage seemed to have been caused by melting, though for the life of him Daniel couldn't imagine what had done it. A plasma cannon would have had a shattering effect, very different from what he saw. He didn't know of a weapon that could provide enough sharply focused heat to turn rock crystal liquid.

"I don't see equipment inside the tower," Hogg said. "Just trash washed in on the tide, it looks like."

The car continued to circle. They were on the undamaged side by now. A seadragon called from out of sight, deeper in the swamps.

"The rooms at the top weren't torn open," Tovera said. "Should I land?"

"Not yet," said Daniel. "I'd like to stay in the air as long as we can. Adele? Does your data unit have enough power to send a signal on four-point-one-three-five into the building from here, or do we have to be inside? That's the frequency that switches on the beacon, so we'll know it's there. Well, the default frequency, but nobody bothers to change them."

"I can relay it through the car's transceiver," Adele said, doing something with her wands. "One moment."

The transceiver in the forward cab popped, then exploded into hissing blue sparks. Three of the four fans shorted out simultaneously. The car started to flip over.

The *bang!* of the exploding transceiver startled Adele. Regardless, she slipped her personal data unit into its pocket without bothering to shut it down; the wands went in beside it instead of being properly clipped to the housing. They might very well jostle loose, but she could use the unit's virtual keyboard if they did.

And anyway, she probably wasn't going to survive more than the next few seconds. None of them were.

Blue sparks blew from the fascia plate, filling the cab. Hogg slammed off the power switch on the console between him and Tovera, then stood. He hauled back on his control yoke with his whole strength.

Three drive fans had shorted out when the transceiver did, but the right rear unit had continued to run until Hogg shut it off by the quickest means possible. The asymmetric thrust would have flipped the aircar over and down, sending it tumbling into the ground instead of just crashing.

"Lean right!" Hogg bellowed. *"Hell bugger us if you don't all lean right!"*

Because Hogg had cut the main switch instead of trying to

find a specific toggle on an unfamiliar control panel, he didn't have servo motors to help with the controls. He was fighting the airstream, using sheer brute force to force the pivoting surfaces on the underside of the vehicle to bite against the dive.

Tovera hauled on her yoke also, copying Hogg. He was the one who'd known what to do, though. The countryman had more experience with vehicles that were just beyond the edge of control than almost anyone else you could name.

Adele smiled faintly. Just as there was no useless information, it appeared that there was no useless experience.

She gripped her side of the car with both hands and leaned as far out as possible. Daniel sprang across the cabin to do the same. The aircar didn't have belts or harnesses for the passengers; given that the vehicle was ex-military, it may never have had them. In the present circumstance, that was good because it allowed those aboard to instantly throw their weight against the vehicle's tilt.

Adele watched the ground coming up fast—rotating up counterclockwise—but the car was more or less on an even keel: her weight and Daniel's, and the drivers' efforts, had stabilized them. That didn't repeal the law of gravity, of course, and without power the vehicle had more resemblance to a brick than to a glider.

The whole business was unexpectedly quiet. An occasional splutter from the destroyed fan motors—insulation must still be burning—and the soft *woo-woo-woo* of the blades of the right rear unit were the only sounds besides Hogg's mumbled curses. A seadragon shrieked querulously in the distance.

Half of the surface below glittered in the sunlight—standing water in which reeds grew, not grass on dry land. In the flat angle of the bow camera, Diamond Cay would have looked much more dangerously solid.

Adele smiled a little more broadly than she usually did. She would still rather be viewing this as an image; ideally from a considerable distance away.

"Adele!" said Daniel. His back was toward her, but she had no difficulty understanding him. "When I tell you to, jump!"

"But—" Adele said. Her instinct was to stay with the hard-shelled vehicle, but that meant she would be slammed *into* that hard shell when it hit the ground. Whereas the surface—

"Jump!"

As Daniel shouted, he lifted himself on his hands, threw his legs forward over the side of the aircar, and flung himself clear. Adele could appreciate the grace of the movement, but it would have been a joke to imagine she could duplicate it. She tried to roll herself out, hoping to belly flop in the water.

The right side of the car began lifting again as soon as Daniel's weight no longer forced it down. The toe of Adele's left boot caught the edge and threw her into a flailing somersault.

Her right hand clamped over the data unit, though the press/seal pocket flap should hold it; she thrust her left arm out with the fingers spread. It made as much sense as anything else she could do. This wasn't the sort of thing librarians trained for.

Adele was upside down when the aircar slapped the wet ground like a huge fish sounding after a leap. Water, reeds, and viscous mud billowed up around it.

Things flew out. One of them was Tovera.

Adele hit in a sitting position with her legs splayed. The

shock knocked all the breath out of her; her vision blurred. She bounced forward, limp as a rag doll.

She hit again. The turgid wave from the aircar's first impact picked her up and threw her a third time. She saw a bright light and didn't move for a time.

"Adele?" someone called from a distance. "Adele, can you hear me?"

Her vision cleared. She was lying on her back in water. *Why am I floating?*

She opened her mouth to answer. Her tongue moved, but there was barely enough air in her lungs to wheeze. She flailed her arms and found mud just below the surface. Closing her eyes for an instant to focus, Adele lifted herself into a sitting position and opened them again.

Daniel stood fifty feet away in knee-deep vegetation. His utilities dripped brown-black mud, but he must have found a pond of cleaner water to wash his arms to the elbows.

"Adele!" he repeated and began stumbling forward. He seemed to gain strength and equilibrium with each step.

Either a sitting posture or the effort of rising into it allowed Adele to breathe again. Her lungs felt fiery, but there was nothing sharp that might have meant broken ribs.

She could feel her personal data unit through the fabric, but she didn't take it out yet. The case was sealed against the environment, but that didn't mean Adele was going to bathe it in clinging mud to no purpose. There would be time enough to check it after she'd cleaned herself off to a degree.

Adele took a deep breath. She stuck her hands into the muck and tilted her body forward, then hunched to her feet.

She had been fairly certain that her legs weren't strong enough yet to manage it alone.

Even so it was a near thing not to pitch onto her face again. Still, she was standing upright and fairly steady when Daniel—who had broken into a shambling trot—was able to put a hand on her shoulder.

"That was too close," he said. He smiled, but for an instant the expression reminded her of a skull. "Let's find the others. I don't see—no, there's Tovera."

Adele turned. The aircar was more than a hundred yards away, its crumpled bow sticking straight up. From the disturbed terrain between Adele and the vehicle, it had skipped twice more before it stopped. Mud-rimmed craters of brown water quivered in the green of marsh grass.

Tovera limped around the side of the wreck. Her arms were before her, each hand grasping the opposite wrist as though she were cradling something. Her face had no expression, but the skin was drawn over her cheekbones.

A seadragon called. The beasts always sounded angry. Of course it was likely enough that they *were* angry at the invasion of their territory.

Adele tapped her tunic pocket. The pistol was still where it belonged. She bent carefully—and even then paused to gasp with pain—and splashed her hands in the shallow water. She was likely to need the pistol before she needed the data unit.

"Tovera?" Daniel said. He tried to put the usual cheery lilt into his voice, but he wasn't completely successful. "Have you seen Hogg?"

"I'm here, Master Daniel," Hogg called as he too came out

from behind the vehicle. His clothing was mud-splashed, but unlike the rest of them he hadn't been completely doused in muck. "Just seeing what I could salvage, which is bloody *zip*, it is. Every bloody thing went flying but me, and that was a near one too."

Adele looked at Hogg as he massaged a lump on his forehead. The blow hadn't broken the skin, but he would have a bruise there shortly.

"How did you manage to stay in the car?" she asked.

Adele's memories of the crash were like pictures painted on glass and then smashed. One vivid fragment was of seeing the aircar shortly before the second impact: upside down as it flipped endwise.

Hogg shrugged. "Don't rightly know, mistress," he said, and from the frown as he concentrated that was probably true. "Hung on like I'd hooked a pot of gold, I remember that. Braced a foot whichever direction it looked like we were going to hit the next time—which meant the frame of the windscreen the onct, and it held but I sure wouldn't have bet on that."

"Glad to have you back with us, Hogg," Daniel said, clasping hands with his servant. "Or I suppose I should put it the other way around, since it was me that left."

Hogg's grimace was probably meant for a smile. He said, "If she'd landed flat on her back, I'd a' been screwed and no mistake. But the way she was hopping around, I don't guess there was much risk of landing flat any whichway?"

"No chance at all!" lied Daniel heartily. "Well, I guess we're none the worse for wear. The next thing to do is to decide how to get off this island."

"I've sprained my wrists," Tovera said simply. Everyone looked at her. "Or broken them, I suppose. I wasn't able to hold on."

She turned to Hogg and made a tiny bow.

"I'll splint them with a few stems and my shirttails," said Hogg gruffly. "I checked the panel in the cab where the first aid kit was supposed to be, but I guess it's been empty since the gods know when."

He trotted toward the starbursts of feathery leaves growing nearer the crystal ruins. As he moved, he snicked open the blade of his knife.

Adele eyed the structure musingly. If the car had been flying toward rather than beside it when the motors failed, they would surely have been killed. Except perhaps Hogg, who had really remarkable reflexes in a crash. Though how could even he survive driving into a large mass of rock?

"I've got a satellite communicator in my attaché case," Tovera said. She must be in a great deal of pain—the redness and swelling in her thin wrists were startlingly obvious—but her voice was grimly whimsical as usual. "Which unlike the impellers will float. But *where* it may be floating is another matter."

They surveyed the undulating green landscape. It was a mile or more to open sea in the direction the aircar had been travelling when it hit the ground, but a rectangular case could have bounced in almost any direction. It depended on which corner touched down as the case spun.

"Oh, it won't be hard to find!" said Daniel; this time the enthusiasm sounded real. "We've got a fine vantage point on the tower of the castle there, fifty feet at least, wouldn't you say? We'll find the case and call the *Sissie* to come pick us up. And then—"

His voice changed.

"—we'll deal with the person who sabotaged the car. Commander Gibbs, I shouldn't wonder."

"Yes," said Adele, suddenly brighter herself. "And learn why he did it, which is more important. Though perhaps not as satisfying."

She looked at the castle. The head of a seadragon lifted from the top of the tower and stretched toward Hogg. The creature shrieked like a stone-saw. It was by far the largest they had seen on the island, easily the thirty feet long which Adele's records gave as the maximum length.

Nearby was a puddle which was at least translucent if not clear. Adele stepped to it and rinsed her hands again.

Then she took the pistol from her tunic pocket.

CHAPTER 14

DIAMOND CAY, ZENOBIA

"Look at me, snake!" Tovera shouted from midway between the wreck and the base of the crystal tower. "I'm going to steal your eggs and eat them in front of you!"

Adele smiled minusculely. She had told her servant to shout to call attention to herself. It didn't matter what the words were or even if they were words. It didn't surprise her in the least that Tovera was acting as though the seadragon could understand the threats, however.

"Are we ready, then?" said Daniel. They had circled to approach the tower from the opposite side. He spoke quietly so as not to call the dragon's attention away from Tovera's fine performance, but his smile seemed satisfied and genuine.

He's really looking forward to this, Adele thought. *Of course, he grew up fishing in the ocean—and Hogg was teaching him.*

Adele *wasn't* looking forward to the business, though she wasn't really afraid. If things went wrong she would probably be killed, but she thought Daniel and Hogg would be able to escape. So long as she wasn't endangering others, the risks didn't greatly concern her.

"Ma'am?" Hogg said. He reached into his left pocket and lifted his pistol partly into sight. "Are you sure you wouldn't like mine?"

Hogg wore the steel-mesh mittens which he needed to handle his length of fishing line weighted on either end with a deep-sea sinker. The beryllium monocrystal was thin and flexible, but you could lift an aircar with it—if you attached the line to a metal part. It would cut plastic—or flesh—like a knife.

"Yes," said Adele. "I'm sure."

Though compact, Hogg's pistol was about twice the size of her own and threw osmium slugs instead of Adele's light ceramic pellets. It was a better choice if you were trying to knock the target down, but this seadragon was much too big for that to be possible.

If Hogg had carried a service pistol, Adele might indeed have borrowed it. The combination of high velocity and heavy slug would shatter the creature's skull; after that they could simply wait for the beast to die. Neither of the available pistols—nor Tovera's, which was much like Adele's—were sufficiently powerful, however. Therefore, she had suggested a different plan....

"I'll feed your eggs to pigs, snake!" Tovera shouted. She had made a flag by tying her tunic to a sturdy reed. She managed to waggle it in the air by clamping her forearms together with the staff between them. "You'll have no offspring ever!"

The seadragon screamed at her. Its nest must be in one of

the upper rooms, but it used the top of the tower as a vantage point. So long as Tovera called and capered, the beast was likely to remain where it could see her.

"Let me get half a circuit ahead," Adele said quietly. She stepped through the entrance and started up.

As Hogg had noted before the crash, a helical ramp six feet wide served the tower instead of a staircase. There was no railing nor sign of where one might have been. The central well was more than ten feet in diameter.

The ramp circled clockwise instead of being counterclockwise like a ship's companionways. That didn't matter in the present circumstances, but it felt subtly wrong.

The seadragon called again. There was a hole in the roof at the ramp's upper end. If there had ever been a door or other cover, it had vanished in the millennia since the tower was abandoned.

Hogg led Daniel into the tower, having scrupulously waited till Adele was opposite the entrance and one level higher. The fifty-foot height was divided into eight levels, so the rooms—though spacious—were far too low-ceilinged for a human to find them comfortable. The entrances were arcs almost ten feet broad at the base. As with the roof opening, there were no doors.

Light wicked through the tower's walls and flooded its interior, but the refractions and reflections of the crystal created shapes and emptinesses. Their movements kept Adele on edge; but not, she judged, significantly more on edge than she would otherwise have been when approaching a thirty-foot reptile with a pocket pistol.

Adele was wearing RCN boots. They were thin enough to wear inside a vacuum suit, but their soft soles gripped even on the oily deck plates of a starship. That was perfect for the pebbled, gently rising surface of the ramp. It circled four times from the ground-level entrance to the roof.

On her second circuit, she reached the point where the building had been breached; had been melted away, if Daniel was correct. The room with no outer wall was brighter. By contrast, Adele could see that the light passing through the crystal had a bluish cast.

She continued at a steady pace. She wasn't looking directly at the roof opening: the bright light might blur her vision when the seadragon started down. Its body would curtain the hole. When the beast moved above on the roof, she saw it as shadows at the corners of her eyes.

The floor of the tower was covered with what Adele took for broken pottery when she first risked a glance downward. *No, crab shells.* She had assumed that the seadragon had chosen the tower simply as a safe place in which to lay its eggs, but the quantity of debris suggested that this was a permanent lair. Its stench was noticeably different from the vegetable miasma rising with every step in the muck of the marshes.

Perhaps they—she and Daniel—could collaborate on a scientific paper on the life cycle of the Zenobian seadragon. After the two of them retired. If they lived to retire. And of course assuming that the seadragons were native to Zenobia, though that could be hedged by modifying the title to "The Colony of Seadragons Found on Zenobia."

The whimsy made Adele smile. Anyway the corners of her lips twitched upward.

She paused, half a circuit short of the tower's roof. Hogg

with Daniel behind him were another half circuit below her. They had reached the entrance to the seventh level. Hogg was spinning a yard of his line out in the tower's well with his right hand while his left held the remainder in loose loops.

Daniel was watched her. Adele nodded, then shaded her eyes with her right hand as she looked up at the opening. Hogg whistled, a harsh trill that echoed in the crystal cylinder.

There was a clacking and scrabbling from the roof. The seadragon, its paddle feet spread to either side of the opening, thrust its head into the interior of the tower.

Adele's pistol snapped; the dragon's bulging right eye burst into silvery droplets. Snapped again and the left eye, the instant before an amber lantern, also splashed into darkness.

The weight of the dragon's shriek made Adele flinch backward. The creature lunged toward her. Its jaws were open but the small forelegs were tight against its chest. Its teeth were blunt cones that could crush a human skull as easily as they did crab shells.

Hogg's line looped about the seadragon's neck. The creature took another sliding, hunching step. Hogg drew back with the full strength of his upper body; he'd looped the monofilament around his right glove and gripped the heavy bronze sinker at his end with his left. Daniel had an arm around Hogg's waist and the other arm reaching through the doorway to lock on the wall of the room beside them.

The seadragon surged forward. Not even those two strong men could have overcome the infuriated creature's mass, but they pulled its blind head toward them across the tower.

The dragon took another step and slipped off the ramp. It

screamed like a siren as it plunged toward the crab shells forty feet below.

Hogg bellowed in agony. The dragon's cry ended in a hiss and a gout of blood that spattered the roof: Hogg hadn't been able to release the looped line, but it had decapitated the seadragon before the creature's weight pulled both men down with it.

The seadragon smashed to the floor. The body flopped and flailed for nearly a minute, and for longer yet occasional twitches dimpled the ton of flesh.

Adele knelt, waving her pistol gently to cool the barrel before she put it away. The seadragon's jaws clopped shut and opened in tetanic convulsions.

Adele didn't let herself blink. If her eyes closed even for an instant, she would see that great head stretching forward to crush the fine, organized brain of Adele Mundy.

Daniel didn't think the seadragon had reached Adele, but the motionless silence in which she knelt on the ramp made him worry as he trotted up to her. Had the tail slapped her as the creature went over the side? He wouldn't have noticed with all the other things that were going on at the time.

"Perfect marksmanship, Adele," he said cheerfully. "As expected, of course. I regret the danger to you, but you were right that there was no better way."

Adele put her pistol away and rose. "I wasn't in danger so long as it was you and Hogg with the line," she said. She sounded like her usual imperturbable self, but Daniel still had the feeling—it was no more than that—that something had disturbed her. She glanced past him and said, "Hogg? Are you all right?"

"I won't be shaking hands any time soon," Hogg muttered. "Nothing that won't heal, but it hurts like bloody blue blazes right now."

Daniel looked over his shoulder. He'd felt as though the creature's weight was going to pinch off his right arm against the doorjamb he'd hooked it around. Hogg had shouted at the same time, but that had seemed a natural reaction to his effort in holding on to the line. In his concern for Adele, Daniel hadn't realized that Hogg was injured.

He was holding his right hand up—keeping it above his heart. He'd taken the mesh mitten off his left hand and put it back with the coiled monofilament into one of his pockets, but the mitten was still on his right. It looked as stiff as an inflated bladder.

"It's my own fault," Hogg growled. "I didn't trust to be able to just hold the sinker, so I gave the line a wrap around my hand. I figured the glove'd save me."

He smiled ruefully at his raised hand. "And I guess it did," he said, "but it was a near thing. If the line hadn't of sawed through the lizard's neck when it did, I don't bloody know what was going to happen."

Adele nodded crisply. "Thank you, Hogg," she said. "The Medicomp should be able to take care of the problem as soon as we get you to the *Princess Cecile*."

"I'd do it the same way again, ma'am," Hogg said with a real grin. "I still don't trust I wouldn't let go if I just had the sinker to hold. And Tovera'd shoot me sure as sunrise if I let something happen to you."

"It wouldn't be anything so quick," said Tovera from the outside door. She still held the flag; Daniel supposed she must have had Hogg tie it to her arms. "But I don't expect that to happen."

"Right," said Daniel, speaking more sharply than he normally would have. He *really* wanted to end the discussion. It hadn't told him anything about Tovera—or Hogg, really— that he hadn't known before, but it made him uncomfortable to dwell on it. "Let me take a look at your hand, Hogg."

"Naw," said Hogg. "Let's find the case, bring the *Sissie* in, and slap me under the Medicomp like Mistress Mundy says. Till then, I keep the glove on, right?"

Daniel thought about it. "Yes," he said, "all right."

He grinned as he stepped briskly up the remaining short length of the ramp. He'd been afraid he was going to lose his grip so that the seadragon would pull Hogg off the ramp. He had determined that he'd let his arms be torn from their sockets before he let his friend and servant down.

It shouldn't have surprised him that Hogg had felt the same way about failing Adele. The four of them functioned less as a team than as a close-knit family whose members would rather die than fail the others.

It was a good group to be a part of. The best, by heaven!

The tower roof was very slightly domed, and there was no coping around its edge. Rain would run off it down the smooth crystal sides, splashing on the ground fifty feet below.

Daniel glanced back. Hogg was still inside, left-handedly cutting Tovera's arms free, but Adele had followed.

"I wonder if this place was built by spacers?" he said, grinning.

She shrugged. "Or by birds," she said. "At any rate, it doesn't appear to be designed for human use."

Daniel felt his lips purse. "There are eccentric humans," he said, "but I take your point. Still, that's a question for the future. What we need now is to find Tovera's case."

Adele unexpectedly sat on the rooftop and took out her personal data unit. She gave his puzzlement a tiny smile. "I was afraid that I might lose the control wands in the crash," she said. "I didn't, so I guess this was my lucky day."

She isn't joking, Daniel realized. His smile spread slowly. Of course Adele hadn't been concerned about being killed. Her troubles were over if that happened.

He turned quickly to survey the boggy landscape. He didn't want Adele to see the sudden grim cast of his face. *Her* problems might be over with her death, but Daniel Leary's would become much worse. Perhaps insupportably worse.

A wedge of faint violet lines, a hologram projected by Adele's data unit, suddenly overlay the terrain before him. Its apex was the wreck of the car. He glanced toward her.

"The axis of the triangle extends from the line between where the car hit before the last bounce," Adele said, "to where it lies now. The edges are fifteen degrees to either side."

She shrugged. "That was a guess," she said, "but I thought it might help to refine the search area."

Hogg and Tovera came up through the oval opening. Hogg looked pale, but his face was set in lines of glum determination.

"Yes," said Daniel with satisfaction. "That will help a great deal, I think."

He lowered the visor of his commo helmet. Its optics would give him not only magnification but other viewing options. A sweep in the infrared would make the case stand out if it were even slightly warmer or cooler than—

"There it is," Hogg said, pointing with his whole left arm. "Eighty yards out and behind that tussock of sedges. It looks like it's…yeah, it's floating. There's a pond or something there, maybe a slough."

Daniel blinked. For a moment he felt as though he'd been insulted; then he burst out laughing.

"What's the matter, young master?" Hogg said, frowning in surprise. "You see it there, don't you?"

Daniel lifted his visor again. "Yes, Hogg," he said, "I see it now that you've pointed it out. Though I'd have found it eventually on my own, I'm sure."

"Of course you would've," Hogg said in amazement. "It's about as bloody obvious as a deacon in a whorehouse, isn't it?"

He grimaced. "Want me to go fetch it, then?"

"One moment," said Daniel, lowering his visor. A poacher's experienced eye was a remarkable shortcut if you happened to have one available, but technology still had its place.

The case was floating with only one corner above the surface of the pond; it looked like a miniature dark-gray iceberg. It was 238 feet from where Daniel stood—Hogg was slightly behind him, of course—and seven feet out from the shore.

It was also about six feet to the right of Adele's fifteen-degree estimate. The bank must be fairly sharp, because the vegetation cut off abruptly at the water's edge.

"I might be able to wade to it, I guess," said Hogg. He knew

243

that Daniel wasn't going to let him and his injured hand go after the case, but he still lobbied for that solution. "Anyways, it won't be much of a swim."

A seadragon slid under the attaché case and curved out of the field of Daniel's magnified optics. It was about five feet long and had feathery gills along the sides of its neck.

"It's a nursery pool for the dragons, Hogg," Daniel said as he widened his field of view slightly. The water had an amber tinge from tannin, but it was clear enough to show movement close beneath its surface. "I can see half a dozen of them. They seem to have territories."

"Do they come up for air, maybe?" Hogg asked hopefully.

"No, they've got gills," Daniel said. He lifted his visor and faced his servant directly. "I'll need your knife."

"I could—" Hogg said tentatively, but he was reaching into a pocket. It was on the right side of his trousers, but they were baggy enough to let him tug a handful toward him.

"No," said Daniel, "you couldn't."

"Yeah, I figured," Hogg mumbled, handing over a folding knife with a knuckle-duster grip and a spike on the butt. It should have been clumsy, but Daniel had seen Hogg throw it with perfect accuracy. "Bloody hand."

Daniel beamed at the women; they had been waiting patiently. Adele and Tovera were urbanites. They had no idea of what the hunters were discussing, but they knew to hold their tongues when they were ignorant.

"Now," said Daniel. "Adele, you'll guide us from up here while Hogg and I go to fetch the case. And Hogg, little though you like it, you'll have to wear my commo helmet so that you can listen to Adele's instructions."

"Aww...," Hogg muttered. "Well, I guess it serves me right for getting hurt."

More brightly he added, "Let's get the *Sissie* here. Because I'm really looking forward to interviewing an assistant commissioner about what happened to the car's motors!"

"The mistress says we're getting off to the right," Hogg grumbled. "What *I* say is that if I didn't have this bloody pot on my head, I'd be able to find my bloody way around like I have since before I started walking."

The ground had seemed solid from the top of the tower, but there were mud-filled swales in which the two men squished knee-deep. So far as Daniel could tell, the vegetation was indistinguishable from that which grew on firmer soil, but the buglike parasites sucking juices from the stems here were bright orange instead of the yellow with brown speckles that he'd seen close around the tower.

"I appreciate you wearing the helmet for me," Daniel said, holding the flag up in his left hand.

In truth, he and Hogg both knew that it was almost impossible to keep a straight line in a marsh like this, and an unfamiliar marsh besides. The tower was the only high fixed point. Without a second point for triangulation, you could wander miles off course.

The commo helmet had a compass function, of course, but it wasn't worth trying to teach Hogg how to use it. He'd always gotten along without equipment, and by this time of his life he wasn't going to change easily.

"She says go straight through these reeds," Hogg said. His pistol was in his left hand. Because he was walking a pace back from Daniel, he kept the muzzle in the air. Unlike Adele, he didn't shoot equally well with either hand. Until he spent some time connected to the Medicomp, the pistol was less useful than the knife would have been.

It kept Hogg from feeling useless, though. Tovera would have made a better commo relay person, but for Daniel to have told Hogg to wait in the tower would have been a crushing insult.

Daniel reached out with the pole to part the reeds; the knife was withdrawn in his right hand to disembowel anything that lunged at the flag. "Right you are, Hogg," he said cheerfully. "And there's the case."

They had reached the lagoon. The bank was undercut and eighteen inches high. The meandering body of water was forty feet across near where they stood. As best Daniel could tell without falling in, it was five or six feet deep. That range would be the difference between swimming and wading.

A juvenile dragon curved close to the bank and darted out again. It didn't come within a foot of the surface, so it would be a waste of time to shoot at it.

"Little bastard," Hogg said morosely. "We don't want to eat your dinner. If you'd just leave us alone, you could grow up to be big and strong."

"I'm showing disrespect for it by moving into its territory," Daniel said. He smiled, but his amusement was tempered by knowledge. "Which isn't a great deal different from us and the Alliance, is it, after all?"

"Well, we've taught the wogs to back off plenty of times," growled Hogg. "I don't mind teaching a lizard, though I still think it ought to be me doing it."

"Warn me if something comes up, Hogg," Daniel said instead of bothering to respond directly. He sat on the bank, letting his feet hang in the water. He could swim with his clothing on if he had to—certainly he could swim the few yards necessary here—and the tough cloth of the garments would be some protection. He slid into the lagoon.

The bottom wasn't quite as deep as he'd feared, but his boots raised shovelfuls of silt to cloud the water. The attaché case rocked away, but not far.

A juvenile seadragon banked sharply and arrowed toward the disturbance. It drove itself with its long, flattened tail, keeping its legs close to the body except when it thrust one or more of the paddle feet out as rudders.

Daniel slapped the flag into the water to his left. The seadragon made a ninety-degree turn as smoothly as water running through a pipe elbow. It rotated onto its side as it struck, ripping the fabric; the teeth were blunt, but the creature's powerful jaw muscles were intended to crush them through crab shells.

Daniel flipped his arm sideways, trying to toss the dragon onto the bank. He got it half out of the water; then the pole broke. He ducked as the creature writhed through the air where his head had been an instant previously.

It slapped the water, tangled and half-blinded by the flag wrapping its head but snapping furiously at whatever was close. Daniel stabbed the creature just in front of its external gills and twisted the knife.

The seadragon continued to thrash, even after Daniel lifted its torso above the surface. Its jaws snapped three times very quickly; then the eye he could see glazed. The legs and tail were still moving, but they were uncoordinated.

Using the knife as a gaff, Daniel hurled the creature farther into the lagoon. The motion took a great deal of effort; the short fight had wrung more out of him than he had expected. He waded deeper and caught the handle of the attaché case with the water barely touching his chin; then he slowly forced his way back to the bank and tossed the case onto land.

"Here you go, young master," Hogg said, grasping Daniel's left hand with his own. Daniel braced his right boot as far up the back as he could reach; then, with Hogg as an anchor, he heaved himself up and stood.

Daniel wiped the blade clean of mud and blood on his pants leg, then closed the knife. "Thank you, Hogg," he said, offering the weapon in the palm of his hand.

Hogg picked up the case instead. "You keep it till we're back with the mistress," he said. "I'm bunged up, and it seems like you know how to use it."

I had a good teacher, Daniel thought as he followed his servant back to the tower.

At the end of the day, Hogg had been right: animals, including humans, did fight territorial battles. People like Hogg and Daniel Leary had thus far fought better than any of the rivals they had faced.

* * *

Adele, seated on top of the tower, took the satellite communicator from the attaché case while Tovera watched with an unfamiliar tight expression. Adele realized that she had never seen the case fully open before. Tovera hadn't exactly hidden the contents, but she was a private person who avoided displaying any aspect of her life.

The pistol-sized sub-machine gun had pride of place in the center of the lower half of the case, but around it and in separate pockets in the lid were a variety of other miniaturized devices. Adele didn't recognize all of them. The information specialist in her wanted to begin questioning Tovera, but that would be both a waste of time and an insult to her servant.

The communicator was obvious, though this one was the smallest that Adele had seen. It was a blunt, flat-based cone the height of her index finger; there were three bumps just below the apex and a dimple above the base. She set it before her on the top of the tower.

"The base will stick," Tovera said, leaning slightly forward as though she were about to snatch the unit away from her mistress. "If you—"

Adele touched the dimple, causing micropores in the cone's base to exude a quick-setting adhesive. If it was the type she was familiar with, a sharp ninety-degree twist of the cone would break the seal and the adhesive would sublime, but that was a question for later.

"Yes," she said, touching the three bumps in turn to release the antenna prongs. "Does the unit require an authorization code?"

Tovera laughed harshly, a very different sound from her not-infrequent cruel giggle. She said, "No, mistress. It's just a communicator. I didn't see any reason to make it more difficult to use than it had to be."

She coughed. "And I apologize."

Adele paused and looked up at her servant. "I don't care to have other people poking around in my files, Tovera," she said. "If I were to break my wrists, I might have to; but I wouldn't be happy about it."

She resumed the process of connecting her data unit with the satellite communicator. Zenobia's network was rudimentary but sufficient to the planet's traffic. Shortly after the *Sissie* landed, Adele had carved a dedicated circuit for RCN use out of the system—just in case. Unless the satellites were destroyed or someone equally capable undid her work, she had access to the entire planet so long as she could connect with the network to begin with.

Tovera coughed diffidently. She said, "I don't think my wrists are broken, mistress, but thank you. I'll go sit with Hogg, if you don't mind."

"Not at all," Adele said without looking up again. Hogg had been wobbling when he stepped out onto the roof with the attaché case; Daniel had instantly ordered him back inside. It was a sign of how much pain Hogg had been in after the climb had raised his blood pressure that he had obeyed without argument.

Adele got her connection. "Daniel, would you care to . . . ?" she said.

He shook his head with a grin. "You're the signals officer, Mundy," he said.

Nodding, she said, "Mundy to *Princess Cecile*. Please reply, *Princess Cecile*, over."

Daniel stood beside her, looking around with a pleasant smile. He appeared to be viewing the landscape in idle curiosity, but Adele noticed from the image on her display that he always watched her out of the corner of his eye.

Does he think I'm going to fall off this roof? Adele thought in irritation.

The hard line of her lips relaxed into her version of a smile. Well, yes, Daniel might very well be concerned that she would fall off the roof. The smooth surface, lack of railing, and the fact the top sloped down on all sides made it quite dangerous unless you were—as she had suggested—a bird.

"Mistress, thank the gods!" said Cazelet's rushing voice. *"Break!"*

There was a pause, about long enough for the acting signals officer to pass the information on. Then Cazelet's voice resumed, *"Mistress, Elspeth—that is, Lieutenant Vesey—says we're three minutes out. What is your situation, please, over?"*

Adele was using her data unit's speakers, but Daniel would have been able to listen anyway through his commo helmet. He frowned with surprise at the news.

"We have a couple minor injuries," Adele said. Hogg and Tovera had reappeared in the roof opening, but they didn't step out. Tovera was surreptitiously keeping an eye on Hogg to prevent him from overreaching himself. *"Princess Cecile,* how do you come to be approaching, over?"

"Mundy, this is Three," said Vesey, taking over from the midshipman. *"When we lost contact with you, Lieutenant Cory brought up recently viewed sites."*

They shouldn't be able to recover my viewing history! Not

251

even Cory and Cazelet should be able to break the encryption!

"He informs me that your history was irrecoverable, but that Six had recently tried to view a site also. By using imagery from ships in Calvary Harbor, Cory was able to pinpoint Six's coordinates as Diamond Cay in the Green Ocean, the direction in which your aircar was seen leaving this morning. I issued an alarm, and we were able to lift in seventeen minutes. Over."

Daniel caught Adele's eye, then pointed to himself. Adele nodded and switched the *control*.

"Lieutenant Vesey, this is Six," said Daniel, using his commo link instead of speaking directly to the data unit. *"We will await your arrival with great pleasure. Land at the base to the crystal structure, if you will; the walls will protect us from the exhaust."*

He paused without signing off, then continued, *"And Vesey? Will you please relay my appreciation to the officers and crew of the Sissie? This was work in the best tradition of the RCN. I have no higher praise to give, over."*

"Roger, Six," said Vesey. *"Three out."*

Adele started to pack her equipment, then decided to wait. It wouldn't take long, and she preferred not to be out of communication just now. She could already hear the rumble of the corvette's thrusters.

"You've trained some good ones, Adele," said Daniel, his hands in his tunic pockets as he looked eastward. "And so have I. I used to worry that Vesey was indecisive."

He chuckled. "Mind," he added, "I suspect the ship's undercrewed, though there's likely forty drunks stretched out at their action stations."

The *Princess Cecile* was visible now, thundering along just high enough that the iridescent plume of her exhaust didn't lick steam from the wave tops. The gun turrets were unlocked. The paired cannon were depressed slightly to fire at such ground targets as might present themselves.

"They didn't know what they might be getting into," Adele said. In moments like these, she thought she knew what other people meant by love. "But they came anyway. Of course."

"Of course!" agreed Daniel in surprise.

In the lagoon where Tovera's case had floated, birds with sharp teeth and clawed forelegs ahead of their two wings were fighting over the corpse of the juvenile seadragon. The thunder of the *Sissie*'s plasma motors drowned their shrieks.

Adele smiled faintly, wondering whether Zenobian scavengers found human carrion edible also. Assistant Commissioner Gibbs might give her an opportunity to answer that question.

CHAPTER 15

CALVARY ON ZENOBIA

Hogg had procured the vehicle, so Daniel let him drive the squad of Sissies through the dark streets of the city. He wasn't a very good driver, but none of them were; and it had been the right choice to make for other reasons. Hogg was whistling "Lilliburlero," cheerful and completely himself for the first time since he'd injured his hand.

"Hey, Hogg, what is this thing?" Barnes called from the back. "A hay cart?"

The vehicle had an electric motor and balloon tires—of four different sizes, granted, but nonetheless reasonably quiet on the brick streets—so it was possible to talk inside without bellowing. Even the thrum of the drive belt, slanting from the cab down through the floor of the back—there was no partition—wouldn't have been noticeable if its rumbling surface hadn't been unshielded for most of its length. Spacers were used to things that could snap off a finger or a whole leg, but the experienced ones didn't let themselves forget about such dangers.

"The fellow has a general hauling business," Hogg said. "I put him onto a good thing, and he's letting us use the truck for as long as we need. Nice one, isn't it?"

Daniel's helmet projected a route in front of the driver. As Hogg spoke, the hologram indicated a corner coming. He turned more quickly than the street did, but the curb on that side was low. Both the pole and the side of the vehicle had brushed things in the past.

Woetjans muttered, "Bloody hell!" as she rocked in the back. That was mainly because she didn't like surface transportation, however. Her hands were tight on opposite ends of her truncheon. Even she couldn't make the high-pressure tubing bend, though.

This *was* a good vehicle, though, especially for the purpose. The back had high sides; they'd rigged a tarp over the top so that people looking down from third-floor roofs couldn't see what was going on, but even that wouldn't have mattered.

Daniel hadn't asked—and wouldn't ask—for details on the "good thing" Hogg had mentioned. It looked to him as though the new battery clamped beside the motor had been RCN issue, though he was pretty sure it hadn't come from stores that Captain Daniel Leary had signed for. Even if the situation was what he suspected it was, the RCN was getting value from its supply budget.

"*Daniel*," said Adele through the commo helmet. "*It's going to take us—*"

"Us" meant Cory and Cazelet under her direction, he supposed. Daniel didn't object to or even ask about the tasks Adele gave his officers. The business was a stark violation of

RCN regs, but it worked extremely well.

"—*days or weeks even to get through the material on Gibbs' personal database, but he seems to have preserved every contact he had with the plotters. He recorded all his conversations with his Palmyrene handler, both personal and by phone. I can't imagine what he was thinking of!*"

She paused, then added, "*Of course, the archivist in me is very pleased. We might not even need Gibbs in person.*"

"Oh, we need him," Daniel said, feeling his smile harden. He wasn't a cruel man; he wasn't even hard, by the standards of people like Hogg and—there was no point in denying the bald truth—Adele. Nonetheless, he was a Leary and an officer of the RCN: those who attacked him and his would pay.

He cleared his throat and said, "Adele, is the password 'Shirley' still correct, over?"

"*Yes,*" said Adele. "*It's his mother's name, according to his file in Navy House.*" Without changing tone she added, "*You're approaching Gibbs' residence. I'm shutting off his exterior surveillance system now. Actually, I've switched off the entire system. Ah, over.*"

Hogg switched off the power, turning the electric motor into a brake: the only brake the vehicle had so far as Daniel could see, except for the spade outside the cab on the driver's side. That could be pivoted to dig into the street on either an up or down slope, though it seemed of limited utility on bricks unless the driver carefully wedged it into a crack.

"We're here, young master," Hogg said. He started to get out. The street was so narrow that there was barely room to walk around the vehicle to either side. The narrow-fronted row houses were of two stories. They had stone foundation courses and were brick above that.

"Stay with the car," said Daniel, "or I'll make Barnes the driver. Your choice."

Hogg grimaced. "I'll drive the bloody thing," he muttered. "Go on, have your fun."

"Come on, Sissies," Daniel said quietly. The cab didn't have doors, and the squad in the back had already thrown down the wooden tailgate. "No sound till I tell you!"

Gibbs lived without servants, though until he began his dealings with the Palmyrenes there'd been a cook/housekeeper on the premises. He'd dispensed with her then, apparently from security concerns. His electronic files were more damning than if he'd published his plans on billboards across from the Founder's Palace, but presumably he hadn't expected to run into Officer Adele Mundy.

Daniel rapped on the door with the knuckles of his left hand. Anyone watching from neighboring houses—and there must be some; vehicles weren't common in this district— would notice his commo helmet; that was unusual but not specifically identifiable. The six Sissies with him wore the loose, nondescript clothing that they worked in—just like every other spacer and most common laborers besides.

"Gibbs!" he growled. "Open up! Shirley! Shirley! It's going to go tits-up if we don't move fast!"

"What's happened?" Gibbs cried through the door in a muted squeak. Metal rattled, a key or a drawbolt. "I saw the bloody corvette come back!"

The door started to swing in. Daniel shoved it hard with his left hand. It banged against a chain bolt. "Woetjans!" he shouted.

The bosun kicked the door where the bolt was anchored, ripping it out of the wood. The panel slammed Gibbs back into the room and knocked the pistol from his hand. Slithering on his back, he reached for the gun.

Daniel stamped on Gibbs' diaphragm, doubling him up like a salted slug. He began to vomit.

Woetjans burst in with the rest of the team behind her. "Don't hit him!" Daniel shouted. "Where's the bag?"

Dasi pulled the tarpaulin sack from under his belt. He slipped it over the head of the prisoner; his partner Barnes pulled the drawstrings.

"If I'd wanted him dead, I'd have shot him!" Daniel grumbled. He stuck his index finger under the edge of the sack and jerked it looser. "We don't want him to suffocate, right?"

"All right, load him in the van," Woetjans said. Four spacers grabbed handfuls of Gibbs and carried him into the street. Any of those present could have handled the prisoner unaided, including—

Daniel grinned with satisfaction.

—Captain Daniel Leary himself.

Light through the open doorway spilled onto the bricks. Daniel pulled the door to, then climbed into the cab beside Hogg. No point in encouraging the neighbors to come look.

"Back to the *Sissie* after a good night's work, Hogg," he said.

"The night's still young, *I* say," said Hogg as the van accelerated slowly forward. There wasn't room in the street to turn around. "I'm kinda looking forward to hearing what Master Assistant Commissioner has to say."

He glanced over his shoulder, then added, "And encouraging him, if he has trouble finding his tongue."

Hogg's right hand was in a lightweight cast from which the fingers projected. He tapped it against the steering wheel in a jaunty rhythm.

Adele gave the prisoner her usual dispassionate appraisal. Viewing a subject the way a butcher looks at a hog had more of a softening effect on some people than growled threats did.

She behaved as she did because it was natural to her, not for some "practical" reason. Though in truth, she couldn't imagine anything more practical than behaving the way she felt like.

"You're making a mistake!" said Gibbs. Even with the hood off he couldn't manage much bluster. Then he said, "What are you going to do with me?"

His wrists and ankles were strapped to a chair in the Captain's Suite—her home and Daniel's again now that the Browns had been delivered—with cargo tape. The chair in turn was bolted to the deck, like all furniture on a starship.

"We're not going to torture you, if that's what you're worried about," Adele said, her face probably showing the disgust she felt at the subject. "I have a few questions for you, and my colleagues—"

She glanced over her shoulder to indicate Daniel and the two servants on jumpseats against the wall behind her.

"—may have additional ones. Then we may request your help. If you're completely helpful, we'll turn you over to the authorities on Stahl's World."

"If I'm *helpful*?" Gibbs snarled. "They'd hang me and you know it!"

Adele shrugged. "Perhaps," she said, "but I don't believe that's certain. The Republic is at peace, and in any case you were intriguing with an allied power rather than with agents of the Alliance."

"I didn't intrigue with anybody!" Gibbs said, trying to regain ground he'd already surrendered in his fear. "I don't know who you've been talking to, but I've been doing my job as well as anybody can in this bloody backwater. That's all!"

"Here's a list of amounts paid to you by your Palmyrene handler," Adele said, ignoring the outburst as she projected a hologram of the records where Gibbs could read them. Though she used her personal data unit as a controller, the imaging system of the suite's console provided a crystalline display at any level of resolution she wanted. "He uses the name Bimbeck with you and claims to be a Zenobian merchant, but he's actually named Erzolan and has the rank of Squadron Leader in the Horde."

"How...?" said Gibbs. "H-how did you...?"

His face had become sallow. His limbs tensed against their bonds, but it seemed to Adele that it was a subconscious reaction to blind panic. Gibbs was smart enough to realize that he couldn't break tape that was meant to immobilize cargo through violent landings.

"There were flaws in your system," Adele said. "Obviously. But even if there hadn't been, I assure you that your Palmyrene friends fall a great deal short of civilized standards of security. Whatever possessed you to trust barbarians like them?"

"Oh, gods," Gibbs muttered. He closed his eyes and probably would have cradled his head in his hands if he could. "Oh, gods."

In fact the security of the computer in Gibbs' home was of a very high order. The only reason Adele had been able to get into it quickly was that the assistant commissioner had three months ago accessed it from Cinnabar House and hadn't reset the encryption afterwards.

But everything she said about the Palmyrenes was completely true. Their data wasn't as complete or well organized as Gibbs', but it would have been quite sufficient by itself to hang him.

"You know, Gibbs," Daniel said judiciously, "you weren't really in such a bad place even if your plot had been uncovered. Oh, the Zenobians would've been upset, but we'd have gotten you off-planet to try you ourselves."

He chuckled. "Fancy letting a passel of wogs try a Cinnabar citizen—and an RCN officer besides!" he said, sounding exactly like the sort of hearty, prejudiced officer that so many of his colleagues were in fact. "And sure, the charge would be treason—but treasonously trying to take a world away from the Alliance isn't the sort of business an RCN court martial gets too worked up about, not so? Certainly not to the point of hanging anybody."

"But then you decided to murder two RCN officers," said Adele. Gibbs' head jerked toward her again. "Not to put too fine a point on it—us. That's a different matter."

"That was quite a clever piece of work, you know," Daniel said, nodding in appreciation. "Keying the shorting strips to the test frequency of the portable landing controller that you added to the files before you turned them over to Brown. You know, it seems to me you might have gone high in the RCN if you'd put your cleverness to better use."

"Gone high?" Gibbs said bitterly. "Don't make me laugh! I was going nowhere. I was going to rot here on Zenobia for the rest of my life—unless they found a worse posting for me."

"And it wasn't clever to try to kill us by a method that pointed straight to you when it failed," Adele added. She wasn't acting: Gibbs was getting a clear view of the reality of the way her mind worked.

She coughed primly. "Just as you needn't worry about torture," she said, "you needn't worry about a court martial. If you refuse to cooperate, we'll simply release you."

"From a thousand feet over the Green Ocean," Daniel said. "Fair is fair: that's what you tried to do to us."

"What is it that you want from me?" Gibbs said in a monotone. His eyes were closed. He opened them and added with more animation, "Can you let me loose, please? My legs at least, so I can move them?"

"You'll remain as you are until you've satisfied us," Adele said. The corner of her mouth quirked. "Or fail to do so, of course. Tell us precisely what the Palmyrenes are doing, if you will."

Gibbs looked at her in amazement. Did he think she was mocking him by being courteous? She had been raised to be courteous. She regarded the practice to be basic to civilization.

Adele smiled at the man, in her way. She was perfectly willing to shoot him, of course. She had shot people who simply happened to be standing in the way when she needed to move fast. They had been enemies by political definition, of course, but they were complete strangers to her personally.

But she wouldn't have mocked those people, living or dead. Nor would she mock Gibbs.

Her train of thought may have shown on her face. The prisoner seemed to swallow something sour.

"I bought land for them three hundred miles south of the city in Commissioner Brassey's name," Gibbs said. "It's just called the Farm. I pretended that I was just a flunky and that Brassey was milking the secret account to create a retirement estate for himself. Of course there wouldn't be any recourse. The Alliance wouldn't extradite him to Xenos for trial, you see."

"Go on," Adele said. There were many references to "the Farm" in the information she had gathered, but she hadn't had enough time to process them. Besides, she hadn't had a context. Without a context, it was very possible to mistake a grocery list for an attack plan—or vice versa.

"The smart part was me—pretending to be Brassey, I mean—developing the land illegally," Gibbs said. "So the secrecy and the bribes to customs officials—and to the Alliance Resident—everybody understood. The Commissioner was bringing in advanced farming equipment that he'd bought with embezzled money, so of course he'd want to keep it quiet!"

Gibbs leaned toward his listeners, obviously proud of how clever his plan was. Adele wondered if he might not have approached the Palmyrenes rather than the other way around. Carefully sifting the documentation would answer the question, though the genesis of the plot didn't matter at this point.

What mattered was that if the plan went forward, it almost certainly meant a renewal of open warfare between Cinnabar and the Alliance. Palmyrene files were just as porous as she had said they were, so when Alliance agents began looking, they would immediately learn that the Cinnabar Commissioner had been instrumental in what had happened.

"What were you bringing in from off-planet?" she said aloud. Her references were to "shipments" without detail on what they included. "Troops?"

"No, no!" said Gibbs in irritated contempt. "There has to be preparation, don't you see? They had to build a base first. There was a missile battery and plasma cannon on mobile mounts in the first shipload, along with cadre to manage the whole business. Since then they've been building barracks. Do you see?"

Adele considered for a moment, then gave an honest answer instead of temporizing. "No," she said, "I don't. Why are the Palmyrenes building barracks?"

Gibbs was looking for a chance to brag. Letting him do so was the best way to get information out of him, though every aspect of the man's personality seemed designed to make her want to slap him. This was a matter of searching for jewels in sewage.

"The troops will be packed in for the passage here," Gibbs said. "The best transport you can find in the Qaboosh is only cattle boats, and not even very big cattle boats. So if they don't have some time to settle in and recover before they go into action, they'll be sod all use in a fight. The Farm gives them that, and their heavy weapons have been brought in bit by bit and set up there ahead of time."

"How many troops?" Adele asked calmly. The intercepted data didn't give strength figures—didn't even refer to the contents except as implied by the word "shipments."

She kept her delivery calm, almost disinterested. If she sounded excited, she would subconsciously tell the prisoner that his information was important. That wouldn't make any long-term difference, but it might delay the process somewhat.

Besides, Adele preferred keeping emotion at bay. For most of her life the only emotion which she felt regularly was anger; and while her mental state had improved since she met Daniel and became a member of the RCN, the red blur was never very far beneath the surface of her mind even now.

"There're barracks for a thousand," said Gibbs. "They look like barns and chicken sheds, you see. But they have to bring in more than they'd planned because the Founder is so set against them and he's popular. They'd hoped to bring him around, you see, but Hergo hates all Palmyrenes and he hates Autocrator Irene like poison. Now they're going to shoot him along with the Resident first thing, then make another of the Councillors the new Founder."

"How does the Autocrator expect to land a thousand or more troops in front of the Fleet contingent?" Daniel said in a measured voice. "Have they bribed Lieutenant Commander von Gleuck?"

"That one!" Gibbs said in disgust. "I met him when he arrived, thinking—you know, two navy men? But he was so full of his bloody honor that he threatened to whip me if he caught me anywhere near his quarters or the Palace, either one. I warned Bimbeck that the stiff-necked bastard would shoot anybody who tried to put him into some easy money."

"There's some of them like that," Daniel said in a tone of commiseration.

Adele looked at him sharply. Daniel himself was very much like that. Aloud she said, "How *are* they getting around the Fleet, then, Master Gibbs?"

"Because it's none of the Fleet's bloody business, that's how!" Gibbs crowed. "Customs and Excise are under the Resident, and Tilton let von Gleuck know that if he started making spot checks of ships in orbit, any knocking shop or bar that served Fleet spacers was going to be shut down. Lieutenant Commander Tightass doesn't like the Resident one bit, but he doesn't get in his way."

"No," said Daniel with a bright smile. "I wouldn't expect those two would get on well."

"Look," said Gibbs, "it's a mercy taking the planet away from the Alliance anyway, right? Not just because it's the Alliance and that's always a good thing for us Cinnabar citizens—"

Adele didn't allow herself to smile. The way the expression would have looked on her face would silence Gibbs faster than a blow.

"—but because all the wogs here hate the Resident so bad. If it wasn't Hergo keeping the lid on, a mob would've lynched Tilton long since. I know some of the Councillors are with the Autocrator on this one, and once she lands here to take possession, they'll all come over!"

Until a squadron arrives from Pleasaunce, thought Adele, *and along with battleships brings a detachment from the Fifth Bureau.*

Aloud she said, "When will this coup take place, Master Gibbs?"

"It's—" Gibbs said, then unexpectedly caught himself. "Ah,

I don't know for sure, you see. But, ah...I think it's going to be pretty soon. Not from anything they said to me, exactly, but just the way they were talking to each other, you know? Bimbeck and the CO from the Farm, Mehdi Nasrullah."

"Days?" said Adele. "Weeks? What?"

"I'd guess days," Gibbs said. He licked his dry lips. "I thought I could, you know, wait. But I'd heard about you, Leary—"

He looked at Daniel; his face worked in misery. Daniel gave him a gentle smile.

"Anyway," said Gibbs, "I couldn't trust you wouldn't try to put a spoke in the operation. And then the Autocrator would blame me, sure as shit stinks. They impale people, the Palmyrenes do, and it takes a long time to die."

"I see," Daniel said. "Tell me, Gibbs—you know the ground here pretty well after so many years, I'd judge? Since your little prank destroyed the Commission's vehicle, what other trustworthy aircars are there on Zenobia?"

"Well, the Founder's got one," Gibbs said, frowning. "It's old but von Gleuck had some of his mechanics work it over. He and Lady Belisande, she's the pretty one, they've gone jaunting about."

"But that car is marked, is it not?" said Daniel.

"Oh, Hell, yes," said Gibbs. "Great big Zenobian Cross on the bonnet, and a Belisande coat of arms on both sides."

"So," said Daniel dismissively. Adele didn't know where the discussion was going; but knowing Daniel, it was certainly going somewhere. "What unmarked vehicles are there?"

"Not a bloody one," Gibbs said. "Not if you don't want to walk back. Some of the Councillors own a car for show, but they only run them in ground effect. There aren't any mechanics you could trust here. Even a new car would go to crap in a year with no maintenance."

"There's one car," Adele said.

Gibbs looked at her. "You don't think the Resident's going to lend you his?" he sneered.

"Yes!" said Daniel. "Thank you, Adele! Yes, that unmarked black limousine is perfect!"

"You want me to steal a car, young master?" Hogg said. The smile he gave the compartment was beatific, in its way.

"No," said Daniel. "That would be an act of war, which is just what we're trying to prevent. But I'm going to speak to a friend and see what he might be able to arrange."

His sudden smile was just as broad as his servant's.

CHAPTER 16

CALVARY ON ZENOBIA

"It's a pleasure to see you again, Leary," said Lieutenant Commander von Gleuck at the door to the study of his private quarters in the city. He wore loose trousers and a tunic, both striped in pale blue diagonals on white. It might be a style from Adlersbild; certainly it wasn't Zenobian. "Podnits, you may turn in. Captain Leary and I can pour our own drinks."

The servant who had admitted Daniel was bald, stocky, and dour. He looked doubtful, but he obeyed. Hogg's demeanor had been very similar when Daniel told him to wait in the van.

"I'm sorry about the delay admitting you," von Gleuck said. "I'm afraid Podnits wasn't convinced that it really was an RCN officer in civilian clothes who was banging on my door."

Daniel closed the study door firmly behind him. "I can imagine Hogg having similar doubts," he said. "I was afraid to call ahead, you see, so I drove here straight from the harbor."

He gave von Gleuck a rueful smile. "Trundled from the harbor, I should say. Unfortunately, time is important."

Three of the walls were decorated with Zenobian tapestries in which figures in garish costumes hunted across wooded terrain. The wall facing the door, however, was a hologram of a mountain fastness. The scene moved slowly, as though a person standing on a height was turning to his right to view the entire panorama.

There were four chairs, each with a leather back and cushion on a frame of rhodium-plated steel; the table matched, though the leather top had been treated with a hardener. That wasn't Daniel's idea of comfort, but he could appreciate von Gleuck's determination to re-create the world he'd grown up in.

The computer console in the far right corner faced the door. It appeared to be a Fleet Standard unit, functionally identical to what Daniel would expect to find on the bridge of the Z 46. Or, for that matter, on the *Princess Cecile*.

"All right, Captain," von Gleuck said with a cold smile. "Speak."

Daniel opened his left hand palm up, as though offering something to his host. "Look, von Gleuck," he said, "we're both officers, and we're not going to forget that ever. But just for now, Daniel Leary of Bantry would like to talk off the record with his friend, the Honorable Otto von Gleuck. Can we do that?"

Von Gleuck's smile broadened minusculely. "We *are* doing that, Daniel," he said. "Part of the delay before I admitted you was to make sure all the recording devices in my quarters were switched off. Apart from anything else, Posey's maid Wood is a member of the Fifth Bureau, and it would not surprise me to learn that her duties included reporting on my potentially treasonous contacts."

Daniel laughed. "Neither of us will be committing treason," he said, "but it's certainly possible that our superiors may decide to hang us as a result of this business if it goes wrong."

He smiled again. This would work: von Gleuck was the man he'd seemed to be. They might all die, but they'd die trying.

"Of course," Daniel said, "if it goes *very* wrong, I won't be around to learn about it. But I'm wasting time. Otto, I need the use of a trustworthy aircar that doesn't have visible markings. I'm told there's only one of them on Zenobia. The matter means peace or war between our nations."

Von Gleuck pursed his lips. "That," he said in a musing tone, "isn't what I expected to hear. I'll admit that I hadn't refined the possibilities very far, but from your reputation I thought it might have something to do with a woman."

"I've had various problems with women," Daniel admitted. "But no serious ones. That may be because—until recently, at least—I had no serious interactions with women."

He cleared his throat. Von Gleuck hadn't answered the implied question, but that didn't mean he hadn't heard it.

"Otto," he said, "after this is over, I will give you all the details. I can't do so now because if I did, you would be honor bound to act on the information. I give you my word as a Leary of Bantry that my proposed solution is the one I believe most likely to lead to a good result for the Alliance and the Republic both."

"Yes, all right," von Gleuck said. "Ah—though the car in question isn't marked, anyone in Calvary is likely to recognize it, you realize?"

Daniel nodded. "Except while coming and going...," he

said, "I won't be anywhere close to Calvary. And I won't be dealing with Zenobians."

He grinned. "Or citizens of the Alliance, either one," he added.

"No," agreed von Gleuck with a similar grin, "you're leaving that to me. And a good thing you are, since my brother the Count tells me that the levies to pay for the recent war between our nations has created a great deal of unrest on Adlersbild. Further taxes might have unfortunate results."

He hadn't asked why Daniel wasn't stealing the Resident's aircar himself, and he wasn't objecting to the personal risk. There wouldn't be a war because a Fleet officer stole a Resident's aircar, but there might very well be a hanging. More accurately, a shot in the back of the neck. That was the technique preferred by the civil authorities of the Alliance.

Naval officers accepted personal risk as a given of their profession, though that didn't ordinarily mean a chance of being executed for treason. Still, the most likely result if the wheels came off this business was that Daniel Leary would be buried in an unmarked grave in the wilds of Zenobia. Or possibly vaporized; Gibbs had mentioned mobile plasma cannon, after all, and Daniel knew from the other side of the muzzle what a bolt at short range would do to an aircar.

He smiled wider. But what a thrill when a plan like this came together! And similar plans had come together in the past, they surely had!

"Where do you want the vehicle delivered, then, Daniel?" von Gleuck said.

"Alongside the *Sissie*," said Daniel. "Alongside my ship. And ASAP, of course."

"Of course," von Gleuck agreed with a nod. "My people should be able to manage that within an hour. As soon as they do, I think I'm going to call an emergency drill to see how quickly my ships can lift off."

"Very wise," said Daniel. "On a posting like this, crews get bored because nothing happens."

Daniel turned toward the hall. Before the door swung closed behind him, he heard von Gleuck bringing his console live.

Both men were chuckling with excitement.

A squall drove across Calvary Harbor as a line of foam on the dark water, then spattered the quay. Adele turned her back on it. Her expression didn't change, but her thoughts were grim.

She smiled.

"Adele?" said Daniel in surprise. He had just lowered his head and squinted at the brief gust. She supposed he was used to being out in this sort of weather while hunting. Well, she was used to it too, from poverty; but she didn't like it any better for the familiarity.

"I was just thinking that the normal, ah, tenor of my thoughts fitted the weather very well," Adele said with the smile still twitching around the corners of her mouth. "Which in turn struck me as amusing."

"Adele...," Daniel said with an informality that he usually avoided when they were in public—as they technically were, since Sun as well as Hogg stood with them; Tovera was in the van, watching Gibbs. "I won't pretend I understood that, but quite a lot of what goes on in your mind is beyond me. It's a bloody good mind, and I'm glad you're on our side."

Adele's smile remained a trifle longer. Her RCN utilities were rainproof, though if she'd wanted more protection she could have spread the cape and hood from the collar—they were cut from sailcloth, tough, thin, and next to weightless. She didn't especially mind getting wet.

But she couldn't read in the rain. Paper soaked quickly to uselessness, and though her data unit was sealed against the weather, the droplets—or even worse, fog—disrupted the holographic display. Anything that limited Adele's ability to receive information aroused her severe dislike.

She had her ordinary senses, of course. She had long ago come to terms with the fact, however, that she preferred to use technology to filter her contact with the world.

"Bloody wish they'd come," muttered Hogg, hunched beneath a poncho of raw wool. There was nothing high tech about it, but it was warm and the lanolin kept the rain out. "If they're coming."

He looked up at Daniel. "You're sure about that, young master?"

"I trust Otto," said Daniel equably, "and he trusts his crew. The car is coming."

"In going over Alliance manning lists, Daniel...," Adele said. Another splatter of rain raked the water, then the quay. She barely noticed it, because she was now back in her proper element: information. "I found something I perhaps should have mentioned to you sooner."

Well, she'd only found the information this evening while reviewing data Cory and Cazelet had marked for her after she left for Diamond Cay. And there *had* been other, more pressing, matters to deal with.

"The cruiser *Sachsenwelt* was stationed on Zenobia," she continued aloud. "The *Z 42* and the *Z 46* under von Gleuck were sent to join it three years ago."

Daniel was frowning slightly. "Sent to replace it, I suspect," he said. "The *Sachsenwelt* was over eighty years old and was withdrawn immediately for scrapping on Pleasaunce."

"The ship was withdrawn," said Adele, "but over two hundred of her crew were transferred to the destroyers. In exchange a hundred and ten of the former destroyer personnel returned to Pleasaunce with the *Sachsenwelt*. I suspect that Lieutenant Commander von Gleuck has more reason to trust his crews than most Alliance captains at this stage of the war."

Daniel guffawed and clapped his hands in delight. "So he not only stripped the trained ratings from the junker, he got rid of the slum drafts that Porra's been using to fill out the Fleet's crews!" he said. "By heavens, that—"

He paused to let his grin spread. He said, "You understand, I trusted Otto anyway. But now I know why I was *right* to trust him."

"There's an aircar coming," said Sun, looking eastward into the city through the visor of his commo helmet. "Yeah, there's the lights. Hey, it's coming fast."

Adele looked up, though it was a moment before her unaided eyes caught movement against the lights of the waterfront bars and other establishments catering to spacers. She didn't like the feel of commo helmets, and the sensory boost they gave experienced users simply didn't interest her.

The car was indeed coming fast. When the driver started to slow, the bow rose dangerously before he managed to restore equilibrium. It was the correct vehicle, at least. It made a half turn, putting it broadside to the quay, and then banged down with a *graunch* from the skids that bounced it into the air again. The driver jerked his steering yoke to the right and screeched to the surface again, finally stopping with half the left skid hanging over the water.

"If they land like that as a general thing," Hogg said musingly, "they better know how to swim."

"Yes," said Daniel. "But my guess is that they don't fly aircars any more often than Barnes does."

Adele had already been thinking of the period when Barnes was the closest thing to an aircar driver aboard the *Princess Cecile*. But Barnes was a very good fellow to have beside you in a fight, and that had been sufficient recommendation enough before Tovera taught herself to drive. She wasn't very good either, but she was generally a great deal less exciting than Barnes had been.

Five tough-looking spacers got out of the aircar, each of them rocking the vehicle on its skids. They wore Fleet utilities; the sodium lights on standards along the quay turned the drab green fabric into a brownish purple. Adele thought the one who'd been driving was female, though she wouldn't have cared to stake anything valuable on that guess.

Adele was interested to see that they were in uniform rather than nondescript slops: they were making the explicit statement that the Resident's aircar had been stolen by Fleet spacers. One way or another the events of the next few hours would make the point moot, but they—and von Gleuck, who must have ordered them to wear utilities—were taking that on faith.

The leader was a warrant officer with a broad black beard and a rigger's maul thrust through his belt. He was of average height, but the width of his shoulders made him look like a dwarf.

"You're Leary?" he said.

"I am," said Daniel. He stepped forward, his left thumb pinching a 20-florin coin against his palm. He reached toward the warrant officer. "For your trouble, sir."

The big man recoiled. "We're not doing this for pay!" he said. "The Old Man asked us for a little private favor, so we did it for him!"

"Nor am I offering to pay you, my good man," Daniel said. He spoke sharply, but he didn't withdraw his hand. "I'm hoping that some fellow spacers would have a drink on me the next time they're in a dram shop."

"Don't get your back up, Porker," growled the female spacer. "He's all right even if he *is* Cinnabar."

"And I'd just about murder a drink," said another man. Then, hastily, "When we stand down, I mean. Don't get your knickers in a twist, Porker, I'm not planning to get blitzed with an alert on."

"Hogg here will drive you to your ship," Daniel said. "And though I realize you didn't do it for our sake, I assure you that I do appreciate your trouble."

Porker palmed the coin, peeked at it in the hollow of his hand, and nodded approvingly. "Thank *you*, sir, and sorry about getting shirty there. Anyway, it wasn't much trouble."

"Warn't any trouble a'*tall*, I say," said one of his companions, a rangy fellow with a long face and merry eyes. "I could've handled both them blowhards myself, and that wouldn't have been trouble neither."

"The Old Man said he'd see us right," said the woman. It seemed to Adele that her tone was prayerful, albeit that of a believer praying. "*He* won't let us down."

"Master Daniel?" said Hogg pleadingly. "You know, they could just take the van themself and I could go along with you, you know?"

"You don't belong on this mission, Hogg," Daniel said. "We have to look official. Please—drive our friends here to the Z 46."

"Come along, lads and lady," Hogg said, striding toward the cab of the van. He sounded cheerful again. "I wouldn't mind hearing just how you pulled this off."

Gibbs had gotten out of the van, probably at Tovera's direction. He looked more miserable than the weather justified. Adele felt contempt for people whose problems were self-inflicted; but then—her hard smile quirked—she felt contempt for most people. And she didn't like herself very much.

Daniel watched the Alliance spacers climb into the van. "Right, then," he said cheerfully. "Let's go. Tovera, you're all right with this?"

"Yes," Tovera said. She held her arms up and rotated her hands while flexing the fingers, showing that everything worked. There was a thin sheath over either wrist.

The Medicomp had made Tovera functional, but she wouldn't be capable of delicate manipulations for some while yet. Fortunately, her driving skills had never risen to delicacy—and Adele was sure that Tovera was still a good enough shot to put down anyone she wanted dead.

As Tovera got into the cab, she said to the gunner, "Hey, Sun? Keep an eye on our friend Gibbs, will you?"

"Oh, I say!" Gibbs blurted. "That's not necessary! I'm on your side now, I assure you."

"Sun, ride up front with Tovera if you will," Daniel said. "Adele and I will keep Master Gibbs company."

Adele got into the closed vehicle. The interior was done in black with silver highlights, presenting a slickly unnatural ambiance. She found it comfortable.

Daniel followed Gibbs in behind her. "Does your man have to carry that rifle?" Gibbs said, sounding petulant. "Does he plan to shoot his way into the Farm, is that it?"

Daniel closed the door. Tovera increased power to the fans, but she didn't try to take off until she had a feel for the controls.

"Sun would carry an impeller if we were visiting for the purpose we'll tell Nasrullah we're there," Daniel said cheerfully. "He's seen a good deal of combat, Gibbs. We all have. So we're going to give Nasrullah and his personnel the sort of people he'll expect when we identify ourselves."

The aircar slid forward and lifted, climbing at a steep angle. Adele suspected that this vehicle was much more powerful than Tovera was used to driving.

"Because," Daniel said, "that's really who we are."

CHAPTER 17

THE FARM, SOUTHEAST OF CALVARY

Tovera was slowing the aircar gradually in response to the commands from the ground, but her attempts to reduce altitude led to a series of bumps. Daniel felt as though he was riding a bicycle down a staircase.

Gibbs glared across the cabin and said, "Blazes, Leary! You should have let me drive!"

Daniel smiled mildly. "Oh, this isn't so bad, Gibbs," he said. "We've gotten here, after all."

If I'm ever tempted to take advice from a traitor, he thought, *it won't be advice to put my life and my associates' lives in his hands.* Daniel guessed that Gibbs was too great a coward to sacrifice himself while plunging his enemies into the ground, but there would be no benefit in taking that chance.

"*All right, you can land,*" the controller from the Farm growled. "*But keep right in the square between the barns or you'll wish you had, over.*"

"*Roger,*" Tovera said, using a throat microphone linked to

the aircar's communications system. *I see the landing zone. I'm coming in now, over.*

"The two apparent haystacks covered with black film at either end of the main house...," said Adele. The Resident's limousine was so quiet that the passengers could talk comfortably without the need of intercom or shouting. "Are automatic impellers which are tracking us. The control station is in the cupola of the house."

Gibbs kneaded his fingers together and began to mutter under his breath. Adele looked at him and said, "Don't worry, Gibbs: the guns can't fire now, though I haven't otherwise interfered with their operation. And they were doubtless aimed at you every time you visited here in the past. You *did* visit, didn't you?"

Gibbs nodded miserably, but he didn't look up. His hands continued to writhe.

Daniel looked through the windows with a cold expression. He was acting now, but the part—a disdainful RCN officer— wasn't much of a stretch.

The car slid over what looked like a rambling house with attached sheds on both wings, then down into a square formed by three high barns and the back of the house. Tovera landed, not hard but with too much throttle. The drive fans made the car hop its own length forward. Gibbs cursed.

Tovera shut the fans off at the crest of the jump. This time the car did slam, but not as badly as it might've done.

The dust Daniel had expected didn't bloom up around them. Though the square looked like bare dirt, the surface had been plasticized into a hard mat.

Daniel released his shock harness; Adele was sliding her data unit away. Sun and Tovera flung their doors open and stepped out. The gunner kept his left arm inside the cab, on the receiver of the impeller that he'd stuck upright between the separate front seats.

A heavyset man in gray clothing and a floppy hat stalked to the aircar from the veranda of the house. The two men flanking him were also dressed as laborers, though with bandanas rather than straw hats; they carried mob guns openly.

"Gibbs," the leader said, bending to speak through the window, "what are you playing at?"

He switched his glare across the cabin to Daniel; his ginger moustache fluttered. "And you, buddy!" he said. "Who the bloody *hell* are you?"

Daniel got out of the car. Over the roof of the vehicle he said, "You'd be Colonel Nasrullah, I take it? As for what Gibbs is doing, he's obeying the orders of his superior officer—me. And I'm Captain Daniel Leary, Admiral Mainwaring's aide and commander of the troop convoy's RCN escort. If there is a troop convoy. That's what Admiral Mainwaring sent me and my staff to determine, don't you know? Whether or not he allows the convoy to proceed."

"What?" said Nasrullah. He stepped back as though Daniel had spat in his face. "What do you mean, if it proceeds? The convoy *is* proceeding!"

"Only if you convince me," Daniel said. Adele had slid across the cabin and gotten out on his side, but Gibbs remained in the car. "And I must say, all these threats and nonsense—"

He gestured to the guards. One of them simply blinked

stupidly, but the other quickly lifted the flaring muzzle of his weapon skyward.

"—don't impress me very positively. And impellers tracking us as we came in! That's exactly the sort of thing the captains are worried about—and why they're refusing to land."

"What?" said Nasrullah. "By Moses' balls, man, we've got to take precautions, don't we? Did you think we were going to let you just waltz in here as though we were running a tavern?"

He broke off and waved his left arm at the limousine. "And where's this car from?" he demanded. "How were we supposed to recognize it when we've never seen it before?"

Daniel opened his mouth to reply, but the Palmyrene officer had just been taking a breath. "And what do you mean 'the captains are worried'?" he said. "What captains, and who *cares* if they're worried?"

"Let's get inside," Daniel said curtly, gesturing toward the house. "It's unlikely that anybody will notice, but there's no reason to risk that a ship landing in Calvary Harbor will pick up imagery of RCN officers in uniform visiting what's supposed to be a civilian agricultural establishment."

"That's impossible!" said Nasrullah. "Is this a joke?"

"If I thought it was worthwhile arguing with people from the Qaboosh Region," Adele said in a thin, disdainful tone, "I would demonstrate that it's quite possible. Perhaps not for a barbarian, of course."

"*What?*" Nasrullah said.

"Come along, Colonel," Daniel said, cupping his hand behind the Palmyrene's elbow in friendly fashion and starting toward the house. The guards followed, continuing to look puzzled. "We'll talk better inside."

For a moment Daniel had wondered if Adele had overplayed her part. Still, Nasrullah had to respect and fear them if this bluff was to work. By behaving as a Cinnabar aristocrat with enormous technical skills—which she was in fact—Adele would achieve that.

If Nasrullah didn't shoot them out of hand. Well, try to: the Colonel himself certainly wouldn't survive the first exchange of shots.

Half a dozen people, all men, waited within the building; their expressions ranged from cautious to worried. None appeared to be guards, but Daniel suspected they all—like Nasrullah himself—were military personnel.

The central hall was open but unadorned, a place to gather but not to impress or entertain; the ceiling was normal height instead of encroaching into the second story. Sliding partitions closed off the wing to the left, but the right-hand side was open. Within was what seemed to be a command center, though the electronics appeared to have been pieced together from salvage.

The bridges of their cutters are probably the same, Daniel reminded himself. *It doesn't prevent them from doing things in the Matrix that I couldn't match.*

As the two groups took stock of one another, Daniel glanced at Nasrullah and said, "You mentioned the previous aircar, Colonel. It's at the bottom of a swamp in the Green Ocean. You're welcome to it if you want to dredge it out. And as for why Admiral Mainwaring sent me—"

Daniel's reversion to an unimportant earlier question

had thrown Nasrullah off-stride as he intended it should. Nonetheless, the Colonel broke in with, "Your Admiral Mainwaring has nothing to do with this. The Autocrator has ordered it, and we take *only* her orders."

"Perhaps you do," said Daniel, giving his surroundings a disdainful look, "but the ships on which your troops are travelling are Cinnabar registry, and their captains have their own opinions on what they're willing to do. You knew that, didn't you? That the ships are ours?"

Nasrullah looked over his shoulder to his staff, his expression worried. The oldest man of the group, easily sixty and badly overweight, stood by the slid-back partition. He shrugged massively and said, "Well, sure, that's right, Albay. They were the biggest ships in the region. For hell's sake, it'd have taken a fleet of cutters for two thousand troops! And anyway, it seemed, you know, good to be using Cinnabar hulls."

Daniel nodded curtly. Adele had established the fact from the data she'd gathered, but the reasons had been speculative until now. *The Palmyrenes had decided it would be good to involve the Republic in an attack on the Alliance. These* barbarians *had no conception of what they were dealing with*.

Adele walked into the "control room" and dragged a stool over to a table spread with tools and components. She took out her personal data unit and cleared a small space for it.

Tovera stood behind her with an empty expression, letting her eyes search in all directions through tiny movements of her head. Her attaché case was unlatched but closed. The fat Palmyrene by the partition—probably a non-combat member of the Horde's staff, knowledgeable but low-status compared to the fighters—watched them with silent concern.

"Cinnabar hulls come with Cinnabar officers," Daniel said. That wasn't necessarily true, but he was pretty sure that nobody here at the Farm could disprove it. "And those officers aren't willing to land their ships out in the middle of nowhere with—"

He gave Nasrullah a patronizing smile.

"—shall we say, the local talent aiming missiles at them. My staff and I are here on orders from Admiral Mainwaring to view your weapon control arrangements. Unless and until I report to him that the arrangements are satisfactory, the convoy will not be landing."

"Now *look*, you bugger!" Nasrullah shouted. "You don't give me orders! You get your poncing asses back to Calvary or wherever the hell till you can show me authorization from the Autocrator! Those're the only orders I'll accept!"

Daniel lifted an eyebrow. "Very well," he said calmly. "You can discuss the matter with the Autocrator yourself, then. She's not in my chain of command, you see."

He gave the colonel a smile that would have frozen a lighted furnace, then glanced toward Adele. "Come along, Mundy," he said. "We have to get back to Stahl's World soonest to inform the Admiral that the Zenobia operation has been cancelled."

He turned. Sun waited near the front door, standing between the Palmyrene guards. He'd left the heavy impeller in the cab of the aircar, but he cradled his right fist in his left palm in front of him: that meant he was wearing a knuckle-duster. If trouble started, Daniel was pretty sure that Sun would shortly be using a mob gun.

"Wait!" said Nasrullah.

Daniel turned, raising an eyebrow again. Adele had risen from the stool, but she wasn't really planning to move: her data unit was still live.

"Look," said Nasrullah. He had begun to sweat. "I've got orders from the Autocrator, you see? If I violate them, she's likely to have me impaled—even if I'm right!"

Daniel shrugged. "I'm afraid that's not my problem," he said with a dismissive smile. "I report to Admiral Mainwaring. And unfortunately for you, so do the captains of the troop transports."

He paused, then said, "So, which is it? Do my gunner and signals officer check out your operation here? Or do we go back to Stahl's World and tell the admiral that the operation has been cancelled?"

Nasrullah twisted his hat in both hands, then ripped it across. "All right, all right," he said in a guttural voice. "Get on with it and get it over with."

The Farm's electronic security was every bit as bad as Adele had expected it to be, but she was finding it remarkably difficult to navigate through Palmyrene disorganization. A good code was a completely random arrangement of symbols, and the staff here at the Farm had through sheer incompetence made a better stab at bewildering Adele than some very sophisticated systems had done.

In the background of her awareness, Colonel Nasrullah plaintively said, "What's she doing, then? It looks like she's knitting."

Daniel said, "Sorry, chappie, but that's not really my line of territory. Technical folderol, don't you know? I'm a fighting officer."

Adele smiled faintly as she worked. Daniel did a flawless job of acting like a bluff, brainless RCN officer. She herself could don the persona of Lady Adele Mundy, upper-class virago, but it wasn't the same thing. She really *was* that other person if someone scratched her the wrong way.

The smile faded. Adele's mother would be pleased and surprised to learn that Lady Mundy still existed. Esme Rolfe Mundy had been disappointed in her bookish elder daughter, though she was too courteous ever to have expressed that feeling.

Adele wasn't interested in the Rights of Man—or in dancing, fashion, or polite conversation. She might have been a tradesman's daughter; and while tradesmen were quite all right in their place, Adele was a Rolfe and a Mundy with responsibilities to her class.

More of Esme's teaching had stuck than either mother or daughter would have guessed. Perhaps Esme now nodded with heavenly approbation every time Adele led the dancing at a rout on a distant world, executing the estampes and sarabandes and gigues with as much precision as she fired her pistol.

Logically there must be a heaven. Certainly there was a hell, because Adele entered it every time she dreamed.

She smiled again as she worked. The expression was as grim as her silent joke had been.

The Farm's personnel records were a subdirectory of the supply inventory. Perhaps that had made sense to someone, but it was equally probable that it was a mistake made when the database was set up and that nobody had bothered to correct it.

According to the records, the Farm had a cadre of eighty-two personnel, but Adele didn't trust the figure. She had never seen a military organization on the fringes of civilization where the officers weren't inflating their personnel strength and pocketing the excess pay themselves. It was even more common than cheating subordinates on their food.

The defenses included four batteries of anti-ship missiles emplaced on high points within the two-hundred-acre tract. Adele plotted the locations on the *Princess Cecile*'s orbital imagery but found nothing until she compared them with images from a freighter which had landed in Calvary Harbor five months earlier. The missiles were covered—she couldn't tell whether by netting or film—so skillfully that only the slight increase in the hills' elevation was noticeable even when Adele knew what to look for.

Adele kept the interaction in the main hall in a corner of her display, in case something occurred that required her attention; something for her pistol rather than her data unit, likely enough. She glanced at the image of Colonel Nasrullah.

He and Daniel were now seated on opposite ends of a simple bench. It appeared that Nasrullah knew his business as a construction supervisor, or at any rate his staff did and he didn't get in their way. Adele had to assume that every member of the cadre was as skilled as the people who had emplaced the missiles clearly were.

A vehicle with a small two-stroke engine drew up behind the building, popping and ringing. A moment later Sun reappeared beside the Palmyrene officer he'd gone off with some while before. Hours before, now that Adele happened to think about it.

Sun was beaming. Adele let her data unit continue to mine information—she had found the claimed inventories of the twenty-seven ships which had landed at the Farm since its purchase by "Commissioner Brassey." Instead of turning her head, she expanded the real-time image of what was going on in the main hall.

"All right, Six!" the gunner said exuberantly. "This is a lot better than I thought it was going to be. Captain Farouk here—"

He jerked his thumb toward the Palmyrene who'd been escorting him. Farouk, young and noticeably sharper than his fellows—even though they all wore the same loose work clothes—flushed with pleasure.

"—went to the Sector Academy on Knollys—"

Knollys was Cinnabar's administrative and naval headquarters for the Thirty Suns, the region closest to the Qaboosh which one could describe as "developed" or "civilized," depending on your frame of reference.

"—and they're using an RCN gunnery console for the director. Okay, it's older than any of us here—"

The console had been built on Cinnabar fifty-seven standard years before and had been partially gutted, though Sun probably didn't know that.

"—but it'll handle ground-to-orbit missiles with no trouble. I wouldn't worry one bit about the missiles on director control."

Adele *always* worried about deadly weapons which someone else might be pointing at her, because she—based on experience—doubted the competence and judgment of all but a few of the people she had met over the years. With that general proviso accepted, she agreed with the gunner's assessment.

Colonel Nasrullah wiped his forehead with a sleeve. "All right," he said, "all right. You will bring the troops here and all is well. There is no need to inform the Autocrator of our visit, that is so?"

"Not so fast, fellow!" Sun said. "Don't get ahead of yourself."

He was obviously relishing the opportunity to lord it over a foreign officer. His terminology would probably have been "stick it to a jumped-up wog," however.

"Sir," he continued to Daniel, "they got individual controls on each battery and a two-man crew. Farouk took me around to three of them, but the fourth was way the hell out and anyway, I didn't need to see it after I'd seen the others."

He took a deep breath and made a theatrical gesture back the way he'd come. Farouk looked worried; Nasrullah got to his feet and snatched up half the hat that he'd torn.

"Sir," Sun said forcefully, "those site crews, I wouldn't trust them to pour piss out of a boot! Not that they'd bother to. You know what they're doing, sir? They're crapping right there in the battery pits, and from the number of empty wine bottles all around they're mostly drunk besides."

"That's not true!" said Farouk. "Not nearly so much do we drink!"

"You're a bloody liar!" Nasrullah bellowed. He stepped toward Sun and cocked his fist.

Adele shifted on the stool for the first time. She'd set down the wand in her left hand. She sensed Tovera moving behind her.

Daniel caught Nasrullah's wrist. The Palmyrene tried to jerk loose—but couldn't.

"Careful, Colonel," Daniel drawled. His voice perfectly

mimicked that of a well-born twit to anyone familiar with Cinnabar accents. "You wouldn't want your clumsiness to be mistaken for an attack on one of my officers, would you?"

"He's a liar," Nasrullah repeated, but this time he muttered it as he stepped back.

"And it's not a problem anyway," Daniel said in a cheerful tone. "Mundy, lock the batteries onto director control, if you'll be so good. That takes care of the matter."

"Yes," said Adele, picking up the wand again. She had already deleted the firing command from both the director and individual instruction sets. All she was doing now was preventing the battery crews from slewing the missiles.

"Wait," said Nasrullah. "Can't you let us use them against surface targets? The director can't observe all the ground that the individual batteries can."

Of course I could, Adele thought. Aloud she said, "No, that's impossible."

It amused her—grimly—to realize that she felt more uncomfortable about lying to the man than she would have been if she'd shot him in the head. On the other hand, his face wasn't likely to reappear at 3 A.M., muttering, "You lied to me."

"Very good, Mundy," Daniel said. "When you're ready, we can return to Calvary and lift to meet the convoy."

"I'm ready," said Adele, putting away the data unit before she got to her feet. She joined Daniel and they strode, side by side, out the front door. Tovera and Sun followed.

"And we *can* join the convoy," she said very quietly to Daniel as they arrived at the aircar. "Because I now have its course and its expected time of arrival on Zenobia."

CHAPTER 18

THE MATRIX, BETWEEN ZENOBIA
AND PALMYRA

Daniel lived with enthusiasm and liked most of what life had brought him. What he felt on the hull of a ship in the Matrix was on an even higher plane than sex or a perfect piece of ship handling, however. It was—

Well, Daniel believed in the gods—of course. One just did; and the fact that he was pretty sure that Adele did not—it wasn't a matter they discussed, of course—was more disturbing to him than if she occasionally turned green and grew horns. He wasn't what anyone would call a religious man, however, and he shared the normal RCN disquiet about the occasional captain who really was a temple-haunting zealot.

But when he stood here on the hull, watching the infinity of separate universes dusted across his field of view, he truly felt that there *were* gods. And in the back of his mind was a thought that he had never spoken: that any human who saw and felt what Daniel Leary did in this moment *was* a god.

But that wasn't accomplishing the mission nor training

Cory, either one. *We can hold a prayer service later*, he thought with a rueful grin, though he half suspected that the lieutenant would join him if he suggested it.

Daniel put the communications rod to the waiting Cory's helmet and pointed with his left arm. "Follow the line R386, R377, P915. Got that?"

Cory lifted his own left arm; he had reached around his helmet to hold the rod with his right hand, allowing him to mimic Daniel's gesture. After a moment that proved he wasn't just chattering, he said, "Yes, I have it."

"Now, do you see the distortion across the first two?"

The bubble universes which Daniel had described by their four terminal digits were blotches of yellow-green in a fainter wash of the same color. An Academy scientist had told Daniel that the colors and relative brightness were artifacts of the viewer's mind; they were tricks his consciousness played on itself to impose order on what was really chaos.

And perhaps that was true, but Uncle Stacey had taught his nephew to see those variations, and Daniel in turn had taught others. Not, he had to admit, all others: apparently to Adele, "glowing chaos" was a sufficient description of what she saw from the hull.

But what Daniel saw was real enough to refine his astrogation beyond what was possible for those who had only the Academy's training. And in the present instance, it had permitted him to find the track of what he hoped was the Palmyrene convoy.

"Yes, sir," said Cory. "I do."

"The disruption is someone moving through the Matrix," Daniel said, "and on the same course as we are."

He lowered his arm, but it was a moment before Cory mirrored the movement. He was desperately eager to succeed. The thing that amazed Daniel was that Cory *was* succeeding, to a degree that very few astrogators could equal.

"Being on the correct course doesn't prove that they're the convoy we're looking for," Daniel said, "but it isn't unlikely. There's very little direct traffic between Palmyra and Zenobia."

They stood just astern of one of the hydromechanical semaphores by which the bridge transmitted orders to the hull when the ship was in the Matrix. Now the six arms clacked upright in an attention signal; then four vanished in line with the support pillar and the remaining two flared to starboard, informing the rigging crew of the new sail plan.

A moment later the port and starboard antennas shook out their topgallants in a coordinated shudder. When Daniel was seven, Uncle Stacey had shown him the Matrix for the first time, from the hull of a freighter being rerigged by Bergen and Associates.

Uncle Stacey could tell what the masts and yards were doing simply from the vibration through the soles of his magnetic boots. That had seemed like magic to the young Daniel...and maybe it was. But it was second nature to him as well by now.

"Now, what I *think*...," Daniel said, "is that the track is too diffuse to be that of a single ship. But I can't swear to that. I may be inventing the, the *blurriness*, because that's what I want it to be."

A Palmyrene cutter captain would know for sure, he thought. The Palmyrenes might be barbarians—blazes, they *were* barbarians!—but they were spacers also, like none in

Daniel's previous acquaintance.

"Yessir," said Cory, though if Daniel read his tone correctly through the vibrating brass rod, the lieutenant wasn't really agreeing. "But, sir? I don't think you're wrong."

Daniel frowned, though his companion couldn't see the expression since they stood side by side. He expected a great deal from his officers—but he didn't expect flattery, and he wouldn't have it.

"Sir," Cory continued, "my dad paves roads. It's what he's done all his life."

"I'd been told that, yes," said Daniel guardedly. According to Adele, Cory's father was the largest paving contractor on Florentine. That made the boy's decision to join the RCN rather than, say, getting a suite in Xenos and chasing women, to be both puzzling and honorable.

"Dad can look at a stretch of concrete once it's had a little while to wear and tell you to a cupful how much cement was in the batch."

Daniel was still frowning. He pursed his lips, then said, "All right, I accept your word on that."

"And that's you out here in the Matrix, sir," Cory said earnestly. "I've watched you, believe me, I have, ever since I was assigned to the *Hermes* when you were First Lieutenant. And I've never known you to be wrong about the Matrix. Maybe you can't say how you know, and maybe you don't even know how yourself—but you *do* know. Sir."

Daniel thought for a moment. At last he said, "Cory, I appreciate your confidence, but I think we'll change the subject."

He coughed and continued, "We won't know for certain

whether we're on the convoy's track until it drops into normal space and we can join it. Or them, whatever we're following. It would be quite possible to make the run from Palmyra to Zenobia in one stage, but I don't expect freighters that're saving on the pay bill by sailing short-crewed to do that. Especially not in convoy. But—"

"Sir, the track stops in P915," Cory interrupted, and a bloody good thing he had. "They've extracted into normal space."

Daniel snapped, "Good man, Cory!" He thrust the communication rod back into its belt sheath, then he lifted the cover from the head of the semaphore pillar, exposing the keyboard. There had to be a way to send messages from the hull to the ship's interior, but Daniel didn't recall having seen the apparatus used more than a half dozen times in his RCN career.

Cory watched in awe as Daniel hammered the pad with his gauntleted fingers. The keys were stiff, as there couldn't be any boost for the strokes for the same reason radios couldn't be used on the hull: an electrical discharge would be trapped by the sails and induce oscillations from the intended course.

That didn't matter. Daniel always pounded when he typed. The fascia plate onto which his console projected its virtual keyboard sounded like a drum set when he was inputting data.

Daniel closed the cover and started for the airlock, gesturing Cory to accompany him. With luck, Vesey would already have extracted the *Sissie* into sidereal space before he reached the bridge. Daniel usually found transition to be an unpleasant or occasionally very unpleasant process, but he didn't think he would notice it this time.

He would be *far* too busy.

* * *

Adele was going over inventories of material unloaded at the Farm when, without warning, Cazelet said, *"Ship, prepare to extract in thirty, repeat three-zero, seconds,"* over both the PA system and the general push.

Adele straightened in surprise. There must have been a—

She checked: yes, Daniel had used the keypad on the hull to order Vesey to enter normal space to intercept another ship or ships. The hydraulic signal was converted into electrical impulses in the *Sissie's* interior, but it had bypassed her normal oversight.

Adele felt as though she had been slapped. She immediately bent to correcting her error.

"Signals, this is Three," said Vesey. *"We'll be extracting into what we believe to be the convoy we're hunting. They may be hostile. Officer Mundy, I want you to handle the communications at your own discretion until Six returns to the bridge, over."*

"Yes," said Adele. "Out."

Well, Vesey's orders gave her something to do other than to worry about getting instant awareness of messages sent through the hydraulic keypad. The first order of business would be to determine the structure of the convoy. If it was simply five freighters—or however many of the original five had navigated well enough to keep station—then there was no problem. If they were accompanied by Palmyrene warships, it became a question of deception or force depending on the strength of the escort.

Adele suddenly understood why Vesey had passed the duty to her. No one could doubt Vesey's competence as an astrogator or shiphandler, and when she inspected the stores you could trust her inventory to the last pulley.

Violence seemed to blind her. Vesey wasn't in any sense a coward: she faced dangers without hesitation, and so long as she could consider battle a matter of moving electronic elements on a display, her attack plans were unexceptionable. Vesey would hesitate before opening fire, however, and her stomach would turn if she had to shout threats at a barbarian who understood no other language.

Adele didn't have that problem. She might balk if duty required her to destroy a Pre-Hiatus book, but as yet that situation hadn't arisen.

While Adele made her preparations, Vesey was alerting Sun and Chazanoff. Not that the gunner and chief missileer wouldn't have been alert: both men regularly set up attacks even when the *Sissie* transitioned into Xenos orbit, just in case.

This time, however, Vesey had cleared Chazanoff to open the doors to the missile launching tubes and told Sun to unlock his guns. Though she would never be a "fighting captain" in the traditional sense, she was working hard to act the part.

"Extracting...now!" a voice said. It was probably Cazelet, but Adele was busy checking her equipment. The *Sissie* had multi-lens laser communicators bow and stern. She made sure that the heads were set to target multiple ships...as of course they were, but she checked anyway.

The *Sissie* dropped into sidereal space. The discomfort affected Adele only in that for a moment her right and left sides seemed reversed. She froze her hands on the wands: better to wait a fraction of a second than to make a mistake that her excellent mind couldn't avoid because it was that mind which was being distorted.

Adele's smile was minute, but real. For an instant she'd felt a flash of resentment that the cosmos would do that to her. She had known Cinnabar nobles who generally reacted that way when things went wrong, but she preferred not to be one herself.

Then the *Princess Cecile* was back in the sidereal universe, and Adele Mundy had new data to collect and collate. If the ship was vaporized in the next instant, she would die content. She told herself that her "content" was what other people meant when they said they were happy. Sometimes she was able to believe herself.

Five transports with Cinnabar registry were grouped closely, the nearest about twelve thousand miles from where the corvette had extracted. The convoy was surprisingly tight for civilian vessels. Either they had been proceeding by very short stages with frequent positioning sights in normal space, or the skill of the Palmyrene astrogators had brought out the best in the Cinnabar officers who competed with them in the Qaboosh. And speaking of Palmyrenes—

Two cutters flanked the convoy like dogs working a herd. In all likelihood both were units of the Horde, but Adele couldn't see anything distinctively naval in their electronic signatures. The sloppiness of the data she'd gathered at the Farm was repeated in spades on vessels whose personnel had no reason even to pretend to be interested in record-keeping.

The visual imagery showed them to be more or less the same as the cutters Adele had seen in harbor on Stahl's World. Both had an exterior pulpit from which to conn the ship;

she knew to look for that because Daniel had spoken of the fittings with such enthusiasm.

And each cutter had a basket of free-flight rockets on the dorsal hull, well ahead of the single ring of antennas. That wasn't ominous in itself—ships were always armed, unless they sailed fixed routes between the most settled stars—but the bundles of external cargo these cutters carried on the after portions of their hulls appeared to be reloads for their launchers.

Still, it would have been surprising if the transports didn't have a Palmyrene escort, and a pair of cutters was a negligible concern. Apparently the Autocrator intended to keep her presence to the background until the troops were on the ground.

What Adele hadn't expected was the last ship present, the armed yacht RCS *Philante*. Because she was an RCN vessel, her particulars flashed onto the display unbidden: 1600 tons, armed with two 4-inch plasma cannon on the dorsal bow and two organ guns on the stern quarters. The latter were aggregations of eight 1-inch plasma cannon, directed energy equivalents of the rockets which vessels on the fringes used against pirates—and for piracy.

The *Philante* was configured for cruising at moderate speeds, escorting merchantmen against pirates. She had a crew of forty and only two mast rings, sufficient to keep up with her charges. She didn't mount missiles and would be only a target if she tried to fight even a small true combat vessel like the *Sissie*.

The problem was that the *Sissie* couldn't fight the yacht. The *Philante* was a Cinnabar naval vessel like the *Sissie*, and to engage it would be treason.

"RCS *Philante*, this is RCS *Princess Cecile*, Captain Leary

301

commanding," Adele said. "Put your commander..."

She paused to check internal communications aboard the yacht, to make sure that the Navy List was correct. It was.

"...Lieutenant Caplan on, over."

The laser communicator would have allowed Adele to call the *Philante* without letting the others eavesdrop on the conversation—well, unless they were a great deal more skilled and technologically sophisticated than Adele thought they were. In this case, however, she *wanted* the Palmyrenes and the civilians alike to know what was going on.

The outer airlock doors released, the *cling* and *whirr* had grown familiar to Adele from frequent repetition. She also heard the rumble of the gun turrets.

Vesey had ordered Sun to unlock his guns from the axial, zero elevation setting in which they travelled, but the gunner was going beyond orders to lay his cannon on the Palmyrene cutters. Adele would have predicted Sun's decision—and under the circumstances, she was in whole-hearted agreement with him.

"This is Caplan," replied the worried voice of Lieutenant Terry Caplan, who surprised Adele by being female. *"Princess Cecile, we are on orders of RCN Station Palmyra. What are you doing here, over?"*

According to Navy House files, RCN Station Palmyra was a room in the Admiralty in Tadmor, the planetary capital. It was simply a liaison office granted by the Autocrator as a courtesy. The *Philante* or a similar ship of the Qaboosh Squadron was usually based in Tadmor Harbor to provide an RCN escort to Cinnabar-flag vessels which requested it.

In the particular instance, the request had probably

come—perhaps indirectly—from the Autocrator herself. The *Philante*'s presence was intended as further proof of Cinnabar support for Irene's capture of Zenobia.

We'll see about that.

"Lieutenant Caplan," Adele said in her usual tone of cold dispassion, "Captain Leary has been sent by Navy House to take charge of this convoy in order to avoid an international incident. You will—"

"Ma'am, the wogs are slewing on us!" Sun shouted on the command channel.

"Open fire!" Adele said with as little hesitation as she showed when a target filled the sights of her pocket pistol.

She would apologize to Vesey as soon as she had an opportunity, but Daniel and a rigging watch were still outside. The corvette's hull could shrug off even the direct hit of an 8-inch rocket, but fragmentation warheads intended to shred sails would turn human beings into cat's meat, even if the victims had been wearing hard suits. Adele wasn't going to let the chain of command lead to that result.

The bow turret fired instantly, a *clang! clang!* from just back of the forward rotunda. The guns themselves were a danger to spacers out on the hull; but not a great danger when firing at high elevation as they were now to track the nearer cutter. Side-scatter from the *Sissie*'s 4-inch weapons was unlikely to injure a spacer who wasn't almost in line with the bore.

The massive 8-inch guns of the *Milton*, the cruiser which Daniel had commanded in the Montserrat Stars, had had a much wider cone of danger. Regardless, this was war and war had risks.

The image of the nearer Palmyrene cutter blurred. The plasma bolts may not have breached the hull, but they detonated the nose fuse of at least one of the rockets. When that warhead exploded, it set off all the others—including the bundles of reloads. The cutter's bow section stayed more or less together, but the stern was reduced to sheet metal with occasional larger chunks, all drifting away in a cloud of the ship's atmosphere.

A half second after Sun fired, the *Sissie* rang again as Rocker, the technician in the BDC striking for gunner's mate, fired the ventral guns at the other cutter. He may initially have been waiting for Vesey to confirm the order, but he followed suit when his chief began shooting.

The second cutter was over 200,000 miles distant, too far for bolts from 4-inch weapons to affect even so lightly built a target. Nonetheless Rocker—joined by Sun as soon as the bow turret could swing onto the new target—continued to fire until the cutter escaped into the Matrix.

The *Philante* disappeared into the Matrix as well. Adele had expected the yacht's captain to demand an explanation, but she must have begun insertion procedures as soon as the shooting started. That showed Lieutenant Caplan to be decisive and furthermore to have good judgment—the *Philante* had no place in a fight against a warship with a full missile armament.

Nonetheless, Adele didn't think Daniel would have decided to run if the positions had been reversed. Nor would any officer serving under Daniel, at least if they hoped to be serving under him in the future.

The inner door of the airlock opened; Daniel stamped from it onto the bridge with Cory behind him. Riggers followed.

Both officers had taken off their helmets before the ship's systems thought the pressure was equalized with that of the interior, but even an experienced spacer required several minutes to get out of a rigging suit. No matter: the control consoles could be adjusted to deal with that eventuality.

Adele added the 20-meter emergency frequency to the *Sissie*'s output. Civilian vessels, especially in a place as distant as the Qaboosh, might not have working laser or microwave suites, but they had to have at least shortwave if they were to receive landing instructions.

"All Cinnabar vessels receiving this message...," she said. Her proper business was communications, not space battles. "Hold your course and do not attempt to enter the Matrix. I repeat, hold your present course and do not attempt to avoid the directions of the duly authorized agent of Admiral Hartsfeld, Chief of the Navy Board."

That was stretching the truth well beyond its breaking point, but the underlying implication was correct: if the civilians tried to flee, they would regret it. Very likely the *Princess Cecile* would open fire, and three or four of the freighters were close enough that plasma bolts would damage their rigging.

Daniel sat down, the plates of his suit clattering against the frame of his console. Before Adele handed off to him, she added, "All Cinnabar ships, respond immediately, over."

"*Unidentified vessel, don't shoot!*" responded the nearest vessel. "*This is* Mary Ann, *cleared from Palmyra to Zenobia. Do not shoot, we are lying to, over!*"

"Adele, keep going!" Daniel said, bellowing to be heard over the piercing buzz of the High Drive. His commo helmet hung from one short arm of the wheel that adjusted his console's relief, but he hadn't taken the time to don it. "I've got course calculations to make!"

The *Birdsong 312* and *Maid of Brancusi* were responding on 15.5 megahertz, the emergency frequency; their communications ran as text on a sidebar to Adele's display. Both captains were falling all over themselves in their public obedience to whatever the corvette ordered.

The cutter's destruction had been spectacular, particularly since most of the civilians would never have seen anything like it. For Adele, as for the other Sissies, it had been a familiar sight. And all the present crew were survivors of the *Milton* when a missile had ripped the cruiser's stern off...

On tight-beam microwave the *Sarah H. Gerdis* replied crisply, "Princess Cecile, *we are lying to as ordered. The ships you have attacked are Palmyrene navy vessels which were escorting this convoy, over.*"

The fifth freighter was the most distant of the lot, straggling a good hundred thousand miles behind the next ahead. It was sending also, but Adele didn't have time to determine the content by an optical enlargement of the vessel's laser head.

"Freighter *Bonaventure*," she said tartly, "switch to shortwave immediately or correct the alignment of your laser communicator. All ships, hold for revised course data which we will transmit to you shortly. Acknowledge this communication, over."

Daniel hadn't exactly said he was refiguring courses for the transports, but that seemed likely. Rather than give fuzzy information, Adele was adding concrete details which would make what she said believable. The civilian captains were certainly confused and probably terrified, but they had to be made to obey the *Princess Cecile* implicitly. Otherwise—

Firing on Palmyrene cutters was an act of war against a nation which was officially a Cinnabar ally. Still, Daniel would get away with that if a court martial resulted—as it might—so long as he could provide proof of Palmyrene intentions. They were, after all, foreigners; and uppity foreigners at that.

Firing on Cinnabar transports was a different matter; especially if one or more of the ships were owned by Senators, as was often the case. There was a great deal of money to be made on the fringes of civilization. The fact attracted investors with the power and connections to get away with cutting corners.

Speaker Leary almost certainly invested in that sort of operation. Adele smiled like a crack in an ice floe. Well, they could probably square him through Deirdre.

"I'm ready!" Daniel shouted, leaning forward to grab his commo helmet. He settled it on his head and, doing so, for the first time adjusted the console so that the bulk of his rigging suit didn't crush him against the virtual keyboard.

"Cinnabar vessels," said Adele, "hold for Captain Leary. Captain Leary, go ahead."

Her job wasn't over, of course: she simply reverted to the data collection which was ordinarily her first priority in a potentially hostile situation. Her equipment was copying information from the transports' databases—mostly logs and course data and not important. It was good to have it against necessity if it were available, however.

Adele frowned, then felt her lips move into a smile of sorts. She assumed anything unfamiliar was potentially hostile. She liked to believe that she was less paranoid than Tovera, who always considered who to kill first—if necessary—when she met a group of people, but in truth mistress and servant shared a similar mindset.

Neither of them was going to change. They were very useful to their associates the way they were; and anyway, they probably couldn't change if they'd wanted to.

"*Fellow spacers,*" said Daniel in a formally friendly tone, "*I regret this inconvenience, but the security of Cinnabar demands it. You were being used by unscrupulous foreigners in a fashion which would certainly have led to your execution as traitors to the Republic.*"

He paused to breathe, but he wasn't giving up his virtual podium. The captain of the *Bonaventure* had adjusted the freighter's sending head, but its packets of coherent light were still missing the *Sissie*'s receptors.

No matter: the civilians had nothing important to say except "Yes, *sir!*" The combination of dire threats coupled with unmistakably lethal force should be sufficient to frighten them into doing just that.

"*I am transmitting course calculations to you,*" Daniel continued, "*now.*"

He hit a virtual key, dispatching the material he'd queued before taking over the communication duties. Adele wondered if the *Bonaventure* would be able to handle the change—any change. In fairness to the captain, the freighter hadn't been so terribly out of position when it arrived at this present stage of the voyage.

"*This will take you to your planned destination, Zenobia,*" Daniel said, "*but in a single transit. The* Princess Cecile *will wait till you're under way, then meet you in Zenobia orbit and give you further instructions. Under no circumstances are you to land on Zenobia or to do any other thing than what I have told you. Please acknowledge your receipt and acceptance of my orders ASAP, over.*"

Three ships responded instantly with versions of "Received and accepted." The *Bonaventure*'s reply was so curt that it could scarcely have been anything else—though the actual message would have to wait for Adele to run the visual imagery through a conversion program.

The captain of the *Gerdis* said, "*Captain Leary, you have no authority over my vessel.*"

"*Break!*" said Daniel. "*Sun, one round and don't hit them, over.*"

The freighter captain was saying, "*My orders come from—*"

"*Roger, Six!*"

"*—the agent from whom I received my contract. It seems to me you're acting more like a pirate than—*"

WHANG!

"*Bloody hell, Leary!*" The civilian's hectoring tone of an instant before had risen to a bleat.

"*Gerdis, I don't have time to argue,*" Daniel said in a voice like an avalanche, "*and neither do you. Either you will accept my orders, or I will launch missiles, and if by some chance you escape them, I will infallibly hunt you down and hang you. I'm a Leary of Bantry, and you have my word on it! Over!*"

"*Received and understood,*" the civilian said. "*Preparing to execute the course change.* Gerdis *out.*"

Daniel gripped the fascia plate of his console for a moment, his eyes closed. When he opened them, he looked toward Adele and grinned. She acknowledged with a nod, but as usual she was watching her friend's image inset onto her display.

"*Ship, this is Six,*" Daniel said over the general push. "*We'll wait till all the transports have gotten under way, then proceed to Zenobia to meet them.*"

He cleared his throat, then continued, "*Now—I won't pretend that it's going to be simple after we extract in the Zenobia System. I expect the Palmyrene forces to keep their distance for the present because the transports won't be able to land if the planetary defenses are alerted. If I'm wrong, we may find the whole Horde waiting for us. We'll deal with the situation as it arises. Up Cinnabar, Sissies!*"

"Up Cinnabar!" rang through the ship. Adele shouted also. This sort of display no longer embarrassed her. Yes, of course it was a tribal bonding ritual—but she was no longer Esme Rolfe Mundy's daughter, she was a valued warrior of her tribe.

She couldn't imagine how Daniel would go about fighting the entire Palmyrene fleet if that was what they found above Zenobia, but she was sure he would try.

And Signals Officer Adele Mundy would be fighting beside him.

CHAPTER 19

ABOVE ZENOBIA

"Extracting in thirty, repeat, three-zero seconds," said Cazelet. Daniel had left Vesey in control of entry into Zenobian space, and she had apparently passed the duty on to the midshipman under her in the Battle Direction Center.

"Extracting!"

Daniel's body jangled excruciatingly, as though all of his bones had shattered and the splinters were migrating outward through his muscles; he felt his breath catch. Then the *Princess Cecile* was in sidereal space, a Plot Position Indicator filled the center of the command display, and the ripping, *blazing* pain was done for the time being.

Each extraction was different. Daniel didn't recall one of what were by now many hundreds which he could describe as pleasant, though many hadn't been really painful. He'd been in the airlock when the *Sissie* dropped onto the Palmyrene convoy; that time he'd felt as though his body had dissolved into soap bubbles which were leaking through the joints of his hard suit. That had been disconcerting but not awful.

He shook himself. *This* time had been awful, but it was over and he had work to do.

The destroyer *Z 46* was in powered orbit around the planet, holding at 1 g to maintain the health of her crew. She was already hailing the *Princess Cecile*. A text crawl across the bottom of Daniel's display read, UNIDENTIFIED VESSEL, THIS IS *AFS Z 46*. STATE YOUR BUSINESS, OVER.

More interesting to Daniel as a tactician was the *Z 42*, the other element of the Fleet's Zenobia detachment. She was in freefall orbit, trailing the outermost of Zenobia's three tiny moons closely enough that vessels with poor sensor suites might not distinguish ship from satellite. Daniel hadn't been aboard a Palmyrene cutter, but similar vessels in the local trade of other regions had poor electronics throughout.

Adele was already speaking forcefully to someone on the other end of her connection, but Daniel knew that only by the way her lips moved. She'd raised the sound-cancelling privacy curtain around her console, and she wasn't copying him on the transmission.

Cory, at the astrogation console, looked groggy from the extraction, but his voice was firm as he said, "Z 46, *this is Cinnabar yacht* Princess Cecile *returning to Zenobia. Please hold for Captain Leary, over.*"

Cory had copied his transmission to Daniel on a two-way link instead of using the command channel to inform the other officers as Adele might have done, but that wasn't so serious a problem that it had to be corrected immediately. Captain von Gleuck *could* be a serious problem. Daniel didn't need close-up imagery to know that both Alliance destroyers were targeting the newcomer with guns and missiles.

"AFS *Z 46*, this is Daniel Leary, over," Daniel said. His voice had the cheerful lilt that came naturally to him. He was juggling a great number of plates, but for the moment they remained in the air.

"*Go ahead, Leary,*" said a different voice through the modulated-laser link. "*This is von Gleuck, over.*"

"Otto...," said Daniel. He'd hoped that von Gleuck himself would be on the circuit—hoped so hard that he could almost say that he'd counted on it. Though if necessary, he would have managed; it was an article of faith with him that he would manage. "Very shortly there'll be five Cinnabar freighters—"

A red caret pulsed on the PPI at a point 280,000 miles from Zenobia. Nothing was at that place now. Vesey had highlighted the disruption in sidereal space-time which indicated that a vessel was preparing to extract from the Matrix there.

"—arriving, and I think one is doing so as we speak. I ask you as the senior Alliance officer present to allow these ships to land on Zenobia under my supervision. You have my word that this course will have the best long-term result for the continuance of the present friendship between our nations. Ah—and for the independence of Zenobia also, though that isn't my primary concern at present. Leary over."

The problem—which Autocrator Irene had very carefully contrived—was the transports. While the troops aboard them were clearly hostile and could be dealt with as violently as von Gleuck pleased, the hulls and at least some of the ships' officers were entitled to the protection of the Republic of Cinnabar.

There had been Senators, and there were many Cinnabar citizens, who opposed the Treaty of Rheims. The destruction of Cinnabar ships and lives would almost certainly reignite the war.

There was a noticeable silence, during which the caret on the display became a blip bearing the legend *Sarah H. Gerdis*. Someone aboard the Z 46 hailed the transport: the signals officer, most likely, operating on the instructions he'd received when the destroyer took station.

Cory would have done the same. Adele, however, would have been auditing the captains' discussion and might have let the challenge wait.

But Adele was otherwise occupied. Well, whatever she was doing was in the best interests of the Republic; and in this case, probably the best interests of the Alliance as well.

"*Captain Leary,*" von Gleuck said at last. "*I trust you, and I'm going to act on that trust. If I'm mistaken, I hope my ghost drags you down to Hell, because I don't expect my body to survive this afternoon. Z 46 out.*"

"Leary out," said Daniel. "Break. *Gerdis*, this is *Princess Cecile*. Acknowledge, over.*"

"*Princess Cecile, this is Cinnabar vessel* Sarah H. Gerdis," said the freighter's captain in a tone of tightly controlled anger. "*We have carried out your illegal instructions to the letter. Are we clear to land, over?*"

Daniel grinned despite the situation. The captain of the *Gerdis* had balls, and he and his crew were surprisingly able to have arrived so soon after the *Sissie*. Granted, Daniel had remained almost four additional hours at the way point until the *Bonaventure* finally got under way; but even so, a civilian vessel's economically small crew simply couldn't shave minutes in the Matrix by taking advantage of minute variations in the gradients between universes.

I'll buy him a drink after this is all over and done with, Daniel thought, grinning even wider. *Assuming, of course.*

Aloud he said, "*Gerdis*, I am transmitting landing instructions which you need to follow. If you attempt to land in Calvary Harbor, you'll probably be destroyed by an anti-ship missile. If you try to land anywhere else on the planet save the point I have marked, *I* will destroy you. Acknowledge, over."

"*Acknowledged,* Princess Cecile," the captain of the *Gerdis* said. He didn't bluster or threaten at this point, but Daniel had no doubt that he was framing a blistering complaint to his putative employer, to be passed on to the figures who used that employer to insulate their noble selves from any shady deals in which the freighter could be proved to have been involved.

A moment later, the *Gerdis* added, "*Coordinates received. We will transit into close orbit, then brake for a landing as ordered.* Gerdis *out.*"

"*Princess Cecile* out," Daniel said mildly. The freighter's distance from Zenobia made it reasonable to reenter the Matrix, but the captain was making a point by not asking for permission. Daniel had matured enough—and had enough real power—that he could view dominance games by weaker men with amusement, but the fellow was pressing his luck.

Daniel took a deep breath. Vesey was careting another point in empty space; somewhat farther out than the *Gerdis* had managed, but not bad. Thus far matters were proceeding quite well. Assuming, of course, that the caret was a Cinnabar transport and not the *Piri Reis*.

Daniel chuckled; he had a few seconds, after all. He keyed his transmitter with, "Z 46, this is *Princess Cecile*. Otto, I assure you that if things don't go as I intend, your spirit won't have to search far to find mine. Leary out."

The freighter *Mary Ann* coalesced into sidereal space, filling the caret. *So far, so good.*

"Extracting in thirty, repeat, three-zero seconds," said Cazelet on the general frequency. Adele continued to sort her data. The way she presented it depended to a certain degree on the situation on the ground in Calvary.

"I'm ready, mistress!" Cory said on a two-way link.

Of course you're ready! Adele thought. *If I'd had the slightest doubt of that, I wouldn't have directed you to handle ordinary communications duties after we extracted.*

"Yes," she said aloud.

Much depended on where Posy Belisande and her brother were. The Founder Hergo probably wouldn't accept Adele's unsupported word, but Posy on the other hand—

Extracting, a voice was saying, but Adele had suddenly become a block of clear ice. She stood beside herself, seeing light passing through her body and refracting from tiny cracks and impurities.

What does the process of returning to normal space do to my brain that causes these illusions? Or—are they illusions?

Adele was back in her own skin. She no longer had time for philosophy—because that's all it really was, philosophy.

Philosophy was never a useful occupation for someone who was concerned with objective reality.

The *Princess Cecile* had extracted 127,000 miles out from Zenobia. The High Drive had kicked in as usual, to counterfeit gravity. In addition, the corvette retained its velocity from when it had most recently left sidereal space, the way point where they met the transports.

If Adele linked directly, she took the risk of being cut off by orbital motion or planetary rotation. She instead used the circuit she had prepared in Zenobia's constellation of communications satellites.

It made her feel smug, though that fact irritated her and intellectually she knew it wasn't warranted. Many people wouldn't have been ready for the present situation—but that was because they were fools who hadn't done the obvious, not because Adele Mundy had anything to boast of.

Lieutenant Commander von Gleuck had overseen the laying of a fiber-optics line between the console in his quarters in the Fleet Reservation and Lady Belisande's bedroom in the palace. The dedicated line couldn't be tapped, but Adele could—and had—entered the public levels of the console itself. She called through it while her wands located the other people on her list.

"*Yes?*" Posy said breathlessly. "*Otto, what is it? Are you all right?*"

Adele blinked. She had rather expected a long wait. Either she had been very lucky, or Posy was camped on her terminal.

"Lady Belisande," Adele said, "this is Adele Mundy. Lieutenant Commander von Gleuck is all right at present, though I expect there will shortly be a battle which he may not survive."

It struck her that she was being overly precise for most people's taste and that she was potentially confusing people who read too much into her flat statements of fact. Which was almost everyone she had met. Well, it was too late for her to change.

"The *Princess Cecile* will be aiding his ships in battle, of course, and we may not survive either," she said. "In case all goes well, Otto will want you safe to greet him. That's what I'm trying to achieve now. Please listen to me."

"I'm listening, Adele," Posy said. Her voice was even higher than it had been when she first answered the call, but it was controlled. *She* was controlled. Adele's tentative good opinion of the woman was being borne out.

"The Autocrator Irene is preparing a coup against Zenobia," Adele said. "The allied Alliance-Cinnabar squadron will deal with external threats to the degree possible, but there is already a Palmyrene infrastructure on Zenobia, a combination of traitors and Palmyrene agents. If that infrastructure is removed, I don't believe the coup can succeed regardless of what happens above the planet."

"Yes," said Posy. *"What do you want me to do?"*

"I want you to go immediately to your brother," Adele said. "He's in his office on the ground floor now. Tell him to confirm to anyone who calls him the orders I will have given, pretending to be you. I'm going to call various security personnel. It simply isn't practical in the time available to give you the information and have you pass it on."

"Yes," said Posy. *"Otto had suggested that we should be ready for trouble, but he didn't give us details. Hergo has put*

the Founder's Regiment on alert and told the captains of the militia companies to be on call, but he didn't want to cause a panic without more information."

She cleared her throat. *"Shall I go to Hergo now?"*

Without knowing anything whatever about the woman who had replaced this one in Porra's bed, Adele was quite sure that he had made a bad bargain. Men had different priorities, of course; but even there the Guarantor was unlikely to have shown good judgment.

"Yes," said Adele aloud. "I'll contact you in the Founder's Office if necessary. And if you would, please don't get separated from your maid."

Posy laughed. *"Never fear, Adele,"* she said. *"Wood is very much of the same opinion. Dear, you've actually made her smile!"*

Adele could imagine the smile. She'd seen it on Tovera's face often enough; and sometimes in the mirror.

"Yes," she said. "See your brother at once."

Without bothering about polite closings, Adele broke the connection and chose the next name from her list: the Honorable Jan Belisande, Marshal of Zenobia. He was by background a wealthy banker with no military experience whatever.

Adele could not have chosen a better man to head the planetary militia—the Forces of Zenobia—in the present crisis, though: Marshal Belisande was Hergo's first cousin. He would certainly be executed by the new regime if the coup succeeded, and he ought to be smart enough to know that.

"Jan," Adele said, "this is Posy. There's an emergency. I'm calling you for my brother."

She had listened to conversations between the cousins; they

were on terms of informal friendship though not intimacy. Rather than try to counterfeit Posy's voice—Adele's skills as a mimic weren't up to that—she subjected the transmission to severe compression so that her gender was all that came through to the person on the other end.

"Posy?" the Marshal said. *"I didn't know you had access to this line. How did you get this line?"*

"Jan, I'm calling for my brother!" Adele said. Despite his business success, Cousin Jan wasn't raising the family's intellectual average. "You must mobilize the entire militia, the Forces, immediately. The Palmyrenes are planning to invade. And—"

"What! What!" the Marshal said. *"The Palmyrenes are invading? Is that what Hergo meant when he told me to have my officers available for summons? Why didn't he say it was the Palmyrenes?"*

Biting off a series of comments that wouldn't have been in the least helpful, Adele said in calm, measured tones, "Do you have any troops already mobilized?"

"Well, yes," said the Marshal. *"I thought after talking to Hergo that as a, well, training exercise I'd stand to the First Company of Calvary District E. They're assembled at their muster point right now."*

Adele had noted the militia muster points as a matter of course. She superimposed them on her current display, a schematic of the city with a caret at the location where her call was being received. It was too obvious even to bring a smile that the muster point for Company E1 was the courtyard of Jan Belisande's townhouse.

"Wonderful!" Adele said with false heartiness. "Bring

them here to the Palace immediately. If you're not here in ten minutes, it may be too late."

"But!" said the Marshal. *"But Posy, you have the Founder's Regiment! What will happen to my house if I abandon it?"*

"Jan, we're facing a Palmyrene coup!" Adele said. "If you don't get your troops over here immediately, the only thing you'll own is six feet of dirt—and that's if the Autocrator bothers to bury you! Do you understand?"

"I—" the Marshal said. *"I..."* Then, *"I'm coming at once. But you have to tell me what's going on!"*

"As soon as you get here, Jan," Adele said soothingly. She broke the connection. She had much more to do, but for a moment she put down her wands and rubbed her temples with her fingertips.

It took conscious effort for Adele to raise her voice. She would have found it much easier to draw her pistol and shoot Marshal Belisande...though of course she wouldn't have done that even if they'd been facing one another across the table.

Not without greater provocation, at least. Somewhat greater provocation.

The trouble, the thing that brought Adele so often to the brink of cold fury, was that people didn't listen to what she was saying unless she shouted at them. They reacted to tone, not substance, like so many infants to whom words meant nothing.

The statement, "You will die unless you do this thing," would be ignored or disputed if one—if Adele Mundy—said it in a calm, logical voice. Screaming was more effective than waving a pistol.

The human race couldn't be wrong: this was the way the

species had evolved over hundreds of thousands of years. But it certainly proved that Adele herself was of a different species, though deceptively human in her physical appearance.

She sighed and picked up her wands. Oh—and one further thing.

"Rene, this is Adele," she said to Midshipman Cazelet. "I need you to check on a militia unit, E1. It should be moving shortly from its muster point to the Founder's Palace. If it isn't doing so in ten minutes, tell me and discuss the matter again with Marshal Belisande. The captain's call sign is—"

"*I have it, mistress,*" Cazelet replied from the BDC. "*And if necessary, I'll try to put the fear of god into them before I bother you. Out.*"

I should probably have cleared that with Daniel; or perhaps with Vesey. Well, another time. She called the next name: Major Aubrey Flecker, commander of the Founder's Regiment.

Flecker had been a captain in the Grand Army of the Stars, but he had resigned his commission after being discovered in intimate contact with the twelve-year-old daughter of his commanding officer.

Knowing Flecker's background didn't make Adele warm to him, but he appeared to have been extremely able professionally. The Founder was willing to use him, so Adele was forced to do so.

She smiled minusculely. And there was always the chance Flecker would be killed in the near future. That was reason for hope.

"*Flecker,*" said the voice on the other end of the connection. He didn't shout, but he spoke with the authority of a man used to being heard and obeyed. *"Is this Lady Mundy, over?"*

Well, that's unexpected. "This is Officer Mundy, yes," Adele said. "Have you spoken with Lady Belisande, Major?"

"I'm in the Situation Room with her and the Founder, Your Ladyship," Flecker said. *"The Founder has ordered me to take your orders as though they were his own. Go ahead, over."*

Adele wondered if Posy was holding a gun on her brother. Though she would probably have delegated that sort of duty to Wood.

"I have Marshal Belisande on the way to the Palace with his company of the Forces," Adele said without preamble. She smiled slightly as she wondered whether her musing had been entirely a joke. "While I don't imagine a company of militia will be what you or I consider an efficient military unit, they should be at least equal to anyone who might attack the Palace in the immediate future."

"Your Ladyship, I've got my whole unit under arms," Flecker said, sounding more distressed than angry at what he took to be an insult. *"Believe me, we don't need a hundred and fifty armed civilians running around to keep the Founder safe. Ah, begging your pardon, over."*

"Yes," said Adele, "but *I* need your troops for more important purposes than sitting on their hands until somebody's ready to attack them. I'm transmitting a list—"

Her wands moved, sending the data not only to the Situation Room—what had been the conference room of Flecker's suite in the Palace—but also to the console in the Founder's suite. She didn't mistrust Flecker, but she had decided it was best to give Hergo the option of following up with the militia in case something went wrong with the professional response.

Neither computer was secure or anything close to secure; Adele could only hope that the plotters were as inept at communications intelligence as the security forces were. Regardless, the information would be unimportant in a few hours, one way or the other.

"—of forty-one names and the subjects' present locations where I have them. In all cases I'm attaching their home and business addresses. When the subjects have guards or employees who are likely to be armed, I'm attaching that information as well. You are to oversee the arrest of all these persons and all persons who are with them at the time of arrest, whether or not the additional parties are on the list."

Adele paused. She could hear Flecker speaking to someone in the room with him, then a response. Flecker said, *"The information has been received, Your Ladyship. Ah—Marshal Belisande has called, saying that he'll be arriving in a few minutes with his troops, as you said. Over."*

"Yes," said Adele. She felt considerable relief that Marshal Belisande really had gotten his militia company moving. *She* wasn't concerned about Palace security—Wood alone could probably handle anything that the plotters, reacting in panic, were able to attempt—but she'd been afraid that Hergo wouldn't release his professionals to the real work unless he had someone close by to hold his hand.

Mind, Posy had thus far proved very convincing.

"Also send a squad to Cinnabar House and escort the Commissioner and his family to the Palace," Adele said. The Browns were completely neutral in what was going on, but in a coup attempt there was simply no safety except being in the midst of a military force. "I'll warn them to expect you."

"All right," Flecker said. *"Anything else, over?"*

"Major," Adele said, "I won't tell you your job, but make sure you use sufficient troops for each pickup. There are several Councillors on the list who will have a squad of personal guards, and the employees of the Palmyrene business people listed will very likely include military personnel who are prepared to act as a fifth column in Calvary."

Flecker snorted. *"Thank you, Your Ladyship,"* he said, *"but I figure my people can handle a bunch of monkeys, even if the monkeys think they're soldiers. Privates in this regiment are paid at the rate of non-coms in Alliance service, and I trained 'em so they earn their money. Can we get on with it now, over?"*

Adele smiled coldly. It was a pleasure dealing with professionals, even if you didn't particularly like them as human beings.

"One further matter, Major Flecker," she said. "It may be that you won't be able to capture some of your targets alive. In that case you are to kill them, using such force as is necessary. If you blow up the building they're in, at the very worst they won't dig out in time to be a factor in the coup attempt. Do you understand?"

"Bloody hell!" Flecker said. *"I heard you were a hard bitch, and they weren't kidding, were they?"*

Adele's faint smile spread a trifle wider. She said, "I've told you your duties, Major Flecker. All you need do is carry them out. You can be quite sure that I will carry out mine. Good day, sir!"

She broke the connection, then set up the call to Cinnabar

House. Not only would the Browns be safer in the Palace, they were also evidence of Cinnabar good faith. If the Belisandes and von Gleuck didn't have doubts about the game she and Daniel were playing, they were fools.

Adele thought about Flecker saying she was—accusing her of being—hard. Well, perhaps so, but counter-coup activities were a hard business on which she was an expert. After all, she'd studied every detail of how Speaker Leary had crushed the Three Circles Conspiracy, right down to where the heads of her parents and sister had been nailed on Speaker's Rock.

"This is Commissioner Brown," her console said. Then, *"Who is there, please? This is the Cinnabar Commission?"*

Adele returned from ancient murders to her present business. Of murder.

CHAPTER 20

ABOVE ZENOBIA

Daniel watched with satisfaction as the *Maid of Brancusi* dropped toward the surface of Zenobia. Plasma wreathed the hull as her thrusters cut in some thirty seconds before he would have expected. Though—

It didn't really matter, but the question had piqued his curiosity. Daniel called up the imagery which the *Sissie* had gathered as a matter of course on all five transports at the waypoint. There was quite a good view of the *Maid*'s underside. Magnified, it showed that only four remained of the six High Drive motors that the transport had been fitted with in the builders' yard—and they appeared ratty even at a distance.

A High Drive's exhaust spewed out a certain amount of antimatter which hadn't recombined within the motor. In an atmosphere, the explosive cancellation of waste particles ate away the High Drive itself. A captain ordinarily was willing to accept the minor erosion that would occur down to twenty miles above a habitable planet, because the output of the High

Drive was greater and much more efficient than that of the plasma thrusters.

The *Maid*'s captain must have decided to nurse his motors. Daniel suspected that he was right to make that decision—assuming, of course, that his thrusters weren't in equally marginal condition.

"Sir?" said Cory, who had been doing an exemplary job as signals officer. *"If I may ask—are you going to put all five transports down on Diamond Cay, over?"*

Daniel glanced toward the astrogation console. Lieutenant Cory smiled—but toward Daniel's image on his display, not at the man himself a few feet away. *He's aping Adele...but all right, that's perfectly proper behavior in a signals officer.*

"Yes, that's right, Cory," Daniel said. "I've directed the captains to dump their reaction mass as soon as they're on the ground. That won't harm the ships, but it'll take a number of hours before they can even think of lifting again. The troops can't walk anywhere, and even if they have a few vehicles aboard, the Green Ocean will stop anything but aircars. You couldn't ferry a couple thousand troops with all the aircars available in the Qaboosh Region. Over."

"Yessir," said Cory. *"But, ah, sir? The buildings on Diamond Cay are really unusual, aren't they, over?"*

"They're unique, so far as I know," Daniel agreed. He grinned. "And I know what Officer Mundy has told me, which I suspect means I have all information available in the human universe."

He paused, going back for a moment to the pleasure he'd taken in the material Adele had provided when they returned from Diamond Cay. "That crystal castle is certainly Pre-

Hiatus," he said, "but it seems to me—from negative evidence, I'll admit—that it's pre-settlement and probably a long time pre-settlement. The biota of the island, including the shallows around it, isn't natural to Zenobia, you see, and it certainly wasn't introduced recently. Perhaps when this is over, I'll have some time to explore it in a less, ah, directed fashion. Over."

Daniel wasn't really an antiquarian, but oddities interested him: things that weren't where or what they should be. The building on Diamond Cay was that, and the biota was that in spades. The seadragons weren't unnatural—they, the pin crabs, and the vegetation the crabs ate were a seamless whole and quite ordinary.

But not ordinary for Zenobia. The fact that Adele hadn't been able to locate the planet from which the creatures were introduced didn't prove anything, but it certainly suggested a considerable distance in time or space from the planet today. It was a fascinating problem, and one which was unlikely to be solved in Daniel's lifetime.

"But that's what I mean, sir," Cory said. *"Those transports are landing on an unprepared surface without ground control. Frankly, there's a couple of them that I wouldn't trust to land in Harbor Three without screwing up, as bad as their commo suites are."*

He paused to clear his throat and perhaps to order his next words. Daniel was smiling. Cory was being more than a little unfair to the freighters' captains: communications equipment was—properly—a good ways down the list of a civilian owner's concerns. But the standard of maintenance of the drives and the rigging of these ships wasn't up to what Daniel considered reasonable standards either, save for the *Sarah H. Gerdis*.

"Sir, what if one of them crashes right on top of the castle?" Cory blurted. *"Crashes or lands—the thermal shock from the thrusters would be as bad as the kinetic shock of just dropping, I suspect. The whole thing will be destroyed! Over."*

Daniel's smile faded. Cory was a good man and a good officer; he deserved an answer.

"Right, that's a risk," Daniel said, "though not a great one. I was familiar with Diamond Cay and knew that it was suitable for my purposes—that is, to isolate the invasion force in safe if not particularly congenial surroundings."

Another caret appeared on the PPI, this one trailing the planet by 330,000 miles. That was at the edge of the volume included in Daniel's display, though he'd set the console to alert him to ships arriving anywhere within a light-year of Zenobia's star.

"And you see, Cory," he continued, "I'm an RCN officer first. I will regret it if a transport destroys the castle, but I'll regret the loss of several hundred lives even more than the loss of the building, and I'll consider them acceptable also. We're in a war, or we will be if things continue to go in the direction they're headed at present. Things get broken, people die."

The red caret became the dot of a ship with the legend BONAVENTURE. She hadn't been the last to arrive after all, though the distance she extracted from the target point of the course Daniel had given her was marginal at best.

"Cory out," said the acting signals officer. *"Break. CS* Bonaventure, *this is RCS* Princess Cecile. *Acknowledge on this frequency, over."*

Daniel felt his smile returning. Cory was hailing the freighter on 15.5 MHz; twenty meters was the only shortwave band on which the *Bonaventure* seemed able to receive and respond. Cory did have a point about the freighters' wretched commo gear.

Vesey placed another caret in the PPI. If this was the missing *Birdsong 312*, then the initial problem—the safety of the Zenobian government—was solved. The troops on Diamond Cay could be disarmed and sequestered at leisure by the planetary forces. The Horde might not even enter the Zenobia system since ships in orbit couldn't affect the situation on the surface.

The caret resolved to a point. The legend read 114G2929L, a responder code rather than a real name.

The ship probably didn't have a proper name: it was a Palmyrene cutter. The dozen carets appearing all around it were almost certainly more of the same. The Horde had arrived, summoned by the escort which had escaped when the *Sissie* captured the convoy.

UNIDENTIFIED VESSEL, read the crawl at the bottom of Daniel's display, THIS IS *AFS Z 46*. STATE YOUR BUSINESS, OVER.

Von Gleuck was quite properly taking charge of the situation. He was the senior naval officer on station, dealing with an incursion of hostile warships.

Adele finished downloading a blind file containing full details on the Farm's defenses and personnel to the Founder and Major Flecker. In three hours the file would open with bells and flashing lights on both consoles.

The delay was to prevent either man from deciding to make

the Farm the first priority. The Palmyrene base was of minor importance so long as the troops it was meant to serve were sitting in a swamp a thousand miles away, but civilians and tactical officers like Flecker might see the situation less clearly than Adele did.

The enemy already within Calvary was the real danger. Thanks to Resident Tilton's behavior, there was enough popular discontent that riots might sweep out the Founder and his Alliance masters even without the help of foreign troops.

Tilton would remain as a serious problem, for the Belisandes and for the Alliance both. So long as Cinnabar couldn't be linked to the trouble, that was none of Adele's business.

She might be tempted to arrange an accident when the *Princess Cecile* returned to Calvary Harbor, however. The city would be in chaos, even if Major Flecker's arrest teams had had no more trouble than they could solve with small arms. Almost anything which happened under those conditions could be blamed on the coup plotters.

But that was for after the present business was concluded, and it required that the *Sissie* and those aboard her—Hogg would probably be the choice to cause Tilton's accident—survive until then. Survival was therefore the next item on Adele's list.

Using a single laser lens and copying Cory and Cazelet, Adele said, "*Princess Cecile* to Alliance squadron commander, over."

Cory or Cazelet might have to replace her as signals officer. Ordinarily the crew of a ship as small as a corvette would live or die together in battle, but a freak chance might take Adele and not one of the male officers.

Adele didn't inform Daniel, even with a text crawl on his display, because he neither knew nor cared how his signals went out. Adele appreciated the fact that though Daniel had a tendency to be his own missileer and gunner, he never tried to second guess her decisions about commo.

A voice that was male but not von Gleuck's replied almost immediately, "Princess Cecile, *this is* Z 46. *How do you come to use this code, over?*"

Adele smiled with chilly pleasure. Competence pleased her, even competence in an enemy; and she supposed she shouldn't think of the Alliance as "the enemy" for at least the time being.

"Z 46," she said, "I cannot vouch for the security procedures of RCN vessels based at Palmyra; therefore I must assume that the Horde can read any signals passed using RCN codes. I suggest that signals between the *Princess Cecile* and Alliance vessels be sent using this obsolete Alliance code. Even though it's outdated, I believe it will be safe from Palmyrene interception, over."

"Hold one, *Princess Cecile*," said the Alliance signals officer. He sounded as though he'd been kicked in the stomach.

Adele's smile quirked slightly wider at the thought. *As well he might.*

She had been careful to refer to the code as obsolete, but it had in fact been the Fleet's active code three months before. Though it had been superseded, the signals officer of the *Z* 46—and his superiors in Pleasaunce—probably thought it was still good.

The Alliance battleship *Oldenburg* had been so badly hammered in the Battle of Cacique that the automatic systems which were supposed to destroy the code generator had failed, and the entire bridge crew was killed. RCN technicians sifting through the wreckage had found the generator, and Mistress Sand's specialists were able to bring it back on line.

The information remained closely held, even in Mistress Sand's organization. Adele was using it now because secure communications among the three warships was absolutely necessary if any of them were to survive. Even so, she knew that some—perhaps including Mistress Sand—would fault her for disclosing it.

The saving grace of Adele's action was that in all likelihood, the *Princess Cecile* and the Alliance ships would be destroyed anyway. In that case, the secret would remain safe.

"Princess Cecile, *this is von Gleuck,*" said a different male voice. *"Am I speaking to Lady Mundy, over?"*

Adele grimaced. "This is Officer Mundy, Lieutenant Commander," she said in a consciously withdrawn voice. "Over."

"I've directed my command to use the code set which you recommend, Lady Mundy," von Gleuck said. *"I felt it necessary to assure myself that the* Princess Cecile's *operator would be able to handle the non-standard procedure. Your presence, which I was not willing to assume, of course convinces me. Von Gleuck out."*

Lady Mundy indeed. He's determined to make his point— stiff-necked aristocrat that he is. Adele's frown bent into a wry smile. *And it takes one to know one, I believe the phrase is.*

She went back to work, analyzing the internal communications of the Alliance destroyers. They were friends and indeed allies at present, but circumstances change.

And anyway, Adele didn't want to die with the regret of having twiddled her thumbs while there was information she could have gathered and collated.

CHAPTER 21

ABOVE ZENOBIA

Daniel's lips pursed: the first Palmyrene cutter appeared some hundred and ten thousand miles from Zenobia, though on the opposite side of the planet from where the *Sissie* was orbiting. That would be very good astrogation for an initial extraction after a voyage of probably fifty light-years or more.

Except that it probably wasn't astrogation but rather pilotage. The Palmyrene captain had sailed to the Zenobia system—a planetary system was a large target, even using what was by Cinnabar standards a very rudimentary computer—and then felt his way inward to Zenobia itself.

It was no accident that the cutter extracted only two thousand miles above Zenobia's second moon, an irregular lump of rock no more than fifty miles in diameter on any axis. Slight as it was, the moon cast its shadow into the Matrix. The cutter's captain had used that as his target.

Even a judge friendly to the Palmyrenes would have admitted that a single vessel appearing in that fashion could be chance. Three more cutters followed almost immediately, none of them more than a hundred miles out from any of her fellows. That was beyond chance, and far beyond the skill of any spacers whom Daniel had ever heard of.

Von Gleuck repeated his challenge. The Z 42 was holding station against the third moon silently, but Daniel no longer thought that the destroyer might go unnoticed. The Palmyrenes were barbarous, certainly, but the forces of civilization had nothing to teach them about sidereal space or the Matrix, either one.

"They're signalling to one another with handheld laser communicators," Adele said on the command channel. *"I can't read the messages—they appear to be in clear, but I'm only able to pick up fragments because the power is so low; the beams don't scatter from the hulls brightly enough for even our optics to pick up. They appear to be discussing a rendezvous—"*

The first cutter slipped back into the Matrix. Her three companions withdrew moments later, in perfect unison as they had appeared.

"Yes," said Adele in satisfaction. *"I believe they're meeting the Autocrator."*

As an obvious afterthought, she added, *"Over."*

"Gleuck to Leary," said the command console. Cory—or had Adele resumed commo duties?—was passing the signal directly through instead of querying Daniel or converting it to text. *"How do you interpret the Monkeys' withdrawal, over?"*

"Leary to Gleuck," Daniel replied, grinning. *Should I refer to our Cinnabar allies as "Palmyrenes," or should I say "Wogs" to demonstrate solidarity with an officer who will shortly be my brother in arms?* "My staff informs me that the leading cutters discussed joining the Autocrator Irene, who will make the decision about further proceedings. You know the Palmyrenes and the Autocrator better than I do, but I personally doubt that the lady will choose to withdraw at this stage, over."

"*Roger, Leary,*" von Gleuck said. "*Break. All Force Posy elements—*"

Finessing the question of what elements those were and where they were located.

"*—you are free to engage interloping Palmyrene warships at will with gunfire, but do not, repeat, do not, launch missiles until I give specific orders. Cinc Posy out.*"

Daniel grinned again. *Does Lady Belisande know that her gallant is going into battle waving her name like a banner?* Well, with luck, there would be someone around to tell her about it after things quieted down.

The frame of Daniel's PPI pulsed orange, then settled to a thin haze that brightened to the upper right of the display. He expanded the image volume, letting it find its own boundaries which would include the ships that had just appeared.

The *Piri Reis* with seven, then twenty, and finally thirty-one cutters had extracted forty light-minutes out from Zenobia's sun. The cruiser was about the same distance from Zenobia itself. Daniel frowned, wondering why in heaven the Palmyrene fleet was appearing *there*.

When he switched the region to a cartouche in the lower right corner of his display, then increased the scale, he understood. A large comet was inbound from the cloud of debris orbiting a light-year out from the sun. The *Piri Reis* had extracted near the comet, and the cutters had formed on the cruiser.

Text at the bottom of the display told Daniel that von Gleuck was ordering the *Z 42* to clear for action, stripping the ship to a minimum sail plan to give the guns better fields of fire. Missiles could be launched regardless of the rig: they were kicked straight out by a jet of steam and didn't light their High Drives until they were well clear of the vessel, whereupon their internal computer guided them on a preset course.

A plasma cannon, however, firing at maximum rate as it followed an incoming missile, could easily traverse into a sail or even an antenna which the bolt would destroy in a fireball. Worse than the direct damage was the risk that the missile would proceed unhindered into the ship which had wasted her defensive efforts on her own rigging.

Daniel wondered briefly that the Alliance signals were appearing in real time on his console. He had expected von Gleuck to be somewhat more circumspect in his dealings with an RCN corvette.

Regardless of the implied comradeship, Daniel didn't intend to step on Alliance toes in a situation as fraught as this one. "Leary to von Gleuck," he said, making it clear that he was speaking man to man. "Commodore, I ask your leave to approach the Palmyrene squadron in an effort to calm this business down, over."

"*Posy Cinc to* Princess Cecile," von Gleuck said after a moment. "*As Alliance commander in the system, I will not interfere with the movements of neutral vessels sailing under civilian registry.*"

He cleared his throat and added, *"Speaking as a friend, however, Leary—it's not worth getting yourself killed trying to deal with Monkeys. I recommend that you take yourself to Stahl's World as quickly as possible and inform your superiors of the situation. Gleuck out."*

"Leary out," Daniel said, letting his brief pique melt under the realization that Otto didn't really expect him to run away from a fight. It was just the proper thing to say under the circumstances, so—being a gentleman in all senses of the term—Otto had said it. "Break. Ship, prepare to insert in thirty seconds, out."

He'd already programmed a course to the Palmyrene fleet. Another handful of cutters had joined those already around the *Piri Reis*. A second large vessel, the destroyer *Turgut*, had appeared about 80,000 miles outsystem of the cruiser.

Relative to the cutters, the *Turgut* had the same disadvantage as the *Princess Cecile* did: it couldn't be conned from the hull. Even so, Daniel hoped he could maneuver more accurately than the destroyer had done. Furthermore, he was pretty sure that Admiral Polowitz would have something to say to the *Turgut*'s captain. Palmyra being the sort of place it was, the word "beheading" might appear in the conversation.

"Inserting," Daniel said as he sent the *Sissie* into the Matrix by rolling a vernier beneath his thumb. Light crinkled, faded, and briefly broke into polarized sheets across which Daniel tried to look sideways. Then the corvette was a universe of her own again, sailing past and through an infinity of other bubble universes.

Most captains simply pressed the Execute button after they

had set up the insertion. The console then brought the ship's charge into balance with the Matrix, squeezing the vessel out of sidereal space. Extraction involved the same process, in reverse.

Daniel had begun to believe that entering and leaving the Matrix were as capable of refinement as astrogation itself: that the right human touch could make the process smoother and impose less strain on the vessel as well as those aboard her. For the past year he'd been experimenting with a dial control instead of letting the computer drop the ship like the trap door beneath a gallows.

He chuckled as he advanced the vernier against a pressure which might be only in his mind. He felt a white-hot microtome slice from his scalp toward his heels at precisely the same rate as the dial moved.

Daniel knew that in his heart he wanted control of every aspect of the *Sissie*'s movements among the stars. Not because he could do it better than the computer could—not entirely, at least. He wanted to *own* the stars rather than merely traverse them like other spacers.

Which was silly and arrogant and various other reprehensible things, he supposed, but by the gods! he loved what he did, and he loved what he felt when he rode the cosmos aboard a ship of his own. RCN officers and indeed spacers generally were expected to be eccentric. Captain Daniel Leary's eccentricity made him better at his job, so nobody was going to complain.

Daniel's muscles quivered. Though the blazing pain of insertion had been entirely mental, his brain had transferred the impulses to the portions of his body which had seemed to be affected, and they in turn had responded.

The ship creaked as her antennas rotated, sliding the corvette along her programmed course. Daniel couldn't be out on the hull to finesse the transit, but over such a short distance even the captain of a tramp freighter should be able to arrive within a thousand miles of his intention.

When the *Sissie* extracted, Daniel would try to prevent a war. He didn't expect to succeed, but he had to try.

And he very much hoped that he and the *Princess Cecile* would survive the attempt.

Daniel was saying—or perhaps he had said it and the word was echoing in her mind?—"*Extracting*," but Adele felt as though she were slipping into a vat of ointment. Her thoughts seemed greasy and faintly astringent, and they smelled of crushed aloes.

Then the *Princess Cecile* was in normal space again. Adele's console was alive with fresh inputs, and her momentary bout of synesthesia was over.

It felt different every time she entered or left the Matrix. Adele sometimes thought of entering the particulars of each transition so that she could correlate them at leisure and see whether there was a pattern. She had never done so, because she didn't remember the details if she waited even as much as a few minutes after an extraction. As a general rule she had something extremely important to do in those initial minutes.

Certainly she had important duties now.

The *Princess Cecile* had returned to sidereal space some two hundred and ninety-one thousand miles—effectively one light-second—insystem from the Palmyrene flagship *Piri Reis*.

The destroyer *Turgut* trailed by another eighty thousand miles.

Cutters hung about the cruiser in a ragged cloud, spreading and slowly falling behind. Though the *Piri Reis* was accelerating at 1 g to maintain the semblance of gravity, many of the cutters were either in freefall or accelerating under lesser impulse to conserve reaction mass. Regardless of how skilled the Palmyrene spacers were, their little vessels really weren't intended for long voyages.

Adele didn't see any signals pass among the Palmyrene ships, but four of the cutters slid into the Matrix with the smooth grace of fish curving to the surface of a calm sea and submerging again.

"Palmyrene vessel Piri Reis...," Daniel said. *"This is* RCS *Princess Cecile, Captain Leary commanding. I wish to speak with the Autocrator, as representative of the Cinnabar Republic, over."*

His voice, though calm and matter of fact, hinted at friendliness. Adele wasn't sure how Daniel managed that. Perhaps it was because he was so naturally engaging that he projected warmth even when it wasn't in the words or even his tone.

Adele hadn't been certain that the Autocrator was aboard the *Piri Reis*, but a quick view of the cruiser's logs showed that Irene hadn't seen any reason to confuse possible enemies by remaining at a distance from her fleet, in a cutter or even at a ground base somewhere. As before in viewing Palmyrene files, the problem was clutter rather than security precautions.

Indeed, the clutter was so general that Adele wondered why the Palmyrenes even bothered to keep records. After all this was over, perhaps she would have the opportunity to meet a

Palmyrene librarian. Or at least to enquire as to whether such a person existed.

"You are the Captain Leary who insulted me on Stahl's World, then?" said the distinctive voice of Autocrator Irene. *"You have turned traitor as well as being a fool, Leary?"*

Daniel waited three long beats to be certain that Irene was through speaking. He didn't want to interrupt her in the middle of a diatribe by assuming that she wasn't bothering with communications protocol. This was a bad enough situation as it was.

Adele, who had gone over logged conversations between the Autocrator and cutter captains, many of whom were Palmyrene nobles as well as being officers in the Horde, knew that Irene ignored protocol—indeed, that the Palmyrenes in general did. That didn't mean that Daniel might not have interrupted her, however—nor that the Autocrator wouldn't have reacted in fury to an interruption.

Adele felt a faint smile touch her lips. For the first time in her life she actually appreciated the usefulness of the protocol which she was prone to ignore.

"Your Excellency," Daniel said, *"nothing I have said or done was meant as an insult to you, who are by far the greatest figure in the region."*

Adele frowned as she heard that. Hogg would have said that no Palmyrene was fit to scrub the latrine of a Cinnabar citizen...and despite the upbringing Esme Rolfe Mundy had given her, Adele found her thoughts turning in similar directions.

I must be extremely *angry about the poor state of Palmyrene record-keeping. Which isn't fair. Entirely fair, at least.*

"And it's because of the friendship between our two nations," Daniel continued, *"that I've come to beg you to let this present business drop while it's still possible to ignore. My Republic is bound by treaty and would be forced to support the Alliance if open war broke out."*

Adele was echoing Daniel's display. Three carets appeared on it, close around the point that was the *Princess Cecile.* Vesey had lighted them pulsing red this time.

"At present nothing has happened, and we can all go our separate ways without involving anyone on Cinnabar or Pleasaunce. Please—"

Adele, listening on the internal circuits of the *Piri Reis,* caught the signal to the cruiser's missile stations before there was any external sign of what was happening.

"Ship!" she said as the fastest way to get word to anyone who might need the information—which was everybody aboard the *Sissie,* come to think. "Cruiser is launching four missiles! Out!"

"Break!" said Daniel, reflexively proper in his commo protocol. *"Gunners, take out the incoming cutters! Vesey, insert us as soon as the plasma charges dissipate! Six out!"*

Even as he spoke, the *Sissie's* guns began hammering. Sun must have turned the stern ventral turret over to Rocker because with four targets—another caret had appeared on the PPI—the turrets had to operate separately to hit all the enemy vessels as quickly as possible.

There wasn't any need for the corvette to concentrate its fire anyway. The *Sissie's* 4-inch guns were the minimum size that could potentially nudge incoming missiles away from a target vessel. At point-blank ranges against ships as light as the cutters, however, they could be devastating—the more so because the cutters' captains were on the hull, with no protection against plasma bolts unless a sail chanced to get in the way.

The gunners had laid their weapons on before the cutters reentered sidereal space. The precursor effects, the twisting of normal space-time as something forced itself through from other dimensions, were as easily identified as real matter or energy.

Sun and Rocker could only guess at what the incoming vessels were, but they were obviously willing to kill on the basis of that guess. If the *Birdsong 312*, still missing, happened to appear close by the *Princess Cecile* at this moment, then it was the transport's very bad luck.

Adele continued to monitor Palmyrene communications; that was her duty, after all. She echoed the insets Daniel ran on the top of his PPI, however: the four ships entering sidereal space around the *Sissie*. None of them was as much as three hundred miles away from the corvette, and the closest was within thirty.

That one escaped the first bolt because Sun opened fire before his target entered normal space. Turret guns were linked so that one of a pair fired a full second after its mate; otherwise the charged path of the first bolt would distort the line of the second.

Sun's second bolt struck the cutter squarely amidships. The hammerblow of charged particles blew in the thin plating, then ignited the interior in the vessel's own atmosphere.

Three masts shook from their steps and flew out from the fireball. The fourth mast spiraled, snapped around by half the cutter's belly and the attached outrigger.

Rocker's target was almost as close, but through bad luck—like Sun, he was firing before the target was more than a blur—his first pair of bolts struck the cutter's dorsal mainsail and its starboard mast near the base. Most of the sail vanished with little harm to the ship proper. The mast step breached the hull, driven downward by the vaporized section of tubing just above it.

The cutter tumbled. Anyone on the hull was either dead from the bubble of gaseous steel or had been shaken into the void. Palmyrenes were probably less likely even than spacers in civilized navies to wear safety lines. In the event some had, they were pirouetting in vacuum like so many tetherballs.

The dorsal guns cycled and hit the cutter again. Shreds of the hull and rigging spun out like sparks from a fireworks display. Rockets on the hull had probably exploded, but that could not add anything to the effect.

The upper turret was slewing. Sun hadn't bothered to fire a second burst into his initial target and instead was bringing his guns to bear on one of the remaining threats. For a moment the last cutter to arrive was only a distortion against the starscape beyond; then it became as sharp in the corvette's excellent optics as it would have been if Adele had been looking across the quay at a ship floating in the next slip.

The cutters were carrying topsails and topgallants on both flanks, but topsails alone on the dorsal and ventral antennas. The rig was intended solely to direct the cutters through the Matrix, not to protect the vessels' hulls from plasma bolts.

If the captains had been thinking of combat, they would have spread a full suit of sails. The sheets of metalized film would stop a plasma bolt—though only once. Replacing a sail was much easier than repairing damaged hull plates, and steel boiling outward from the hull when a jet of ions struck it would ruin furled sails anyway.

The Palmyrenes hadn't expected combat—or rather, they hadn't expected to fight gunners who had a great deal of experience in using their plasma cannon offensively. Most gunners trained to defend against missiles, a delicate art but suitable for rote learning: all incoming missiles had the same characteristics, and they generally approached from a great distance.

Bringing the guns to bear on a vessel in space or on a ground target were completely different skills which demanded speed rather than subtlety. Freighters not infrequently carried a single four-inch gun as defense against pirates, but they rarely had a specialist gunner. No civilian vessel would have a gunner with the skill and experience of the *Sissie*'s. The Palmyrenes had underrated their enemy, and they were dying as a result.

Which didn't make them any less dangerous, however. The four cutters probably hadn't come—or hadn't been sent, though Adele hadn't seen any form of signal—to attack the *Princess Cecile*. They merely wanted to be on hand to attack if the corvette proved hostile.

The *Piri Reis* was now signalling, *"Attack them! Destroy the Cinnabar scum!"* in clear on the 10-meter band. The cruiser's beam was directed toward the *Sissie* and the cutters extracting around her, though other vessels of the Horde were close enough to pick up the signal also.

At least a dozen of the cutters which were trailing the cruiser now slid into the Matrix. Several attempted the pointless exercise of launching their free-flight rockets while they were still a light-second away from their target.

Those rockets would arrive somewhere, eventually; but the corvette's crew would have died of old age before that happened. Besides that, normal dispersion over such a distance made it unlikely that any of the volley would pass through the ship's present location.

But the cutters which were inserting would become a problem in a few minutes. And the pair which were already alongside—

Sun locked his pipper on the last cutter to extract. The target had a ragged look: one topsail was thirty percent smaller than the other three and was cocked at a sharper angle to the ship's axis; tags of cordage dangled from several of the yards, and the hull had either been painted in motley or been patched with plates taken from ships with different decorative schemes.

Two crewmen were cranking handwheels to swing the rocket basket toward the *Princess Cecile*. Another at the pillar nearby was entering data into a computer designed to be used by people wearing rigging gauntlets.

Adele had seen similar rocket launchers often in the past, but this was the first one she'd seen that was aimed from the exterior of the hull. The ship was very small, even by the standards of Palmyrene cutters, and this installation may simply have been a response to the lack of interior volume.

WHANG!

Sun's first bolt stove in a hull plate some ten or fifteen feet back of the prow. Gas swelled in a light-scattering haze, but the charge didn't have enough energy to convert the interior of the cutter into an inferno.

WHANG!

The second bolt hit the basket of eight rockets end-on. The warheads went off simultaneously, though the crew had already been cooked and shredded by the whiplash of ions.

An orange fireball of high explosive enveloped the vessel: there was no atmospheric pressure to contain the bubble of hot gas. It continued to expand, thinning to a faint haze through which Adele could see the cutter's bow and stern tumbling in opposite directions. Amidships, the hull had been reduced to scraps spreading away from the blast.

The remaining cutter was very close and bow-on to the belly of the *Princess Cecile*. The dorsal turret couldn't bear on the Palmyrene, and the ventral guns had been delayed when Rocker needed to fire a second pair of bolts at his initial target.

Daniel was superposing targeting displays over the high-resolution imagery of the cutters. Adele saw the pipper slide onto the nose of the cutter. As it did so, the target blurred with the wreathing exhaust of its own rockets.

WHANG!

"*Cease fire!*" Daniel ordered. "*Cease fire so we can—*"

WHANG!

"*Cease fire, Rocker, or I swear you'll never again sail in the RCN!*" Daniel shouted. Adele saw that he'd engaged the gunnery override on the command console, but a fraction of a second too late to prevent the second bolt.

Which might be unfair to Rocker. The turret guns were intended to fire as a pair in quick sequence. It was possible to fire one tube at a time—Sun had done it, and she remembered Daniel doing it also—but it wasn't easy.

And until the instant that the first bolt struck the cutter's bow and shoved the vessel's whole axis outward in a starburst, Rocker had intended to fire both tubes. The second packet of plasma created a sudden fluorescence in the gas ball where the cutter had been, unnecessary but harmless in itself. The charged track and the side-scatter of ions clinging to the *Sissie*'s rigging prevented her from entering the Matrix until it had dissipated, however.

Readouts from the BDC told Adele that Vesey was thrusting at her display's Execute button with both thumbs. That was pointless—the button was virtual, not something that could stick and be forced to respond by greater effort—but a natural enough response to desperation.

The cutter's rockets were racing toward the corvette, on ballistic courses now that their propellant had burned out. The warheads were just as deadly as ever.

"For what we are about to receive . . . ," murmured someone over the command net. *"May the gods make us thankful."*

It was Daniel. Adele wasn't sure he knew that he'd been speaking aloud.

The hull rang to a heavy blow, then a spiteful tinkle like that of glass breaking on a tile floor. It sounded like a gong, not an explosion, because the warhead had detonated in vacuum.

"Inserting!" Vesey said.

Adele felt a familiar prickly queasiness. She thought, *I never imagined I'd be pleased to be entering the Matrix.*

There was another deafening *clang*. Adele's console became a pearly glow as the *Princess Cecile* left behind all external inputs. They were in the Matrix, safe from all the troubles of the sidereal universe.

Adele smiled wryly. Unfortunately they had to return to normal space at some point. She very much doubted that trouble would have vanished while she was absent, but she supposed it wouldn't do any harm to hope otherwise.

CHAPTER 22

ZENOBIA SYSTEM

"Everybody got out of the way when we saw them launching," Woetjans said, gripping her end of the communications rod so fiercely that Daniel wondered if she subconsciously believed she was squeezing the words through the brass tube. "As much as we could, you know. We had a good twenty seconds—not enough to get all the way to the other side, but there could've been wogs shooting there too. But to get behind a mast, you know, or Griswold behind the fairing for the belly airlock."

Daniel and his bosun stood toward the stern of the *Sissie*'s underside, between the E and F mast rings. He'd left one rigging watch on the hull when he extracted to plead with Autocrator Irene. He'd been concerned about the cruiser's 15-cm plasma cannon, but he'd considered the risk marginal at a light-second's range.

If the negotiation went badly—as he had expected—he wanted to be able to maneuver in the Matrix with precision. He'd seen enough of Palmyrene skill to know that any obvious attempt at escape risked having the *Piri Reis* extract alongside later.

It hadn't occurred to Daniel that cutters would close with the corvette the way they might have done with a merchant vessel. Attempting that with a crack ship like the *Sissie,* whose RCN gunners were using a warship's equipment, would be obvious suicide.

But it *hadn't* been obvious to the Palmyrene captains, because they hadn't faced a warship from a major power before. With all respect to Admiral Mainwaring's command, the patrol sloops of the Qaboosh Region weren't in the same league as ships of the RCN's main force squadrons.

The Alliance destroyers *were* first-rate combatants, especially with an officer like von Gleuck leading them, but the Horde hadn't seen them in action. Daniel suspected that the Autocrator had a nasty surprise coming there, too.

But the fact remained that the cutters of the Horde, supported by the heavy Palmyrene vessels, would be able to crush Zenobia's defenders unless Admiral Polowitz was completely incompetent. From what Daniel had seen of the admiral, that wasn't the case. Regardless of his strategic ability, the way he'd extracted the cruiser alongside a comet after a considerable voyage proved that he was no more a slouch at ship handling than his cutter captains were.

The immediate result of the way the Palmyrenes underestimated the *Princess Cecile* was that warhead fragments had done moderate damage to the sails and rigging of the ventral antennas, and there was a serious dent in the starboard outrigger. Also, Rigger Griswold, a phlegmatic man of fifty—not quick in any sense, but steady—was now dead.

"The rocket hit the other side," Woetjans said, pointing to the dimple in the three-inch hull plating.

Fragments of the warhead casing had scribed an asterisk around the point of impact, skewed slightly toward the half dome of the fairing. That too was scarred.

If Griswold was squatting, as he probably was, he would have been completely out of sight of the cutter. He should have been safe.

Both rigging watches were now repairing damage: reeving cables to replace those which had been severed and swapping fresh sails for those tattered by the blasts. A squad of technicians under Pasternak was adjustng a sheet of bright pink structural plastic broad enough to cover the seams started on the outrigger. When they had it in place, they would glue it down.

The bosun's mates were in charge of the riggers, though the *Sissie*'s veterans didn't need direction for work so cut and dried. Daniel wanted to know what had happened to Griswold; Woetjans was the best witness as well as the victim's line supervisor.

"I hunched down behind E Ventral myself," Woetjans said, ringing the knuckles of her glove against the antenna she referred to. "I heard the rocket hit—bloody hell, they could've heard it in Harbor Three it was so loud. The hull leaped up and swatted my ass, and I mean to say!—hard suit or not, it whapped me good. A chunk of shrapnel banged the antenna, and I thought, 'Bloody good thing I was on the other side of this tube.' That's what I thought."

Daniel turned to look sideways, keeping his end of the rod against his helmet. The dent was small but deep, visible as a bright gouge against the patina of corrosion. The fragment had hit where a band had been shrunk onto the tubing to support the deadeyes to which the lower stays were attached.

"And I didn't give a thought to Griswold," Woetjans said, "because he had the whole fairing between him and the bang. Good thing it didn't hit the E tube instead, because it'd have cut him up for doll rags."

She struck the antenna again, this time a slap that would have spun a man's head around like a top. Her reinforced gauntlet rang against the steel tubing.

"So we finally insert," Woetjans said, "and I take a deep breath because whatever you say about a miss being good as a mile, that *hadn't* been any bloody mile and I was glad there wasn't more wog rockets coming in. I steps around the antenna to see how much damage it'd done, and there's Griswold looking surprised and floating away. And there's a hole in his helmet where that little chunk of rocket casing bounced back and carved off the top of his skull."

"I'm surprised you were able to catch him," Daniel said in a neutral voice. He'd told Vesey to set a circuitous course back to Zenobia orbit, but even so they should be on the verge of extracting. He needed to be on commo when that happened.

He grinned. Adele would be able to handle it, even though he'd only given her a few cursory words as briefing before he rushed onto the hull. Even so, it was his job and he didn't mean to leave it to others.

Woetjans lowered the communications rod for a moment to look straight at Daniel. Then she turned sideways again and brought it back to her helmet.

"Look, Six, I knew I could grab the F Ventral forestay after I got Griswold," the bosun said defensively. "Bloody hell, I been hopping around in the rigging twenty-five years close enough, right? It wasn't risky."

Like hell *it wasn't risky.* Woetjans had jumped from the *Sissie*'s hull, wrapped one arm around the rigger's body—which had probably floated ten feet at least—and trusted that she would be able to seize the slanting cable which supported the sternmost antenna against strains from ahead rather than the usual sideways or rear.

Because of her experience, Woetjans automatically noted the position of all the rigging whenever she stood on a starship's hull; she had leaped after Griswold in full awareness of the forestay. But that same experience would have warned her, as it did Daniel, that the stay might have been all but severed by the blast of moments before.

Then it would have parted, the ragged end dragging through Woetjans' desperate grip. Bosun and corpse would have sailed out into a universe that had no place for humans; becoming two corpses whenever Woetjans choked out the last of her oxygen.

And because she was speaking to an experienced spacer rather than a civilian who wouldn't know the truth, Woetjans blurted, "Six, he was my responsibility. *I'm* the *Sissie*'s bosun. We can send him off the hull as soon as we're back in normal space if you want. Griswold never much liked the ground, so there's no big deal like we ought to bury him in dirt. But I didn't want him, you know—there. Nowhere. Hell, if there's a Hell."

"I understand," said Daniel. Then—because he suddenly

realized it was true—he said, "I'd have done the same thing, Woetjans. Carry on."

He clasped her shoulder with his left hand, then returned the brass rod away in its sheath on his equipment belt. He started around the corvette's hull in a diagonal, moving toward the dorsal airlock in the bow rather than using the lock within arm's length. It was actually easier to get to the bridge this way than it would have been going up six levels of companionways and then striding down a corridor that might be blocked by men or equipment.

Besides, it kept Daniel longer in the light of the Matrix, which he loved. Though like Woetjans—and probably like Griswold, as with every other rigger Daniel had known—he wouldn't want to float for eternity in a place so inhuman.

"Extracting in thirty, that is three-zero, seconds," announced Cory from the console kitty-corner across the bridge.

Adele suspected that Vesey had handed the task off to Cory because the First Lieutenant was involved in complex course computations. Under other circumstances, Adele might have echoed Vesey's console in the BDC to check her guess, but at the moment she was otherwise busy.

The inner airlock sighed. Daniel strode into the rotunda while the valve was barely open enough to pass his—slightly chubby—form wearing a rigging suit. He had already stripped off his helmet and gauntlets; the magnetic stickiness of his boot soles on the decking didn't slow his movements discernibly. He threw himself onto his console, beaming in sudden surprise to find that Adele had already adjusted the seat to fit a user wearing a rigging suit.

He looked at her. She nodded crisply toward Daniel's image, but her smile was satisfied and perhaps a trifle wider than usual. Her job was information, and using information to prepare at least one step into the future.

"Extracting!" Cory said.

Adele blanked her display to make room for the new inputs the *Princess Cecile* would receive in sidereal space. She had been viewing the personnel file of the late Leading Rigger Joshua Griswold.

She recognized Griswold's image, but she hadn't been able to attach it to his name without prompting from her databank. He had twenty years' service in the RCN before he joined the crew of the communications vessel RCS *Aglaia*. Three years later, that ship landed on Kostroma and came to the attention of a librarian named Adele Mundy.

Griswold had been captured during the initial disaster on Kostroma, then freed through the actions of some of his shipmates commanded by young Lieutenant Daniel Leary...with the help of that same librarian. Griswold had joined the crew of the *Princess Cecile* on Kostroma and had followed Daniel from that point onward.

Until now, when he died.

Adele could no more bring Griswold back to life than she could revive her little sister, but she had felt that he at least deserved to have his face connected with the name in her memory. There was no logical reason to do that, but humans were frequently illogical. Perhaps she was trying to convince herself that she was human.

The *Princess Cecile* shuddered into normal space. The return reminded Adele that during transition she had felt as though she were an empty skin, collapsing in on itself. The illusion hadn't been disturbing because she was completely given over to musing on Rigger Griswold, and on life, and on the pointlessness of life.

Her smile was wry, but real. *That* train of thought wasn't disturbing; rather, it was the black pool into which her intellect often dived in the waking reverie during the small hours of the morning. Familiarity gave it a bleak hominess, like the bare stone cell of a prisoner who would never be released.

Adele's console went from a pearly void to a Plot Position Indicator—she was echoing the command console in the center of her display—with communications inputs as flanking sidebars. The *Sissie* was in the same orbit as the *Z 46*, leading von Gleuck's flagship around Zenobia by twenty-one thousand miles. The *Z 42* was still—optimistically—in concealment behind the third moon, and the Palmyrene fleet—most of it, at least—appeared to be where it had been when Daniel approached it. Presumably that would change, probably very soon.

"*Posy Cinc...,*" said Daniel in the usual friendly, authoritative tone of his official conversations. "*This is* Sissie *Six. Over.*"

"*Posy to RCN,*" von Gleuck snapped back almost instantly. Both ships were using laser communicators, so there was no need for significant compression. The Alliance officer's tone was sharp and, if not hostile, at least not obviously friendly. "*Go ahead, over.*"

"Posy Cinc," Daniel said, as warmly as if he'd just been greeted as a long-lost brother. *"I wish to place the* Princess Cecile *under your command for the duration of this action. I believe we'll do better if our efforts are coordinated, over."*

There was no response for ten long beats. Adele was transmitting both sides of the conversation to the *Z 42*. Goodness only knew what the captain of the second destroyer thought of it—*Z 42* continued to maintain communications silence—but Adele believed it was a better plan than trusting to a stranger's good sense not to treat the *Sissie* as an enemy when the shooting started. If von Gleuck had a problem with Officer Mundy's meddling, then he could call on her to discuss honor after this business was concluded.

Adele smiled, in a manner of speaking. She was joking with herself, mostly. But not entirely.

"Captain Leary," said von Gleuck in a very different tone. *"You are senior to me in rank, are you not, over?"*

Yes, of course Daniel is of superior rank—but he's not an idiot. Only an idiot would assume that the Honorable Otto von Gleuck would turn over defense of his mistress to a foreigner.

"Posy Cinc," Daniel said easily, *"we are in Alliance space. Do you accept the offer of our help, over?"*

It was theoretically possible for an observer at the distance of the Palmyrene fleet to follow the track of the modulated laser beam which the *Princess Cecile* was sending to the *Z 46*. Adele wasn't sure that she would have been able to manage that task herself, though, and she was quite sure that the Palmyrenes wouldn't. The region above Zenobia was generally clear of light-scattering debris.

After another pause, von Gleuck said, *"Leary, you've got enough experience to know that this isn't likely to have a good result. Grateful as I would be of your help and advice, a Cinnabar warship has no duty to become involved in what is, as you point out, an Alliance matter, over."*

There's more reason than you'll know, Adele thought, *until the inevitable Alliance investigators uncover Assistant Commissioner Gibbs' role in the business.*

But she knew that didn't really make a difference. Daniel would almost certainly have made the same decision if the Republic's hands had been completely clean.

"Otto," said Daniel, *"I believe that all civilized persons have a duty to stand against barbarians. Do you accept our offer, over?"*

The Z 46 sent a packet of course information. Adele routed it to both the command console and the BDC.

"Roger, Posy Three," von Gleuck said. *"This section of space is about to become infested by Monkeys, I'm afraid, so we'll vacate it for the time being. We'll rendezvous ASAP a light-minute from here and discuss the next move. Posy Cinc out."*

"Posy Three out," said Daniel with a broad smile of satisfaction.

"Six!" said Vesey. *"This is Three. We are ready to execute the new course, over."*

Daniel, who had just opened the course packet, raised an eyebrow. Aloud he said, *"Roger, Vesey. Make it so, out."*

"Inserting in ten, one-zero, seconds!" said Cazelet. The team in the BDC must have started the process even before Daniel had authorized them.

Adele wore a slight smile also. Von Gleuck commanded a pair of crack ships. Vesey was obviously at pains to prove that the *Princess Cecile*'s spacers were better still.

"Inserting!"

As we most certainly are.

Adele's console received no external inputs while they were in the Matrix, but imagery of the Palmyrene fleet taken at thirty-second intervals, with the changes highlighted, demonstrated that the Autocrator had made up her mind. Over the last minute and a half before the *Princess Cecile* inserted, two—then four—then twelve—Palmyrene cutters left sidereal space also.

It irritated Adele that she couldn't be certain how ships of the Horde communicated among themselves. She supposed they were passing the signals from ship to ship with handheld lasers which were too low-powered for her to read them by hull reflection, even with sensors of RCN standard. That should cause a great deal of confusion and garbling, but in fact the Horde appeared to operate with admirable coordination.

She considered the way collectives of hundreds and even thousands of individual birds and fish appeared to move as one. Perhaps she had been wrong about the Palmyrenes being barbarians: they might instead be animals.

Mother would not approve of the joke, Adele thought. But surely the fact she *could* joke under these circumstances was worthy of praise.

"Ship, this is Six," Daniel said. *"I know you're all wondering about the ability of our new squadron commander—you'd*

be fools if you didn't. Posy Cinc apparently noticed that our Palmyrene friends like to form on intrasystem debris when they extract from the Matrix. He's set our rendezvous for a section of space which is completely empty. Thus far he has my fullest approval! Six out."

Adele looked at her friend's image. He glanced toward her and grinned.

How much of what Daniel just said was true, and how much was cheering up his subordinates by putting a good face on matters? Perhaps it was *completely* true; it certainly seemed to be. But he'd retailed it to his crew for morale reasons.

"Adele?" said Daniel on a two-way link. *"I suspect that Otto won't have any idea of the situation on the ground. I'd like you to brief him when we extract, all right?"*

"Yes," said Adele. "As the situation permits."

She hadn't explained to Daniel what she was doing when they first arrived above Zenobia. There hadn't been a great deal of time . . . but she supposed that at the back of her mind was the knowledge that it wasn't the sort of thing that Daniel would want to hear about. Odd to think that a man who had so often struck at the throat of an enemy would be squeamish about political necessities.

On the other hand, Daniel had obviously known what she was doing, and he hadn't objected. And he *was* Speaker Leary's son.

"Extracting," said Vesey. This had been a very short transit, the sort of maneuver which vessels with less skillful astrogators performed regularly to close on their intended destination after an initial extraction well out in a planetary system.

Adele realized that she had been spoiled: she took for granted prodigies of astrogation, whether Daniel himself or one of the officers he'd trained was laying the course. Well, despite the fact that her father had led the Popular Party, the Mundys had always been clear in their awareness that they were of the elite. Adele's frame of reference had changed in the past five years, but her status remained elite within that new reality.

In her mind, the air began to freeze into needles of ice. She thought about the men and women all over Calvary who were being jerked out of their homes and businesses by troops of the Founder's Regiment. Some were traitors; some were Palmyrenes and though not traitors—their allegiance was properly to the Autocrator—were agents of the national enemy.

And some, doubtless, were quite innocent: victims of clerical error, mistaken identity, or simply a semiliterate sergeant who misread a house number or a street name. She assumed— because she had seen this sort of business before—that some would be shot where they stood instead of being arrested. That was particularly true in cases where the neighborhood was hostile and the troops involved didn't want the delay of dragging prisoners through a gauntlet of jeers and bricks.

Adele sometimes wondered why the people whose deaths she caused in this fashion didn't come to visit her in the bleak hours before dawn. She had never pretended that they were not as much her victims as the people she'd shot, some of them so close that their blood sprayed her.

The *Princess Cecile* returned to normal space with all systems alive and humming. The Alliance destroyers hadn't arrived yet.

Adele's smile was as terrible as the curve of a headsman's axe. She was never short of company in the darkness, even without the faces of those she had murdered indirectly.

"Posy Cinc, this is Posy Three," said Daniel a careful twenty seconds after the Z 46 extracted from the Matrix. Even though the Alliance systems would be fully live from the instant the ship dropped back into normal space, the crew—no matter how skilled and experienced—would take a little time to recover. "We have information as to the political situation on Zenobia, over."

The Alliance flagship had already been a distortion when Daniel's mind cleared enough from the fog to take in his console's readouts. During transition he had been chatting with Stacey Bergen and three of his uncle's old shipmates about Palmyrene skill in the Matrix.

The other old-timers ranged from amazed to incredulous at Daniel's stories. Captain Reese—he'd left the RCN for the merchant service and retired when he lost his left arm to a collapsing antenna—said that if the Palmyrenes were really that good, they would have coursed all over human space instead of being stuck in a backwater like the Qaboosh.

Stacey's judgment was that pilotage was an interesting skill and certainly impressive, but that a Palmyrene captain would take a month to sail a route that a proper astrogator could manage in a week. For all that, Stacey would have liked six months to spend on a Palmyrene cutter while he tried to pick up some of the tricks.

It was a perfectly reasonable conversation, one of the sort Daniel had listened to frequently before he went off to the Academy. But Uncle Stacey and all his friends were dead, dead for years. It had been a harmless illusion; but the next time Daniel reentered sidereal space, he thought he would prefer feeling that he was being flayed with hot knives.

"Posy Three, go ahead with your information," said von Gleuck's voice. He sounded tense, but there were many possible reasons for that—and it could simply be that his head was splitting from a bad transition. *"Cinc over."*

Rather than speaking, Daniel pointed his right index finger toward Adele. She nodded to his image and said, *"Commander, the Palmyrene Fifth Column within Calvary has by now been eliminated by the Founder's Regiment. The Founder had a full list of traitors and their probable locations, so there shouldn't have been any difficulty. The Founder's Palace is being guarded by the best of the militia units. I don't imagine they'll even be attacked, but they should be able to shrug off any panicked attempt by somebody who eluded Major Flecker's troops."*

Adele paused to gather data for the remainder of the briefing. Though the details of her display were a blur except to Adele's own eyes, Daniel saw the field from the upper right corner shift into the center of the hologram to replace the previous one.

Von Gleuck seized the momentary silence to blurt, *"Good God! Who are you, please? Is this Lady Mundy, over?"*

Daniel called up the navigational packet which the Z 46 had transmitted when von Gleuck accepted—to give the thing its right name—the RCN offer of alliance. The information consisted of 36 points in space—literally points in vacuum, none of them close to heavenly bodies—each within a light-minute of Zenobia. In addition, there were six points some thirty light-minutes out. Force Posy could displace with no communication beyond a single numerical preset.

It was exactly the sort of preparation Daniel—and Vesey, and probably Cory as well—had separately computed on the run back to Zenobia from the waypoint where they had intercepted the convoy. It reinforced Daniel's existing high opinion of von Gleuck as a fighting officer.

"Yes, this is Officer Mundy," Adele said, frowning slightly— either irritated at being interrupted or more likely chiding herself because she hadn't given proper identification before speaking. Her lack of ceremony hadn't disturbed von Gleuck, but obviously the source of such information was important. *"Now, as you will have guessed, the Palmyrenes intended an invasion with their own troops as well."*

Very likely von Gleuck *had* guessed that, at least after the Horde arrived. He would have noted that the transports were Cinnabar registry. For a politically astute officer—as von Gleuck was—it would be obvious why Daniel had been so close-mouthed about his plans.

The *Z 42* extracted a careful twelve thousand miles from the *Z 46*. Daniel was sure that she would be signalling the flagship, but he was equally certain that von Gleuck would leave those communications to a subordinate while he was listening to Adele.

A few Palmyrene cutters—not nearly as many as had disappeared from the swarm about the *Piri Reis*—extracted in the region above Zenobia. Daniel frowned as he realized something. He touched his display, extending the course that the *Princess Cecile* had been following beyond the point he took her back into the Matrix. Five of the six cutters were within fifty miles of where the *Sissie* would have been if she hadn't inserted. They had tracked her through the Matrix.

That was truly amazing. Uncle Stacey—Uncle Stacey's ghost—might be right about the Palmyrene skills being inferior to real astrogation, but Daniel knew that they would be *very* effective in the close-range combat in which the *Sissie* had made a name for herself.

"The troop transports," Adele was saying, *"are on Diamond Cay, cut off from Calvary and the main continent. Their Cinnabar captains have been warned to remain where they are on penalty of being declared traitors to the Republic. While they may bow to threats from the Palmyrene troops, that won't happen quickly, and by now the Founder's troops should have overrun the Palmyrene base on Zenobia."*

"Lady Mundy…," said von Gleuck. *"You have done all this? A Palmyrene base? I have been on Zenobia for eighteen months, and all this comes from a clear blue sky. You are all I have heard, and more. Cinc over."*

Most of the cutters which had entered the Matrix were now back in close company with the Palmyrene cruiser. They must have realized their prey was gone, so they had returned to the Autocrator without extracting into sidereal space.

Daniel wished he had more knowledge of Palmyrene equipment. He realized for the first time that the cutters' instrumentation must be extremely basic—a fact that his hallucination had put in the mouth of Uncle Stacey. Indeed, a captain conning his ship from the hull couldn't use the sort of sensors that spacers from civilized regions took for granted.

It was quite wonderful that the cutters could track the *Sissie* to her orbit above Zenobia, but they probably wouldn't have been able to locate her by any other means. Whereas Daniel had crisp, complete information regarding the Horde's dispositions across the entire electrooptical band, accurate to one minute at this distance.

But if there was a battle, it was going to be a knife fight. The *Sissie* had been lucky thus far, but that could not possibly continue. Both the *Piri Reis* and the *Turgut* had good sensors; in particular, the cruiser's Pantellarian optics were at least as good as those of the most modern RCN warship. The cutters may have returned to the flagship not only for orders but for information.

"*Yes, well,*" said Adele with a hint of irritation. "*This was really a task for the Resident, not the Fleet, but I'm afraid Resident Tilton himself is much of the problem. As I was saying—the problem on the ground is contained for the time being. If the Palmyrenes are able to bring their heavy ships into the atmosphere to provide fire support and to land crews for the transports, they may still be able to bring off the coup. I don't know how good Palmyrene infantry is, but I have very little confidence in the Zenobian militia. It would be much better if the infantry didn't get off Diamond Cay.*"

The Horde vanished into the Matrix like water soaking into cloth. Starting with the cruiser and destroyer, the displacement rolled across the assemblage. It was complete within thirty seconds.

Daniel started to say something; he didn't have time to. Von Gleuck's voice said, *"Break. All Posy elements, this is Cinc. Execute Course Pack Two. Cinc out."*

"Prepare to insert!" Vesey said. *"Inserting!"*

The *Princess Cecile* shimmered into the Matrix, leaving Daniel's mind hanging for a moment in sidereal space, under the hard separate gleams of the stars.

CHAPTER 23

ZENOBIA SYSTEM

Daniel's mind reentered, meshed with—the process reminded him of registering a transparency over another image—his body. His limbs felt cold, and his eyes didn't focus for a moment.

"Ship, this is Six," he said. The effort of speaking brought him fully back to himself. "I expect the wogs to come after us this time—probably just a few cutters, but maybe the whole fleet. Gunners, after the second destroyer appears, hit everything that extracts. Missileers, we may have a heavy cruiser close aboard in a few minutes. I won't pretend I'm looking forward to that, but I want you plotting trajectories to each anomaly as it forms. If it's a cutter, switch to the next."

Daniel's lips were dry, but he felt a leaping excitement that nothing but battle could give him. This was a terrible situation: the *Sissie* was facing opponents who could clearly beat her at her own game, precise maneuvers in the Matrix and point-blank engagements. But by the gods, if any ship could pull it off, it was this ship and this crew!

372

"If either of the heavy ships appears," Daniel continued, "launch as soon as you have a solution. Chazanoff, I'm not usurping your authority as Chief Missileer, but if the target Fiducia is solving for turns out to be the *Piri Reis* or *Turgut*, he doesn't need to ask your permission or mine either one. Acknowledge, over."

"Roger, Six!" said Fiducia.

"Roger, Six," said Chazanoff. The chief's response wasn't so much an echo as a dull counterfeit of his mate's.

Daniel grinned. He knew exactly how Chazanoff felt. If Captain Leary hadn't had more to do in the early seconds following extraction than any three people could manage, he would be computing missile attacks himself.

And directing the gun turrets also, of course, as Sun and Rocker well knew. Daniel handled the plasma cannon skillfully, but he couldn't pretend he was actually better than the *Sissie*'s gunner or gunner's mate: they practiced constantly while the corvette was in the Matrix, running imagery of past engagements as well as simulations. Even so, it would have required a real effort of will for Daniel not to lock out the gunnery consoles and lay the pippers on target himself.

The Z 46 arrived less than thirty seconds after the *Princess Cecile*. She was shaking out additional sails.

Daniel was running the corvette with a minimum rig: topsails on A and E rings only. If the *Piri Reis* did appear close alongside, he was going to regret not having a full suit of sails to absorb the initial wracking salvo of plasma bolts. A single hit from the cruiser's 15-cm weapons could dish in the *Sissie*'s hull at five thousand miles, and the multiple hits likely if the Palmyrene gunner knew his business would finish the corvette at much greater range.

But the more probable danger came from cutters, and the best defense against them was the corvette's gunfire. Daniel had decided to give his plasma cannon the best field of fire possible by limiting the arcs that sails would block.

Besides, fewer sails meant fewer riggers on the hull to handle their problems. Daniel would much rather have kept his entire crew inside, but the *Sissie* was going to have to maneuver with precision to survive. Woetjans was on the hull—it was the bosun's job, and she wouldn't obey orders to stay inside while some of her personnel were facing danger—with four of her most experienced riggers.

If something jammed, that team would clear it; and if they had *known* that a hail of rockets and plasma bolts would scour the hull clean, they would still be out there. It was their job, and among the Sissies, duty was more important than life.

It made absolutely no sense at all, except to other people who were or had been members of a crack combat unit. Then it made all the sense in the world.

The *Piri Reis*, then the *Turgut*, extracted within a hundred miles of one another and about thirteen thousand miles above Zenobia. Instants later, the Palmyrene cutters began to appear about their heavy vessels like ripples shimmering on a pond.

The Alliance flagship was only a thousand miles distant: Daniel had brought the *Princess Cecile* closer to the rendezvous point than he had the first time because he expected that the little squadron would be better off tight together to supply supporting fire. A single ship might be mobbed by a score of cutters and have her rig blown off by rockets.

Space-time dimpled between the *Sissie* and the *Z 46*. The second Alliance destroyer—

But it wasn't.

"Target!" Daniel shouted, highlighting the cutter which crystallized out of the infinite possible.

"I'm on it! I'm on it!" Sun cried. That wasn't quite true, but the rumble of the dorsal turret rotating the necessary thirty degrees was comforting proof that he would be shortly.

Another anomaly four hundred miles away made the stars beyond it quiver. *"Targeting!"* Rocker said as the ventral turret turned also. *"Targeting, I'm on it!"*

The first anomaly became a Palmyrene cutter, sharp and squarely broadside to the *Princess Cecile* but with her axis cocked up by fifteen degrees. The corvette was drawing ahead under 1 g acceleration in parallel with the *Z 46*, but the cutter's rocket basket pivoted to lead her target expertly.

The Palmyrene captain stood in his pulpit in the far bow. *If I boosted the magnification, his face would be as clear to me as the scratches on his visor allowed*, Daniel thought.

The middle of the cutter's hull went bright, then exploded outward. A single rocket spat out of the conflagration. It vanished from the image area and from the *Sissie*'s concern. Sun's second plasma bolt stirred the luminous gas cloud, but its energy could add nothing to the holocaust.

The recoil of the two shots was echoing through the ship. Daniel hadn't noticed the *Whang/whang!* when the guns fired.

His thumb mashed a key, locking Rocker's firing circuit. "Ventral, hold your fire!" he ordered. "That's the *Z 42*, over."

Two more anomalies shimmered on the display. They were

forward and aft of the cutter, each within two hundred miles. Sun and Rocker divided the targets, but only when the ventral guns had slid off the *Z 42* did Daniel free Rocker's console. The *Sissie* faced enough enemies already without accidentally putting a plasma bolt into an Alliance destroyer—particularly since Daniel was sure that the Alliance gunners were at least as jumpy and ready to shoot as Rocker was.

"Posy Cinc, this is Three-Six," Daniel said. "Over."

His gunners, and possibly his missileers—though the *Princess Cecile* would be reduced to glowing debris in a matter of seconds if the *Piri Reis* extracted alongside with her nine 15-cm guns cleared for action—would handle incoming attackers as well as human beings could. Tactics, or at least advice on tactics, was the job of Captain Daniel Leary.

"Cinc to Three-Six," von Gleuck responded so promptly that Daniel suspected the Alliance commodore had been about to initiate the call. *"Do you have an attack plan, over?"*

The *Sissie*'s turrets fired in such close conjunction that Daniel wasn't sure which gunner had gotten on target first. Two cutters bloomed into fireballs. The Palmyrenes were clearly keying on the corvette rather than on the Alliance destroyers.

"Sir!" said Daniel. He realized as the syllable came out that he was being artificially bright, much as he must have sounded when addressing instructors at the Academy. "So long as we remain within observation range, the Palmyrenes won't be able to land on Zenobia. I therefore recommend that instead of attacking, we—"

A Palmyrene rocket detonated with a deafening crash. It must have hit squarely over the bridge. The air was suddenly hazy with dust and flocking shaken from the insulation. A bank of lights in the port-side ceiling went out, then flickered on again at half their usual output.

"Bloody hell!" Daniel said. "Ah, sorry, sir. That Force Posy shift location every time the *Piri Reis* inserts, but that we not initiate attacks un—"

A second rocket hit, this time in the *Sissie's* ventral rigging from the sound of it. Shrapnel tinkled spitefully, ricocheting in the angles between the hull and the outriggers withdrawn against it.

How many riggers did that kill? But this was battle, and people die in battles. *By the gods, the wogs will pay the score before this is over!*

"Until one of the heavy ships tries to land and we can catch them in the atmosphere, over."

Two plasma bolts from the *Z 46* roiled the gas cloud to which Rocker had already reduced the cutter that had attacked from the *Sissie's* underside. Daniel suspected that when von Gleuck had a moment, he would well and truly ream his gunner for shooting when he did. He hadn't just been late, he'd been pointlessly late. He'd triggered his 13-cm guns in sheer frustration at not having a real target while the *Princess Cecile* was making excellent practice on the wogs. On the Monkeys, that is.

"*Three, this is Cinc,*" von Gleuck said. "*From your reputation, Leary, I'd have expected you to suggest a headlong charge to destroy the cruiser and the Monkey Queen herself. If we kill her, then we've won, not so, over?*"

Daniel grinned, though without the expression's usual warmth. There was a sort of beauty to the idea, but—

"Cinc, this is Three," he said aloud. "I'm not sure that a

377

salvo of ten missiles—" the number of launch tubes in their small mixed squadron "—is enough to guarantee destroying a cruiser, let alone killing the Autocrator aboard her. I *am* sure that if we go down their throat while they're waiting unhampered for us, there'll be no one left between Zenobia and whatever remains of the Palmyrenes. Over."

Nine of the dozen cutters which had sortied now reappeared close to the *Piri Reis*. The other three were debris clouds still dusted with sparkles of plasma.

Daniel wondered if he would have been willing to make that—perfectly accurate—assessment if he hadn't had the reputation of being a hell-for-leather daredevil. How many officers over the millennia had been willing to die—and fail— because they were afraid to be called cowards?

His smile spread wider. *Sure, I'd have said the same thing. It's my duty, after all.*

There was a pause of seconds, a chasm of silence in the present tension. Then von Gleuck said, *"Roger, Three. Cinc out."*

The PPI highlighted movement in bright amber. Daniel moved his cursor quickly, certainly, and brought up a direct visual image: the destroyer *Turgut* was braking to enter Zenobia's atmosphere while the cruiser stood guard in orbit.

Daniel had already roughed out an attack plan. He had begun putting the finishing touches on it when the Z 46 signalled, *"All Posy elements, this is Posy Cinc. Prepare to attack in thirty seconds, over."*

"Ship, prepare to insert," Daniel said, pressing the Execute button that sent his queued course computations to the corvette's other consoles and to the separate computer which controlled the hydromechanical linkages to the rigging.

"*Attack!*" von Gleuck ordered.

Daniel pressed Execute a second time. His heart was filled with leaping excitement.

Still tingling from an insertion which had felt as though someone were tickling the inside of her skin, Adele shifted to the damage control system to get imagery of the A Level corridor. That seemed to her to be the best way to learn what the noise was about.

Rene Cazelet—Midshipman Cazelet—had come from the Battle Direction Center wearing a rigging suit, all but the gauntlets and helmet. As he ran—well, lumbered—he was shouting, "Hester and Blakeslee, you go out with me!"

There was movement among the riggers waiting in the forward rotunda. Adele's wands brought up the crew list reflexively, but she didn't need its prompting: Hester and Blakeslee were senior riggers, both on the list for promotion to bosun's mate if there was an opening. Presumably they were among the eighteen suited-up spacers just outside the bridge.

Cory hunched disconsolately at his console, plotting missile launches on an attack board. Granted that the *Princess Cecile* was about to go into action, it seemed very unlikely that the young lieutenant would be required as a missileer, and it was just possible that Adele *would* need to understand what was going on.

Besides, she was curious—she was always curious—and she had no real duties, which was bad for her state of mind. Palmyrene communications were so chaotic and low-technology that she hadn't been able to imagine a way to delude the enemy and cause confusion in their ranks.

All Adele's ideas had foundered on the Palmyrenes' simplicity. It was like trying to outthink an anvil.

"Cory," she said on a two-way link to the man at the console kitty-corner behind hers across the bridge. "What's going on out there? Over."

"Ma'am, Rene's taking two riggers out to replace casualties, over," Cory said in a miserable tone. He hadn't even bothered to inset her face on his display as he ordinarily would have done.

Adele frowned. The ship's external sensors shut off when they entered the Matrix, but recorded imagery would show the hull as it had been in sidereal space. They'd been hit, by rockets she supposed....

She split her screen—dorsal left, ventral right—and then scrolled back from the moment of insertion. Almost immediately she found what she was looking for—what she wanted, in the informational sense: a ragged black puff swelling from the ventral B antenna, just below the furled topsail. Fingers of dark, dirty orange poked through the smoke.

The sail streamed from the yard in tatters. The two spacers at the base of the antenna slammed against the hull and bounced back. One suited figure caught the ratlines with a hand and then hugged them. The other figure continued to sail outward. Its torso scissored at a sharp angle from the legs and lower body, then separated completely.

Adele blanked the images, returning to a schematic of the enemy fleet. Her display started as the Horde had been at the moment the *Sissie* inserted; it then advanced with the ships' individual courses extrapolated against elapsed time. *Cory taught me to do that*, she thought, looking at the young man's sorrowful face.

"*I ought to be out there!*" Cory blurted. They hadn't closed the two-way link, but Adele wasn't sure that he knew he was speaking to her as well as to himself. "*It was properly my duty, but Vesey sent Rene out instead!*"

The inner airlock closed with its usual series of muted *ching*s, the sound of the dogs seating. The airlocks were much smaller than the boarding hatch which was used while the *Sissie* was on the surface; it was thus less prone to twisting during maneuvers. They mated quietly, and their hydraulic dogs didn't have to strain to bring the seams back into alignment.

Adele hadn't been watching, but she supposed Cazelet and two additional riggers were going onto the hull. She started to check her assumption with stored imagery, but she caught herself. *It doesn't matter!*

Aloud she said, "Cory, I don't understand. *What* is the duty you're talking about?"

"*Chief Woetjans was wounded,*" Cory said. "*You saw that, right? Belachik killed and the chief got maybe a dozen holes in her legs. Her suit sealed the punctures and they must've all been little, but she's not going to be jumping around. There needs to be an officer out there and it should've been* me!"

Woetjans was wounded? Yes, of course: the arms of her suit have blue chevrons.

"Shouldn't—" Adele said before she caught herself. "Oh, I'm sorry, yes."

Of *course* Woetjans should have been brought inside and

hooked to the Medicomp immediately: rigging suits were self-sealing, but human bodies were not. The bosun might very well be bleeding to death right now.

But there was no chance that Woetjans would leave her post of duty so long as she was conscious. Only if she fainted would it be possible to deal with her injuries—assuming she didn't simply drift off into the Matrix, unnoticed until her body was lost forever.

"Six would've sent me," Cory said bitterly. *"You know that. But Six gave maneuver control to Vesey, and she sent Rene out instead of me."*

Adele *didn't* know that Daniel would have sent Cory instead of Cazelet, and she had even less notion of why Cory thought that Vesey would keep him in a place of safety and instead send her close friend—

Adele grimaced. *Give a thing its right name.*

Send her lover, Rene Cazelet, into a place of obvious danger. But Cory did believe both those things, and he was wretched because he wasn't being allowed to risk his life on the hull.

She smiled faintly, because she'd long since learned that human behavior didn't make any sense at all. "Well, Lieutenant," she said. "Given what we're about to do, there's an excellent chance that you won't survive Midshipman Cazelet by even a fraction of a second. Think positively, my good man."

"Extracting!" Vesey warned. The *Princess Cecile* began sliding into normal space—and into the midst of her enemies.

Daniel's system was so charged with adrenaline that the confusion of extracting from the Matrix didn't bother him—

except that he had to pause for a moment while the right and left halves of his body realigned. When they locked together, he was able to view the Palmyrene vessels and to adjust the attack plan based on the locations he'd predicted for them.

There hadn't been a great deal of difference, but a tiny error multiplied by 89,000 miles would mean the *Princess Cecile*'s two missiles—a pitiful salvo to begin with—wouldn't come anywhere close to the target. In all likelihood, no amount of tweaking the missile courses would bring them close at this range. The *Turgut* would be deep in Zenobia's atmosphere by the time they arrived, so the missiles' High Drive motors would be devouring themselves.

"Missiles, you are clear to launch!" Daniel said. Not so very long ago, he would have taken over the attack himself. That he didn't do so now was partly maturity and the realization that other people really might be as good as he was, especially if they'd had longer to plan.

Besides that, Daniel had a great deal on his plate as captain of an RCN ship going into action as the junior member of a Fleet squadron. He was nearly as concerned about what the Alliance vessels were going to do as he was about the Palmyrenes.

"*Launching two!*" Chazanoff said. The *whang!* of steam driving out a five-ton missile truncated his final syllable. The second *whang!* came a minimal two seconds later, so close that there was a risk that the hull's whipping might bind the later missile in its tube.

Reloads began rumbling along the rollerways carrying them from the missile magazines to the launch tubes. Daniel had given strict orders that Chazanoff not start the reloads moving until the initial salvo was out of its tubes. That delayed the second salvo considerably, but it avoided the ratfuck which was certain if one or more missiles didn't launch and several reloads were already in motion.

Besides, this was a hit-and-run attack. The *Princess Cecile* wasn't making a sustained effort involving multiple launches.

The target was Daniel's first priority, but the Horde's defensive response was a close second. He had extracted the *Princess Cecile* not only beyond the effective range of the cruiser's plasma cannon but with the bulk of the planet between them. Even at 93,000 miles—the distance between the *Piri Reis* and the *Sissie*—a 15-cm bolt could charge the corvette's hull sufficiently to prevent her from reentering the Matrix. If that happened, the cutters would have as long as they needed to chew the *Sissie* apart.

It was unlikely that the Palmyrenes had enough big-ship experience to attempt such a move: they were used to dealing in free-flight rockets, not plasma cannon. But underestimating your enemy's skill was about as good a way to get killed in battle as Daniel could think of.

Because the cutters were grouped closely on the *Piri Reis*, the *Sissie* had a comfortable margin of separation from them as well. The closest was at 33,000 miles, too far to be dangerous or for the corvette's 4-inch guns to do any dam—

Whang. Whang. Whang. Whang.

"Gunners, cease fire!" Daniel shouted. "Acknowledge my orders, you bloody fools, over!"

They're wasting ammunition—which didn't matter—*and burning out their barrels*—which did. Had watching the Z

46's trigger-happy gunner caused Sun and Rocker to lose the fire discipline he'd spent years trying to teach them?

"Sorry, Six," Sun said, glancing sideways toward the command console. He looked and sounded contrite. *"Won't happen—"*

Bloody hell! A dimensional anomaly began to form so close ahead of the *Princess Cecile* that Daniel thought he could hit it with a shotgun if he'd been standing on the hull.

"Target, target, target!" Rocker shouted, but his ventral turret didn't have an angle on the cutter, if it *was* a cutter and not one of the Alliance destroyers extracting in just about the worst place possi—

It was a Palmyrene cutter, congealing into empty space like a poisonous insect. Its rocket pod was already aligned with the *Princess Cecile*. Its salvo would rake—

Whang!

The cutter disintegrated. It was a perfect shot, so centered that the four antennas flew out from the gas cloud in precise symmetry. Perhaps to prove that he *wasn't* an out-of-control wacko, Sun didn't spend the usual—but here unnecessary—second round on the target.

"Cease fire!" Daniel ordered. "Ship, prepare to insert presently, over."

He pressed the Execute button, leaving his right index and middle fingers in place. The *Sissie* would transition as soon as the bath of ions which sprayed from her own gun muzzles had dissipated sufficiently. That wouldn't be as soon as Daniel wanted, but almost nothing happened as soon as he wanted it to.

He grinned despite the present situation. *Almost* nothing. He'd met a few girls who were nearly as eager as he was.

Daniel had hoped the Alliance destroyers would extract at the same moment as the *Princess Cecile*, splitting the Palmyrenes' attention and defensive efforts. He hadn't expected that to happen, of course. Synchronized maneuvers in the Matrix were difficult, and it would have taken incredibly good luck for three ships which hadn't operated together before to launch an unplanned attack with perfect precision.

The *Princess Cecile* hadn't been unlucky during this engagement—the fact that she'd survived proved that. But neither had things worked out quite *that* well.

The Alliance destroyers extracted within seconds of one another, however, though they were widely separated in space. The *Z 42* appeared 38,000 miles from Zenobia and over 50,000 miles from the Palmyrene cruiser. She had four missile tubes. She launched a missile from each pair simultaneously, then launched the two remaining missiles after a textbook five-second interval.

Pursued by rockets fired from hopelessly too far out, the destroyer faded back into the Matrix. She was able to make the immediate transition because she hadn't used her plasma cannon, even though several cutters had been within the effective range of the 13-cm weapons.

Von Gleuck brought his *Z 46* in close—within a hundred miles of the *Turgut* and as a result close above Zenobia, deeper into the atmosphere than Daniel thought it was safe to extract. Mind, sometimes you have to do things that aren't safe, but this struck him as being pointlessly risky.

To protect the planet, Force Posy had to survive. Scarring the throats of your High Drive motors could lead to very bad results when battle required full power.

The Palmyrene destroyer didn't launch when its sensors registered the disruption of a ship extracting from the Matrix. That made sense when Daniel thought about it: the Palmyrene captain would expect the anomaly to be a friendly cutter, not an Alliance destroyer.

Even so, the *Turgut*'s guns shouldn't have remained locked in landing position. The buffeting a ship endured on entering an atmosphere from orbit stressed everything which projected from the hull. The Palmyrenes should nonetheless have trained on the anomaly and accepted the strain on their turret mechanisms and elevation screws, just in case it was hostile.

The Z 46 rippled her four missiles with little more than a heartbeat separating one from the next. The third missile came out tumbling and didn't ignite. Daniel suspected that the destroyer's hull had twisted during ejection so that the mouth of the launch tube had nipped the High Drive motors.

More haste, less speed ... but Daniel understood better than most the balancing act that any combat maneuver entailed. Von Gleuck had made a series of reasoned decisions which were different from those Daniel Leary had made, but that didn't mean either captain was wrong.

Four cutters had been keeping close company with the *Turgut*. One Palmyrene, then two more, fired their rockets as the Z 46 was launching her missiles.

The last image Daniel saw before the *Princess Cecile* finally inserted into the Matrix was the destroyer's rigging flying apart. Warheads were bursting into puffs of filthy smoke, shot through with orange fangs.

CHAPTER 24

ZENOBIA SYSTEM

Adele could see clearly again, though her eyes continued to switch between purple and orange as a result of the *Sissie*'s insertion. That would pass, she was sure. More worrisome was the realization that she faced a gap in coverage.

"Master Cory!" she said.

She should have called him Lieutenant Cory or perhaps Six-One, but neither of those naval titles felt proper to her. Simply saying "Cory" would have been adequate to cue a two-way link and wouldn't have bothered Cory himself, but it seemed to Adele to be discourteous. She was punctilious about her honor and would not hesitate to kill someone who treated her with disrespect. It therefore behooved her to be polite to others.

"Mistress?" said Cory, speaking to her image on the astrogation display. He'd begun doing that recently, just as Adele always had.

"When we return to normal space," Adele said, "we'll be one light-minute from where we inserted, won't we?"

"Yes, mistress," said Cory. He didn't ask why she wanted to know or even imply a question in his tone. *"We'll be at Rally Point Three, according to the Course Pack."*

"But the time elapsed in the Matrix will be longer than a minute, won't it?" she said. "That means that we won't actually be able to see what happened immediately after we inserted. Unless we go farther out later and pick it up then..."

As Adele spoke, she considered trying again to access the video log of the *Piri Reis*. It hadn't been working when she tried to enter it before, but perhaps the cruiser's technicians had repaired the problem by now.

And perhaps pigs will fly.

It infuriated Adele when she was balked because other people were incompetent. If the Palmyrenes had demonstrated foolproof security, she would have been rather pleased: it would have given her a goal to strive for, possibly unattainable but worthy of her effort nonetheless.

Instead the Palmyrenes, the *wogs*, were unable to perform basic maintenance. She couldn't read their records because they weren't capable of keeping records!

"Oh, I'll—" Cory said. Then he licked his lips and resumed in a careful tone, *"That is, if you'll let me take control of your console for a moment, mistress, I can set it up. We'll be in transit a calculated three minutes, seventeen seconds, but I think it may be longer by as much as a minute because of the damage our rig took before we inserted."*

He wants to take control of my console! Adele thought. She felt her muscles tense; her right hand closed on the second wand to free her left hand to reach for her pocket.

Then, very deliberately, she said, "Yes, all right, Cory. That appears to be the most practical method."

She smiled with a touch of wry humor. Intellect didn't prevent you from being afraid or even paranoid to the edge of psychosis. But intellect permitted you to act as though you were not afraid...and it might even permit a borderline psychotic to counterfeit sanity, much as Tovera had learned to act as though she had a conscience.

Adele deliberately disconnected her wands, though she continued to hold them. Cory, using the virtual touch pad he favored, set up a series of links among functions on the signals console.

As he worked, he said, *"We won't have the actual visuals, mistress, but if we take imagery of the two and a half minutes we were engaging the enemy, and we then couple that to..."*

Cory punched Execute. He wasn't smiling—he didn't smile any more often than Adele herself did, she suddenly realized— but his face had a look of earnest satisfaction. He'd always been an earnest youth, even when she'd first met him and learned that he could be expected to bungle even the most basic computations.

"To what we see as soon as we extract again," Cory went on, entering a new set of parameters. *"That gives us both ends of each course, you see. For as short a gap as we'll have, say three minutes and a half at worst, well, there's probably only one way they can get from before to after. And the computer will calculate it, you see?"*

Adele let her consciousness play with the words, twisting them about until she saw how their meanings fit together.

"Yes," she said when she was sure her statement was true. "I understand. Thank you, Cory."

"Thank you, mistress," Cory said. He was blushing. *"It's, that is, I've put an icon at the bottom of your left sidebar. You can bring it up any time after we extract. Or, well, you can do it now but it won't—"*

"I understand, Cory," Adele said gently. "Thank you."

What she *didn't* understand—one of the many things she didn't understand—was why people treated her with such deference. She was owed courtesy as a human being who was herself courteous, but she didn't deserve the degree of stumbling embarrassment to which she'd been treated this time and often. Cory was a commissioned officer, far Officer Mundy's superior in RCN terms, and she didn't trade on her civilian rank—

Lady Adele Mundy grinned coldly.

—unless someone pressed her the wrong way. And even then it wasn't her rank but her*self* that the other party found themselves facing, generally to their great discomfort.

Very deliberately Adele said, "If our duties following extraction permit, Cory, I may ask you to help me interpret the imagery as well, since I suspect it will involve more knowledge of shiphandling than I have."

"Yes, ma'am!" said Cory. *"I'll be pleased to, of course!"*

"Extracting!" said Vesey.

Adele split her main screen between the display on the command console—because Daniel would be looking at whatever was most important to the mission—and the communications inputs which were her primary duty.

Ordinarily the latter would consume all her time and more, but the Palmyrenes didn't signal in any sense that was useful to her, and the Alliance destroyers—

Adele felt herself cascade back into sidereal space. This time it was a blazing rush that made her tremble for a moment, an irritating delay before she could resume use of her wands.

As expected, the Plot Position Indicator indicated that the allied destroyers hadn't yet arrived at the rally point, though both had managed to escape from their lunge down the throat of the Horde. The *Z 42* had inserted ahead of the *Sissie*, now that Adele thought about it, but it still wasn't a surprise that the Alliance destroyer was still in the Matrix. She expected Daniel's command to outperform rivals, any rivals.

"Why haven't the cutters come after us this time?" Cory said. The link was still open—and being Cory, he probably realized the fact. *"They're still in place above Zenobia, all of them but one."*

Adele clicked up an echo of Cory's display. He'd overlaid a time-corrected pre-insertion image of the enemy fleet onto the real-time image, with significant discrepancies highlighted in yellow. There was a single bright caret, a cutter which had inserted into the Matrix and which probably meant nothing. Certainly the Palmyrenes hadn't decided to overwhelm the defenders in response to their attack.

The *Turgut* was deeper in Zenobia's atmosphere. The Alliance missiles must have missed, though von Gleuck had launched from point-blank range; the pair from the *Princess Cecile* were still distant from their target. Even if Daniel had aimed perfectly, the Palmyrene destroyer could easily maneuver clear—so long as her crew didn't ignore them in confusion and the press of other business.

Adele watched stiff-faced, then replaced the real-time image with the simulation Cory had prepared. All the missiles had been launched before the *Sissie* inserted, so re-creating the events was, as Cory had implied, a simple matter of physics.

It wouldn't have been simple for me. I have a great deal of technical knowledge, but it's deep rather than broad, and it doesn't include astronomical simulations.

The missileers were chattering on an intraship channel. Something had gone wrong with the starboard rollerway, but apparently it was fixed now: the deep rumble of a missile resumed, then ended with a squeal as hydraulic rams seated the weapon in the launch tube. Moments later the breech closed and locked.

In the simulation, the Alliance destroyers—blue beads— launched missiles, four and three paler blue lines, toward the red bead of the *Turgut*. The *Princess Cecile* was white, and two off-white missiles crawled away from her.

The Z 42, then the Z 46, vanished from the display. Adele frowned in concentration, then tried to magnify the simulation as though it was real imagery. To her delight and surprise— she hadn't given Cory enough credit—the dots expanded smoothly into shapes. She centered the *Turgut* and increased the magnification still further.

Filling the right half of the signals display, the Alliance destroyer had a vague graininess that could have tricked even Adele into believing it was real imagery had she not known otherwise. Apparently the software manipulated the initial image instead of creating an icon of greater precision. She would have to learn more about the system, when she had leisure.

Iridescent plasma wreathed the *Turgut* as thrusters slowed the vessel's plunge into the Zenobian atmosphere. A sparking trail marked its slanting course downward; at lower magnification the ship would look like a comet.

The *Turgut*'s turrets were withdrawn into the hull as if the destroyer was making a normal landing. As Adele watched, the pair on the spine lifted from their secured position. The *Princess Cecile*—any ship that Daniel commanded—would have kept its guns ready for action while attacking a hostile planet, but Daniel had more experience in such situations than most captains. Where were Palmyrene officers trained, anyway?

Before its guns could slew or elevate, the destroyer shuddered violently. Instead of continuing to descend, it hung at the same altitude for a moment, its train of plasma wobbling behind it.

A blue flash on the underside silhouetted the hull momentarily. The *Turgut* began to rotate slowly to starboard on its axis, its nose tilting down.

Two more flashes, vivid and instantaneous, lighted the port side. Half the port outrigger sagged; after a moment it tore from the hull and twisted toward the surface on a separate course.

A section of missile, probably one of the three from the *Z 46*, corkscrewed by so close to the *Turgut* that it appeared momentarily on Adele's closely focused display. The Palmyrene captain had cut in his High Drive to avoid incoming that his thrusters alone couldn't accelerate clear of. He'd been successful in that, but several motors had failed and crippled the destroyer.

Adele nodded crisply, a salute to Captain von Gleuck that he would never see. The *Turgut* would continue down to the surface and probably make a safe landing: High Drive motors were mounted on the outriggers, so their explosive failure hadn't damaged the hull. Even so, the destroyer would not for some while yet be freeing and supporting the troops sequestered on Diamond Cay.

Adele halted the simulation, then shrank it to an icon on her sidebar. Cory's miniature image watched her hopefully from the top range of her display. *I don't need your help after all*, she thought. She might have smiled, but that would have been cruel. The boy—he *was* a boy, twenty-two years old—so desperately wanted to be of service to her.

The Z 42 extracted twenty-one hundred miles sunward of the *Princess Cecile*. Both Alliance destroyers were fully rigged, giving them a plump, bristling appearance. By contrast, the Palmyrene cutters had only a single set of four antennas and wore minimal sails on them.

Adele suspected that in many cases the cutters only owned a partial rig. The little vessels had limited storage volume. If the Palmyrene logistics system was as chaotic as every other aspect of their organization, ships probably went without food, let alone sailcloth and cables. But they certainly could sail in the Matrix.

"*Posy Three to Posy Two,*" Daniel said. Adele had set her console to transmit automatically through a single laser head unless she overrode the default herself. "*Over.*"

"*Posy Three,*" replied the destroyer. The Z 42's captain was Fregattenkapitan Henri Lavoissier, but the speaker was female. *"Resume communications silence unless told otherwise! Out!"*

Adele's face went blank. *I may have something to discuss with one Fregattenkapitan Lavoissier when this is over*, she thought; then she smiled with a sort of humor. It wasn't her business but rather Daniel's, and she knew he would laugh it off. Even more to the point, it appeared unlikely that those aboard the Z 42 and the *Princess Cecile* would be in condition to discuss anything when the business was over, let alone carry on an affair of honor.

"Mistress?" said Cory. *"What happens if von Gleuck is killed? Are we under Lavoissier's command? Because from what Six said about this being Alliance space, we should be."*

Adele felt a suddenly jolt of cold fury. Then she caught herself and chipped out a tiny laugh.

"No, Cory," she said to the excellent, earnest, young lieutenant, "not unless Captain Leary loses his mind as a result of another blow on the head. In which case his loyal officers will regretfully transfer command to an officer who isn't incapacitated, not so?"

"Yes, mistress," Cory said gratefully. *"Thank you, mistress."*

All I did was tell him that Daniel has too much common sense to let protocol force him into a ridiculous situation, Adele thought. *Surely Cory knew that without my saying so?*

But the truth was that people tended to follow rules rigidly when they were frightened. The one disadvantage of a leader as strong and charismatic as Daniel Leary was that if he were removed, some of his subordinates—though exceptional officers in their own right—would be temporarily paralyzed.

Whereupon Lady Adele Mundy would sort things out. She would rather die than lose Daniel, but she would do her duty regardless of how she felt. She had been emotionally empty, *dead*, for the fifteen years immediately following the murder of her family. Meeting Daniel had resurrected her, but she would go on even if she lost him.

She would have a purpose, after all: the complete and ruthless destruction of everyone and everything responsible for Daniel's death.

Smiling, though not everyone would have recognized the expression as a smile, Adele used one of the *Sissie*'s microwave heads to key the circuit she had built into Zenobia's satellite communications system. A light-minute was well within her equipment's capacity, though the satellites were intended to send and receive planetary transmissions only.

Adele began combing the reports from teams of the Founder's Regiment. The arrests—and deaths resisting arrest—were consistent and gratifying. A smile started to spread across her face.

She got to a report filed by the militiamen guarding the palace. At first the significance escaped her.

The idiots!

She opened her mouth to report to Daniel, when the Z 46 finally dropped out of the Matrix nearby. Captain Leary had a battle to win; the other matter could wait.

But when the battle was over, Lady Mundy and her servant *would* take care of it.

* * *

Daniel bared his teeth in an instinctive grimace when he got a good look at the Z 46. Though he knew the appearance was worse than the reality, the reality was bad enough.

Because the destroyer was wearing a full suit of sails, the Palmyrene rockets had a large target. Their warheads were fused to detonate even on sailcloth, and as many as a dozen had done just that before von Gleuck managed to withdraw into the Matrix.

Plasma bolts would have vaporized the sails, blasting them off the hull. Fragments from the rocket casings had instead shredded the fabric with thousands of spinning knives. What was left trailed in strips like clothes rotting from a corpse.

The sails and occasional severed cables could be replaced easily enough. The antennas and yards had probably received very little damage, and the hull would only have been scratched.

The ship *looked* appalling, though, and the black, ripping storm of explosions which tore the sails would have done the same to anyone out on the hull. Most of the riggers on duty must have been killed, and the full rig would have required more than the minimal crew that Daniel had allowed.

The *Sissie* had lost one rigger of four, and Woetjans could no longer move about the hull, let alone climb. The Z 46 might well have lost forty people, leaving too few survivors to clear the damage as quickly as might be necessary. The work was already under way, though.

"*Posy One to Force Posy,*" signalled the Z 46. The voice wasn't that of Captain von Gleuck; presumably it was his First Lieutenant, handling an administrative chore. "*Report damage, over.*"

Responding to that was Vesey's job. Even if it hadn't been, a nearly simultaneous signal from von Gleuck himself said, "*Cinc to Three-Six. What do you think they're up to, Leary? I mean, why aren't they coming after us? Over.*"

Von Gleuck was just out of transition, but he'd analyzed the Palmyrene dispositions and understood the basic problem regarding them. *And* instead of issuing orders, von Gleuck was discussing the situation with an experienced fighting captain. That showed good judgment as well as flattering Daniel's ego.

Smiling—because it *was* flattering—more broadly than he might otherwise have done at the present juncture, Daniel said, "Cinc, this is Three-Six. The cutters can track us wherever we go, but we've done considerable damage to them every time they attacked unsupported."

By "we've done considerable damage" Daniel meant that the *Princess Cecile* had done considerable damage, but he kept the statement neutral both by policy and for the sake of fairness. The Palmyrenes had been coming to the *Sissie*, giving Sun and Rocker most of the opportunities; and during Force Posy's recent counterattack, the Alliance destroyers had kept their guns silent in order to escape more quickly into the Matrix.

"From the delay," he continued, "I'd guess that Admiral Polowitz plans to bring the cruiser in with or just following the cutters the next time. She's as dependent on her sensors as we are, and our personnel are a great deal more skilled in using electronics. I think that if we keep moving, inserting every time we see the enemy inserting, we'll be able to remain a force in being until the Founder's Regiment and the militia have captured the invasion force."

Or massacred it, of course. The Zenobians were as surely barbarians as the Palmyrenes were, and Founder Hergo might decide it was simpler to blast two thousand enemy soldiers into oblivion than to imprison them. Hard lines for the Cinnabar captains and crews if that happened, but it would be a problem for another day.

"I recommend that course of action, over."

A handful of Palmyrene cutters vanished into the Matrix. That meant they had been on the way for a minute already, but Daniel didn't imagine that even the best of them would actually reach the allied squadron in less than two minutes more.

The bulk of the remaining cutters, nearly forty of them, inserted over a period of only a few seconds. Daniel didn't see how the Palmyrenes managed such coordinated maneuvers; it was as though they were insects with some sort of hive mind.

"Posy, this is Posy Cinc," von Gleuck said. Behind the Z 46 spread a cloud of metallized fabric, the remains of sails which desperate riggers had cut away while the destroyer's High Drive pushed her along at a 1 g acceleration. New topsails had appeared on several antennas, but the vessel would be sluggish in the Matrix, scarcely as maneuverable as a freighter.

"Posy Two and Posy Three will proceed to Rally Points Four, Five and Six in succession," von Gleuck continued. He sounded bored. *"They will remain at Points Four and Five for thirty, repeat thirty, seconds only. At Point Six, they will rejoin Posy One. All Posy units will put themselves in a posture of mutual defense at Point Six. As the enemy appears, we will engage him. Acknowledge, over."*

"Sir, acknowledged, sir!" said Posy Two. *"Two out!"*

Daniel received the *Z 42*'s message as text at the bottom of his display. The Alliance captain hadn't copied his reply to the *Princess Cecile*, though that didn't make a practical difference because Adele was the *Sissie*'s signals officer. She must have used reflection from the flagship's hull to read the *Z 42*'s modulated laser signal.

"Three to Cinc," Daniel said, feeling the rush of excitement again. Cory stood beside the astrogation console, donning his rigging suit against the chance that he would have to replace a casualty out on the hull shortly. "Acknowledged, out."

He took a deep breath, then said, "Break. Lieutenant Vesey, execute the squadron commander's orders at your earliest convenience, out."

"Prepare to insert at once!" Vesey said. As expected, she had courses to all the rally points preset by now. *"Inserting!"*

As the lights within the compartment took on the glassy patina that preceded transition, Daniel's PPI display changed. The Palmyrene cutters still hovering about Zenobia vanished into the Matrix, and with them inserted the *Piri Reis*. Autocrator Irene intended to make a final end to this business.

Daniel was smiling faintly. That suited him as well.

"Up Cinnabar!" he called over the *Sissie*'s intercom as they headed again for battle.

Rally Point Five appeared to Adele to be as uninteresting as any other featureless waste of vacuum. Location was important, however; because Point Five was only a light-minute from Zenobia, she could at least survey the political situation there.

Though that was, as she well knew, an electronic equivalent of twiddling her thumbs. The success or failure of the coup would be determined here above the planet where the warships battled. There were details below that mattered to Adele Mundy personally, but she would have to be on the ground to affect them.

She smiled wryly. Which in turn required that she survive. It all came back to the naval battle.

Cory sat heavily at his console; he'd extended the bench to accept the bulk of his hard suit. He looked wanly at Adele's face on his display and said, *"Mistress, these quick transitions stress the ship and they stress me. But the* Sissie*'ll be all right when it comes to cases, and so will I."*

Adele's grin sharpened. "As I recall, the hallucinations I had when we didn't return to normal space for . . . what, something over twenty days' ship's time? That was at least as unpleasant."

"That was during the Strymon Mission, mistress," Cory said, smiling faintly as well. *"That was before I joined the company, but everybody at the Academy was talking about it. I'll bow to your expertise."*

"Though this has certainly been . . . unbalancing," Adele said after a moment's consideration. "I would say that perhaps human beings weren't meant to travel between the stars; but if that were true, I would be unemployed."

Cory laughed. *"Yes,"* he said, *"I'm sure that's why we do it, you and me and all of us Sissies. The RCN pays us so well!"*

That was a joke, of course, but the truth was that all members of the *Princess Cecile*'s crew were rich in their own terms, or anyway could have been rich if they hadn't drunk or gambled or whored away their prize money. Captain Daniel Leary had been the luckiest RCN captain since Captain Anston had captured a convoy of fullerenes.

Anston had gone on to become the Chief of the Navy Board, the head of the RCN. Anston had been a brilliant Chief, a fact which became ever more evident when his performance was weighed against that of his successors. It appeared to Adele that, given time and a degree of maturity, Daniel might follow Anston in that respect as in others. If he did, he would fill the position to the great benefit of the RCN.

Adele's smile didn't quite reach the muscles of her lips. *I wonder if the Chief of the Navy Board has a personal signals officer?*

Being who she was, Adele brought up the Navy House Table of Organization and checked: no, there wasn't a signals officer. The Chief had a broad degree of latitude regarding his staff, however. For example, Admiral Hartsfeld, who had replaced Admiral Vocaine during the change of senatorial leadership that preceded the Peace of Rheims, had a wine steward. Daniel didn't need a wine steward.

Vesey said, *"Prepare to insert!"*

Another ship appeared on Adele's display. She started to call up the particulars, but before she could highlight the newcomer, Vesey said, *"Inserting!"* and the *Princess Cecile* shivered out of normal space.

"Mistress," said Cory, *"it was the Z 42. She isn't able to keep up with us even though she wasn't damaged, but almost."*

In a grudging tone he added, *"This pair isn't bad at shiphandling, though, even if they're Fleet. The Z 46 was chewed up and spit out, which is why Posy Six is going to meet us instead of following."*

For a moment Adele felt as though her legs had disappeared while her head and torso were encased in cold gelatin. She remained motionless for a time—a second? a heartbeat or less?—until the sensation went away.

She frowned slightly. The *Princess Cecile* had completed insertion, so the feeling shouldn't have had any direct connection with that. It seemed rather to be a hallucination like those she had experienced during long immersion in the Matrix.

"Why is the Z 46 joining us at Point Six?" Adele said, working to get her head around the problem. "Will they have repaired—"

Surely not, not such a tangle as the explosions left!

"—their rigging in the interim?"

"Oh, no, mistress!" said Cory, in an amazing mixture of deference and incredulity. Adele teetered between laughter and fury at the tone; neither was appropriate, so she suppressed both responses.

"We're going to ambush the cutters at Point Six, you see?" Cory said. *"Some of them are going to follow us from point to point, extracting the way they do—they're bloody good in the Matrix,* bloody good—*or just tracking us without extracting."*

"All right," said Adele. "But why at Point Six instead of just waiting for them where we rallied after our attack, at Point Three?"

"Mistress," Cory said, *"the cruiser, the* Piri Reis. *She needs an astrogator, not a pilot, so she won't be able to follow till somebody's computed a course. That's maybe ten, even fifteen minutes, I'd guess. It'd take us three or four, or for Six and maybe*

Vesey, well, less. You see? So the cruiser waits till we extract, and it waits till we extract again, and they're getting tired and frustrated, you see? And the cutters expect us to run too, right? And then, blam, they catch us but we're cleared for action and we hit 'em for Six before the cruiser can get under way!"

"Ah," said Adele.

She faced Cory. He turned also, rotating the seat of his console because the hard suit didn't allow him to twist his body sufficiently to look across the bridge otherwise. He looked surprised and more than a little concerned.

"Thank you, Cory," she said, dipping her head. "I do understand now, because you've decoded the signals for me."

Because that was what had happened. There hadn't been any announcement as to the plan: just of the practical measures required to effect it. Cory had understood what was happening, because the training he'd received from Captain Leary and Officer Mundy had turned him into a fighting officer in the best traditions of the RCN.

If I were to have a tombstone, that wouldn't be a bad epitaph to be carved on it.

There wouldn't be a tombstone, of course. Perhaps she could concentrate her will to twist into letters the vapor that would be all her mortal remains, though a phrase of that length was probably unrealistic.

"Extracting!" said Vesey. Daniel was working on a course computation, leaving the immediate maneuvers in the capable hands of his First Lieutenant.

Adele felt as pleased as she ever did when she turned again to her display. The airlock whined open as the riggers withdrew into the shelter of the hull. They would only be in the way in the point-blank firefight that would be taking place any moment now.

Signals Officer Mundy didn't have an obvious role for the immediate future either, but she would be ready if the situation changed. For now she began to review the interchanges she had recorded when she most recently entered Zenobia's communications network. That might be useful, if she survived.

Daniel had inset visuals of the gunners' faces onto his display. Sun looked bright and eager, ready for anything. He might not really be that cheerful, but he certainly seemed to have just climbed out of bed on a lovely morning.

Rocker wore a woozy, blinking expression; he massaged his temples with his fingertips. His eyes were focused on his gunnery board, however, and the worst you could say about him was that the rapid transitions had left him in no worse shape than Captain Leary. If either of the regular gunners had been incapacitated, Daniel would have had a reasonable—a not completely unreasonable—excuse for taking over the position, since he had a demonstrated flair for gunnery.

The flash of disappointment made Daniel chuckle at himself. Paradoxically, that made him feel better. He had more important things to deal with than potting individual Palmyrene cutters with plasma cannon. None of his real duties were as straightforward as running a gunnery console, however, nor as much fun.

Positions were reporting. Technicians slapped virtual

buttons at their stations, indicating that they were alert following extraction, and the bosun's mates were calling in the readiness of their watches. Whether manual or oral, each report became a green light down the left side of the command console and its equivalent in the BDC where Vesey presided.

The rapid transitions hadn't crippled the *Sissie* or her crew, but Daniel could see a rigger collapsed in the corridor and there were doubtless other casualties. It didn't matter how experienced you were; it was disconcerting at the level of nerve impulses to shift back and forth between sidereal space and infinite universes which had no place for human beings nor apparently for life as humans understood the word.

An anomaly began to coalesce into substance less than fifty miles from the *Princess Cecile*. It was at about eighty compass degrees to starboard and so almost perfectly aligned with the corvette's horizontal axis.

"*Dorsal target!*" said Sun, using his whole right fist to slew the turret while his left hand depressed his guns. Both gunners had kept their weapons at a forty-five degree elevation from the hull as a resting position.

"*I'm on it!*" said Rocker simultaneously. The anomaly was almost squarely on the division point between the two gunners, and it might well be that, because an antenna was in the way, the dorsal guns didn't have a clear shot despite the fact that the target was slightly above the midpoint. Most of the *Sissie*'s rig was stowed as though for landing, but sometimes your luck was exceptionally bad.

Even so, Daniel had opened his mouth to shout, "Rocker, give way—"

—when the anomaly became a Palmyrene cutter wobbling at a skewed angle, its stern as much as any part of the hull aligned with the corvette. The *whang!* of Sun's plasma cannon, the left tube only, punctuated the low vibration of the rotating turrets.

The cutter's starboard half spun like a flipped coin away from the fireball which had devoured the remainder of the vessel. Its High Drive hadn't lighted in the seconds following extraction. Without power, the cutter couldn't bring her armament to bear on the *Sissie*.

It wasn't only the Sissies who found the quick transitions racking. *The Palmyrenes may be bloody fine spacers*, Daniel thought exultantly, *but they aren't supermen!*

More of the telltales on his sidebar—amber until toggled by reporting spacers—were flashing green. The *Sissie*'s crew was recovering; if not completely, then almost completely.

"Incoming!" Cory announced, though everyone aboard the corvette with a live display must already have been aware of the six anomalies fluttering about them like flies above a corpse. Five were within a hundred-mile radius of the *Princess Cecile*, while the last was at eleven hundred miles, almost directly off the bow.

Both gunners were shouting. Daniel noted how the two turrets lay at present and which direction they were rotating, then split the potential targets between them with blue and red highlights.

"Gunners, this is Six," he said sharply as he transmitted his assessment. "Red are dorsal targets, blue are ventral, out."

He didn't ask Sun and Rocker to acknowledge, because they were properly too busy to worry about that. They *would* obey, though, or they'd lose their ratings as soon as this was over.

Daniel grinned. Adele would have added, "if we all survive." He didn't think in those terms. It wasn't that he was optimistic; rather, it just didn't occur to him that he and the Sissies were going to fail.

The nearest anomaly congealed into the *Z 46*. Most of her antennas had been lowered, though her crew hadn't had time to furl or replace the sails. They were a mare's nest of tatters that would be the devil's own job to police up afterwards, but at least the gun turrets had clear fields of fire.

Daniel moved to lock out the *Sissie's* dorsal turret, but Sun was already shifting his guns to target red two. He was a small man and very fit, with a wasp waist and close-cropped hair. Sweat beaded on his forehead and the backs of his hands, and he wore an expression of fierce delight.

Sun liked what he did. Everybody Daniel knew who was really good at his job also liked that job. For the specialized gunnery required by the situations into which Daniel put the *Princess Cecile*, there was nobody in the RCN better than Sun.

Four cutters shimmered into normal existence. The dorsal turret fired two shots; both into the Palmyrene's stern, but the target was so frail that it didn't matter that the bolts weren't perfectly centered. The bow spun away like a paper lantern blown by the gases of its own destruction.

The ventral guns whanged, punctuating the rumble from the forward turret as Sun shifted to the next target. Rocker tripped his guns early, but the second bolt grazed the target instead of crackling past as the first had. A grazing hit was good enough, gutting the cutter like a fish and killing everyone in or on her hull.

The *Z 42* came out of the Matrix at 1100 miles, broadside to the *Sissie*'s bow. That was very respectable astrogation, for all that her captain was a stiff-necked bigot.

Daniel completed his computations. More—many more, at least thirty—anomalies were forming close by.

It was beyond question that the Palmyrenes were keying on the *Princess Cecile*. The Autocrator had taken Captain Leary's snub personally. She was reacting as an angry noble, not as a general or a head of state. In the longer term that was probably to the benefit of Zenobia's defenders, but it meant short-term problems for the *Sissie* and her crew.

"All Posy units," Daniel said. "This is Posy Three-six, transmitting new course data for Posy Three, out."

He was dancing on a razor blade. Even if he succeeded, the damage was going to be terrible, *terrible*. The odds were just too long.

Rocker fired; his target exploded violently. The cutter had been so close that fragments of it would probably hit the *Sissie*, though they wouldn't do as much damage as the—

Four rockets went off in quick succession along the corvette's underside. The damage-control sidebar went thirty-percent amber with a scattering of red speckles: seals had strained or failed completely. Daniel heard internal hatches banging shut.

"Cease fire!" he ordered, locking out the guns as he spoke. The gunners would be furious, but he was right and he was Six regardless of whether he was right or wrong. "Ship, prepare to insert ASAP. Inserting ASAP, out."

Six more rockets crashed along the *Sissie*'s spine. More seals and seams were leaking, and the buzz of the High Drive had risen to a ragged whine. Several motors had been knocked out by rockets which had hit the underside, and the outriggers—made of much thinner plating than the hull—would require extensive repairs before the *Princess Cecile* could make a water landing.

The warheads weren't intended to do serious hull damage, but a continued series of hammerblows would reduce the corvette to junk sooner rather than later. "As soon as possible" didn't necessarily mean "soon enough." Daniel kept his finger on the Execute button and under his breath prayed to the gods in whom he didn't really believe at this instant.

The *Princess Cecile* began to slide into the Matrix. The cutter which had fired the most recent salvo was inserting also, preparing to reload her rocket launchers and resume the attack in company with scores of her companions.

Just before the *Sissie* reached the merciless safety of the Matrix, the Palmyrene cutter became a fireball. A 13-cm bolt from the Z 46 had caught it.

Good luck to you and yours, Otto, Daniel thought as blazing needles entered his body with the transition. *And good luck to us Sissies as well.*

The Zenobians didn't need luck: they needed Force Posy. *So far, so good.*

CHAPTER 25

ZENOBIA SYSTEM

Adele continued to puzzle vainly about how the Palmyrenes communicated. Beyond question the cutters inserted and extracted in organized groups, though "squadrons" might be too formal a word; "schools" or "flocks" seemed more in keeping with Palmyrene society.

Perhaps Daniel would know whether there was a collective noun for maggots. That would be even more suitable.

Adele's self-deprecating smile was too slight even to make her lips quiver. She was apparently still angry about the abysmal Palmyrene record-keeping.

A voice somewhere on the fringes of Adele's consciousness said, *"Mistress?"* She ignored it as she ignored the repeated cycling of the airlocks and the sharp but less identifiable sounds coming through the hull.

The Palmyrenes *did* communicate. Unless they were psychic—which Adele wasn't ruling out, though they hadn't shown any signs of psychic abilities on Stahl's World—the hypothesis that best explained the situation was that they were communicating passively.

All that would take was a single low-power laser or even a UHF transmitter: the cutters were generally close enough together to make that possible. The cruiser could send such a signal to a key member of the swarm; that cutter's maneuvers could then be copied by several other ships—clan members? peers who took a whim to follow?—whose crews had been watching the first.

That wouldn't communicate the details of the planned maneuver, but the Palmyrenes didn't require anything more than the signal to insert. The cutter captains were doubtless as able to follow one another as they were to track their prey. They seemed to feel their way through the Matrix.

Adele couldn't see her screen. She froze—*What's happened?*—and realized that Tovera had leaned into the holographic display.

"Mistress," Tovera said. She was wearing an air suit, the light-weight, flexible garment intended for ship's side personnel who for one reason or another had to go out into vacuum. "Captain Leary has ordered everyone to put on their suits before we extract. Woetjans and I will help you into yours."

"No," said Adele, frowning at both the request and the presumption of it. "I'm going to find a way to read Pal—"

Hands gripped either side of her rib cage and lifted her away from the console. Her right heel kicked the couch as Woetjans set her upright beside it, then released her.

Adele spun in cold fury. Tovera held Adele's personal data unit so that it didn't drop to the deck when the bosun lifted its owner away.

Woetjans was wearing an air suit; her face was as gray as a corpse's. Sunken cheeks and dilated pupils showed that she was on heavy medication even though she was no longer hooked to the Medicomp—as she obviously should be.

"Woetjans, why are you in an air suit?" Adele said, the first thing that flashed into her mind after she realized the situation and her anger sluiced away. "I thought you always wore a rigging suit."

"I'm going out on the hull," Woetjans said, turning toward the bridge hatchway. "They need me on the hull."

"Mistress, don't let her," Tovera hissed in what would have been an access of concern in someone who felt concern. Surely a sociopath couldn't learn to feel emotion? That would be like a cripple growing a new leg.

The situation clarified in Adele's mind; she had finally understood. She snapped, "Woetjans, I need you! Help me with my suit or I won't be able to get into it."

Woetjans was in an air suit because fragments of rocket warheads had damaged her rigging suit beyond quick repair. Many chunks of steel had continued on into Woetjans' legs and torso.

"Ma'am?" said the bosun, staggering as she changed direction. "Yes, ma'am, your suit. You got to be suited up, because the wogs're gonna kick the crap out of us, you know? I got your suit...."

Woetjans' face grew puzzled. Adele looked at the deck beyond her and saw an air suit, rolled and packed into its helmet. The bosun must have dropped it when she lifted Adele from the console.

"Here it is," Adele said, stretching to reach the packet. If Woetjans bent, the chances were that she would fall flat. She still had her strength, but the drugs managing her pain left her operating on reflex alone. "You can help me, Woetjans."

The bosun's hands began unrolling the suit. Her blank, black eyes were turned toward the bow, but she didn't appear to be looking at anything.

Fiducia was seated at the missile console. The other bridge stations, including the command console, were empty. Adele blinked and said, "What's happened? What's gone wrong?"

"All the riggers are on the hull clearing the damage," Tovera said. "And the officers with training as riggers; all but Vesey in the BDC."

She smiled faintly, though Adele wasn't sure what the expression meant. "Hogg's out with the Captain, too," Tovera added. "I doubt he's any more use than I would be, but since you stayed on the bridge, I didn't have to make a fool of myself."

I should have been aware of that, Adele thought. *What was I doing? Examining imagery of the Palmyrene fleet, I suppose, but wouldn't I have noticed the bridge emptying?*

"Where is Sun?" she said as took in the situation. "Shouldn't he be at his position?"

"B Dorsal folded over the turret, ma'am," Woetjans said, stretching the air suit between her spread arms. Adele had almost forgotten the bosun's presence. "A bloody rocket sheared the antenna off right at the base hinge, and the stays twisted over the gun barrels when the mess come down. Sun's helping clear it."

Woetjans closed her eyes and swayed briefly, then opened

them again. "You put your suit on so I can go out with them, ma'am," she said. Her voice was as hollow and lifeless as an echo from a catacomb.

Tovera whispered in Adele's ear, "There's nobody else aboard she'll listen to, mistress. I asked her to help me, you see?"

Yes, of course, Adele thought. Aloud she said, "Hold the legs of the suit open for me, Woetjans. I'll put it on."

There were few enough people aboard the *Sissie* who would expect the bosun to take their orders anyway. Not even Daniel could be sure that Woetjans would obey if she thought her duty lay in a different direction.

Adele smiled ruefully. *She* could sidetrack the barely conscious bosun not by force of authority, but because Woetjans knew at the core of her being that Officer Mundy was hopelessly inept. Adele needed to be helped with ship's business which a fourteen-year-old apprentice could handle without supervision.

"Are we seriously damaged?" Adele said as she stepped into the suit, resting her hand on Woetjans' shoulder. She tried not to put any weight on it, but when her right toe caught on the fabric and she started to topple, the bosun caught and steadied her with careless ease.

"The rig's tore up," Woetjans said with mechanical calm. "The one antenna is all, but some yards was hit and the sails is all tore to crap. Even furled, you know? Cut to crap. We'll have to hang a whole new suit, pretty much."

She swayed again. Tovera stepped behind the bosun and leaned into her shoulder blade. For a moment Adele didn't think that would be enough, but Woetjans recovered her balance.

"And the hull?" Adele said, trying to sound brightly interested. Air pressure within the hull seemed to be down, and a damage control party of technicians was spraying bright pink sealant along seams in the corridor ceiling.

"Not my duty," Woetjans said. "They won't have no trouble, though. They can use the scrap sails for the bad patches anyhow, stick them down on the plating. They're not good for anything else, all tore to crap."

Adele had her arms into the sleeves of her suit. She faced the bosun to let her seal the center seam. Instead, Woetjans turned and said, "Got to get out and clear the rig. Tore to crap!"

"Woetjans!" Adele said. "Help me!"

The bosun faced around and swayed. Tovera stepped back, braced to catch but not to steady her. *Better that Woetjans fall than that she go out on the hull in her current state.*

The airlock cycled open. A phalanx of spacers bulled through with Daniel and Sun in the lead. Hogg in an air suit and a grim expression followed close behind his master. Tovera guided Woetjans to the side, but reflex had already started the bosun moving out of the way of incoming personnel.

"Ship, this is Six!" Daniel said, his words echoing from the PA system. He'd taken off his helmet but was shouting into it as he trotted toward the bridge. "Prepare to extract in ninety, that is—"

He banged down onto the command console.

"—nine zero seconds! We're going to well and truly stick it to them, Sissies!"

* * *

Daniel had helped the riggers in pitching Dorsal B over the side instead of strapping it to the hull to be broken down later. In theory Dasi was in charge of the team; but since Six was present, the bosun's mate would probably have tried to salvage the upper two-thirds of the antenna and the attached yards.

That would have been the wrong decision. It would have cost time, and that might have meant losing the whole ship. Daniel's hand signals to the riggers might have been missed in the general haste, but he'd stepped close with his heavy loppers and cut away the shrouds binding the antenna to the hull.

Whereupon the base of the mast rotated free and caught Daniel one hell of a crack on the right thigh. His rigging suit saved him from a broken bone, but he was pretty sure that he had—or anyway, would have—quite a bruise.

That was cheap at the price. If he hadn't gone out on the hull, he'd have been biting his nails at the command console, eaten up with misery that the *Princess Cecile* hadn't reached her extraction point yet. Labor which was physically and mentally exacting was just what Captain Daniel Leary needed to keep sharp for what came next.

Mind, it would have been a *really* bad time to have broken his thigh by pretending to be a rigger when he was actually an out-of-shape officer who spent so much time at a console that he was mostly a liability on the hull in a crisis. Still, it had worked out well enough.

The airlock opened again. Even with both locks crammed full, it would require three cycles to bring in all the personnel on the hull. There wouldn't be time to complete the process, but it would—barely—be possible to get the last group of spacers into the locks and therefore out of the hail of ions and shrapnel which might shortly rake the *Sissie*. That was good enough, because it had to be.

The *Princess Cecile* was taking nearly eleven minutes of ship time to travel less than—slightly less than—one light-minute in sidereal space. Short transits were much less efficient than long ones, but the present ratio would have been embarrassing for a civilian vessel with a minimal crew.

The problem was the sails. Their fabric, charged, blocked Casimir radiation and shifted the corvette among the infinite bubbles of the Matrix. The Palmyrene rockets had done such extensive damage that the *Sissie* wallowed between universes instead of slipping like a seabird in a stiff breeze.

Riggers had hung new topsails on the four C antennas and topgallants on Port and Starboard F to provide leverage to the main driving sails. That wouldn't allow the sort of delicacy which Daniel—and the *Sissie*'s whole company—made a matter of pride, but—nothing else appearing—it would have allowed a crisp, precise transit to where the corvette needed to extract.

Precise it would be because it had to be; the sort of slop that freighters tolerated would mean death and—worse—failure for the *Princess Cecile* in the present situation. It wasn't crisp, however, because the tags of sailcloth which dangled from the yards interfered with the set rig. The transit had been a series of mushy corrections and overcorrections.

There hadn't been enough time to completely clear the tatters or even the bulk of the tatters. The riggers—and at least a dozen technicians from the ship side, who had their own work cut out for them with repairing or at least assessing the damage to the thrusters and High Drive—had done what was humanly possible in the time available.

Very shortly the *Sissie* would receive a further hammering, one which would undo most of the current repairs and very possibly blow the ship to oblivion. But—Daniel's expression was a ruthless smile—if things worked out as he planned, there would be far fewer Palmyrenes present to gloat about it.

The outer airlocks, both bow and stern, closed, sending muted temblors through the hull. A less experienced ear would have missed it.

The sound might have passed beneath even Daniel's auditory horizon if he hadn't wanted so desperately to hear it: his spacers were in from the hull. They weren't safe now, but they were as safe as the *Princess Cecile* herself was.

"Ship, this is Six," Daniel said. The cheerful lilt he heard in his own voice made him smile in amazement. "This is going to be a quick out and in, Sissies; we'll launch missiles and off again. I hope we're gone before the wogs react, but if they're too quick then, well, we're RCN and we came to fight, didn't we? Up Cinnabar!"

There were ragged cheers. Specialists in air suits were running for their action stations, and the riggers waiting in the rotunda were jockeying for position to be in the first lockful when Six ordered them out again. Over their raucous babble came Vesey's voice on the PA system: *"Extracting!"*

Daniel poised, feeling anticipation. His eagerness to try conclusions with Autocrator Irene overrode his subconscious flinch at the discomfort of transition.

Subjective reality rose up and batted him in the stomach.

He felt as though his body was being crushed down to a point; the pain made him gasp. He would have gasped if there'd been time, and if the sound could have fought its way up against the pressure squeezing his lungs from all sides.

The *Princess Cecile* was in normal space, eighty-three miles from the *Piri Reis*. The cruiser had stripped to a minimum sail plan; two of her three triple 15-centimeter turrets could have borne on the corvette. Instead, all her plasma cannon were aimed in the direction of the pair of Alliance destroyers which were battling cutters a full light-minute away.

"*Launching one,*" said Chazanoff. A jolt of high-voltage electricity vaporized a gallon of water. The soft violence of expanding steam shoved the missile out of the port launch tube.

Daniel had set up the attacks before he'd finalized the course plan. It would have taken him or Chazanoff less than a minute of additional computation to correct the missile courses, but there wasn't time for that or for even half that. If the cruiser's big guns got on target at this short range, the *Sissie* would vanish like gossamer in a furnace. To save Zenobia, the corvette had to survive long enough to reenter the Matrix.

The 4-inch turrets were traversing with penetrating hums, though Daniel had locked the firing circuits. He wasn't really worried that either gunner would ignore his orders not to fire, but accidents could happen. Locking the guns from the command console was a way to prevent a mistake which would keep the *Princess Cecile* longer in sidereal space, with fatal results.

"*Launching one!*" said Fiducia. The shock of her release was almost simultaneous with the Chazanoff's. The launches were so close together that the second missile might have bound in its tube—it didn't—or be damaged by the corrosive exhaust of the first. Under the circumstances, it was still the better way to proceed.

Daniel had divided the launch between the Chief Missileer and his mate, not out of fairness but to be sure that the attack would go ahead even if rapid transitions had incapacitated one or the other man. In the event, both missileers had performed flawlessly. Perhaps the chance to practice their specialty against a cruiser had armored them against the hallucinatory misery.

"Inserting!" Daniel said as he pressed the Execute button with his right index and middle fingers. If he had failed, Vesey was ready to back him up—just as the missileers had checked one another. Anybody could fail under the stress of these quick transitions. It wasn't a matter of skill or courage, just the whim of fate.

A rocket detonated on the point of the *Sissie*'s bow. Its ringing *CRASH!* made Daniel rock forward in surprise, though his fingers didn't twitch from the virtual button. The transition was already taking place.

Seams had started—he heard air leaking with a high whistle—but the second and third approaching rockets vanished when Daniel's display went blank. They probably passed through the volume of sidereal space which the *Princess Cecile* had occupied until a second or two previously.

Half a dozen cutters were still accompanying the Palmyrene flagship. Several of them had reacted more quickly than the cruiser's gunners had done. One, even closer to the *Sissie* than the *Piri Reis* was, had launched before Daniel could return to the Matrix.

The frozen moment released; the stress of transition dissipated. Daniel's console showed status displays for the corvette's power train and the less accurate—pointer-actuated—readouts for her rig. The hull vibrated as hydraulic motors turned the antennas in accordance with the astrogation plan; missiles rang and rumbled down the rollerways to reload the launch tubes.

Daniel took a deep breath. What he was about to do was the hardest thing he'd ever faced in a short but eventful RCN career. It was going to be equally unpleasant for everyone else aboard the *Princess Cecile*, but he was the only person for whom it was optional: his finger—his thumb would be on the control.

He barked a rueful laugh. It wasn't optional for him either. This was the only way he could prevent the Palmyrene cutters from gnawing Zenobia's defenders down to nubbins which the *Piri Reis* would devour at her leisure.

"Sissies," Daniel said. "This is going to be rough."

When the circumstances allowed, Daniel tried to keep his crew informed about what was happening. This time, however, he felt that he was apologizing—or confessing—rather than simply explaining. Nonetheless, if every other soul on the *Princess Cecile* rose to object, he was still going ahead with his plan. He was Six.

"We're going back to where we just inserted, off the starboard quarter of the wog cruiser," he said. "Then we're going to start to extract again."

The starboard missile clanked into its launch tube. Rollers continued to spin behind it with high-pitched whines, though they were barely audible until the port missile slid home also.

"That's what you all expect, I know," Daniel said. "We're

RCN, we're the Sissies, and we always go for the bastards' throats regardless of what they're going to throw at us."

There were cheers. Enthusiasm didn't make a lot of sense, but Daniel expected it and he was sure it was sincere. Over the years, RCN ships had won half their battles because their enemies knew they *wouldn't* back off, no matter what the odds. Recently the *Princess Cecile* had been the point of the RCN's lance in several of those engagements.

"But we're not going to extract," Daniel said. "I'm going to hold us in transition for as long as I can. Those cutters that have been following us like fleas on a dog. They're going to extract when they see us extracting, so they think. And they're going to come out right on top of their bloody cruiser which we've just sent two missiles at. I don't think we hit her, but we sure got her attention—and she's going to be spreading that attention around one bolt at a time to her own cutters."

The countdown clock on his display was nearing zero, the point at which Captain Daniel Leary would have to act or not act. He was RCN and a Sissie; he would act.

"Are you with me, Sissies?"

The cheers were real and full-throated; and there wasn't a spacer aboard who didn't know what it meant, but they were cheering anyway.

"Up Cinnabar!" Daniel shouted. He rolled forward the switch beneath his right thumb, just the least hair of a motion.

Daniel plunged into boiling lead. His mouth was open to scream, but pain burned his lips and tongue away—

—and he was RCN. His thumb held the wobbling vernier control, and the pain went on.

CHAPTER 26

THE COSMOS

For the initial millisecond of extraction, Adele felt as though her body was being pulled apart, cell by cell, by tiny pincers. Then, suddenly, she became what for her was Paradise.

Adele had many times been on the hull of starships in the Matrix. Daniel and officers whom Daniel had trained had repeatedly tried to show her what they themselves saw, the shadings of hue and intensity which allowed them to refine or even choose a course.

It had never worked. Though intellectually Adele recognized that the Matrix was a code, her mind persisted in treating it as a splotch of color.

She had never cared a great deal about graphic art. If she could recognize the subject of a painting, she liked it better than she did something described as Abstract. Either way, however, it was a way to cover an area of wall which didn't have bookcases in front of it.

To her, the Matrix had always been a very large wall which

had been painted by an Abstractionist. Adele regretted her inability to see what Daniel did, not because she wanted to conn a starship but because there was a great deal of information which was closed to her.

But no longer. Everything, *everything*, was clear and intelligible.

As the *Sissie* extracted, Adele had been mulling the question of Palmyrene intership communications. Now she *was*—she wasn't watching, she was part of the event—a spacer with long blond hair on the right side of his skull and the left side shaved. He stood on the hull of the *Piri Reis*. His hard suit had been cobbled together from pieces of at least three originals; the suit's left arm and right forearm had been anodized in gleaming bronze.

The Palmyrene was aiming a projector which rested on his right shoulder. The unit was deceptively simple: besides the laser emitter, it had a stabilizer and, built into the hardware of the objective lens, shape-recognition software optimized to pick out starships.

The operator was using keypads in both handgrips with speed and aplomb, despite the awkward position and his heavy gauntlets. The projector was sending his message to a cutter thirty-seven miles away. That cutter's captain was receiving the transmission on a spherical antenna no more than three feet in diameter; a processor converted the signal to voice and piped it down a length of flex plugged into his helmet.

Adele could have given the distance in feet or for that matter angstroms. *Everything* was open to her.

The Palmyrene system was crude but effective, so long as the parties were precise enough to make it work. Adele valued organization above all things and had little appreciation for craftsmanship: knowledge was knowledge, whether it was scratched on a potsherd with a sharp stone or illuminated in gold leaf and lapis lazuli on a sheet of choice vellum. Nonetheless, she found the Palmyrenes' skill to be impressive.

Part of Adele felt amusement, though she no longer had a body which could smile. Perhaps she devalued craftsmanship because she took it for granted. She was never in doubt as to where a pellet from her pistol was going to go, for example.

What are the Alliance destroyers doing?

It was the second question—the first was the location of the Palmyrene vessels—Adele would have set about determining when the *Princess Cecile* extracted. Now the thought was the answer: The Z 46 and the Z 42 were in the Matrix, struggling toward the point that Daniel had informed them was the *Sissie*'s next destination as he left von Gleuck and his consort behind.

The destroyers had been punished by eight or ten rockets apiece, but neither was as badly damaged as the *Sissie*. In part that was a matter of size: each destroyer had twice the corvette's tonnage and more than double its sail area to absorb a similar number of hits. Their sails were in tatters, but their antennas and yards were in relatively better shape than those of the *Princess Cecile*.

The Palmyrenes seemed determined to cripple the Cinnabar vessel and were launching at the destroyers only as an afterthought. When Daniel had taken the *Sissie* back into the Matrix, most of the cutters followed.

Some of them inserted, leaving behind the Alliance vessels at the rally point. The cutters which had volleyed their rockets were reloading their launching baskets. They would send fresh salvos into the corvette as soon as she returned to sidereal space.

Some cutters had tracked the *Princess Cecile* but hadn't managed to attack before their target reinserted. They simply shifted their courses within the Matrix. Their captains made hand gestures. In response crewmen hauled on cables, rotating antennas and spreading or furling sails.

The rigs were worked manually. Not only were the cutters conned from the hull, they dispensed with the hydromechanical linkages on which the vessels of the civilized universe depended.

Do the Palmyrenes think of themselves as a species different from civilized humans? Certainly they had skills that personnel of the RCN and Fleet could not imagine. Though the ability to dance about in the Matrix wasn't nearly as important as being able to organize data, a skill in which the Palmyrenes were sadly lacking.

The *Z 46* extracted almost on top of a cutter which hadn't yet reversed course to follow the *Princess Cecile*. The Alliance gunners were logy from transition. The turret in the middle of the destroyer's belly began to traverse, but not quickly enough.

The Palmyrene cutter was a large one, over five hundred tons; it mounted two launching baskets. Bright yellow exhaust flared from them; an instant later, rockets raked the destroyer's underside.

The *Z 46*'s starboard outrigger ripped in a series of red flashes punctuated by the blue-white scintillance of exploding High Drive motors. The destroyer heeled, pushed by the motors on the port outrigger. They too had been damaged, but not nearly so badly as the other set.

Von Gleuck, as calm as a statue seated on his bridge, tapped keys at two-second intervals even as the rockets were hitting: right index finger, right ring finger, right middle finger, right little finger. At each tap, the *Z 46* launched a missile. Like Daniel, the Alliance captain obviously preferred to carry out his own attacks.

Missiles...

The *Princess Cecile* had launched two in the moments before Daniel took the ship back into the Matrix. The range was very short—they hadn't had time to burn out and separate—but both had missed: by a mile, and by a mile and a half, respectively. Daniel's gamble had failed.

Adele was aware of the relationship of the *Sissie*, the Palmyrene cutters chasing her, and the *Piri Reis*. Each would have been infinitely separated from all others in normal space-time. Viewed from Adele's present unbounded perspective, they were converging on a single point.

What Adele felt was beyond contentment: *all* knowledge was within her compass. Adele Mundy was happy, possibly for the first time in her life.

Though she was not really alive now. That in itself might be why she was happy.

Very slightly Adele regretted not having a body, or at least not having lips to smile with. She remembered that smiling had been a pleasant sensation, one she indulged in more often since she met Daniel Leary than she had in the previous decades.

But now she had knowledge...and Daniel sat on the bridge of the *Princess Cecile*, where Adele Mundy would find him when she returned to being merely human. Besides, she'd found during the past five years that being human was bearable. Perhaps now it would be even better, because she could hope that when she died, there was a heaven in which she could believe.

Again Adele's lips would have smiled... and perhaps her psyche did.

The turrets of the Palmyrene cruiser were rotating, their triple plasma cannon locking on anomalies as they coalesced close aboard the *Piri Reis*. The guns began to fire individually, jets of plasma ripping tracks through the sidereal universe.

The heavy cannon had to cool for at least thirty seconds before they were reloaded. Nonetheless, the energy in a single bolt would have been sufficient to destroy the *Princess Cecile* as a combat unit, even though only a portion of the target was within the sidereal universe when the plasma ripped that point.

The corvette wobbled. It was on the verge of breaking free but still not quite in the sidereal universe. Cutters plunged into the volume of normal space surrounding the point where the *Sissie* seemed to be extracting. They arrived from every apparent direction.

Adele marveled. The little vessels vanished like thistledown in a bonfire, one and another and more, many more. Cutters touched by 15-cm bolts were destroyed completely, leaving only spars tumbling out of an expanding gas ball to prove that they had once been starships.

Don't they realize...? Adele thought. But of *course* Admiral Polowitz and his gunner realized that they were destroying their own cutters. They were shooting at two and three anomalies at a time as they appeared, knowing that at most one—the *Princess Cecile*—could be an enemy: the *Z 42* had extracted near her consort, the *Z 46*, ten light-seconds distant from the *Piri Reis*.

Polowitz understood—and he understood that he didn't have a choice. Half a dozen cutters had been destroyed before the Autocrator Irene realized what was going on, however. When she did—

"Polowitz!" Irene said, standing like a golden statue in the center of the cruiser's bridge. "Do you want to be whipped to death? You're killing our own men!"

The Autocrator's acceleration couch was gimballed at the foot to lift upright and rotate while still in contact with the person in it. Irene didn't have a console of her own, but she could echo any of the consoles to the adjustable display built into the left arm of her couch.

"Excellency," said the Admiral. His voice was firm, but there was sweat on his forehead. Whatever he had planned for his next words caught in his mouth.

Both dorsal turrets crashed; the left stern gun was still recoiling when the central bow gun spurted a thermonuclear explosion down the center of its bore.

The cruiser's bridge layout was circular with Polowitz' station in the far bow beside the command console where the ship's captain sat. All the Palmyrene officers were turned inward toward the Autocrator. On the *Princess Cecile* and most RCN—or Fleet—vessels, all but the command console were fixed to face the bulkhead, though the attached couches could be rotated away at need.

"Have you gone mad?" Irene said. When she was in a good mood, her voice had the timbre of stones sliding; now she shrieked like an angry seabird. "Stop shooting our own men!"

"Excellency, we can't take a chance," Polowitz said in a tone of desperate calm. "A chance with *your* life, Excellency. Leary is a demon, Your Excellency! We cannot—"

Three plasma cannon fired, then a fourth. Moments later, a fifth bolt vaporized a cutter after it completed extraction only twenty miles from the cruiser. Instead of giving independent control to his turret captains, Bailey—the gunnery officer— had put the *Piri Reis* on automated response. A computer was directing the weapons: slewing the turrets, adjusting the tubes' elevation, and tripping the laser array which compressed and detonated the pellet of tritium in the breech of each gun.

The gunnery computer could have been programmed to ignore targets which had successfully extracted unless they were hostile. The cruiser's gunnery officer—Adele had seen him; Bailey, ill-bred and ill-educated, the sort of man one expected to leave civilization to work for barbarians—hadn't thought to do so or hadn't been able to do so. He was ignorant and frightened and a fool.

I wouldn't have understood what was going on if I were human, Adele thought. Afterwards she would have asked Sun or Daniel for an explanation, which they would bubblingly have given. If there was an afterwards.

But now Adele simply *understood* with the whole of her being. She knew *anything* she chose to know. Her human intellect—fine though it was—couldn't encompass the Cosmos in its entirety, but any separate portion was hers when she considered it.

"—let him attack again, he won't miss the second time," Polowitz was saying. "You can see—"

The turret on the cruiser's underside fired, shifted minusculely, and fired again. Two cutters had started to extract, a hundred miles apart but almost in line with one another to the cruiser's guns.

Adele wondered if the gunnery computer could feel satisfaction. Her new state didn't give her subjective information like that; she could only look within herself.

The computer felt satisfaction.

"Polowitz!" the Autocrator said. She turned to the hatchway, where two guards stood. The now-vertical couch must be slaved to the motions of her body. "Shoot this madman before he kills more of our own men!"

The turrets fired in a rippling salvo, one and two and three, then a fourth bolt.

"Cease fire!" the admiral said. He rolled off his couch, trying to hide behind it while he drew his pistol; he hadn't been strapped in. "Cease fire, Bailey, cease fire!"

The guards raised their weapons—mob guns, again; flashy, messy, and a confession of incompetence in the person using it. Adele would have sneered at them when she was a human being; now her omniscient psyche felt a cold disgust.

"Cease fire, Bailey!" the admiral repeated, pointing his pistol toward the gunnery console. Several other officers on the cruiser's bridge were drawing guns, or in one case a long, curved knife.

Bailey bolted from his console, trying to put the Autocrator between him and Admiral Polowitz. A guard stepped forward and clubbed the gunnery officer behind the ear with the stubby butt of his gun. Bailey flew forward, bounced off the arm supporting Irene's display, and flopped back on the deck; his blank eyes were staring at the ceiling.

The guns of the *Piri Reis* fired twice more: Bailey hadn't had time to disengage the program he'd set to run them. Even so, there was silence after the second crashing shot.

The computer had run out of targets. Nearly thirty balls of gas, cooling and expanding, drifted in the cruiser's wake.

Adele's body sucked her psyche back into itself. The signals console was live again with real-world inputs. The *Princess Cecile* floated in vacuum some four hundred thousand miles from the *Piri Reis*. The game Daniel played with the Matrix had caused the corvette to drift significantly beyond the initial extraction point.

Adele felt a profound sadness. *Only human. Until I die.*

ZENOBIA SYSTEM

Captain Daniel Leary had a full if detached grasp of his surroundings, much as a mirror reflects what is before it. Reality touched only the surface of his awareness; he wasn't a part of what he saw.

The bridge of the *Princess Cecile* looked like the aftermath of a gas attack. Hogg had been sitting at the subordinate position on the back of the command console. It was intended for training or, during action, for a junior officer who could take over the duties if the captain were incapacitated.

The *Sissie* had too few watch-standing officers ever to put one on the back of the command console, so Hogg regularly used the position when the ship was in action. A rustic with a stocked impeller had nothing useful to do during a naval action, but he wasn't going to be separated from the young master when people were shooting at him.

Hogg held his impeller, but he lay on the deck as stiff as if he'd been brain shot. He'd been raising his left hand toward his face at the moment he froze; now it hung in the air.

So far as Daniel knew, no one in the past had ever held a ship in transition for—

He'd noted the clock at the right center of his display as he started the extraction.

—twenty-one seconds. Could it be fatal? But he hadn't had any choice. Not if he, if the *Princess Cecile*, was to save Zenobia.

Cory had rotated his couch away from the astrogation display. He sat upright, weeping uncontrollably. He appeared to be staring at Sun at the gunnery console, though that seemed unlikely on the face of it.

Sun wore his rigging suit, though he'd removed his helmet and gauntlets in the airlock on returning from helping clear the dorsal turret. He was now working industriously to clamp the right gauntlet onto his left cuff. The edges wouldn't mate, of course, but the gunner didn't appear to be getting angry. His smile was quizzical and earnest.

Fiducia had gotten up from the missile board and walked against the outer bulkhead. He usually buckled himself onto his couch, so he must have shown enough enterprise to release the harness. He continued to step forward with slow deliberation, seemingly convinced that eventually the hull would give way.

Daniel was confident that if he switched to views of the *Sissie*'s other compartments, he would see similar disruption. Certainly the riggers in the forward rotunda had been stunned as thoroughly as the bridge crew, Daniel included. Barnes was trying with increasing frustration to open the airlock, but he was trying to find the latch on the left instead of the right edge; his perceptions had been mirrored.

The exception to the general chaos was Adele. She was at work, her control wands flickering. She showed no sign of disorientation. Columns of text scrolled up both edges of her display, while the middle section echoed the command console: PPI above and a real-time image of the *Piri Reis* below.

Daniel had intended to send the *Princess Cecile* back into the Matrix when he found that he could no longer bear the, well, *insanity* of transition. He had expected that he would be confused and that some or even many of the *Sissie*'s crew would also be confused. The ship could drift in safety, out of the sidereal universe and away from her enemies, until her captain and crew were functional again.

That was a reasoned, intelligent plan. The emotional impact of reality was so much worse than what Daniel had expected that it bore almost no connection to that plan. He hadn't been able to reverse his thumb pressure, so the corvette had completed her extraction. She now wallowed in easy missile range of the cruiser.

Daniel's mind worked perfectly, or at any rate he thought it did. It unfortunately no longer had control of his body. He couldn't even tap a key to bring up imagery from the cameras in other compartments.

He didn't need to do that, of course. The technicians in the Power Room and the riggers in the lower rotunda would be in the same wretched shape as the Sissies he could see: numb, babbling, unconscious...and perhaps one or two others like Adele, apparently normal except that she was going on with her normal duties in the middle of blind chaos.

What Daniel *did* need to do—his mind told him this with perfect clarity—was to move the *Princess Cecile* out of the path of the missiles from the cruiser. The *Piri Reis* launched five missiles, then four, then five, and finally five more, allowing a reasonable five seconds between each salvo.

That was a poor percentage out of what should have been a volley of twenty-eight missiles total, but it would certainly put paid to the *Sissie* unless she moved. Retreating into the Matrix—there was plenty of time—would be the simplest way to escape, but with 413,000 miles of breathing room, Daniel or any of the corvette's officers could have maneuvered clear in normal space.

If they had been conscious and functional. Which apparently they were not, none of them.

Daniel strained to make his right index finger move. The system was set to toggle the most recent action. At the present moment, simply touching the Execute key would cause the *Sissie* to insert into the Matrix and avoid the incoming missiles.

He might as well wish that Zenobia's moons would fall into the planet: there was no connection between what he wished and the desired result. Vesey and Cazelet in the BDC were probably doing the same thing. If so, they were having as little success as he was.

Cory lowered his head into his hands but continued to sob. It didn't appear that he would come around quickly enough to save the *Princess Cecile* either.

At the signals console, Adele continued to carry on a conversation with someone beyond the volume included within Daniel's PPI. It would take only a light pressure on a virtual control to increase the PPI volume and display the other ship. Daniel couldn't move a finger for that purpose either.

The Palmyrene missiles had reached terminal velocity and were splitting into three segments each. It wouldn't be very long before they destroyed the *Princess Cecile*.

Adele felt sharp, fully in control of herself. That was her normal state, of course.

She realized that she had very little control over anything except herself. She had learned long since that she could shoot other people, but short of that she couldn't really affect their behavior; not even threats of shooting worked very well. She didn't let that concern her so long as she could depend on herself.

Now, after her experience in the Matrix, she felt particularly good. For the first time in her life she had a vision of a better existence that wasn't simply oblivion. She hadn't met God, but something or Somebody had vouchsafed her a view of a heaven in which Adele Mundy could believe.

She smiled wryly as she checked the electrooptical spectrum for incoming signals. Perhaps she would in the future preach a gospel of Deified Information. That, coupled with occasionally killing people, might prove even more fulfilling than her RCN duties. She wondered how Daniel would react.

But she had work to do now. She switched from text to audio as one of the three recently-arrived ships ten light-seconds outsystem from Zenobia said, "...*repeat, RCN Qaboosh Squadron calling Alliance Control in the Zenobia System, requesting immediate consultation with Admiral Mainwaring, over.*"

The ship—the patrol sloop *Dotterel*—was transmitting on 9.275 kHz in the shortwave band, a standard commercial frequency. The beam was directed toward the Alliance destroyers, but the *Piri Reis* would be receiving it as clearly as the *Princess Cecile* did. Adele suspected that the cutters, or at any rate most of the cutters, didn't have shortwave receivers.

Adele directed a bow laser emitter toward each of the new arrivals—the sloops *Dotterel*, *Penguin*, and *Espeigle*; she had probably seen them in the naval basin on Stahl's World, though even now one ship was very like another ship to her—and also, using the stern cluster, prepared to copy the message to Captain von Gleuck's vessels. They were still fighting a handful of Palmyrenes, but most of the surviving cutters—and there were over a score of them—had scattered when they took in the behavior of the Autocrator's flagship.

"*Princess Cecile* to RCN squadron," Adele said calmly. "We have been attacked by Palmyrene pirates who are also attacking the local Alliance squadron which came to our aid. We request immediate assistance against the pirates, over."

That was a compressed statement of the facts, and a strict

literalist might even have described it as a false statement. Adele would make peace with her conscience later; or simply live without peace. She was used to that, after all.

The delay was only slightly greater than the doubled transmission lag. Then the voice of Admiral Mainwaring announced, using tight-beam microwave, *"Palmyrene ship* Piri Reis, *this is Admiral Eliot Mainwaring of the RCN. I direct you in the name of the Republic of Cinnabar to cease fire immediately. Acknowledge at once, over."*

Simultaneously over modulated laser a voice that Adele didn't recognize said, *"Squadron to* Princess Cecile. *Put Captain Leary on at once, over."*

I wish that I could, Adele thought, but it didn't bother her to take charge of matters when they were within her competency. At this moment she appeared to be the only fully competent person aboard the *Sissie*. Even Tovera, seated at the back of the signals console, slumped against her restraints with a line of drool trailing from the corner of her mouth.

Aloud, Adele said, "Squadron, this is Signals Officer Mundy. The rest of the crew including Captain Leary has been incapacitated in action with the pirates. As agents of the Republic we attempted to forestall a pirate attack on an Alliance vassal, in accordance with our treaty obligations. The pirates thereupon attacked us. Over."

That was true in every jot and tittle. Intellectually, Adele didn't believe that telling the truth wiped out the stain of an earlier lie, but she felt better nonetheless.

"Mainwaring, this is Autocrator Irene!" the *Piri Reis* replied using modulated laser. *"The Zenobia System has requested*

to come under Palmyrene protection, which I have graciously granted to them. Return to your base immediately or it will be the worse for you."

The *Princess Cecile* had the best optics available: Daniel had at his own expense replaced the excellent RCN-standard units with a special order from a Pantellarian shop which he believed to be even better. Thanks to them, Adele was able to intercept the laser message even from well off the axis of the sending head.

Adele brought up the particulars of the three RCN vessels. Daniel would have known their statistics off the top of his head, and even in her case the details confirmed her suspicion: patrol sloops had no more business engaging a heavy cruiser than a corvette did. Less if the corvette was the *Princess Cecile*, since the *Sissie* and its crew had experience with such attacks in the past.

Each sloop carried six 4-inch guns in separate mountings. For most warships the plasma cannon were defensive weapons, primarily intended to nudge projectiles off a collision course with the vessel. Twin mountings worked best for that purpose, permitting the gunners to hammer a target in close succession before the effects of previous bolts had worn off.

Patrol sloops were relatively large—bigger than destroyers, let alone the *Sissie*—but they were expected to deal with pirates and disturbances on the ground. Pirate cutters might appear in considerable numbers, but they were individually far less resistant than a solid projectile. The single mountings gave better coverage for single shots.

Each sloop was equipped with two launching tubes and supposedly ten missiles. Adele had seen enough of reality on the fringes of civilization to wonder if the whole Qaboosh Squadron had ten missiles among the three of them. The vessels' most common usage was to land parties of troops or armed spacers, to put down riots or to cow local chieftains into paying taxes and refraining from killing and devouring Cinnabar merchants.

Throwing such ships against a modern heavy cruiser would be suicide. Not pointless suicide, however. The action would be another heroic legend to be taught in the RCN Academy, more useful in a way than a victory. Would-be officers had to learn that one's duty wasn't limited to the way one behaved in battles which could be won.

"All RCN vessels, prepare to engage the pirate cruiser," said Admiral Mainwaring in a tone of bored nonchalance. The statement was a bit of theater: the *Dotterel* continued to use laser commo with one of the emitters directed toward the *Piri Reis.* *"Break. Your Excellency, I must direct you to lay to and await boarding by officials of the RCN, over."*

"You bloody little worms!" Irene said. Even screaming in a complete fury and with her voice compressed for transmission, there was a melodious power to her words. *"I will wipe you from the universe! The Qaboosh is Palmyrene, and I am Palmyra! I will execute every Cinnabar citizen in the region and stack their heads—"*

The Autocrator's rant stopped abruptly. Adele frowned, wondering whether her own equipment or the cruiser's was at fault. She still had a tracking signal, the laser equivalent of a carrier wave, from the *Dotterel,* so—

"Bloody hell!" Admiral Mainwaring blurted. *"They took*

a direct hit! Where did those missiles come from? Milch, who launched those missiles?"

Ah. Because Adele was echoing the command console on her own display, she'd had the answer to what had happened to the signal in front of her all the time. She backed up the image of the *Piri Reis* to the point the cruiser exploded from hydrostatic shock, then let it track forward again.

"Squadron, this is the *Princess Cecile*," she said. She was being quietly polite because at the moment she was a librarian answering an information request. "Captain von Gleuck fired missiles as soon as he extracted into his current location. Because the range was so long, I suppose the Palmyrenes lost track of them in the press of other business."

Adele frowned and pursed her lips. "I wonder," she said, "if that was what Daniel had in mind all along? Captain Leary, that is, sorry."

By this time Adele had more firsthand experience of watching missiles strike starships than most officers in the RCN. The death of the *Piri Reis* was an unusually vivid example, however, because the projectile had been at terminal velocity—a significant fraction of light speed.

The impact was on the cruiser's starboard quarter, coursing forward. The upper stern turret remained attached to the hull; the lower turret was whole but was spinning clear because the frames supporting the turret ring had been blasted away.

Everything ahead of the projectile's entry point was a glare of white-hot gases. The forward portions of the cruiser's hull hadn't burned: kinetic energy had caused them to sublime instantly.

The remnants of the stern flattened as the shock wave

443

of expanding gas flung them away. Acceleration must have killed any personnel in that portion even if the fireball hadn't cremated them.

"Princess Cecile," said the officer speaking from the *Dotterel*. *"You are under attack! By all the gods, spacers! A salvo of missiles is tracking toward your location! Over!"*

Ah.

Yes, of course. While there would be a certain justice in the *Sissie* being destroyed by long-range missiles just as her opponent had been, Adele didn't require that her data be symmetrical; just that they be properly filed.

She looked at her display. Though she could duplicate the functions on it, Daniel might have some obvious markers at his own station.

If not—and "not" was certainly more probable—she could look for a suitable menu. Acceleration? Maneuvering? Precisely how would the spacers who designed the system have indexed the necessary information? She doubted that she could articulate a question at this level in a fashion that the officers of the *Dotterel* could answer.

With a slight smile, Adele rose and walked to the command console. This was an unusual information request. It promised to occupy her fully during what would probably be her last minute or minutes of life.

CHAPTER 27

ZENOBIA SYSTEM

Daniel wondered what condition the *Z 42* and *Z 46* were in. Most of the Palmyrene cutters had followed the *Princess Cecile*, but fifteen or sixteen had remained at the previous stage to batter the destroyers.

The Alliance gunners weren't quick enough in laying their sights on high-deflection targets. They had destroyed a handful of the cutters, but several of those had gotten off a volley of rockets before taking a 13-centimeter bolt.

The pounding from rocket warheads would have stripped most of the antennas and yards from the destroyers. Their outriggers had probably been hammered to scrap by now, and with them all the High Drive motors. A destroyer would carry one or two spare motors, but the level of damage these ships had received meant it might take them days to reach Zenobia orbit without outside help.

Daniel could fault the Alliance gunners, but the missileers who had programmed the attack on the *Piri Reis* had done a faultless job. At the range of the launch, the missile segments spread significantly. Even so, the hit wasn't a fluke: the cruiser was squarely in the center of the pattern.

If Daniel's lips could move, he was smiling; he couldn't be sure. Even with a perfect launch, there was a great deal of luck if a destroyer's meager salvo hit a target at that range. Well, he wasn't going to complain about that. The gods knew that Zenobia's defenders had needed luck.

The cruiser's twenty-one rounds wouldn't require luck to destroy a corvette at a comparable distance, unfortunately, and they bid fair to do just that. It was really a pity that Daniel hadn't managed to drop the *Sissie* back into the Matrix as he'd intended rather than completing their extraction. They wouldn't even be able to claim the *Piri Reis* as a final victory: that was the *Z 46*'s work, pure and simple.

Though the chances were that Cinnabar historians describing the action would shade reality and say otherwise. *That'll leave Adele turning in her grave. Well, cause her vaporized atoms to spin more quickly on their axes.*

Adele walked briskly into Daniel's field of view. She adjusted his couch to the left, making room for her to sit cross-legged on the floor in front of his display, then took out her personal data unit and slaved the console to it.

Daniel suspected that the command console couldn't be taken over that way, at least if you listened to the manufacturers and RCN security personnel. Well, they would never learn otherwise, given the sleet of projectiles approaching the *Princess Cecile*.

Adele was…great gods and little fishes! She'd called up

a Help menu and was asking what commands to give to maneuver a starship in sidereal space! What did she think she was going to find: *Shiphandling for Toddlers? Every Boy's Book of Space Combat?*

Daniel began to laugh. He was *really* laughing: gusts of laughter were racking his body.

Adele looked up at him. "Well, can you do better?" she snapped.

Daniel pressed the Execute button, toggling the corvette back into the Matrix. It would be close, but there was just enough time before the missiles arrived.

"No, my dear friend," he said. "Without you, I couldn't have done nearly as well."

Transition felt like a bath in ice water this time, causing Daniel to shudder. It was good to feel his muscles moving again, after the bodiless horror of the recent past.

At the moment of transition, Adele felt as though her skull was being split with the back of an axe. That or equally unpleasant sensations were among her mind's usual responses to entering and leaving the Matrix, so she supposed she ought to be pleased that things were returning to normal. She got to her feet.

The crew of the *Princess Cecile* was coming around—the members Adele could see, at any rate. She had been willing to accept them as a representative sample when they were unconscious or psychotic, so it was only proper to assume that the recovery was general also.

Fiducia sat at his console again. He looked up, then away with a shamefaced expression when he noticed Adele standing beside the command console.

She frowned. He had nothing to be embarrassed about. An event had occurred which had damaged most of those involved with it. One might as well apologize because one's bullet wound is dripping onto the carpet.

Hogg squatted on the deck; he'd laid the impeller across his knees so that he could rub both cheeks with his fists. He looked angry and unhappy, but he didn't seem to have suffered the physical injury that Adele had feared when she saw his stiff body.

As for Cory, he had rotated his seat back toward the display and was reviewing the record of the minutes before the *Princess Cecile* retreated into the Matrix. That was a very sensible, very professional, thing to do. Adele felt a surge of pride which intellectually she didn't believe was justified.

She smiled; a tiny expression, but more than she would have managed a few years ago. She had a great deal of experience in controlling her emotions, but that didn't prevent emotions from stirring her. It still surprised her to feel anything besides the red fury which had been so long and so close a companion.

"Barnes," Daniel said. Adele wasn't wearing a commo helmet, but since she was standing beside the command console she didn't need amplification. "Take out the starboard rigging watch. I don't have a course yet, but I expect to determine one after I've had a chance to consult with Vesey, over."

He looked up at Adele and grinned. "I was afraid that insertion was going to drop me back into whatever state it was that you

448

laughed me out of," he said. "Instead it seems to have brought all the rest of us back to proper form. Rather like pulling the power and then rebooting to reset a computer, isn't it?"

Adele thought about the analogy. Computers weren't nearly as similar to human minds as people seemed to think they were...but it wasn't a matter to argue about, at least not now.

"Yes," she said, keeping her qualifications to herself. "And as for courses, Daniel, I believe we need to return to Calvary as quickly as possible. Though—will we be able to land in the harbor with the damage?"

Daniel frowned. "A few sheets of structural plastic around the starboard outrigger and it'll hold air well enough to allow a real fix," he said. "But I'm sure Admiral Mainwaring will want to be brought up to speed immediately. Certainly before any RCN vessel lands on Zenobia, at any rate."

Adele made a dismissive gesture with her left hand. "The Admiral can wait," she said. "Commander Gibbs escaped from Zenobian custody during the confusion. He's in Cinnabar House and has taken Commissioner Brown and his family hostage. They'd gone back after the end of the emergency."

Daniel's eyes narrowed. "What are the local authorities doing, Adele?"

"Founder Hergo has ordered his own forces to seal off the area but to take no action," Adele said. "He's waiting for someone from either Cinnabar or the Alliance to take charge of the business so that the Zenobian government won't be blamed for the outcome."

"Ah!" said Daniel, nodding his understanding. "Yes, we should be able to put down within three hours. If there's more of a problem with the starboard outrigger than I foresee, we can use the plaza fronting the Palace. Presumably Hergo can have that cleared. And then we'll decide how to proceed."

Adele felt her lips smile. "I felt that Tovera and I should be put in charge of the negotiations," she said.

"And me," said Hogg, suddenly cheery again. "Neither of you are worth squat beyond pistol range, and I—"

He hefted the powerful impeller at the balance.

"—bloody well am."

Yes, it might be very bloody indeed. Adele's lips twitched again at her unspoken joke.

CHAPTER 28

CALVARY HARBOR, ZENOBIA

Adele had decided to wear utilities on the ground: they were loose, practical, and had pockets for even more equipment than she expected to carry. She glanced toward Daniel, waiting beside her in the *Sissie*'s boarding hold while the ship's exterior cooled enough to allow them to disembark.

Daniel met her eyes. Though she hadn't spoken, he grinned and said, "No, these aren't—"

He fluffed the breast of his second-class uniform. He wasn't wearing either medal ribbons or a pistol belt; both were permissible by regulation but not required.

"—because I'm worried about being called up on charges of being out of uniform. What we're doing qualifies as dismounted duty as sure as riot suppression would. Though I sincerely hope that it won't involve shooting."

Tovera snickered; Adele's face blanked.

Daniel gave them a wry smile and said, "I'm well aware that my hopes aren't controlling in this situation and may not even be realistic. But I'm hoping to convince Gibbs that I'm a fellow officer with whom he can have a calm, peaceful discussion about the best way to proceed from here."

"I know the best way to proceed," said Hogg. Occasionally Adele noticed twinges when the servant moved his right hand, but he seemed to have adequate flexibility in it. Certainly enough to squeeze the trigger of his impeller. "And no, don't you worry, young master, I won't shoot till you say to. But I said back when we got him the first time that the best place for Gibbs was him and a boat anchor wrapped in a fishnet and dropped in the harbor, didn't I?"

"Yes, Hogg, you did," Daniel said. "But since that would *always* be your opinion, I think I can be forgiven for leaving Gibbs under guard instead."

He smiled, but there was a little more edge to his banter than Adele was used to hearing. *He thinks Hogg may have been right this time. Well, it's an easy mistake to rectify.*

The pumps were running with an unfamiliar note. They normally refilled the tanks of reaction mass whenever a ship touched down on water. Adele hadn't been paying much attention to the discussion of repair priorities on the command channel, but she now recalled that one of the feed hoses was to be run into an access port in the starboard outrigger instead of being dropped straight into the harbor in normal fashion. That would more than keep up with the leakage.

The twenty spacers waiting in the hold were quiet. They were ready for anything that might happen, but they had been in similar situations too often by now to show nervousness.

The section was armed with a variety of bludgeons and

knives, but no guns. Very few spacers were good shots to begin with. Since a child was being held hostage, Daniel didn't want projectiles flying about unless he was *very* sure of the person aiming them.

Adele had her pocket pistol; Tovera's miniature sub-machine gun fired the same light ceramic pellets as the pistol. The stocked impeller would punch its osmium slugs through a brick wall, but in Hogg's hands the weapon would do so only if he *wanted* to shoot whatever was behind the brick wall.

Adele glanced at imagery of the main hall of Cinnabar House. Since the console—the only one on Commission premises—was there, Adele had a view of about three-quarters of the hall. Gibbs was pacing around his tied-up hostages.

The former assistant commissioner carried an electromotive carbine, taken—probably bought—from one of the militiamen who were supposed to have been guarding him, and a Cinnabar service pistol which had probably come from a drawer somewhere in the building.

He looked desperate and as vicious as a weasel. *What in the name of heaven does he expect to gain by all this?*

But that wasn't a fair question. The game would end for Gibbs in precisely the same place that it would end for Adele and for every other human being. Considered against the Heat Death of the Universe, Gibbs' hostage-taking made as much sense as Adele's determination to free a decent couple and their child from a nasty little traitor.

The notion amused Adele. It was good that she wouldn't have to justify her decision to anybody else, because in her own mind she was behaving quite irrationally.

Thinking of that, she looked toward Daniel and said, "By the way, you needn't worry about how Admiral Mainwaring is going to react."

Daniel looked at her and raised an eyebrow. "To be honest, Officer Mundy," he said mildly, "I stopped giving Admiral Mainwaring's curiosity any consideration when you told me that a child's life was at stake. I'm sure the admiral will display the same sense of priorities; and if he doesn't . . ."

Daniel gave a shrug of disdain that a perfumed courtier couldn't have equaled. *Daniel is a genuinely good-natured man*, Adele thought, *but I wouldn't want him to catch me mistreating a child.*

Her mind flashed to an image of soldiers nailing the head of her little sister to Speaker's Rock. A shiver danced through her. Until that moment there had been a possibility that Commander Gibbs would survive the coming interview.

"Of course, Daniel," Adele said, deliberately informal despite there being other people around. "I misphrased my statement. I meant to say that I explained to the admiral that I had conveyed orders from a higher authority to you. He stumbled over his tongue in assuring me that he would wait to debrief you until it was convenient. He emphasized that he had no wish to learn anything about your actions which could not be discussed with propriety between two RCN officers."

Daniel blinked. "You told him that I was under orders from . . . ?" Even under these circumstances, he couldn't bring himself to articulate Mistress Sand's name.

"You are being guided by the principles of justice and of protection of the weak," Adele said primly. "Which surely take precedence over an admiral's whim, do they not?"

Daniel guffawed. "Not necessarily in the opinion of the admiral," he said, "but I don't think we need to press that question to a no-doubt busy Admiral Mainwaring."

He coughed against the back of his hand. "Ah—thank you," he said. "Adele."

The dogs withdrew like anvils falling on steel all around the perimeter of the boarding hatch. It began to squeal downward to become a ramp.

"*Bloody* well about time," growled a technician with a long-handled wrench in his right hand. He rubbed the head with his left palm. The wrench jaws were powered, but the man's shoulders and biceps didn't look like they'd need assistance if he had to use the tool today.

The air which puffed through the widening gap was warm and wet; it made Adele sneeze. The flames of the plasma thrusters incinerated any organic garbage floating in the slip, leaving a residue to mix with leftover ozone ions. The result bit and cloyed on the nasal passages in equal measure.

"All right, Sissies!" Daniel boomed. Everyone in the hold could hear him despite the screech of the lowering hatch and the more general chorus of cooling metal. "Officer Mundy and I lead and the rest of you follow as polite as if you were going to divine services. We'll talk to the locals first, and you *will* not under any circumstances make a peep until I give you orders to. Do you understand that?"

"*Aye aye, sir/Six/Cap'n!*" echoed thunderous agreement.

Daniel let the response settle, then added, "Right you are, fellow spacers. There's a little girl's life on this, so keep it calm and don't let anything get out of hand."

The ramp rang into position, resting on the starboard outrigger. Adele shut down her data unit and tucked it away. Her pistol was in its usual place, but she didn't feel a need to touch it at present.

"Sir, they'll make you proud," said Woetjans, standing at the control switch. She looked as though she'd been dragged from her grave. Her weakness was so obvious that she hadn't objected to Barnes and Dasi leading the section. "You know they will."

Daniel gave her a gentle smile. "Of course they will, Chief," he said. "You trained them, after all."

Looking over his shoulder he continued, "Come on, Sissies. We've got a job to do."

Adele kept pace with Daniel down the ramp. Instead of crowding ahead, the spacers followed Hogg and Tovera in a double column. They were in about as orderly a formation as Adele remembered seeing ever in her RCN career. One—one of the few women in a group chosen for brawling ability—was humming "Haul Away Joe," but that was probably an unconscious attempt to keep cadence.

"Is the Founder up there to meet us?" Daniel asked quietly as they reached the floating extension. He didn't point or otherwise call attention to the group waiting at the upper stage of the quay.

"No," said Adele. "Lady Posthuma is, and Major Flecker is with her. The rest are various palace functionaries, department heads or the like. I assume Posy brought them in case you need something specific from the local authorities."

Daniel chuckled, though there wasn't much humor in the sound. "I just need plenty of elbow room," he said. After a moment he added, "I *really* don't want anything to happen to that little girl, Adele."

"Yes," said Adele. She understood being worried, though the feeling didn't make her talkative: she became either depressed or angry. This time she was angry.

Daniel mounted the steps to the fixed portion of the quay in the lead, since there wasn't room for two people abreast. When Adele reached the top, Posy Belisande stepped forward and embraced her. Being shot wouldn't have surprised Adele as much.

"Adele," she said. "You made it possible for Otto to speak to me, did you not? To let me know that he was alive and that you had won?"

Adele blinked. Patching through the call hadn't been difficult, though the process had left her with the belief that the signals officer of the *Z 46* must have some skills besides his professional competence to have advanced to the rank of lieutenant. There had been moments when she had considered sending Cory or Cazelet aboard the destroyer to complete the connection.

"Ah," Adele said. "Yes, I suppose that's correct. But it isn't particularly germane at the moment, ah, Posy."

"Not to you, perhaps," the younger woman said, stepping back with an expression Adele couldn't read. It seemed positive, at any rate. "But we'll speak later."

The spacers were shuffling past and re-forming against the edge of the quay. Occasionally one would adjust the truncheon under his belt or pat the meaty end into his palm, but they projected an air of eager calm.

"I see you have a truck for us," Daniel said, taking charge of the conversation. He nodded toward an articulated goods wagon. The two streets on the route between the harbor and Cinnabar House were wide enough for it, though the vehicle wouldn't have done for much of Old Calvary. "My man Hogg will drive. If you'll see to it that your people will pass us through your cordon, we'll get on with our business."

"I'll ride with you to the post on Nation Way," said Major Flecker. "And wait there with my troops."

"Captain?" said Posy. "Wouldn't you rather have an aircar for yourself and Lady Mundy? I've brought mine. Otto's engineers say it is perfectly safe."

"No, Your Ladyship," Daniel said. "I'll stay with my people. With your permission, we'll be going now."

From the way Posy's eyes widened, she apparently understood the chill in his tone. Adele was sure it was unintended, but...Posy had a great deal of experience with aristocrats. Apparently this was the first time she'd met a war chief leading his troops into battle.

"A moment, Captain Leary," said the dry, precise voice of the woman standing behind Lady Belisande: her maid, Wood. Though she had spoken to Daniel, her eyes were on Adele as she continued, "Might I perhaps be of service?"

Hogg stiffened, then looked at Tovera; Daniel didn't speak. Wood's right trouser leg was cut off at the knee to allow what was either a bandage or a thin cast over her lower leg, but she appeared to move normally.

Tovera grinned at Hogg in a reptilian fashion. She said,

"Don't worry, Wood's on our side. We're all allies now, right? Cinnabar and the Alliance."

And if you think Tovera believes that, Adele thought, *you'll buy the Pentacrest from the first sharper who offers it to you as prime Xenos real estate.*

"But thank you, mistress," Tovera went on to her former compatriot. "We have this covered. And besides—"

She nodded to the cast.

"—you appear to have had your share of the fun already."

Wood grinned back with no more humor than Tovera's expression had indicated. "In that case," she said, "may I offer this?"

She held out a small chest to Adele. It wasn't as large as the attaché case which held Tovera's sub-machine gun when she wasn't wearing it in a hip holster, as now.

"It has a variety of self-propelled viewing devices," Wood said. "Since you may not have brought your own?"

"Thank you," said Adele, taking the chest in her right hand without answering the implied question. "Now, Captain, I believe we are ready."

"Right!" said Daniel as he strode for the truck cab. "Follow me, Sissies!"

Not far behind Adele in the shuffling line of spacers, the tech was singing, "First I had a Dunstan gal, and she was fat and lazy..."

Daniel opened the door from the right—residential—wing of Cinnabar House onto the covered space separating it from the official wing where Gibbs held the Browns hostage. Folks in Bantry would have called it a breezeway; but since it was two floors high and part of a mansion, it probably had a more impressive title.

It was a very run-down mansion, though. The double doors facing the street were solid, but the interior arch gave onto the garden through a pair of wrought iron gates. They admitted plenty of light for the plants growing from the cracks between the patio tiles.

Daniel had brought Adele, Hogg, and half the spacers with him in through the back of the residential wing. Water-damaged plaster had flaked onto the rear hallway, the valances above the curtains in the reception room were rotting, and there was a pervasive smell of mildew. The condition of the upper floor, closer to the leaking roof, could easily be imagined.

"Do they have any servants?" Daniel asked Adele quietly, continuing to watch the door opposite. They were to the left and right side of the vestibule: Daniel standing and Adele seated with her data unit. Hogg sat cross-legged on the floor between them, his left elbow on his left knee to brace the impeller which he pointed toward the closed door of the official wing.

Adele, seated also, continued to watch her display. She said, "They had two, neither of them much good that I could see. Presumably both ran off when Gibbs burst in with a gun."

Daniel shrugged. He was waiting for a signal from Tovera, who'd gone with the team under Dasi to enter through the kitchen at the back of the garden.

"I suppose one can't really blame them for running away under those conditions," he said.

Hogg snorted. "Can't I?" he said. "What d'ye suppose some yobbo would have got if he'd broke into Bantry House to grab you and your mother twenty years ago, eh?"

"Besides me head-butting him in the crotch, you mean?" Daniel said with a grin. "I take your point, Hogg, but I don't think servants with two weeks' service can be held to the same standards as those whose families have two centuries of service."

The vestibule to either wing had a heavy door opening onto the patio and a light one on the inside, the hall side. The outer walls of Cinnabar House were blank brick for their full height; all the windows looked out on the garden.

"Is there any chance we could starve him out?" Daniel asked. He pitched his tone hopefully, but he didn't imagine it was going to be that easy. And he wished that Tovera would signal.

"Cinnabar House was stocked with thirty cases of military ration packs," Adele said primly. "They've been on the accounts here as far back as I can trace them, at least thirty-three years. I suppose they may have gone bad."

This time it was Daniel who snorted. "I've eaten older packs," he said, "though 'going bad' implies they started out better than a civilian might imagine was the case. Why in heaven's name were they stored here?"

"I have no idea," said Adele. "But I've made a note to check the regional records when we return to Stahl's World."

Daniel grinned. "Assuming," he said, in near synchrony with Adele's, "Assuming."

She didn't look up from her display, but her smile would have been noticeable even to someone who didn't read her expressions as well as Daniel did. "I'll admit," Adele said, "that our chances of reaching Stahl's World look better than they did six hours ago."

"Sir?" said Barnes in a quiet voice.

Daniel stepped aside—out of sight from across the courtyard—and looked toward the hall. Barnes crouched in the doorway. Behind him waited the members of his squad in anxious silence.

"We was thinking, a couple of us could go up and come down by the roof, sir," Barnes said. "If he's on the ground floor, you know?"

"Hold what you've got, Barnes," Daniel said, trying not to snarl. It was very hard to keep still in a tense situation, but that was the right course here. "I don't know what Gibbs would do when he heard noise overhead. Regardless, it wouldn't put us ahead of where we are now. We're going to wait until Tovera has a bug in position and then open negotiations."

"There," said Adele. Her data unit projected two images in the air between Daniel and Barnes.

The left half—Daniel wasn't sure whether it was an omnidirectional display or if the rigger was seeing a colored blur—was from the console in the room where Gibbs held his hostages. The commander was drinking from a wine bottle. He held the carbine's grip in his right hand with the butt resting on his hip. He hadn't shaved, and he looked as savage as a starving dog.

The other half of the display was initially a ragged-edged circle. It suddenly expanded to a view of the entire room from the back corner of the wall onto the garden. The bug had drilled in through a window sash. The lens provided an anamorphic image which Adele's software corrected. Daniel was getting what seemed to be a perfect three-dimensional view of the room and its occupants.

Gibbs had drawn the curtains over the windows. The console stood against the outside wall. Gibbs was in front of it; he didn't seem to have noticed the bug grinding its way to a vantage point.

The Brown family lay in the corner—father, mother, child—between the outside wall and the door to the patio. Their legs were tied at the ankles, and their hands, behind their backs, were presumably tied as well.

"I shouldn't wonder if a slug through this wall would nail him cold," Hogg said in a speculative tone. "The civilians are well clear. They'd catch a bit of brick dust, that's all."

Daniel shrugged. "I shouldn't wonder either, Hogg," he said. "I'd give you three chances in four, even without you being able to see the target."

He grinned at his servant, then stepped into the doorway; Hogg immediately raised his muzzle. Daniel said, "The fourth chance, though, is that he doesn't drop clean. That's an automatic carbine. I don't want him pointing it at the Browns and clamping on the trigger."

Hogg grunted. "How about I settle in on the roof of the kitchen?" he said. "If Dasi's people pull the curtains down, I might do some good. Since I guess you'll be standing in front of the door here, won't you?"

Daniel chuckled. He felt very much alive—on his toes almost literally. "Yes, I suppose I will," he said. "Adele, tell the squad in the garden to clear the curtains away if I tell them to go in, all right?"

Besides the patio entrance, the main hall of the official wing had a door onto a corridor in the back. The latrine, a storage room, and a stairway to the upper floor were on the outside of the corridor. On the inside, the commissioner's private office looked out at the garden. At the end of the corridor was a door, also onto the garden.

Daniel was sure that some of Dasi's people were in the corridor, but Gibbs had blocked the door into the main hall with a filing cabinet. A pair of husky Sissies—goodness, any *one* spacer of the present lot—could smash through the barrier, but that would take a little time and make a great deal of noise.

Daniel didn't know Gibbs well, but nothing he'd seen of the commander suggested that the man wouldn't be willing to shoot his hostages. He was beyond question a nasty piece of work.

Daniel took a deep breath, then stepped into the patio. "Commander Gibbs?" he called to the door of the official wing. "This is Daniel Leary, and I'm here so that we can figure out how to get you out of this alive."

"Don't try anything, Leary!" Gibbs shouted. The doors into and out of the vestibule were closed, but Daniel had no trouble making out the words. "I'll shoot these highborn scum and I'll shoot you too!"

"We don't need any shooting at all, Commander," Daniel said. "I don't even have a gun."

He coughed and went on, "Ah, can I open at least your outer door so that we can speak without having to raise our voices? I give you my word as a Leary that I'll not attempt any tricks."

"Bugger your word, Leary!" Gibbs said. Then—because he

464

was desperate but not quite suicidal while the rational part of his mind was in control—he said, "I'll open the inside door but not the thick one. *Don't* try anything!"

Adele was projecting the bug's image past Daniel's shoulder, forming it in the air where he could see it while he faced the door across the patio. The Fifth Bureau had trained Tovera in manipulating the bug itself, but nobody could have bettered Adele's use of the tool's output.

Gibbs unlatched the inner door, then quickly flipped it open left-handed while keeping his body behind the masonry jamb. Significantly, he kept his carbine pointed at the Brown family; the Commissioner wriggled into a sitting position, keeping his body between the gun and his wife and daughter. Hester was crying.

Hogg could have taken him, Daniel thought with a mixture of anger and contempt. But Hogg was across the garden, now, and the reasons not to let him shoot blind were still valid.

"You don't need to worry, Commander," Daniel said calmly. "There won't be any violence at all; that's why I'm here. Set your guns down and come out—or I'll come in, if you're worried. Me and my crew will get you off-planet before the locals have any idea what's going on."

"*You'll* save me?" Gibbs said. "Sure, save me to hang! That's what you mean, isn't it?"

"You're not guilty of a capital offense that any civilized court would recognize, Gibbs," Daniel said. "Or to put it another way, no one but me has evidence of a capital crime against you. I give you my word as a Leary and as an officer of the RCN that if you'll lay down your guns, I won't appear against you."

He was still speaking louder than he would have liked to, but he tried to keep his tone warm and reasonable. He smiled engagingly toward the door. Daniel knew that Gibbs couldn't see him, but it was useful to keep his performance as the brotherly fellow officer on course.

The commander's image drew at the bottle again. It must have been empty, because he flung it across the room in a fury. He didn't speak.

Grimacing momentarily—he wanted this to be a dialogue, not a harangue—Daniel said, "That's why I rushed here, you see: I wasn't going to leave a brother officer in the hands of wogs. The gods only know what Zenobians do to traitors! But you see, if you don't come out, I'll have to lift ship. Then you'd be on your own, you see. So please—"

Gibbs' image pointed the carbine toward the door. Daniel stepped to his right, his face blank.

Gibbs fired, punching a hole near the top of the thick panel. A flying splinter stuck in Daniel's left sleeve; the slug slapped the bricks above his head. Dust drifted down.

"Don't play games, Leary!" the commander said. "Listen to me! This is how we'll do it. I'll come out with the Browns, but I won't give up my guns. The parents'll walk on either side of me, and I'll have a gun to the kid's head! You got that?"

"Commander, this isn't necessary," Daniel said. He smiled ingratiatingly; he was ice cold inside. "All you need to do is—"

"Listen to me!" Gibbs said. "Shut up! Just shut up or I'll shoot the brat now, do you hear? You're going to take me to your ship, me and the hostages, you got that?"

"Of course I'll take you to the *Princess Cecile*, Commander,"

Daniel said in a reasonable tone. "But you—"

"Shut up and listen!" Gibbs shouted at the door. His carbine was pointed toward the Browns; it shook with emotion. "Just shut up!"

"I'm listening, Gibbs," said Daniel. His mind was as clear as Haileywood Creek where a pipe took out the water supply for Bantry.

"I'm taking off in your ship, Leary," Gibbs said. "Me and these."

He kicked Commissioner Brown's thigh. It must have been an instinctive act, because Gibbs didn't seem to know that Daniel was watching him.

"I'll take twenty of your crew, that'll be enough," Gibbs said. "Common spacers, that's all; I'll be the only one aboard who can astrogate. I'll let them loose in Palmyra. The Autocrator will be glad to see me, especially since I'm bringing the yacht she wanted. I'll sell it to her, Leary, since you wouldn't!"

Daniel paused, smothering his first impulse to tell the traitor what had happened to Autocrator Irene. That wouldn't help. Indeed, it might push Gibbs into homicidal fury.

He glanced over his shoulder. With his right index finger he pointed to Hofnagel, a Technician 3 holding a five-foot pinch bar. Daniel crooked his finger to bring Hofnagel—he was built like a troll—forward, and then toward the latch of the door opposite. It opened outward.

"Gibbs...," Daniel said. The big technician slipped past, his bar raised. Daniel touched his shoulder and whispered, "Get set quietly but wait."

"I can't hear you!" Gibbs said. "Speak up, you bastard, or I'll end this right now!"

"I'm very sorry!" Daniel said in a voice they could hear at the harbor. "Gibbs, what you're discussing is suicide. You're a fellow officer and I can't let you do that. Release the Browns and I'll take their place. You can tie me up but we can talk like men ought—"

"I'm through talking!" Gibbs said. He aimed at the center of the door. Daniel was already out of the line of fire, so he didn't move. "I'll start killing them, Leary! I'll start with—"

The carbine muzzle twitched down toward the hostages.

"I surrender!" Daniel shouted. "We'll do it your way, Gibbs! Just tell me what you want me to do."

The carbine wavered. Daniel couldn't see Gibbs' face from either camera angle, but the man had paused. Hofnagel slid the thin end of his bar into the crack between the door and the jamb. The bolt was sturdy, but it didn't have a separate plate to cover it from outside.

"All right, Leary," Gibbs said after a long moment. "I guess you've learned that being lucky doesn't mean that everybody has to bow down and do it your way, right?"

Daniel continued to smile vaguely; he didn't reply. He was perfectly willing to abase himself further if it had seemed to him that would help, but he didn't want to set Gibbs off because he thought he was being patronized.

There were various ways to deal with someone who was both irrational and abusive. Under the present circumstances, minimal response seemed the best of the various poor choices.

On the imagery, Gibbs was using a folding utility knife to free the feet of his hostages. He seemed to have tied them

468

with electrical cord. Daniel frowned, but he supposed it was adequate for the purpose.

From the way the Browns moved, they were tied together at the wrist so that each parent was held within about thirty inches of the little girl in the middle. Had Gibbs planned from the beginning to walk out with the hostages around him?

Gibbs snarled something to them, gesturing with the carbine. Daniel couldn't hear the words through the door panel, but it was obviously a demand for them to get to their feet.

Awkwardly, unable to use their hands, the Browns obeyed. Hester was crying and trying to wipe her tears on her shoulder. They'd all fouled themselves; Gibbs must not have allowed them to move even to use the latrine after he took them hostage.

Daniel poised, though nobody looking at his calm expression would realize that he was running increasingly violent options through his mind. Even if the situation on Palmyra had been what the commander thought it was, the stated plan was impossible. Daniel wasn't going to get the Brown family out of Cinnabar House simply to send them to death in space—or worse, in the Matrix.

Gibbs positioned the Browns in the vestibule. The commissioner was on his left, Clothilde on his right, and Gibbs' left hand gripped Hester by the top of her tunic. The carbine's barrel was short enough that by cocking his right elbow back he could hold the muzzle to the little girl's head.

"All right!" Gibbs said, speaking for the benefit of both Daniel and the hostages. "We're going out now. At the least *hint* that something isn't right, I'm going to blow the brat's head off. Do you all understand? I'm going to kill—"

Commissioner Brown hurled his weight against the carbine, thrusting it away from Hester's head. All four of the group went down in flailing confusion.

"Go!" Daniel bellowed, pointing to Hofnagel. The big technician hurled his full weight into the bar to seat it as deeply as possible, then wrenched outward. The lock burst through the wood as the door swung out. Daniel swept the panel fully open.

The Browns lay in a tangle on the floor; Hester and Clothilde were screaming. The commissioner sat up, trying to kick Gibbs' legs out from under him.

Gibbs had lost the carbine, but he drew the pistol from his belt and pointed it at Commissioner Brown's chest. As Daniel started to dive forward, Gibbs snarled a curse and pulled the trigger.

Gibbs' chest expanded, causing his tunic to bloom outward. Brick dust exploded inside the room. Outside, a spray of chips blasted from the sudden hole, scarring the sod. Even at a slant angle, Hogg's powerful impeller had penetrated the brick wall.

Gibbs' skull deformed. Adele had put two holes in his left temple—if he'd been facing her, she would have shot for his eyes. Tovera stood in the hall doorway behind a glowing haze, the vaporized driving bands of her sub-machine gun pellets.

Daniel hit the commander hard enough to carry them to the floor of the main office, where they skidded. Gibbs was thrashing. His mouth opened and closed, but the impeller slug had blown his lungs through the side of his chest. There were three holes in his right temple also, courtesy of Tovera.

Sissies poured through the doorways and climbed in by the windows. A panel dislodged from a torn sash fell, adding further confusion to the shouts. Daniel got to his feet.

Hofnagel stood over the commander's corpse and raised his pinch bar. Daniel grabbed his wrist and said, "Belay that, Sissie!"

Then, on an impulse, he threw his arms around the big technician. "And a bloody good job you did with it already. *Bloody* good."

Daniel stepped back. The stink was familiar but no less unpleasant for that. *That was a bloody near thing.*

Adele had put away her data unit, but the pistol was still cooling in her left hand. "Thank you," Daniel said. "For both before and after the wheels came off."

Adele shrugged. "I'm glad it worked out," she said.

Barnes had cut the hostages loose, using Gibbs' utility knife. The commissioner looked dazed.

Tovera ejected the loading tube from the pistol Gibbs had tried to use. "The contacts are corroded," she said, sounding amused. "Lucky for you, eh, Commissioner?"

Daniel picked Hester up and cradled her to his chest. This uniform was ruined anyway, not least because of what had splattered from Commander Gibbs' chest when the slug went through it. Hogg would normally have complained about the clothing; but not, Daniel thought, *this time*.

"Hester, dearest," Daniel said. "Your daddy is a very brave man. He just saved your life."

There were other, less positive ways to view what the Commissioner had done, but Daniel didn't second-guess the man on the ground. Esecially when things worked out well.

He smiled. Life was beginning to return to commissioner Brown's face. Daniel kissed the little girl's cheek and handed her to her father.

CHAPTER 29

CALVARY ON ZENOBIA

Adele didn't have a great deal of interest in landscapes or architecture, either one, but she thought she would have approved of the walled garden of the Founder's Palace if she'd seen it a week earlier. Its proportions had been regular, at least. She disliked the raggedness of natural woodlands.

The militia company which had camped here during the recent crisis had reduced the plantings to a state of general raggedness, unfortunately. The low hedges enclosing the four parterres had been crushed down, and the tiled fountain in the center was broken. It appeared that a heavy vehicle had driven through it.

Though there'd been an effort to move the fruit trees in terra cotta planters against the back wall, most of the pots had been cracked in the process. That probably didn't matter to the trees, because their branches had been broken off for firewood. Well, worse things had happened to human beings during the past few days.

Commander Milch came out of the Palace and strode briskly

toward the back of the garden where the tables had been set under a marquee. The meeting hadn't officially started yet, but it appeared that major items of business were being worked out already. Admiral Mainwaring stood in a close discussion with Founder Hergo and with Otto von Gleuck—who to Adele's surprise wore Zenobian national dress in its natural bright colors rather than his Fleet uniform.

Marines and spacers with stocked impellers stood on the palace roof and the walls surrounding the other three sides of the garden. Fleet and RCN personnel were present in equal numbers. They seemed to be getting along well, or at any rate as well as the crews of different ships in the same squadron would get along.

At the foot of the garden, behind the conference table, was a grotto. Over the entrance was a monumental woman's head; on chairs to either side of it sat Woetjans and the Fleet warrant officer who had delivered the aircar to Daniel. Woetjans looked gray; her counterpart's right arm and leg were in casts.

Adele nodded a greeting to Woetjans. Armed guards weren't completely unnecessary—there was certainly a chance of a surviving Palmyrene sympathizer deciding to take some of his enemies with him in a final blaze of glory—but the main reason that the two warrant officers commanded those guards was that it kept them out of the way while their ships were being repaired.

Woetjans wouldn't have been able to simply watch and give orders if she'd been on the *Princess Cecile* now. From the look of her Fleet counterpart—and the fact that he was here—Adele presumed that he was from the same mold. The kind of exertion that both took for granted would be crippling or fatal in their present physical condition.

Daniel was chatting with other space officers. Vesey and Cory and personnel from the Qaboosh Squadron were around him, but there were several Fleet uniforms also.

Fregattenkapitan Henri Lavoissier of the Z 42 stood apart with two young officers, probably his own juniors. Either he was unwilling to pollute himself by contact with RCN personnel, or else he had decided he would be unwelcome in a group of celebrating victors. If Adele were to guess, it was probably the latter reason—though Lavoissier would claim it was by his own choice.

Adele suppressed a smile at a thought. The RCN had its share of stiff-necked fools. They didn't like Captain Leary any better than Lavoissier did.

Accompanied only by the silent presence of Wood, Posy Belisande was standing at a slight distance from Hergo, von Gleuck, and Mainwaring. She turned to Adele, seated at the far—low-ranking—end of the tables, then walked toward her.

Commissioner Brown sat across from Adele. He wore a suit which was suitably formal for this gathering; he'd probably bought it when he learned he had been appointed commissioner to Zenobia.

The table was wide enough that a low-voiced conversation probably couldn't be heard across the scarred wood, but Brown's eyes had a thousand-yard stare anyway. His mind was in a different place and time.

Adele didn't shut down her data unit, but she shrank the display and smiled pleasantly. Well, she hoped it was pleasant. She rather liked Posy. She had been a perfect surrogate for

Adele in the Palace when the trouble started.

Besides—Adele's smile changed slightly—it was Lady Mundy's task to winkle information out of Lady Belisande. At this point Adele was nearly certain that success was impossible, but she owed it to Mistress Sand to make an effort.

"Do you mind?" Posy said, gesturing to the chair to Adele's right. "I keep thinking this business is going to start but they delay yet further."

Adele shrugged. "If there are assigned seats, they haven't told me," she said. "Mind, I think that if I tried to sit at the head of the table—"

She nodded.

"—someone *would* have told me."

Posy walked around behind her, which meant that Tovera had made way. Adele had chosen the side of the table facing the Palace because that put her back to the brick wall. While a powerful impeller could shoot through bricks, as Hogg had proved the previous afternoon, it made Tovera more comfortable.

Adele suppressed a wry smile. The situation now was that Wood would be standing behind Posy and therefore behind Adele, and vice versa. That wasn't going to do anything positive for *either* bodyguard's state of mind.

Posy settled onto the chair, a pair to Adele's though there were several different styles around the table. These were of pale wood with cushions of light suede and seemed surprisingly comfortable. Which might mean more to Lady Belisande than it did to Adele.

Founder Hergo sat down at the head of the table. Otto von Gleuck took the seat on his right, and Admiral Mainwaring sat to his left. Daniel was on Mainwaring's left, displacing Milch by one seat. Lesser officials began scrambling for chairs.

"They wouldn't want me up there either," Posy said. She glanced toward Commissioner Brown, who remained in another world.

A thin Zenobian with a pointed beard and maroon velvet garments tried to take the seat beside her. Posy put a hand on the chair back and said, "Wood, sit here if you will."

"Mistress...," Wood said doubtfully, glancing at Tovera. The Zenobian Councillor looked startled, then concerned when he realized who Posy must be. He didn't take his own hand off the chair, however.

"Tovera, please step around to the other side of the table," Adele said. "You'll have a better view of what might be happening above us on the wall."

Tovera had been smirking at Wood's discomfiture. That expression blanked, then reappeared with a wry twist. "Whatever the mistress wishes, of course," she said as she walked around the table.

Wood touched the official's wrist. In a voice as dry as rustling paper, she said, "I won't cut your hand off, because that would spatter blood on Lady Belisande. But I will break your wrist, and then both your knees."

"What?" said the fellow. "*What?*"

Whatever he saw in the servant's eyes answered his question. He blundered off backward because he was afraid to turn his head.

Wood slid the chair back slightly as she sat. Now she could keep Posy—and Adele—in her peripheral vision without turning her head.

"All right, we'll start now," said Hergo. He'd raised his voice, but the acoustics of the garden were surprisingly good: the walls and the back of the Palace provided clean reflections. "While the internal governance of Zenobia is a matter for her Founder and Board of Councillors alone, we—and I speak here for the Board as well—"

Six civilians at the long table nodded in various mixtures of solemnity and enthusiasm. Though four were dressed in slightly dated Pleasaunce fashions, they and the seventh man now standing in back of the Founder—the fellow Wood had run off—were unmistakably the Councillors. The ones who'd survived the attempted coup, which explained their present subservience.

"—are aware of our debt during the recent difficulties to Zenobia's friends and allies, the Alliance of Free Stars and the Republic of Cinnabar. I have called all parties together here as a mark of our respect."

"My brother understands the situation," Posy murmured, leaning sideways so that she was almost speaking into Adele's ear. "In front of the other Councillors he has to pretend we're independent, but he won't give Guillaume any reason to impose direct rule."

Though the combined tables—at the Founder's end, one from the banquet hall of the Palace; and joined to it one from the refectory of the Founder's Regiment—seated almost forty, many more people were watching from behind plush ropes. A Palace functionary stood at the passage to the tables, but four spacers in liberty suits lounged nearby. Their utilities were so covered with ribbons and embroidered patches that only by their caps could Adele tell which pair was Fleet and which was RCN.

The spacers' cudgels differed according to individual taste, but all four were serious weapons. From their banter, and from Adele's experience of the breed, they were looking forward to having somebody try to push past the rope.

"I think your brother is fortunate that you were in Calvary when this plot was uncovered," Adele said. She tried to keep her tone neutral, but she was pretty sure her opinion of Founder Hergo was evident in her tone. Still, thick and parochial though Hergo might be, he had shown enough intelligence to take his sister's direction during the crisis.

The people at the head of the table were introducing themselves. Adele wondered if the process would continue beyond the polished wood. If it did, she would be Signals Officer Mundy and let those who didn't know her wonder how she rated a seat.

And what will Wood say? Adele's lips twitched.

"Hergo's a good sort," Posy said, though she wasn't really protesting. "He's never approved of me, but neither did he try to run my life. And he never pretended that I couldn't be smarter than him because I'm a woman."

"He's gone up in my estimation," Adele said truthfully.

It's harder to notice something that is missing than it is something which has been added to a familiar array. Adele frowned as she looked at the head of the table and said, "Why isn't Resident Tilton here?"

Posy turned slightly toward her. "Ah," she said. "There was an incident during the coup. The Resident—"

"I think that will do for introductions," the Founder said forcefully as the uppermost member of the Council rose

478

to make what—from his sheaf of notes—was a speech. "I believe the first order of business is to inform everyone that the Alliance Resident, the Honorable Louis Tilton, was foully murdered by Palmyrene agents. I'm sure you all—"

"Murdered!" said the Councillor with the sheaf of notes. "How did that happen? He had an army of guards, didn't he?"

Nobody spoke for a moment. Then Posy said, "My understanding is that this was a well planned operation which began when a bomb went off in the wing of the Residency where the guards were quartered."

Everyone at the table turned to look. Posy was a striking woman, and the very simplicity of her dress set her head and shoulders above the other Zenobians present. The local women had at best overdressed for the occasion.

"The Resident and the three guards who had escaped the explosion," she continued, "were killed by the attackers in what I'm told was a hail of gunfire."

"There must've been forty of them," said Major Flecker. "Resident Tilton didn't have a chance. But I figure we got all the bandits and traitors when we did the cleanup of their hideouts later in the day."

Tovera looked over the table at Wood, who shrugged without speaking. Adele caught the exchange and said quietly, "Your Ladyship, do you know how many bullets hit the victims?"

Wood turned to look past her smiling mistress. "Three each," she said in her dry voice. There was a discussion of the situation at the head of the table, several people talking at once, but even without the background noise the words would be barely audible. "At the top of the breastbone."

That must be Fifth Bureau training, Adele thought. Though Tovera was more likely to center her three rounds on the bridge of the target's nose.

"As I was saying," Hergo resumed, "I'm sure you all share my deep sense of loss at Resident Tilton's death."

Adele half expected somebody to burst out laughing at that, but apparently the events of the past day and a half had frightened all the humor out of the Great and Good of Zenobia. They looked at their hands or made their faces rigidly blank.

"The office of Resident has therefore devolved on the senior member of the Alliance present on Zenobia," Hergo said. "The Honorable Otto von Gleuck, who in order to take up this civilian position has resigned his commission as Fregattenkapitan in the Fleet. I'm pleased to announce that the interim Resident has announced his intention to settle permanently on Zenobia and to marry one of our fairest flowers—if I may be allowed to voice my pride: my sister, Lady Posthuma Belisande."

"Hear hear!" said Daniel and began to clap.

There were cheers around the table and from the lesser lights gathered in the garden. Admiral Mainwaring called, "And you couldn't have found a prettier gel or a sharper one, von Gleuck!"

"By heaven, man!" said Commander Milch. "I bow to no man in my appreciation of a pretty face—"

He glanced down the table and dipped his chin to Posy.

"—but you've won a brilliant victory here. Wouldn't the lady travel back to Pleasaunce with you? Because you're sure to be promoted, aren't you? Even with our great nations at peace, as I'm glad we are."

There was frozen silence from the junior Alliance officers, and a look of incredulous anger on Founder Hergo's face. Admiral Mainwaring stared at his aide in frustration. Daniel pursed his lips, evidently searching for a way to cover the gaffe.

"Not at all, my friend," said von Gleuck, apparently the only person at the upper table who hadn't been horrified or angered by the question. "To be quite honest, I've grown tired of spacefaring. On my homeworld Adlersbild, I would get in the way of my brother, the Count. On Pleasaunce, well, I'm sure I'd find myself in somebody else's way. I'm confident that Zenobia will give me enough challenges to keep me interested. It will also allow me to work for the betterment of the Alliance at a considerable distance from the seats of power."

The seat of power, singular, Adele thought. Guarantor Porra had sent a potential rival to the fringe of the galaxy. Should that rival come back a greater hero even than he went, well...there was a place from which no human had yet returned.

Quietly to Posy she said, "Many RCN officers are smarter than that, Your Ladyship. And in fairness to Milch, nothing in his normal duties requires him to be familiar with the political realities of Pleasaunce."

Posy gave a brief, silvery laugh. Her face *settled*. In a falsely light tone she said, "I wonder if Otto would stay if he *could* go back to Pleasaunce? Even for those of us who were born here, Zenobia is a rather limited place. Though I don't really mind having to live out my days here...."

She met Adele's eyes.

"As of course I must, by Guillaume's direction. Though I suppose I ought to call him 'the Guarantor' now that we've ceased to be friends."

Farther up the table, Councillors were enthusiastically reopening matters in which they felt they had been unjustly treated by Resident Tilton. Hergo was letting them talk, and von Gleuck listened with what seemed to be an equable expression.

Adele eyed Posy. Because of the way they were seated, the younger woman was in part profile. Her features were as perfect as if stamped from a die.

Sometimes when people asked the kind of question Posy just had, they wanted reassurance rather than an answer. If that was the case here, Posy was less perceptive than she had seemed.

"I don't know," Adele said. "I'm not an authority on human relationships."

She thought in silence. Though she didn't understand feelings, she *was* skilled at analyzing data and making recommendations based on that analysis.

"I think you make suitable consorts for one another," Adele said. "You're both intelligent and pragmatic; you're willing to make the best of situations which aren't what you might have wished. As for your specific question rather than the general one it implied—"

Posy's expression remained calm, but Adele thought she saw a sudden hint of tension. It wasn't quite fear, but it tended in that direction.

"Have you been to Adlersbild?"

"Otto's home?" Posy said. "No, Your Ladyship. I met him here on Zenobia when I returned, only a few months ago."

"I accompanied my mentor, Mistress Boileau, there," Adele said. "To inventory a library which had been bequeathed to the Academic Collections. It may be that you think of Adlersbild as a smaller version of Pleasaunce since it's an equally old world and was an original member of the Alliance?"

"Yes, I suppose I do," Posy admitted guardedly. "Though I haven't really thought about it very much. Why do you mention it?"

"The Great Houses of Adlersbild perch on high crags," Adele said. "Contacts among them are limited and formal. Social life is centered on hunting parties."

She cleared her throat. "I don't think the Honorable Otto will miss the social whirl which you encountered on Pleasaunce; he wouldn't have been exposed to it on Adlersbild or as Fleet officer on active duty. And I suspect there are parts of Zenobia which lend themselves to hunting if he gets nostalgic for home. From personal experience, I can say Diamond Cay is suitable."

Posy laughed again and patted the back of Adele's hand. "Thank you," she said. "I suppose I—"

Both women had been speaking in low voices, but they suddenly realized that the chattering further up the table had ceased. Posy's laugh had rung in silence.

Founder Hergo looked at his sister, then turned toward Daniel and said, "While I'm very thankful for the help which the Republic of Cinnabar provided to us during the recent crisis—"

"It was critical," said von Gleuck firmly. "We couldn't have defeated the invaders without the aid of Captain Leary."

"Yes, I have accepted that," Hergo said to his soon-to-be brother-in-law with a hint of a frown. "I don't want to seem ungrateful, but I remain puzzled. Captain Leary, why did you risk your life to become involved in a business which you might have honorably walked away from?"

"Yes, Leary," said Admiral Mainwaring, turning to stare at Daniel beside him. "I was going to ask you that when we had a chance to talk, but I'm willing to have an audience. What in bloody *hell* were you thinking of when you got mixed up in this?"

He frowned toward Hergo, then added, "Though I'm not saying you were wrong, not after the way things worked out."

"Ah," said Daniel, tugging down the right sleeve of his tunic. His eyes met Adele's and he smiled.

Returning his attention to the head of the table, he said, "Yes, I've been wondering how to answer that question ever since we turned out to have survived. You see, it's this way..."

Daniel had been dodging Admiral Mainwaring ever since the *Dotterel* landed six hours ago. Though the *Princess Cecile* and her captain were not part of the regional chain of command, the reality was that Mainwaring and everybody in the Navy House bureaucracy would expect Daniel to provide a full explanation to the commander of the Qaboosh Squadron—which he had just embroiled in a war with a Cinnabar ally.

Daniel was willing to do that, but he'd hoped and prayed he could do so publically rather than in a private conference with the Admiral. Mainwaring's reaction would be muted in front of a foreign head of state, albeit a barbarian, and—more important—officers of the Fleet. If the Admiral were alone with a junior captain during the discussion, it might be kitty bar the door.

But the explanation was still a minefield.

"Your Excellency," Daniel said, realizing that he didn't know what honorific was proper for a Founder of Zenobia. He dipped his head toward Hergo in something just short of a bow, hoping that the gesture would make up for it if he'd gotten the rank wrong. "My Republic has no desire for additional possessions in the Qaboosh Region. But..."

He swept the table with what he hoped was an apologetic grin.

"Inevitably there are rumors and suspicions. Cinnabar and the Alliance, though at peace now, have been at war for most of the past decade. My former Fleet counterpart across this table—"

He nodded again, this time to von Gleuck.

"—and I have spent almost all our service careers in trying to kill one another and one another's colleagues. Peace has come and I personally welcome it, but I'm afraid that trust won't arrive for some considerable time."

Admiral Mainwaring looked restive and was verging on angry at what he saw as a lecture; Founder Hergo was intent but obviously puzzled; and the other Zenobians present looked as though Daniel had lapsed into unintelligible singsong.

Von Gleuck, however, wore a hard smile. He—alone at the upper table—understood what Daniel was saying.

"Commissioner Brown found certain anomalies when he inventoried the records of his new posting," Daniel said, gesturing toward the man as he spoke. Brown straightened when he heard his name, but he still looked like someone who was desperately trying to hang on to life after a fatal wound. "He brought them to me as a fellow Cinnabar official."

He grinned. The thought amused him, but he reacted openly because it struck him as politic to do so.

"We were rather thin on the ground here before the *Dotterel* landed, you'll recall," he said. "At any rate, I put my staff to work on the question—"

Daniel very deliberately didn't glance toward Adele as he spoke. Half the other RCN officers present did, however, but then jerked their eyes in any other direction. Admiral Mainwaring was one of those who did the double-take.

Which means I've won, Daniel thought with a rush of triumph. He hadn't realized until that instant how nervous he had been about the Admiral's reaction.

"—and learned that Autocrator Irene's agents had laid a false trail that would have made it seem that the Republic's government was involved in the Palmyrene invasion. This forced me to act. Because there was very little time, it forced me to act without consulting either my superiors—"

Daniel nodded to Mainwaring...who technically wasn't his superior, but who would appreciate the reference.

"—or to the Zenobian authorities. I sincerely apologize to those whom I slighted in my haste."

He had brought Adele into the discussion deliberately, though not by name, because of the effect the reference would have on Mainwaring. The Admiral obviously suspected that Mistress Sand had, on the basis of secret intelligence, ordered the bluff, honest RCN officer to act in the fashion he had. Mainwaring wouldn't push for an answer that might uncover matters that he didn't want to know about.

Daniel had never met a real space officer who was comfortable with spies. Certainly Captain Daniel Leary was not; though he thought of Adele Mundy as a friend with a different background who helped him solve problems.

"I don't know what you're apologizing for," the Founder said gruffly. "If it wasn't for you, we in Calvary would've been screwed with a barge pole no matter what happened in space. Those names and places you had your signals officer send us, they saved our asses. Didn't they, Flecker?"

The major looked sour, but he said, "The information we got from the yacht in orbit saved us a certain amount of time. Though I assure you, sir, you'd have found my troops equal to the problem."

"The Militia alone would have crushed the uprising, Hergo!" said the man seated just below Otto on the Founder's right. He wore a uniform of forest green with blue lapels, heavily encrusted with gold braid and buttons. "Let's not make a bigger thing out of this than it was. The foreign help was welcome—"

From the way he glared first at Major Flecker to his right, then at Daniel across the table, *he* certainly hadn't welcomed it.

"—but Zenobia easily would have maintained her own independence against the Palmyrene dogs."

Hergo looked at the fellow—his cousin, if Daniel remembered correctly what Adele had mentioned in passing about the militia commander. He said, "Jan, your boys did bloody well and I'm thankful for them. Now, drop the subject, all right?"

Jan reddened, but he didn't speak again.

The Founder turned back to Daniel. "Leary," he said, "this is all well and good—there was a plot and you uncovered it. But why did you *act*? I may be a rube from the Qaboosh to you lot—"

His eyes swept the table. Daniel, along with all the Cinnabar and Alliance officers present, put on a blank expression.

"—but I'm not stupid enough to think that the Cinnabar navy goes around doing good for the sake of its soul. What does Cinnabar get out of this? What do *you* get out of this?"

The Founder is rather sharper than I've given him credit for being, Daniel thought. Aloud he said, "No, Your Excellency, neither the Senate nor the RCN is a priestly order. If I'd learned that your—"

He gestured across the table. Daniel wouldn't have gone out of his way to repay Jan for sneering at the Cinnabar contribution to his head remaining on his shoulders, but since an example was needed anyway...

"—your militia commander was plotting a coup against you, I'd have passed the information on to my superiors at the next opportunity. And I'd have slept perfectly well knowing that nothing—I suspect—would be done about it."

"You're bloody well told that nothing would be done about it!" Admiral Mainwaring said. "The RCN doesn't meddle in politics, and certainly not politics in a—"

He caught himself and closed his mouth. After a swallow, he resumed, "Politics on a world well outside the Republic's sphere of influence."

Lieutenant Ames, standing on the other side of the plush ropes, grinned from ear to ear. Daniel suspected that after the story had been retold a few times, Mainwaring would be reported as saying, "The RCN doesn't meddle in the politics of a satellite of Bumfuck Major," or words to that effect. Which in fact would more accurately describe the Admiral's thought than the phrase he had used.

"But it wasn't an internal problem, it was the action of a so-called Cinnabar ally," Daniel said. "Furthermore, the Autocrator had falsified evidence to make it appear that the RCN was behind her grab. Since she chose to bring us into the business, then she could take the consequences of her decision."

Daniel realized that by the end of that sentence his tone had become harsher than he'd intended. He was looking at Hergo, but that meant Mainwaring was in the corner of his eye. He breathed another sigh of relief when the Admiral slapped the table with his palm and said, "Hear, hear!"

Posy Belisande laughed musically, drawing all eyes to her. "Thank you, Captain Leary," she said, "for reassuring me that Cinnabar policy is not determined by altruism. I would have felt spiritually inferior to you. Pride, on the other hand, is an emotion which we in the Qaboosh understand quite well."

There was a moment's frozen silence before Daniel, Mainwaring, von Gleuck, and the Founder all laughed— together, but in a striking variety of styles. *If that girl was sitting beside me, I'd have clapped her on the back*, Daniel thought. *Well, if she'd been a man, I would.*

Admiral Mainwaring leaned back in his chair. He lifted his saucer hat—like Daniel and Milch, he was wearing Whites— and rubbed his brow with the back of his hand.

"All right," he said. "I understand. I'd have approved your

actions, Leary, if you'd had time to warn me. Hell, I might have done the same bloody thing myself when I was a young fire-eater. I only hope I'd have been as lucky as you were. But—"

Mainwaring gave the table a challenging look. Daniel laced his fingers on the tabletop before him and looked at the Admiral with bright interest.

"But this has been a quiet region, ladies and gentlemen," Mainwaring said. "I liked it that way. That's good for trade and it's good for people. The only thing it's not good for is promotion, and if you want to think I've gotten soft because I don't like the thought of a lot of people being killed to put another stripe on my sleeve—"

He tapped the single ring around his right cuff. It was the silver of a rear admiral, not the gold that served for lesser ranks.

"—then you go ahead and think that."

"No one at this table," said von Gleuck, "is such a fool, Admiral. A soft man does not attack a cruiser with a sloop."

Mainwaring looked at him. "Thank you for that, Resident," he said.

Sweeping the assembly again but settling his eyes on Founder Hergo, Mainwaring continued, "The thing that's done the most to keep the Qaboosh quiet is Palmyra. With the Autocrator dead and probably half her nobles besides, political stability there has gone to hell in a handbasket."

He spread his hands, then clenched them and scowled. "That means piracy," he said, "and the gods alone know what else. I don't look forward to it, and I suspect neither does whoever takes charge of the Zenobia detachment now that Fregattenkapitan von Gleuck has stepped upstairs. Not so?"

"Quite true," said von Gleuck, nodding. "But wearing my current hat as Interim Resident, I have a more pressing problem involving Palmyra: the troops on Diamond Cay. I believe there are two thousand of them?"

The Fleet aide standing behind von Gleuck started to call up a field from the data unit hanging from his belt. "Roughly," said Adele. "More accurately, nineteen hundred and twenty-three. As of this morning."

Von Gleuck looked startled. When he saw Daniel grinning at him, he relaxed and smiled back.

"Thank you, Officer Mundy," he said. "They can't stay on Diamond Cay, of course, or on Zenobia—"

"They must be shot!" said the militia commander. "Or—they're all in one place, after all. We can bomb them. Or shoot them with cannon. Resident, I guess your ships were pretty badly damaged, but the Cinnabar navy will help you, won't they? After all, they're enemies of all of us!"

He looked from Mainwaring to Daniel. His tone, Daniel would have said, had been more imperious than imploring.

Von Gleuck's expression as he stared at the fellow was a mixture of disgust and amazement. He didn't reply, but his mouth worked.

Before the Interim Resident could come out with something that he would later regret saying to a member of the planetary nobility, Daniel said, "That would be quite impossible, Marshal Belisande. It would leave the galaxy with the impression that Zenobia was no better than a rookery of vicious animals."

The marshal opened his mouth but shut it again. By now he had realized that the temper of the conference—the civilized members of the conference—was not with him.

"That's all well and good," said Hergo, "and we've got a little time to think about it now that Irene's dead. But we don't have forever—they'll get off the island if we don't do something about them fast. When it comes down to cases, I'm more worried about my life than my reputation back in Xenos."

He looked at von Gleuck; he wasn't quite glaring. "Or on Pleasaunce. I want to hear a solution."

"There is a solution," said von Gleuck, smiling; again the affable gentleman. "The troops aren't a threat if they're a thousand light-years away. I'll arrange on behalf of the Alliance of Free Stars that they be transported to Caftan—"

The nearest Alliance Central Base. It had facilities for a battle fleet and was garrisoned by at least a division of troops.

"—where they'll be enlisted as auxiliaries in the Grand Army of the Stars. I think the Palmyrenes will be agreeable to that outcome, as an alternative to the sort of treatment which they, as barbarians, expect from the victors."

"Now, wait a minute, Commander," said Milch. "We captured those troops, not you, so the Land Forces of the Republic should get them. Besides which they're on Cinnabar-registry ships. You can't—"

"If I could have a moment, Commander Milch?" Daniel said.

"Leary," said Admiral Mainwaring loudly. "This is a regional matter now, and I'd like you to leave it to the regional authorities, all right?"

Daniel's face froze. Mainwaring was correct: it *was* a regional matter. But if it were left to regional interests making their parochial arguments, the best result would be the decades of piracy and fear that the Admiral himself had prophesied.

"Unless Cinnabar is asserting a claim to Zenobia...," von Gleuck said. He didn't raise his voice, but you could have used it to crack walnuts. "Then the only authority to be considered is mine. I have—"

"Brother!" said Posy Belisande.

Daniel sat up as stiffly as if he were a cadet who'd been caught napping; even Admiral Mainwaring jumped. Von Gleuck and the Founder straightened with similar expressions of startled concern.

"Am I correct in recalling...," Posy said. Her voice was still cutting, though she had reduced the volume now that the initial whipcrack had brought silence. "That this is the conference which you called as leader of the independent world of Zenobia?"

Von Gleuck looked at though he wanted to speak. His eyes met Posy's; his tongue touched his lips. He closed his mouth again.

"Yes, sister," said Hergo in a conciliatory voice, "but without the support of—"

"Then may I suggest that you call on my friend Lady Mundy," Posy said as though Hergo had stopped after the second word. "She has a proposal which will not only solve our problem but—"

She gave Mainwaring a look you could have speared an olive with. Daniel kept a straight face.

"—will address a situation which the so-called regional authorities have described but which they don't have the wit to solve."

Daniel was glad that he wasn't expected to respond to Lady Belisande. Posy had spent years at the highest level of Pleasaunce society—the standard by which even Cinnabar measured sophistication—but it appeared that she remained a woman of Zenobia at heart. Daniel doubted whether anyone at the conference table would have guessed that until the present outburst.

"Ah...," said Hergo with a hunted expression. "Lady Mundy?"

He hasn't connected "Lady Mundy" with the RCN junior officer at the end of the table.

"Officer Mundy," Daniel said. "Will you please give your recommendations to the company?"

"Yes," said Adele. She held her control wands, and her personal data unit's display was a blur before her, but she remembered to raise her eyes and turn toward Founder Hergo.

"The best choice...," she said. "Clearly the best choice, I believe, is to repatriate the troops to Palmyra. If there were a practical way to send the heavy weapons captured at the Farm along with them, that would be even better, but I think in this region it would take too long to arrange shipping on vessels of sufficient displacement."

Daniel concealed his smile: Mainwaring, and possibly von Gleuck as well, would have suspected that the smile was mocking instead of simply showing amusement at what Adele's words had done. She couldn't have gotten a greater effect by rolling a live grenade down the table. Everyone was chattering, and at least one Zenobian Councillor shouted.

"If you will all be silent!" Posy said. "Lady Mundy will explain her reasoning!"

Adele rarely—or never, in Daniel's experience—raised her voice; Posy didn't feel that constraint. Here, sharp words were more acceptable and very possibly more effective than the alternative Daniel *had* seen his friend use to get attention: drawing her pistol.

The babble died down, though it didn't completely disappear. Adele said, "There's a political vacuum on Palmyra, as the Squadron Commander pointed out."

She nodded to Admiral Mainwaring. Because she was speaking at an ordinary level, the whispers and muttering ceased. Those present were more interested in what Lady Mundy was saying than in the sound of their own voices.

"If we do not take a hand, one or another of the surviving space captains will eventually gain the throne," Adele said. "He and his peers will have turned to piracy to recruit a maximum number of followers against his rivals. Piracy is the only way for a cutter captain to make money quickly."

Von Gleuck suddenly smiled. Admiral Mainwaring must have seen where the explanation was going at the same moment, because he clapped Daniel on the shoulder with a delighted guffaw.

"General Osman, who was to command the invasion of Zenobia," Adele said, "seems to be an intelligent man. Further, he's able enough to have kept his troops in check after Captain Leary landed them on a large mudbank. The Cinnabar transports they arrived in are unharmed, as are the crews. And those troops are far and away Palmyra's best."

Von Gleuck's Fleet aide, and the junior officers standing behind Mainwaring and Milch, suddenly buried themselves in their data units. The Zenobian Councillors looked puzzled, but Founder Hergo had relaxed. He might not understand the details of what was being said, but he was satisfied because his sister was nodding with approval.

"If Osman returns home with two thousand troops who owe their lives to him," Adele said, "he will take the throne. Perhaps even without fighting, since not only Autocrator Irene but also Osman's most active potential rivals have been killed in the recent battles."

"He's a soldier, not a spacer," said Mainwaring. "That by itself is likely to make him less interested in building the Horde back up to strength. Though—"

He pursed his lips.

"—will he be able to keep his captains in harness?"

"He will if their families remain on Palmyra," said Adele with the chilling dispassion she always displayed in discussions of this sort. "I suppose we—"

She glanced at von Gleuck.

"—or the Fifth Bureau can provide Osman with advisors if he is more tenderhearted than I've found to be the norm among barbarians. Or soldiers, either one."

She's thinking about her little sister, Daniel realized. *And probably about Speaker Leary, who ordered the Proscriptions.*

Daniel Leary, RCN officer, wasn't sure that the Proscriptions had been necessary, and he *was* sure that he wouldn't have ordered them. Lady Adele Mundy, however, saw things in a very different fashion.

"I suspect that Autocrator Osman will have his hands too full at home," von Gleuck said, "to be planning foreign adventures. Certainly I believe that my host, Founder Hergo—"

He nodded to Hergo in pleasant deference. *He'll make a very good Resident.*

"—and I will be fully occupied for quite a long time in returning Zenobia to calm after the attempted coup and invasion."

"Milch," said Admiral Mainwaring, "put together a team to survey the transports and determine what they'll need to become spaceworthy. I don't imagine that parking in a swamp has had good effects on their seals and environmental systems. Besides which—"

He looked across the table to von Gleuck.

"—they'll need rations, and that the RCN can*not* help with."

"We lifted in a bloody hurry when the *Philante* raised the alarm," said Milch, speaking while he keyed notes into his data unit. "Well, we thought it was an alarm, Leary."

He looked at Daniel with a wry smile. "One of our own ships turning pirate was what it looked like to me. Anyway, we're transferring cereals from the *Espeigle* to the *Dotterel* right now or we wouldn't have bread."

"There must be troop rations stockpiled at the Farm," said von Gleuck. "We can transport them to Diamond Cay."

It wasn't clear to Daniel whether Otto was speaking as a Fleet officer or as Resident when he said "we," but it didn't matter until Marshal Belisande said, "Everything captured on Zenobia is our property. We'll sell the rations to any friendly power which wants to purchase them, of course, but—"

"The Government of Zenobia hereby makes a free gift to the Alliance of all loot captured from the Palmyrene invaders," said Hergo gruffly. "Jan, make sure the Resident gets whatever he wants. *No*, come to think."

He switched his glance from his cousin to the mercenary seated beside him.

"Major, *you* take charge of the Farm with your troops. And make bloody sure that there's no delay in getting food or whatever else the Resident asks to Diamond Cay. I want those Palmyrenes to go back home as fast as they can get there, and I'd say travel rations were a bloody cheap price for that."

"Speaking of necessary supplies," said von Gleuck, smiling—but not in an entirely friendly fashion—at Daniel. "My destroyers are the major defense of Zenobia against attack by Palmyrene survivors who haven't gotten the message, but their rigging is badly cut up. When we landed, we found that virtually all the sail fabric in Calvary Harbor has been commandeered by our friends and allies in the *Princess Cecile*. Including the sails of civilian vessels. I think a redistribution is called for, do you not, Captain Leary?"

"Ah," said Daniel brightly. Apparently Vesey and the Sissies under her direction had applied in a very literal fashion his direction to make the ship right ASAP...which he approved. But he could see Otto's point.

Daniel paused to frame an answer. He suspected that the patrol sloops, which hadn't been engaged, could spare some sails, but he wasn't going to suggest that until he'd had a moment to beg the Admiral's indulgence.

Posy and Adele rose from the table; Adele was putting away her data unit. They walked toward the grotto with Posy in the lead.

What in heaven's name are they doing? Daniel wondered. But right now he had more pressing questions to answer.

CHAPTER 30

CALVARY ON ZENOBIA

"My dear," Posy murmured in Adele's ear. "Would you care to visit the grotto? Since I doubt you're any more interested in discussions of sails and ration packs than I am."

"The information.may be significant," Adele said, shutting off her data unit. "But I don't see that I would gain anything by listening to the decision being arrived at."

Arrived at by thoroughly childish argument, she thought but did not say. The relative allocations were being treated as matters of honor, not pragmatic questions of need and availability.

She got up and put the data unit away. "This grotto?" she said, nodding minusculely toward the gate in the wall behind them. Because the conference table was in the left corner of the garden, the central entrance was less than twenty feet from their end of the table.

"Yes," said Posy, leading by a half step. Wood flanked them. Her face had no expression, but Adele read concern in it. Perhaps she was projecting her own puzzlement.

The warrant officer commanding the Alliance guard contingent leaned forward in his folding chair to look down at them. Woetjans had risen to her feet and braced her right hand on the monumental head which would otherwise have blocked her view of what was going on. Adele looked up at the bosun and nodded—reassuringly, she hoped.

Posy touched the gate with an electronic key. The bars were woven from beryllium monocrystal: it would be easier to blast through the stone wall itself than to cut them. Wood started in ahead of her mistress.

"Wood," said Posy. She didn't shout, but there was no give in her voice. "Wait outside, if you will, and prevent anyone from disturbing Lady Mundy and myself."

Wood glanced from Posy to Tovera, then back. She didn't move from the gateway.

"Wood," Posy repeated.

"Tovera," said Adele with a faint smile. "Please keep your colleague company. Perhaps you can talk about old school days with her."

"Yes, mistress," said Tovera. "Pillow fights in the dormitory and cheering the field hockey team. Rah rah, eh, Wood?"

Posy lost her composure enough to frown in surprise. Wood, however, broke into a glacial smile and stepped aside. She said, "As Your Ladyship wishes."

Dim lights built to a glow as Adele walked forward. The path bent sharply to the right and descended, curving around so that in twenty feet they would be below the garden. She heard Posy *cling* the gate closed, then lock it before walking briskly to join her.

"If we go to the end," Posy said, nodding the way forward, "I don't believe any device outside the grating can overhear us. And I had Wood check this morning to be sure that nothing had been concealed within."

Which is only proof if I trust you, Adele said; but in fact she did trust the younger woman. Besides, Adele had no intention of saying anything that she would mind everyone on Zenobia overhearing.

"All right," she said. No doubt Posy would explain what this was about in good time; and as an alternative to listening to a wrangle over ship fittings, she would prefer to watch concrete set.

The passageway ended in a circular room which must be directly under the garden's central fountain. It was amusingly similar to the rotundas onto which starship airlocks opened, including the relatively low ceiling. Faint green glow strips marked the floor and outlined twelve small alcoves—peepholes, really—set into the walls at eye level.

Posy gestured to an alcove. "When this was built in the last century," she said, "those showed exotic scenes. I don't suppose they work now."

Adele walked to the nearest; she couldn't see anything within. She moved to the next. "The gates looked more recent than that," she said.

"My uncle, who preceded Hergo as Founder, added the gates," Posy said. "He used the grotto for private parties. He wasn't a nice man."

The second alcove lighted when Adele stepped close. A giant arachnid chased a nude woman with flowing blond hair through a forest glade. Its clawed forelegs gripped her and threw her down.

Adele's lip curled. The creature's intention wasn't to devour the girl after all.

"The person who built this place," Adele said, facing Posy in the center of the room, "wasn't a very nice man either. What did you wish to ask me, Lady Belisande?"

The younger woman grinned crookedly. "Posy, I hope still," she said. "Adele, was Captain Leary telling the truth about why he stopped Autocrator Irene?"

Adele didn't speak for a moment; her right hand toyed with the outline of her data unit in its thigh pocket. *Why would she trust me to tell the truth? She* knows *I'm a spy.*

But Adele *would* tell the truth. She said, "I think the matter was a little simpler than Daniel made it sound for Admiral Mainwaring's benefit, Posy. He believes that the Republic needs peace, and he also believed that the Autocrator's action would lead to a resumption of hostilities between us and the Alliance. If he put it that baldly, though..."

She shrugged. "Well, the Admiral could see that Captain Leary's action might lead to unrest in the region for decades. Whereas the larger questions are speculative and aren't the concern of the Qaboosh Squadron anyway."

The greenish cast of the glow strips gave Posy the look of a corpse and presumably did the same to Adele's appearance. *Exactly what kind of parties did the previous Founder hold here?*

Adele turned her hands palms-up, then down. She said, "Daniel therefore put the matter in terms of an insult by barbarians to the majesty of the Republic, which made it more palatable to the Admiral."

"And do you agree that Cinnabar and the Alliance need peace, Adele?" Posy said.

"Yes," Adele said simply. "I believe human civilization needs peace between us and the Alliance."

Posy sighed and turned away. Adele waited, trying to keep from frowning. She understood that people sometimes wanted time to think, though she hadn't noticed that it helped them very much. She wouldn't have minded if she could take out her data unit and get on with other business, but that wouldn't help her learn what Posy actually had in mind.

When the younger woman faced Adele after a moment, she had become Lady Belisande, stiff and imperious. She said, "Are you familiar with Tattersall, a world in the Forty Stars?"

Adele reached for her data unit, though she didn't switch it on yet. She would have to sit on the floor to use it.

"I've heard of it," she said. "I can become familiar very quickly."

Posy laughed harshly. "No doubt you can," she said. "There'll be time for that shortly. For now, all you need to know is that Tattersall is a Friend of Cinnabar with an RCN squadron stationed there. Her nearest neighbors and trading rivals are Associates of the Alliance, as Zenobia herself is."

"Go on," said Adele, though by this point she probably had all the information she needed to start digging for more on her own. She waited because Posy might have a unique insight. More important, it was courteous to let her have her say.

"Soon," said Posy, "and I don't know more than that, but I

think only a few months. Soon Tattersall will be invaded, and the new government will ask for admission to the Alliance of Free Stars. This hasn't been planned by, by Pleasaunce; but Guillaume knows about it. There will be a cruiser squadron nearby to protect the new government from outside interference."

"I see," said Adele. "You haven't asked, but I assure you that your name won't be brought into this, Posy."

Once you had information, it was easy to find additional pathways to the same point. No one but the two principals would know where Adele's report had originated.

"I don't care!" Posy said, her face anguished. "Captain Leary did what was right and honorable. Why shouldn't *I*? Why shouldn't everybody?"

Everybody should. But a woman who expects to spend the rest of her life with a former Fleet officer should also have better sense than to do so openly.

Aloud, Adele said, "You've done your part, Posy. It's in my hands now."

And Daniel's. Which had been good enough to settle matters in the Qaboosh Region, after all.

Posy looked to be on the verge of tears; in her mind, she had come very close to treason. Adele put her hand on the younger woman's shoulder and said, "Come along, dear. I doubt that anyone's missed us. I want to keep it that way."

And so will Lady Belisande by tomorrow morning.

"So, young master," Hogg said as Daniel finally rose from his chair. "You going to tell Vesey that she shouldn't've took all those sails from the ships whose asses we saved? Because I don't have to tell *you* what was going to happen to everything in the harbor when a gang of wog pirates landed."

"No, you don't have to tell me," said Daniel, smiling. "They ought to be happy that the captains' liquor wasn't looted too."

He'd deliberately waited till everybody else had left the conference table. This way he wouldn't find himself in private conversations that he didn't want to have until he'd sorted out the possibilities. Adele would be able to tell him what the sail lockers of the Qaboosh Squadron held, as well as give him an inventory of the stores on Stahl's World.

"Which they wouldn't've been so lucky if I'd been in charge, but I'm here being a loyal retainer while my master listens to folks talk bumf to hear their own voices," Hogg said.

He glowered in the direction of Woetjans. From what he'd said earlier, Hogg was aggrieved that the bosun had been allowed to carry a stocked impeller, while personnel except for the guard detachment were unarmed. He added, "Well, at least you got a chance to look pretty in your Whites."

"Which I will be out of as soon as we get back to my cabin, I assure you," Daniel said. He might have worn a second-class uniform for this conference, but his best set hadn't outlived Commander Gibbs by more than a fraction of a second. Whites had been a better choice than ragged Grays, let alone Grays which still showed the marks of blood and brains. "Where—ah, there she is!"

He had missed Adele after the conference. He'd begun to think that she had left the garden, and why shouldn't she have? Instead, she was seated on the far curb of the fountain, her feet in the cracked, dry basin. The personal data unit was on her knees, and she was lost in her work, as usual.

Tovera, standing behind her mistress, reached through the top of the holographic display and then withdrew her hand. Adele looked up coldly, then smiled. She shrank her display, but she didn't shut down the unit and rise as Daniel had more or less expected she would.

Adele wouldn't be doing this if she didn't have a reason. He sat carefully beside her. The curb was lower than a normal bench, which put additional strains on the knees and seat of his trousers.

It was actually a good place to hold a private discussion. Workmen—only a few of them wore white and purple palace livery—were clearing the conference tables. Members of the gardening staff, identifiable by their grief-stricken expressions, were going over the damage to the hedges and plantings. The eldest, a bent little man with a halo of fine white hair, mopped his eyes with a polka dot bandana.

Some of the attendees were still in the garden, talking in pairs and small groups, but they avoided everyone else rather than trying to overhear conversations. More interestingly, Commissioner Brown skirted the shattered fountain on the way to the Palace and the street beyond, walking between his wife and his little girl. Brown smiled wanly when Daniel gave him a friendly nod, but Hester waved her free hand with enthusiasm.

Clothilde Brown didn't notice anyone else. She was leaning close to her husband and circled his waist with her left arm.

If Brown survives, Daniel thought, *the business with Gibbs will have done his relationship with his wife quite a lot of good. But that's a big if.*

"Daniel," said Adele, "I've been looking at the situation in the Forty Stars, based on information I've gathered recently."

She looked to the right, then the left, seeing where their servants stood. Hogg was watching half the arc around them, his right hand in a pocket and a murderous scowl on his face. Tovera had the rest of the circumference. From a distance her expression might seem blank, but anybody who passed close enough to overhear the conversation would sheer off even more abruptly than they would from Hogg.

"I knew Vondrian in the Academy," Daniel said. "He has a destroyer in the Tattersall Flotilla, where he's found slots for two other mutual friends. Ames here was planning to become Vondrian's Second Lieutenant, and since I haven't seen Ames since the *Fantome* landed this morning, I suspect he may already be on his way to Tattersall."

"Yes," said Adele crisply. "I believe that Tattersall faces attack by her neighbors with substantial after-the-fact support from the Alliance."

Daniel opened his mouth, then closed it. If Adele hadn't been sure, she wouldn't have spoken. For her, the interrogatories which he would have thrown at anyone else who had made such a statement would be improper and insulting.

"If a substantial RCN squadron were to arrive at Tattersall in the next short while," Adele continued, "ideally including a battleship...?"

"Two battleships are home-ported to the Sector Base at Kronstadt," Daniel said carefully. "That's within five days of Tattersall, perhaps four. But not four for the *Schelling*, I fear."

He paused, calculating courses. "Orders would have to

come from Xenos, of course," he said. "But Cinnabar is almost on the shortest route from here to Kronstadt anyway."

He coughed. "Ah, if Navy House agrees."

"I think that will be possible," Adele said. "I will endeavor to pass the information on through channels which will get the prompt attention of Admiral Hartsfeld."

She turned to face Daniel. "I believe that if an RCN squadron appears over Tattersall before open trouble breaks out," she said, "it will be possible for people with the correct skills to root out the plotters there."

"Right," said Daniel. "A coup like that depends on speed, which means there has to be an infrastructure on the ground. Just like here."

"Yes," Adele said. "Just as happened on Zenobia."

Her smiles didn't always mean she was amused at something, but Daniel thought this one did. She said, "Technically, I suppose this information should go by courier vessel, but...?"

Daniel laughed. "On your feet, Officer Mundy," he said. "We'll lift in three hours and complete our repairs during the voyage. The day the *Sissie* can't better the time of any courier built, I'll retire to Bantry and fish!"

They strode side by side toward the Palace and transportation to the harbor. At the end of the garden, Daniel turned and bellowed, "RCN forever!"

"I'm not sure that was appropriate," he muttered to Adele. Everybody present was staring at their backs.

"It's always appropriate," said Adele. Daniel rarely heard her express pride, but it was evident in her voice now.

ACKNOWLEDGMENTS

Dan Breen continues as my first reader, thank goodness. I give each of my works multiple passes. Despite this, Dan consistently catches things—and sometimes extremely obvious things—which I nonetheless had missed. Besides, he laughs at jokes in my manuscripts that most people are going to miss.

Dorothy Day (under difficult circumstances) and Evan Ladouceur helped enormously with continuity. Such problems as remain are merely a hint of the mess things would be in without them.

Dorothy and my webmaster, Karen Zimmerman, archived my texts in widely separated parts of the country. Only somebody who kills as many computers as I do can appreciate the sense of relief that gives me.

And I'm not sure that anybody else *does kill* as many computers as I do. This time it was my backup machine, which got rained on and then crushed. My son Jonathan set me up with a new backup, a laptop whose screen my grandson

Tristan had broken. (Apparently the computer-slaying gene has skipped a generation.)

Besides archiving texts, Karen (a cybrarian) searched material for me. I now have (for example) several versions of *The Ring That Has No End*, though none of them is quite what my friend Manly Wade Wellman used to sing with banjo-picker Obray Ramsey in his cabin in the mountains.

The only things that matter in a book are the things that matter to the writer himself. Details of that sort matter very much to me.

My wife Jo took care of me, the house, and the dogs while I wrote. I mentioned that knowing my texts were safe brings a sense of relief. Knowing that my nest is safe is far more important.

My sincere thanks to all those mentioned, and to the many other people who brighten my life by their presence and support.

ABOUT THE AUTHOR

David Drake was attending Duke University Law School when he was drafted. He served the next two years in the Army, spending 1970 as an enlisted interrogator with the 11th Armored Cavalry in Vietnam and Cambodia. Upon return he completed his law degree at Duke and was for eight years Assistant Town Attorney for Chapel Hill, North Carolina. He has been a full-time freelance writer since 1981. His books include the genre-defining and bestselling *Hammer's Slammers* series, and the nationally bestselling RCN series including *What Distant Deeps*, *The Road of Danger*, and *The Sea without a Shore*.